THANK YOU
MERCI
GRACIAS
ARIGATO
DANKE

Mercury's Rise

Books by Ann Parker

Silver Lies
Iron Ties
Leaden Skies
Mercury's Rise

Mercury's Rise

A Silver Rush Mystery

Ann Parker

Poisoned Pen Press

Copyright © 2011 by Ann Parker

First Edition 2011

10 9 8 7 6 5 4 3 2 1

Library of Congress Catalog Card Number: 2011926975

ISBN: 9781590589618   Hardcover
       9781590589632   Trade Paperback

Poisoned Pen Press
6962 E. First Ave., Ste. 103
Scottsdale, AZ 85251
www.poisonedpenpress.com
info@poisonedpenpress.com

Printed in the United States of America

Dedicated to sisters, and especially to
Alison
With love and hugs, stretching over the miles and over the years.

Acknowledgments

First, I'd like to thank the usual suspects: My family—near and far—for their unending support and encouragement, and especially Bill, Ian, and Devyn (who have to live with all this!).

Then, there are friends, writers, critique partners who patiently stood by me as I thrashed through this next Silver Rush epic. Special thanks to Camille Minichino and Dick Rufer for providing a "hide out" for focused writing; Dani Greer, who, at the eleventh hour, put the virtual knife in my hand, said, "You must kill your darlings," and pointed me toward some egregious examples (less purple prose herein as a result); and other critique partners/early readers/proofers who read pieces or the whole: Colleen Casey, Janet Finsilver, Staci McLaughlin, Carole Price, Penny Warner, Mike Cooper, Margaret Dumas, Claire Johnson, Rena Leith, Jane Staehle, Gordon Yano, and the "nagsisters." I owe much to various e-groups who made it possible for me to write "apace" and who share my passion for history and accuracy, including Book-in-a-Week (where writers write together...one page at a time) and Women Writing the West. A special acknowledgment goes to my webmistress Kate Reed for wonderful design and customer service, and to Michael Greer, for the wonderful map of Manitou and environs.

Special kudos to the experts, hither and yon, who gave of their time and knowledge (sometimes on very short notice, and always with grace and courtesy). Experts in Colorado and Manitou Springs and times Victorian: Doris McCraw, Berry Jo Cardona, Deborah Harrison, Dianne Hartshorn, Chelsy Murphy (Colorado Springs Convention & Visitors Bureau, who set up an *awesome* info-packed area tour for me), Bret Tennis (Garden of the Gods), and Donald McGilchrist (The Navigators). Experts in Civil War, medical, and gun "stuff": Steven and Amy Crane, and George McCluny. Special thanks to researcher Jeanne Munn Bracken, and Profs Michael Grossberg (Indiana University) and Hendrik Hartog (Princeton University) for information on divorce issues/philosophy/laws in the 1800s, and others who provided resources/advice over the years on this "sticky issue," including Christie Wright and Ruth Rymer. If I've gone astray with my facts, these wonderful people are not to blame; rather, it's my own darn fault (or, in some cases, intention).

Where would we be without libraries and historical societies and museums? In the wilderness, that's where, learning as we go, without easy access to areas and the past beyond our own experience and memories. My gratitude goes out to all, particularly to Lake County Public Library (esp. Janet Fox and Nancy McCain), Pikes Peak Public Library District/Penrose Library (esp. Dennis Daily), Manitou Springs Public Library, Livermore Public Library, and Denver Public Library. The historical societies/museums that helped me fashion this, the latest story in my Silver Rush "saga": Colorado Historical Society, the Pioneer Museum in Colorado Springs, the Manitou Springs Heritage Center, and the Old Colorado City Historical Society. A heartfelt plea to readers: Support your libraries and historical organizations! They carry the light from the past to the future and cannot keep the flame alive without our help.

A proper curtsey and bow to The Cliff House in Manitou Springs for its elegant hospitality and for being the inspiration for my fictional the Mountain Springs House, and to Glen Eyrie and its gracious staff for access to their research library and a lovely overnight stay in General Palmer's "castle."

To those whose names and/or characteristics I employed with enthusiasm, thanks for giving me permission to "borrow you" for my nefarious fictional purposes—Robert Calder; Sharon Crowson; the Pace/Cummings clan (kids: if you don't like what I did, blame your mom, she gave permission!); and the one and only Dr. Aurelius Prochazka.

Finally, hats off to those at Poisoned Pen Press: extraordinary editor Barbara Peters, publisher Rob Rosenwald, associate publisher (crack the whip!) Jessica Tribble, and Marilyn, Nan, Annette, Elizabeth. Thank you for bringing Inez and her tales to the wider world.

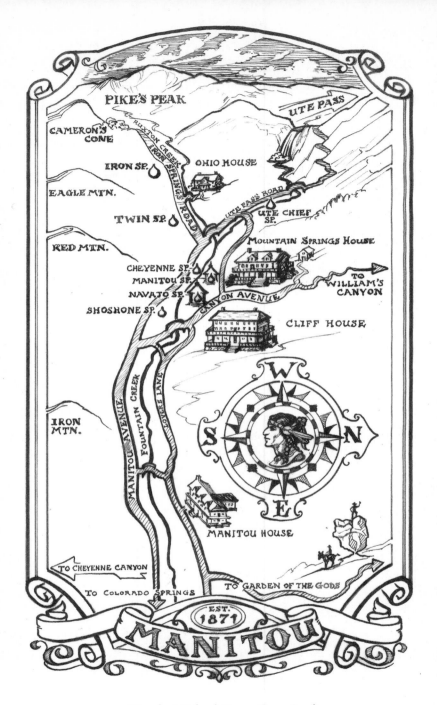

Map by Michael Greer, Greer Studios

"Learning is like mercury, one of the most powerful and excellent things in the world in skillful hands; in unskillful, the most mischievous."

—Alexander Pope

Chapter One

August 1880

Inez Stannert had nowhere to run. Nowhere to hide.

Since she couldn't escape the purgatory that was the confined and crowded stagecoach, Inez tried to let the droning voice of the man seated across from her wash over like the water in a mountain stream. But Edward Pace, Boston businessman and investor questing after yet more wealth in the West, went on and on. His monologue was interrupted only by the occasional screech from one of his three children—pushed beyond endurance by the heat, the cramped quarters, the dust—or punctuated by the muffled shout of "G-long!" or "H-up!" from the coach driver on the seat above them.

Mr. Pace's voice accompanied the rhythmic cadence of horses' hooves as they pounded mile after mile of red dirt roads. Yesterday, the coach had stopped only for short rest breaks and a non-restful scant handful of hours sleep at a "hotel" in Fairplay. Today, the hapless passengers continued their journey, crammed together shoulder to shoulder, thigh to thigh, as the coach steadily lengthened the distance from their starting point in Leadville and drew ever closer to their destination of Manitou.

The coach was now edging toward Florrisant, and the final descent out of the high peaks of the Rocky Mountains to the lesser lands at the edge of the mountain range.

The end of the trip could not come soon enough.

Inez clenched her hands, fingernails biting through thin leather gloves. The backs of the gloves were covered with the fine dust that swirled throughout the interior of the stagecoach. A rusty tinge painted every surface and every passenger—Inez, her friend and traveling companion Susan Carothers, the Pace *paterfamilias*, his wife, their three children, and the unintroduced nanny. Inez fervently wished the dust would simply choke Mr. Pace into silence. But Lady Luck was betting against her, and the businessman appeared impervious to the dust's strangling effects.

Behind Inez's traveling veil—which had proved almost useless in keeping the airborne dirt at bay—sweat trickled from her hairline, down temples and cheeks to drip off her chin.

The clattering stage rocked forward, back, forward, back: a metronome in motion, a mother's nudge to a cradle.

There was a sudden, violent pitch forward, a sharp jerk back, a whistle from the driver above, and the snap of a whip. Inez, crammed on the leather seat between her friend Susan and the nanny, clutched Susan's arm to keep from falling forward into Mr. Pace's lap. As the stage lurched from rut to rock, a hard jolt shuddered through the thinly padded leather seats. Pain raced up Inez's back, tracing the corset laces, and set her teeth rattling. She bit the inside of her mouth to keep from uttering an oath that, most likely, would have stopped the businessman dead in his oratorical tracks.

The two older Pace children—a girl of about five and a boy of perhaps three—yelped. Mrs. Pace turned to them with a "shush," her brown-gold hair a muted flash beneath her own dust-coated veil. The youngest child, a baby planted in the nanny's lap, uttered not a peep. A strand of drool made a rusty wet streak across one chubby cheek.

Crowded by Susan and a stray hatbox on one side, and by the ample proportions of the nanny on the other side, Inez felt her temper rise from a simmer to a boil. She prayed more fervently than she had in a long time that the next stage stop was near. *If I must endure many more hours of this, I fear I'll do something fatal to my reputation.*

Undeterred by the howls of his progeny or the ruts of the road, Pace leaned toward Inez, his knees jostling her own, nearly spitting at the net covering her face. "The air is so vile in Leadville, it is a wonder that the entire population is not sickened to the point of disease."

Behind her veil, Inez's upper lip curled as Pace continued to vilify the town they'd left yesterday. She glanced at Mrs. Pace. Sitting at her husband's side, the woman appeared immune to her husband's vitriolic speechmaking and instead whispered urgently to the boy and girl beside her, who alternately squirmed and jabbed at each other. After one particularly hard poke to the ribs from his sister, the little boy lashed out with a grimy laced-up boot, leaving a dusty streak on the nanny's long skirts.

"Enough!" the nanny snapped. The boy froze, sullenness stamped on features a miniature of his father's.

The sister smirked.

Inez reflected that, given the history of the past hour, the two would be back pinching and jabbing each other within a space of minutes.

And there had been some very, very long hours since leaving Leadville the previous morning.

Inez had stepped up into the coach sent to bring them from Leadville to Manitou's Mountain Springs House if not with a high heart, at least with a hopeful one. It was a journey she had long been anticipating: In two days, she would rejoin William, her not-quite-two-year-old son whom she had not seen in a year. The sweat beneath her travel clothes damped the locket stuck to her skin, the locket holding a photograph of William at eight months.

Inez shifted on the seat. Her hip bumped the nanny, who managed one evil glance before turning to the baby in her clutches. "There's a little dumpling," she cooed, rocking him with her knees in time to the coach's sway. The infant's head lolled on her lap.

As far as Inez could tell, the "little dumpling" was out cold, no doubt thanks to the liberal dosing he'd received of Ayer's Cherry Pectoral. Inez had sneaked a peek at the label as the nanny had struggled to uncork the bottle while baby Pace was engaged in one particularly intense infantile fit. The tonic had effectively rendered mute his non-stop screaming, crying, and coughing.

"Furthermore, the mines in Leadville are played out." Pace settled back against the coach seat, pulling out a limp linen handkerchief from his wilted travel suit and mopping his pale, dust-streaked face. "The management of such is lackadaisical and not prepared to handle the workers with the firmness required. Witness the strike of May. Poorly handled, all around."

Unable to stand it any longer, Inez said loud enough to drown him out, "Pardon, Mr. Pace, I am curious as to what brought you to Leadville to begin with, if all it held for you is a dark and bleak vision more suited to Hades' world than our own?"

Pace stopped talking. She was pleased to see that her words, or perhaps it was her tone, had done what the road's ruts and rocks could not.

For a blissful moment, his mouth hung slack and without sound. His dark mustache, no longer so impeccably groomed, was streaked with damp and dust. He looked as astounded as if the leather side curtains had suddenly given voice.

Susan's black-gloved hand crept over to cover Inez's balled fist, a mute warning to watch her tongue.

Pace removed his Homburg and swiped at his streaming forehead.

Inez noted with a nasty curl of satisfaction that although his mustache was carefully blacked, his hair was iron-grey. That, and the lines on his face, placed him on the far side of fifty, at a guess. She risked a sidelong glance at the veil-shrouded missus beside him. Inez had judged the wife and mother at about five-and-twenty, no more. Inez's brow contracted in sympathy. There could only be money behind this union. His or hers, she wondered.

Inez had seen Mrs. Pace without her veil a few times now, the longest stretch of time being the previous evening at the Fairplay hotel, where they had stopped for the night.

Having vowed to not imbibe on the trip, Inez had found the Fairplay evening, apart from the respite of the coach ride, less than stellar. The food was wretched, and the company for the most part dull. Excusing herself early, Inez had repaired to the room she was sharing with Susan for the night to do a more thorough wash than the hurried splash of hands and face she had managed before supper.

Inez was brushing her hair when Susan had knocked and entered an hour or so later. Inez set her silver-backed hairbrush on the simple desk that served as a dressing table and said, "I am sorry I suggested taking the stage to Manitou, Susan. If we had gone by train, as I originally planned, you would not have to endure this miserable trip."

"Oh, no, Inez, I'm enjoying it. Well, mostly. The dust is quite something, isn't it?" Susan took a clothes brush and vigorously attacked her travel cloak, hanging on a wall peg. "Some of the scenery is wonderful. I'm making notes for later. Too, I'm thinking, there's a spot east of Leadville that is perfect for capturing the city with a stereoscopic camera. I could sell stereoviews like Mrs. Galbreaith's views of Manitou."

She stopped brushing and pulled a stereoview card out of her coat pocket, examining the twin stereoscopic image on the front. "I'm so honored that Mrs. Galbreaith offered to share her photographic techniques and that I can stay in her boarding house for the duration." She flipped the card over. "It is quite clever of her to list the different springs in Manitou on the back, along with their mineral compositions. I shall have to think of something similar to say about Leadville. 'Manitou Springs—Saratoga of the West' sounds so romantic. Maybe I could offer up 'Leadville—Silver Sensation of the Rockies.' Or 'Leadville—Cloud City of the West.'"

Inez sighed. "I just wish things had worked out as I had planned. I had thought we would have the coach to ourselves and be able to stop whenever you wanted. I had not counted on the Paces appearing, seemingly out of nowhere, and demanding passage to the Mountain Springs House as well. Now, there is no stopping to gaze at the scenery, and I am sorry for that."

"It is all right, Inez. We still have the train ride back to Leadville, at the end of the trip. This way, we get to see more of the country. I truly appreciate you underwriting this trip and supporting my efforts to expand my business. "

"You have a rare talent. I cannot imagine a better way to invest my money than in helping you with your enterprise. Others may grubstake prospectors and pray for a silver bonanza. I prefer putting my money into a surer operation." She smiled briefly at Susan. "I have seen you as you weathered good and bad times. You are careful with your profits and minimize your losses. Your business sense is sound."

Susan blushed in the light of the oil lamp. "Thank you. That is high praise from one of the most successful businesswomen in Leadville."

A sudden jolt brought Inez back to the confines of the stagecoach.

Mr. Pace was saying, "Well. Since you ask, Mrs. Stannert, my business in Leadville involved an exploration of possible investment opportunities. My wife's father has much to do with metals and thought I should investigate."

In a gesture that mimicked Susan's, Mrs. Pace placed a gloved hand over his. His fingers, clamped tightly atop his bony knee-cap, visibly relaxed beneath her touch. Behind her veil, Inez raised her eyebrows, intrigued.

"And, you, Mrs. Stannert?" He spoke stiffly, as if unused to making polite give-and-take conversation. "Do you and your husband reside in Leadville?"

Susan's hand gripped tighter as Inez's fist spasmed. "Indeed," she said, ignoring her growing rage. "We, that is to say, Mr. Stannert has a number of business ventures in town."

"Indeed." He echoed her and gave her that odd look again. It was a cousin to the one he'd provided at their introduction. On hearing her name, he'd done a visible double-take, then stared with increasingly narrowed eyes, before finally offering her a stiff short bow. She had held her breath, to see if he would add anything damning, such as "You are that harlot who runs the saloon on Harrison and State streets!" He didn't, but for that moment, it seemed as if he knew her, or knew of her, and not in a positive way. Inez had racked her mind, but could not recall having seen him in the Silver Queen Saloon. When he said nothing after his bow, she had decided to let it pass.

Realizing her musings had taken her mid-explanation from the conversation, she added belatedly, "What with all his various undertakings and his many investments in Leadville, Mr. Stannert decided it was best for us to remain in the city year-round. To keep an eye on things."

"Leadville is a hard place for a gentlewoman," Pace remarked, glancing at his own wife.

Inez smiled tightly. A sudden flash of memory from the previous week: her reflection in the Silver Queen Saloon's dressing room mirror, hair in place, evening gown a rustle of satin and silk, diamonds glistening at her neck, brandy goblet on the washstand, and pocket pistol tucked safely in a hidden pocket. Her regular Saturday night visitors waiting across the hall for her to appear and for the late-night high-stakes poker games to begin.

"You are staying at the Mountain Springs House for the rest of the summer season, then? Are you intending to take the waters?" The wife's question could scarcely be heard over the creaks of the coach, the squeaks of horse tracings, and the clatter of hooves.

"Miss Carothers and I are staying in the area for a short while. I imagine we will sample the mineral springs while we are there." Inez started to say more, then stopped.

No need to explain her personal business to these people. No need to tell them that she was on her way to see her sister Harmony and her own son William, whom she had not seen since the previous August. Definitely no need to explain that the reason her husband, Mark Stannert, was not in the coach beside her was because she had threatened to put a bullet through him if he were to accompany her to Manitou.

Chapter Two

Leadville

Inez's nightmare had begun eight days before the trip to Manitou. Memories of that early morning still burned like acid through her waking hours and her restless dreams. She had said her good-byes to Reverend Justice Sands at the Malta station, a few miles from Leadville.

The train waited, prepared to carry former president and Civil War general Ulysses S. Grant and his entourage onto the next stop of his Colorado tour. Darkness still shrouded the sky while Grant, his family, and others descended from their carriages and buggies. In the sheltered interior of the hired hack, Inez and the reverend exchanged one long kiss and lovers' promises and counterpromises.

"Less than a month, and I'll be back," he said.

She'd closed her eyes, focusing on his voice, his touch as he traced the line of her cheek.

He continued, "I would not leave you now, but I promised the General—"

She placed a finger on his lips, stopping his words. "Justice Sands, you made a promise. You must honor it. No need to worry about me. The worst is over. What else can happen? I'll be here, waiting for your letters and your return."

Weeks ago, Grant had asked that Reverend Sands accompany him on his much-publicized Colorado tour. Such a request from his former commander-in-chief and supporter could not be refused.

Reverend Sands took her hand in his own, kissed her fingers. "Still, all the trouble of the past days, and now, your home is gone. Burned to the ground. I don't like leaving you to deal with all this alone."

"Nonsense." She forced herself to speak lightly, glad that the dark interior hid the yearning that she was certain showed on her face. "It's nothing I can't handle. I'll settle into the second story of the saloon for now. That will keep me busy. That, and sorting through to see if anything escaped the fire. Besides, I'm not alone. I have Abe to help with the business. Susan for friendship. The church for solace. I also have another meeting scheduled with the lawyer, to see what the next steps are in obtaining a divorce. He has assured me it will be simple. With no husband around to fight my suit on the grounds of desertion, how complicated a process can it be?"

His grip on her fingers tightened. "The sooner you are free of the past, the sooner we can forge a life together. I love you, Inez. From the moment I saw you. Meeting you was a gift from God."

"Well, let's not give thanks to the Almighty quite yet," she said. "You may yet have cause to curse falling in love with a saloon owner and soon-to-be divorced woman."

"That will never happen."

Shouts from outside, the whistle of the train: it was time for him to leave.

Inez and Reverend Sands descended from the hack for a more formal farewell and parting.

Afterwards, back in the carriage alone, Inez watched with an aching heart as the train swallowed her lover, along with Grant and his followers.

Returning to the Silver Queen Saloon, Inez had felt weary to her very bones. Yet, with the graying of the sky toward dawn, a lightness lifted her spirit. She was finally looking forward with something approaching anticipation and hope. Thinking about her plans to see her little William and her beloved sister

Harmony, in less than two weeks. Thinking about promising business deals, recently made, glinting like newly minted silver coins and shining bright with promise. Thinking about her impending divorce from her husband, Mark Stannert, who had been missing for well over a year. At last, she was moving forward with purpose in her heart.

Inez unlocked the door to the Silver Queen Saloon and walked into the gloomy interior. She could just make out the tables with chairs resting upside down upon them, creating a forest of wooden limbs. The rising sun hadn't yet penetrated to the corners of the room.

By the backmost table, in the darkest shadows, a figure stirred, stood up.

Inez tensed, then relaxed, identifying a familiar black hat, pulled low, on a black-garbed figure. *Did the reverend change his mind? But I saw him get on the train.*

Then, a voice.

A voice she hadn't heard in over a year.

"Hello, darlin'."

He removed his hat.

Inez froze. For a moment, it felt as if all the blood had left her body, leaving her an empty shell, ready to collapse. Then, all that missing blood suddenly rushed back to her head and chest.

"No," she whispered, willing it to be a bad dream. "It can't be."

Mark stepped out of the shadows. "Not the kind of welcome I was expecting from my wife after one year, two months, and fifteen days."

"You! You can't be here!" She swayed. The room swirled around her, darkness grew behind her eyes, blocking her sight. Inez reached out blindly for something to support her.

She heard the thump of a cane on the floor as he moved forward and grabbed her elbow to steady her.

More than his touch, it was Mark's overwhelming familiar scent— sweat, travel, even the same pungent cinnamon-almond Macassar hair oil—that brought the old days stampeding back.

Sight clearing, Inez yanked her arm out of his grasp. "Stay back!"

He held the offending hand off to one side, as if trying to assure a jittery poker opponent that he was unarmed, with no cards up his sleeve.

Inez grabbed a nearby chair leg for support. At that moment, the forest of chair legs looked for all the world like a wooden audience, arms high in shock and horror.

"I stopped at the house," said Mark. He eased both hands over the head of his cane and leaned on it. "When I saw nothing but a burned plot of ground, I feared the worst."

She closed her eyes. She could block the sight of him, but not the sound of his voice, the soft Southern accent blurring his words, smoothing them out until they were like silk wrapped around her throat.

The sun began to cast its light within. She opened her eyes and took a hard look, still not quite believing that her errant husband, who had been gone for so long, was standing there before her. Not a ghost, but real. A few things in his appearance registered as different from before. New lines creased his face, and he was lean in a way that spoke of illness, past or present. A scar extended from the corner of the left eye and disappeared beneath his light brown hair. He leaned upon a walking cane.

He smoothed his sandy mustache, which, she noticed with an odd detachment, was still the same. "I must ask—William?"

"He's well."

His shoulders loosened as he sighed, a sound of relief. "You're both alive and safe. My prayers are answered then. When I first realized that you were still here in Leadville, I thought that William was…" He shook his head. "But then, when I got to town and saw the house gone, I imagined the worst. So I came here to wait. Waiting, for what, I didn't know. So, where is he, our boy?"

The concern and relief in his voice sounded real. Or was it all for show? Even in the old days, even after ten years of marriage, sometimes she wasn't sure. Her love and jealousy had so often blinded her to where the truth lay.

She slipped a hand in her coat pocket. "You need to leave."

The cane was suddenly against her wrist. He took one limping step closer. "You still in the habit of carrying that little Smoot pocket revolver, darlin'?" The cane pressed lightly, testing her.

"The Smoot," she said coldly, "went up with the house."

With the cane resting against her arm, she slowly extracted a ring of keys. The cane slid away as she held one up before him at eye level.

"This is the key to the dressing room behind the office." She saw him glance up toward the second floor. She continued, "*My* room. I'm the only one with the key. We—Abe and I—changed the locks to the office and dressing room some time ago."

She stared past the key, straight into his eyes, willing him to recognize the depth of her seriousness. "Speaking of the Smoot and such, do you remember what you impressed upon me, early on, in our marriage? Shoot first, ask questions later. If you gain entrance to *my* room through any means whatsoever—pick the lock or copy the key—I will shoot you with your old Navy revolver, which I just happen to have up there. I'll shoot first, deal with the questions later. Actually, I doubt there will be questions. I will simply claim I didn't know it was you, that I thought you were an assailant, breaking in."

She pressed her lips together and stared, daring him to call her bluff, hoping he wouldn't.

To her surprise, he nodded, and took a step back. "We need to talk, darlin'. Not now, but soon. I know you've got questions."

"No questions." She started toward the stairs and the office. "I'm tired. Leave."

"Just tell me," he said, "and I'll go for now. Is my son up there?"

My son.

One foot on the stairs, she turned. Her hand gripped the handrail so hard she felt her knuckles shift. Finally she said, "William is back East with my sister. He's safe. He's well."

With that, she continued up the stairs without another look back.

Once in her room, she waited by the window. A few agonizing minutes ticked by. Finally, she saw his lean figure appear on the boardwalk below and, with that unfamiliar limp, cross the street to the Clairmont Hotel.

Inez paced from one end of the modest room to the other, trying to calm herself. She thought of all the plans she had put into motion, with the expectation that her husband was dead or, at least, not returning. Her plans to obtain an uncontested divorce from an absentee husband. Her ever-closer liaison with the reverend. Her plans to reconnect with her young son, William.

My God, he's back. Why? Why now?

She had arranged to meet her sister Harmony and William in Manitou, less than two weeks hence. Keeping those plans secret from Mark would be impossible. Once he knew that William would be in Colorado and that Inez would be traveling to see him, he'd insist on coming. *Maybe I can insist that I must go to Manitou first, alone, to prepare Harmony. She thinks he's dead. Good God, I thought he was dead.*

Inez stared at the silver lamp sconce on the wall, unlit, her mind racing. *Does he expect to just pick up where we left off before he disappeared?*

She went to her fainting couch and gripped the tasseled pillow in both hands. Underneath, Mark's Civil War Navy revolver lay in cold, dark stillness. Loaded. Ready.

Inez twisted the pillow viciously, as if strangling it.

"God damn you, Mark Stannert!" she hissed. "God damn you to hell. You can't just waltz back in here and expect me to forgive your sins and kiss your wounds. I don't care *what* happened to you! I will not let this happen. Not now. You will not ruin my life. The life I have planned. I'll kill you first."

Chapter Three

Inez became aware of Susan, gently patting her hand, and shook her head, disengaging from the past. Susan knew Mark, knew of Inez's reluctance to revisit those days of chaos after his sudden and recent return. But apart from all that, something about the Paces also urged Inez to caution.

Early the previous day, the Paces, their entourage, and their confusion of trunks, hat boxes, carpet bags, and travel cases had unexpectedly popped up at the Leadville stagecoach office as Inez and Susan were boarding the hotel's private coach to Manitou. Mr. Pace had strenuously demanded seats, and got them. After the tense introduction, Inez had decided not to divulge any more than necessary during the journey.

"Leadville is played out," he snapped. "There are no decent opportunities for growth and investment. Only fools invest there." Pace paused, tugging on his collar as if it was too tight. "But Manitou, now that is a place of great interest and promising growth."

"Miss Carothers, are you also going to Manitou to take the waters? Or are you meeting relatives there?" Mrs. Pace's voice flowed over her husband's rant.

Susan sat up straighter and Inez could imagine the smile radiating from behind the net covering her face. "I'm a photographer, Mrs. Pace. I will be spending some time with Mrs. Galbreaith, who is a photographer in Manitou. She's promised to introduce me to the natural wonders of the area, including the Garden of the Gods. With Mrs. Stannert coming down for a holiday it was the perfect opportunity for me to accompany her and bring my equipment."

The stage slowed, then creaked to a stop. A few muffled thumps and bumps punctuated the sudden silence, along with the snort of the horses and jingle of the traces. The door flew open and the driver pulled down the kerchief covering his nose and mouth, showing a definite demarcation between dirt-red skin on the upper half of his face and weathered brown below. "A few minutes, mistresses and sir, whilst we be changin' the horses," he said, as he helped Susan, then Mrs. Pace, Inez, and the nanny disembark. "Timest to walk the kinks out."

It was the same speech he had delivered at the previous two stops of the day, and at the four stops on the day before. Inez accepted the driver's proffered hand as she stepped down out of the stage and observed Susan and Mrs. Pace chatting as they repaired to the facilities by the shabby way station. As she watched, Mrs. Pace paused and set a protective hand over her midsection. At Susan's apparent inquiry, the young wife shook her head, and the two women continued on to the water closets.

Another little Pace on the way? The thought crossed Inez's mind, in a desultory fashion, as she added the inadvertent "tell" to other signs she'd gleaned on the trip.

Inez strolled across the hard-packed ground, grateful for a moment's release from the rolling motion of the coach, and lifted her veil up and over her hat, breathing deeply. The lungful of air carried with it the hot summer scent of pine, dust, and well-exercised horseflesh. She wandered around the back of the carriage to the banks of the South Platte. Sunlight, inclining toward the west, glinted ferociously off turbulent water. Its rushing sound—cool and full, like the roar of wind through a forest—carried her to a rare peacefulness. Inez closed her eyes and tipped her head back, feeling the strength of summer sun heat her eyelids.

"Manitou Springs is the coming place, you know. This physician, Dr. Aurelius Prochazka, he knows what he is doing."

Inez's eyes snapped open. She turned to Mr. Pace, trying to contain her irritation. The businessman had pulled yet another pocketchief from the depths of his jacket.

"Well, sir, as you appear to be well-versed in such things, you *would* know." She hoped he would take the hint and leave her to a moment's tranquility.

"Oh, yes." Pace rocked on his heels, gazing at the river. "There is no doubt. I have spent many a summer at the health spas and watering holes back East. My wife, you see, is declining in health, but determined to chase the cure and I am in complete agreement. None of this 'keep in closed rooms, dose with cod-liver oil, and pray to God nonsense.' Begging your pardon, Mrs. Stannert, if you are a devout woman." He didn't even look her way to register her reaction.

Inez's temptation to turn and walk away melted in the sudden torrent of personal information pouring from the businessman. She had wondered about Mrs. Pace, thought that, on top of her possibly delicate family condition, there was something else behind the deep cough that occasionally rattled her otherwise healthy-seeming frame. And here was the good husband, spilling all to a stranger.

"In Manitou, I see the seeds of growth. Nay, not just seeds, for they have already sprouted, but a healthy sapling, which has taken root and flourishes. Mark my words, Mrs. Stannert, there are fortunes to be made in Manitou. I am certain of it, and I have the nose for a going proposition. I am most hopeful concerning Dr. Prochazka and his formulations and his prescribed regimen of exercise, fresh air, healthful food, and the mineral waters. Truly, it is as if a miracle had…"

Inez spared a glance from the river.

He looked old. Older, Inez corrected herself. His shoulders slumped, lines of worry cutting even deeper alongside of his mustache as he frowned. His face still streamed with sweat, despite their being freed from the confines of the stage and the slight breeze that whispered over the waters.

"I should not have brought her with me on this side trip, to the pestilence of Leadville. It was a mistake. A mistake. Her cough had lessened in Manitou, and now, listen to her. We were warned. We were told it was not wise. But she insisted on coming. One error in judgment breeds another. I was most foolish, and now, we will all pay the price." He seemed to be talking to himself.

Inez was surprised at the sudden flash of sympathy that softened her disdain of the bombastic businessman.

"All aboard!"

The shout from the driver indicated it was time to continue the journey.

Pace jumped, then looked at Inez, his countenance filled with fear and something more. Guilt? Self-loathing? It was gone before she could dissect it further, and his face flooded with embarrassment.

To spare him further discomfiture, Inez lowered her veil and disappeared into anonymity, saying, "Well, we will be in Manitou by tonight. Once we reach Ute Pass, it's a steep ride down the other side, and we shall be there, in the shadow of Pike's Peak."

Pace turned with her to the coach and suddenly slumped, one knee to the ground.

Inez grabbed his arm. "Mr. Pace, are you unwell?"

The rust-coated driver and the veiled Mrs. Pace were hurrying toward them.

"Leadville. The air, the night, it must have made me ill." He took out his kerchief with a trembling hand and held it to his mouth. "I'll be better once we are moving again."

"Edward!" Mrs. Pace took one of her husband's arms. Inez stepped away, and the driver took the other. "What is it?"

"Tight. Like a band. Here." He slashed a hand across his chest.

"Perhaps we'd best get you back in the coach, sir," said the driver. "Soonst we start, soonst we'll get to Manitou. There's nought here to help." He glanced around the low sage, the small way station, the primitive facilities. "All the proper pill-rollers and practitioners of physic are in Manitou. We've a fresh team of horses rarin' to go. Just need to crest Ute Pass, then it's down we go. Shouldst be there by nightfall."

The trip to the pass was, if anything, worse, with the heat of the afternoon pouring onto the lurching coach. The children squabbled and whined with growing intensity. Conversation faltered as lips parched.

Then, the rains came.

It started with a bit of thunder, barely audible. Before long, the air around them thickened, and closed in. The first few drops whipped in the windows, slapping those nearest with a cold awakening. Curtains, which had been opened for the cooling breezes, were hastily drawn down. The interior sank into premature night.

The patter of rain became an insistent drumming on the wood frame. The coach canted forward noticeably as they began descending the snakelike road on the other side of the pass.

Mr. Pace drew out a silver flask and after shaking it, turned to his wife. "You have the tonic still?"

Inez was alarmed by the odd, almost breathless rasp to his voice.

"Of course. I finished a bottle this morning, and have several still untouched."

"Inside? Here?"

Every word seemed to cost him.

Mrs. Pace nodded, then said, "Edward, do you think it wise? The formulation is specifically for me. The doctor and nurse made it clear that each condition has its own remedy, based on symptoms, gender—"

"Said…for…pulmonary…" It was all he could wheeze out. He gestured, an impatient give-it-to-me snap of the fingers. Mrs. Pace, who like the other women had pulled her travel veil back in the dark interior, looked alarmed. She leaned toward the nanny. "My valise. The tonic. Quickly."

The nanny handed the infant to its mother and yanked a soft-sided valise out from under her seat. She rummaged around in it, even as Mr. Pace's breathing changed, taking on an ominous wheeze.

The nanny finally pulled out a small, dark bottle. Mrs. Pace snatched it from her. The seal gave with a small crack, and Mrs. Pace handed it to her husband. "Dr. Prochazka says a teaspoon to ease the breathing."

Mr. Pace shook his head and tipped the bottle into his mouth. Brought it down, wiping the back of his hand across his mouth. "Air." He wheezed.

The nanny to one side of Inez and Susan to the other rolled up the leather window curtains. Rain gusted in, causing the children to scream even louder.

Mrs. Pace rounded on them, clutching the baby tight as it began to wail. "Quiet!" The one word held a surprising edge of steel. The children immediately ceased, except for the baby, who continued a high-pitched screeching that seemed to require no intake of air. She jiggled the baby, asking her husband, "Did it help? Can you breathe easier?"

In answer, Mr. Pace raised the dark amber bottle and drained it. Mrs. Pace cried, "Edward…no! That's too much!" as the nanny simultaneously squeaked, "Sir!"

The small bottle fell to the rattling wood floor of the coach. Coughing violently, Pace grabbed at his cravat with both hands, tearing at it so savagely that the detachable collar popped off at one end.

He leaned toward Inez, almost as if he were executing a deep bow in preparation for asking her hand in a dance. Instead, he reached out, grabbed her knee. The iron grip of his hand pinched the skin beneath the intervening layers of travel skirt and petticoats. Inez inadvertently yelped, and Mrs. Pace covered a scream with her one free hand. The nanny tried to rise in the confines of the swaying, accelerating coach. Pace vomited, splashing bloody flux over Inez's black travel skirts and shoes.

He collapsed half against her, half on the rocking coach floor.

His eyes stared, wide open, but Inez knew they saw nothing but blackness.

Chapter Four

The stunned silence in the coach vanished under a torrent of pandemonium.

Mrs. Pace stuffed the baby under one arm and, with near superhuman strength, hauled her husband up off the floor with the other. Inez, recovering from shock, grabbed his lapels, heedless of the ominously red fluid now dribbling from his mouth and all over her gloves, and helped Mrs. Pace push him back into his seat. The nanny put her energy into screaming. "Stop! Stop! For the love of Jesus, stop the horses!"

The baby howled from its inverted station under his mother's arm. The toddler boy, who had gaped as his father pitched forward, now added his cries to the baby's. The girl stuffed her gloved hand into her mouth and chewed on the fabric. Susan half rose in the pitching coach and, holding herself steady with one hand on the window frame, began pounding on the ceiling. Wooden echoes rattled inside the confined space, like a staccato drumbeat. Keeping one hand on Mr. Pace's chest to hold his slumping form upright, Inez turned to the nanny and snarled, "Stop yelling! The driver can't hear you!"

The nanny, hands over her ears, continued wailing.

Inez was ready to lean over and slap her hard, chancing a fall onto Mr. Pace's lap in the lurching carriage, when Mrs. Pace said, "Miss Warren. Shut up."

It wasn't said at the top of the lungs. It wasn't said in anger. All the same, the tone behind those four words carried the authority of a direct order from a general to the army. Had the words been "forward march," the inhabitants of the coach would have marched straight into a death's hail of bullets.

Miss Warren shut up.

"Assist Miss Carothers," Mrs. Pace said.

Miss Warren aimed a meaty fist at the ceiling and added her own unsyncopated beat. Inez heard a muffled bark of the driver. The team's rhythmic canter faltered along with the sudden drag of a brake applied.

Mrs. Pace turned to the children beside her and, with only a modicum less of intensity, said, "Mathilda, Atticus, quiet!"

The admonition was completely unnecessary, as they had silenced at their mother's first order to Miss Warren. The only one still carrying on was the baby. Mrs. Pace thrust the infant out—not to the nanny, but to Inez. "Take him. Please."

Inez automatically clutched the drooling, hiccupping babe to her best traveling cloak. His warm weight against her arm and chest, the soft head of hair brushing her chin, brought memory flooding back of the last time she had held her son William. He had been eight months old. She'd handed him to her sister Harmony in Denver, knowing she would not see him for a long, long time. The feeling of having her heart ripped in two.

Mrs. Pace leaned toward her husband, lifted his chin off his chest, and using the same imperious tone, but softer, with desperation, said, "Mr. Pace. Edward! Can you hear me?"

By this time the coach had creaked to a stop, nearly throwing the nanny on top of Mr. Pace's inert form. There was a slight clatter from above, a dip and rise of the compartment as the driver jumped down from the box.

The far door swung open. Atticus and Mathilda shrank back from the rain that drove in through the gap.

Mrs. Pace spoke. "My husband, Mr. Pace, he's unconscious."

The driver's head disappeared, the door slammed shut. A moment later, he was on the other side opening the opposite door. Mr. Pace, now leaning half against the coach wall, half on the door, almost toppled out despite his wife's fist balled onto his jacket sleeve. The driver caught the man's form and half carried, half dragged him out into the open air.

Mrs. Pace slipped out after him. Inez turned to the nanny and said, "Here." She popped the baby into the nanny's doughy arms like handing off a hot potato from oven to plate, squeezed past the woman, then paused on the coach step. She half-turned and addressed the interior. "Miss Carothers, would you stay with the children?"

Susan moved to sit by Mathilda and Atticus. Inez heard her voice, low and comforting, balm to the children's fear and confusion.

Inez stepped carefully onto the hardpacked road, now skimmed with mud. The roaring of an unseen river racketed about in the narrow confines of Ute Pass. The driver had spread an oilcloth tarp on the ground and was setting Mr. Pace upon it. Inez drew close. Mr. Pace's face was slack and white in the dying light, eyes open and empty.

Mrs. Pace crouched on the edge of the tarp, murmuring her husband's name over and over. She'd removed his glove and was chafing his hand.

Hand to her neck, holding her travel cloak closed in the insistent wind, Inez knelt on a flapping corner of the tarp, searching for the right words to say.

She had seen too many dead men in her time to not recognize another.

"He has never fainted in his life," Mrs. Pace said. "Never, ever. It must have been the altitude. Perhaps something he ate. When he returned to the hotel from his meetings last night, he seemed unwell."

Inez looked up at the driver, crouched on the other side of Pace's body. He was squinting westward. The sun had slipped away and dark clouds blanketed the peaks. His eyebrows, bleached nearly white by constant exposure, were furrowed in a frown. He tipped back his soaked wide-brimmed hat and pulled down the neckerchief that protected mouth and nose from the elements, revealing a long drooping mustache covering compressed lips.

He glanced at Mrs. Pace, then her husband, and finally at Inez, with eyebrows raised, telegraphing a unspoken question. Inez shook her head slightly. Mrs. Pace had not the ear nor heart for the truth right then. It would be the ultimate cruelty to insist she face it, straight out, in this God-forsaken spot of road.

The driver removed one long gauntlet glove and reached over to close Pace's staring eyes against the driving rain.

"Ma'am, I can wrap him in the oilcloth and set him up top by me, so'st not to alarm the young'uns."

"No, no, that will never do." The wind whipped tangled loops of honey-blonde hair about her ears and tugged at the lifted travel veil. "He needs to be kept warm, inside. He needs time. Time to recover."

The driver opened his mouth as if to argue. Then, he closed it and instead exhaled a long sigh through his nose.

"Wrap him up," Mrs. Pace continued, suddenly all business, "and set him next to me. We've a fur coat in one of our trunks. If we can find it and wrap that over him…How close are we to Manitou? He needs a doctor!"

The driver folded the oilcloth over Pace and stood, looking around at the terrain. "We have crested Ute Pass. Just need to make the journey down to town. No needst to get into your things, ma'am. I've got a buffalo robe at hand wouldst keep him well covered."

"He needs rest," she said, with conviction. "He just needs to rest."

The road stretched in both directions, as empty as the eye could see.

Inez stood from her half-crouched position. "Let me help you back into the coach, Mrs. Pace," she said. "Our driver, Mr.—" She looked at him, at a loss for his name. He'd introduced himself back in Leadville, but that seemed so long ago.

"Morrow. Gene Morrow."

"Mr. Morrow will get the blanket for your husband."

She handed the tiny woman back into the coach as Morrow went to the rear and pulled the heavy skin from the boot. Inez stepped away from the coach, hugging her elbows against the chill. Before entering the coach to wrap the dead man, the driver looked again at Inez and shook his head once, a quick side-to-side motion.

He would drive as quickly as was safe, she knew. It would be her job to keep panic and hysteria away and maintain some semblance of calm in the coach, even if it meant denying the horror that had just occurred.

Inez waited until Morrow had tucked the robe around the body before venturing back inside. The two Pace children had changed seats to give their mother and father more room, and were now huddling between the nanny and Susan, who had draped a protective arm over their shoulders. "Did you really see a red injin savage?" the little girl asked.

"Indeed I did," said Susan. "When I was no older than you are now. But his skin was no more red than our driver's. There were many Indians close to the town where I grew up in Nebraska. This one, he was hardly a savage. He liked to take tea with my father, who ran the town's newspaper, and they would talk. Why, he even wore a top hat!"

"Stop your prattling, Mathilda," said Mrs. Pace sharply. "Your father needs his rest."

Nanny Warren was whimpering as if they were all on their way to the underworld. She clutched the baby, pillowing it to her bosom, and rocked back and forth. "Missus. Oh Missus."

"Shhh!"

"Here," said Inez injecting a no-nonsense tone to her voice. "Why don't I sit on the other side of Mr. Pace, and we'll just make sure that he stays covered and comfortable."

"Thank you, Mrs. Stannert." Mrs. Pace suddenly sounded far more subdued.

"What's wrong with Papa?" Mathilda wanted to know.

Susan was staring at Inez through the darkening coach. Inez gave a slight shake of the head, cousin to the one from the driver to her.

"Your father has taken ill," said Mrs. Pace.

"We'll see what the doctor says when we get to the hotel," Inez added.

Mathilda looked dubious. "The medicine made him sick."

"Papa?" said Atticus uncertainly.

Nanny Warren left off whimpering and began to whisper. Inez, sitting across from her, caught "Blessed is he whose transgressions are forgiven, whose sins are covered. Blessed is the man whose sin the Lord does not count against him."

In her turn, Inez prayed fervently that the road to Manitou would be smooth and swift. But no matter how fast the horses ran, she feared the questions and sorrows rattling within the coach would keep easy pace and only loom the larger at journey's end, not fade away.

Chapter Five

The ageless sound of racing water kept them company down the pass, across the clatter of a wooden bridge, and into the flats at last. A change in the tempo of hoofbeats alerted Inez that the coach was slowing down. Inez pulled back a corner of the coach curtain, relieving the pitch dark inside. The two oldest children, huddled next to their nanny, stirred. Inez heard one snuffle, then yawn.

Inez eyed the dark shape beside her: Mr. Pace, bundled in a tarp like a caterpillar in its chrysalis. Only, unlike a caterpillar, he was not going to emerge in a new form, unless one counted the journey from life to death as the ultimate transformation.

Mrs. Pace leaned over and gently shook her little girl's shoulder, whispering to wake her. Inez's heart constricted at the sight of the children, beginning to stir. Inez became aware of a pale filtered light coming through the curtain and the motionless state of the conveyance, just as her friend Susan said softly, "We're here."

A hasty crunch of feet on gravel, accompanied by low male voices outside, stopped. The coach door creaked open. Weak light resolved into a partially shuttered lantern held aloft. The shaft of light revealed the holder of the lamp—a barrel-chested man, dressed formally in a black frock coat but no hat. Thinning hair on top was offset by an impressive pair of white muttonchops, which, like a pair of parentheses, embraced a round and somber face. He gazed at the stirring forms in the coach, before taking in the wrapped figure by the far door.

He said, "Ah," then turned to the driver. "Mr. Morrow, please fetch Dr. Prochazka. He's in the clinic, of course." He returned his attention to the travelers. "I'm Mr. Lewis, that is Mr. Franklin Lewis, hotelier and owner of the Mountain Springs House. You must all be exhausted after your journey. Please, allow me to escort you inside."

"Are our rooms readied?" Mrs. Pace asked.

"Indeed, Mrs. Pace, they are." He held out a hand.

Mrs. Pace, now holding the toddler boy, clucked to her daughter. The young girl tentatively disembarked. Mrs. Pace, holding her son, followed. Susan exited, and the nanny with the baby squeezed past Inez and the body of Mr. Pace to hasten out the door.

Inez risked a final glance at the lonely shape bundled on the coach's seat, then rose and moved to the door to take Franklin Lewis' steadying hand. A gangly figure behind Lewis scampered to the boot of the stagecoach. Inez caught a glimpse of a youngster hauling out hatboxes and piling them into a three-wheeled handcart.

Lights gleamed through lower windows set under a deep porch, backlighting figures within. The upper floor was mostly dark. Here and there muted illumination bled through drawn curtains. Beyond this half-lit façade, all was blackness, although Inez sensed the hotel sat on a saddle in a rise and the hill continued, in some fashion, behind.

Blessedly cool air caressed her cheek. Inez inhaled as deeply as her sweat-loosened travel corset would allow, and let the sound of the vigorous waterway wash over her. The air seemed heavy compared to Leadville's thin atmosphere, full of moisture, and redolent with sage and a hint of something sweet and blooming, some kind of rose. The sharp, bracing scent of mint tangled among other scents she could not identify.

Entranced, temporarily distracted from the sorrows of the trip and complications of her life, Inez lingered a moment longer in the welcome air. The small knot of travelers huddled around the lantern and guided by Lewis, drew further away, ever closer to the hotel proper. Inez fell further behind, seeking a few minutes alone before having to face whatever commotion waited inside. She finally turned from the light toward the invisible river and stood still, listening, wishing the water could simply sweep away all problems with its rushing sound.

The loud crunch of hasty footsteps on the gravel behind her belatedly reached her awareness. A hand fell heavy on her shoulder with a stern voice saying, "Nurse Crowson! I need you now."

Inez's own hand had flown to her pocket at the instant of the touch. Her new pocket revolver was out, even as she wrenched away and turned. In the confusing light, she looked up.

Tall as she was, Inez was not used to encountering men whose eyes were a handspan or more above her own. Wrapped in a loose white coat, the thin rail of a man took a hasty step back. Reflected light flashed off oval spectacles and touched a head of wild hair, which looked as if its wearer had faced off a windstorm without the aid of any pomade.

"Madam, calm yourself! I mistook you for someone else." Without further ado, the white shadow brushed past her and stalked toward the carriage, a ghost crossing the gravel pathway.

The knot of travelers had reached the porch and disappeared inside. Lewis was hurrying back in her direction, lantern bobbing. Inez, slipped the pistol back into its hiding place, trying to stop the shaking in her hands.

"Mrs. Stannert." He positioned himself at her side. "Please, come with me." Holding the lantern high, he gestured toward the hotel. Inez risked a final glance back over her shoulder. The white-coated figure knelt by the prone shape that was Mr. Pace, with the coach driver standing nearby. Another involuntary shudder ran through her frame.

Lewis took her elbow. "I am sorry that you and Miss Carothers were party to this sad event. Forgive me, but you are shaking like a leaf! The shock of the incident, I'm certain. Come, it's warm inside and I can supply something to calm your nerves."

I do hope it is something with a high alcohol content. She allowed him to guide her to the inn.

One of the hotel staff opened the door for them as they came near. Eyes dazzled by the light, Inez looked around. A wide staircase faced them across the lobby, its long sweep guarded at the top by an impressive bronze statue of Hermes, complete with winged helmet, winged feet, and caduceus. She was willing to bet, although it was too dark to be certain, that the statue also sported the obligatory fig leaf.

To her left, a reception desk was flanked by twin marble pillars. Behind the desk and above the shadowed letterboxes and key board, the antlered heads of what looked like a veritable herd of elk or deer graced the wall. On the right, the lilt of a string quartet drifted to her from behind a set of closed dark-wood doors.

The doorman, a young man with slicked-down blond hair and a "face-spanner" mustache with ferociously waxed points that looked lethal in their sharpness, closed the hotel's front door with a muted click. Lewis asked him in a soft undertone, "Where is Miss Carothers?"

"In the ladies' parlor, as you suggested." The words rolled out in well-schooled syllables that spoke of top-drawer schooling in England. "The fire's made up, and I am off to prepare the tray."

Lewis nodded. "Excellent. Thank you, Mr. Epperley."

Epperley bowed to Inez saying, "Madam," and moved briskly past the music room and staircase, vanishing down a hallway to the right.

Lewis said, "Mr. Terrance Epperley, my manager. Came to Manitou for the waters at his physician's orders and decided to stay. Many similar stories here at the springs."

He guided her to the left of the staircase, away from the music and the lobby and down a hallway punctuated by gaslights set in sconces at regular intervals. Pausing before a door leaking bright light from underneath, he remarked, "Here we are," and pushed the door open.

Susan looked up from a cushion-filled settee. Other chairs and a divan or two dotted the room, set further back from a fireplace that, despite its painted screen, radiated heat. Susan's travel coat and hat hung on the coat rack by the door. Inez felt beads of sweat popping out along her hairline, the layers of clothes and overgarments suddenly stifling. On top of it all, she had a raging, overwhelming desire for a glass of something that would take the edge off the day's events.

Inez unclasped her travel cloak, and allowed Mr. Lewis to slip it from her shoulders. "Mr. Lewis, is there something to drink?"

"Refreshment is on the way. Epperley is preparing it."

Coat off, Inez gazed down at her skirts. A crust of dried vomit and blood blotted the dark wool from knee to floor. She bit back a groan. The skirt, she feared was a lost cause.

Without her cloak, she felt a coldness penetrate to her bones despite the heat in the room. Shivering, she moved to the fireplace, standing to one side of the screen. A mantle clock ticked loudly into the silence as Lewis took her cloak to the coat rack.

The door swung open, admitting Epperley with a tray of crystalware and a decanter. He handed Inez a cut-crystal goblet before moving to Susan. Inez took a large gulp, only to have the liquid fizz in her mouth, delivering an overwhelming taste of ash and salts. She swallowed reflexively, and almost gagged. She stared at the glass in disbelief, then looked at the hotelier.

"What *is* this?"

Lewis appeared proud, obviously taking her shocked distaste for admiration. "Mineral water from Manitou's famous Ute Iron spring. You all have been through an extremely difficult event, and no doubt you find yourself much disturbed in temperament and humors. The carbonic acid and carbonate of soda of the waters here in Manitou are known to have a calming effect, soothe inflammations, and relieve dyspepsia, that is, the imperfect actions of the digestive powers. Certain of the springs also address symptoms of nervous exhaustion and those of a," he averted his eyes, "delicate nature. "

Her stomach did a flip-flop, feeling like it was back on a badly rutted portion of the coach road. She set the goblet down with a decided *click* on the mantelpiece.

"Something stronger, Mr. Lewis, if you would," Inez said tersely.

"As you wish. Nurse Crowson makes an excellent mint tea, that does wonders for the nerves."

"Stronger than tea. If you please."

He looked around the room, as if at a loss. "We have some wine."

Inez narrowed her eyes. "I was thinking more along the lines of whiskey. Or brandy."

Susan froze in mid-sip, crystal glass raised. Lewis' mouth dropped open. He looked as shocked as if she'd slapped him. No one moved, except for Epperley who set the decanter of spring water on a side table and silently exited the parlor.

Finally Lewis spoke faintly, "Pardon me? Whiskey?"

His horrified stare only enraged her. "Surely, surely, if you haven't a decent whiskey in the house, the gentlemen in this fine hotel take an occasional glass of after-dinner brandy with their cigars. That will do nicely. Minus the cigar, of course."

Although her gaze was fixed upon Lewis, she caught sight of Susan who was shaking her head in a determined fashion. Inez could almost hear her wordless remonstration: this isn't Leadville. You are not in your saloon. This is a different place, a different class, with different expectations.

It all began to close in on her. The present. The past.

The lingering aftertaste of the mineral water.

The heaviness of her skirts, soiled with Mr. Pace's dried blood.

All that awaited, and all that went before.

It felt as if someone had yanked on her corset stays, tightening them to the point where she could no longer draw a full breath.

The sudden tightness gave her an idea. Placing the back of one hand to her forehead, she murmured, "Oh," and swayed slightly.

"Mrs. Stannert?" Lewis sounded alarmed. "Are you ill?"

"Just...faint."

Inez very quickly found herself hustled to the settee, pillows plumped around her, Susan's arm about her shoulders. Lewis hovered before her, a vial of smelling salts hovering below her now stinging nostrils.

Alarmed that her bit of stagecraft had been so readily accepted, she held up a hand, fending off the salts. "Forgive me, please. The long day, the sudden shock of a warm room."

"Madam?" It was Epperley, at her elbow, holding a goblet that, she was relieved to see, held an amber liquid that she knew well.

Inez accepted the brandy snifter and cradled the bowl between her hands. She swirled the trapped liquid gently to release the dark, smoky aroma and inhaled. Closing her eyes against the anxious faces, she lifted the glass and allowed the first taste to slip between her lips and down her throat. A dark and velvet heat spread down and out to her limbs. She sighed in contentment and release. Upon opening her eyes, she discovered everyone in the room looking at her anxiously, except Epperley, who seemed to be trying to hide a smile beneath his mustache.

Epperley said, "I say, looks like the brandy did the trick."

She looked down at the empty snifter. "Forgive me. The trip, the travails, must have weakened me and sent me into this state. My apologies."

She snuck a sideways glance at Lewis, to see if her explanation would do.

"It is quite understandable," the hotelier assured her. "Such a shock. Do you have these spells regularly?"

It dawned on Inez that admitting to an occasional fainting spell might be the ticket to obtaining "something stronger" than the ghastly mineral water—say, the welcome medicinal draught of brandy—without censure during her stay.

Susan said, "No!" just as Inez said, "Yes!"

Lewis tsked-tsked and said to Epperley. "Perhaps a little more brandy, to be certain the chills have departed."

Epperley picked up the empty snifter from the occasional table. "But of course, sir." When Lewis turned his attention back to Inez, Epperley looked at Inez from behind his employer's back, one eyebrow raised in question or perhaps amusement.

Inez said, "That would be wonderful."

Epperley exited again.

"What about Mrs. Pace and the children?" Susan asked.

Lewis said, "She asked they be taken directly to her rooms."

He hesitated, looking from Susan to Inez. "The town marshal will probably want to talk with you both about what happened in the coach. Dr. Prochazka is understandably concerned about what happened as well."

"Is it really necessary?" Susan asked.

Mindful of more brandy in her future, Inez gave a mock shiver. Lewis ventured to pat her hand timidly. "We shall make it as painless as possible for you both and for Mrs. Pace. But, such unfortunate circumstances require a certain amount of inquiry. I'm certain it will add up to little. Mr. Pace was of an age that I'd not advise him to take such an arduous journey, and his wife—" He caught himself. "Well, I am no physician, I leave all that to Dr. Prochazka. However, I've seen my share of ailments and conditions here in Manitou over these past few years, and, I can assure you the climate of Manitou and the therapies of the good doctor are truly miraculous."

He ventured another hand pat.

Inez wanted to whop him.

"We have had customers and clients come from all corners of the country and Europe, with complaints of consumption to colitis, hysteria to neurasthenia. They come through our doors, take the therapies and follow the doctor's instructions, and recover."

He stopped as Epperley returned and offered Inez another brandy, saying, "Should madame require anything further, I am at your service."

Lewis added, "Epperley is my right-hand man. If there is anything that you need or something does not meet your satisfaction, do not hesitate to call on him or myself."

The second glass did much to augment the benefits of the first. She had barely finished when the parlor door flew open. Inez looked around, expecting to see Epperley with yet another offer of more brandy.

Instead, hands clasped before her pale satin evening dress, eyes large and liquid in the dim parlor light...her sister.

Harmony.

Chapter Six

Momentarily forgetting her role as invalid, Inez rose to her feet. Harmony's face brightened. Inez held out her arms. *Has it truly been a year since I last saw her?*

Harmony moved forward, evening shoes making no sound on the deep carpet.

The sisters embraced. Inez closed her eyes, feeling the slight frame of her sister solid and real within her arms.

"Mrs. Jonathan DuChamps. Let me look at you." Inez pulled back to put Harmony out at arm's length.

The first thing Inez marked was how pale Harmony was, nearly as pale as the antimacassar lace on the back of the settee. Far paler than she'd been the previous year. The second thing Inez became aware of was her sister's youth: twenty-two, and three years married.

At thirty-one, Inez felt suddenly old.

Harmony's smile seemed to bring light to the room, then her expression sobered. "I heard about your travels, and the Paces. We met them here at the hotel before they set out to Leadville. They have been at the Mountain Springs House most of the summer, so they told us, and were doing so much better in this climate and under the doctor's care. Oh, poor Mrs. Pace, and the children. I cannot imagine." She stopped, wiped a tear with one hand. A diamond bracelet sparkled at her wrist. "But that is not for us to talk of now." She turned toward Susan, who was now standing. "Is this your traveling companion?"

"Mrs. DuChamps, may I present my dear friend from Leadville, Miss Carothers." Inez, still holding her sister's hand with her own, took Susan's hand as well, drawing her forward to meet her sister. "Miss Carothers is a photographer. Only in the West, I'd imagine you're thinking. Yet, talent finds a way, no matter where it resides, and Miss Carothers has considerable talent. She is also my dear friend and confidant in Leadville, and has been like a sister to me."

Inez looked from one woman to the other and was struck by the resemblance. Both were of modest height, with dark hair and eyes. Harmony had even adopted a stylish frizz of curls bordering her forehead, much like Susan. They differed in their costume, Harmony's elegant eveningwear and diamonds contrasting sharply with Susan's plain, travel-worn clothes. But the most striking difference to Inez was in their skin tone. Susan's face exhibited the rosy flush and darker hue of someone who, despite bonnets and parasols, was no stranger to the sun. By comparison, Harmony's pallor would have suited an alabaster statue.

Her sister's paleness troubled Inez, putting her in mind of invalids lying under blankets and shivering despite fires roaring in the grates. Inez mentally shook off the grim vision.

Harmony took Susan's free hand and said, "My sister's letters mention you often. I look forward to getting to know you during this short time in Manitou."

Susan smiled. "I look forward to that as well, Mrs. DuChamps. I will only be at the Mountain Springs House for tonight. After that, I'll be staying at Mrs. Galbreaith's Ohio House." She glanced at Inez. "I should retire and leave you two to talk. Inez? You'll be all right?"

Harmony looked a question at Inez.

"Fine, fine." Inez said hastily. She added to Harmony, "A momentary faintness. Nothing serious. The travels and the strain, I suspect."

After Susan said her goodnights and departed, the two sisters sat on the settee.

Harmony said, "The arrival of the carriage caused quite a stir among the staff. I had been expecting you, so was more sensitive to their whisperings than others who were in the music room. A tragedy. Those poor children, and Mrs. Pace."

"Sad indeed."

Harmony hesitated, then said, "I have much I need to talk to you about, but it can wait until tomorrow."

"As I have with you." The weight of Mark's return sat like a mountain upon Inez's thoughts.

The mantel clock began chiming. Inez glanced at the time: midnight. "I should be retiring. But, I'd like to see William first."

"Of course!" Harmony paused. "He's sleeping, but we could wake him."

"No need," Inez said. "I just want to see him."

A discreet knock at the door and Lewis entered, key in hand. "Mrs. Stannert, your luggage is in your room, and the warming stove is stoked. Feeling better, I hope?" His eyebrows raised to his nonexistent hairline.

"Much." Inez stood, moved to the coat rack, and gingerly folded her cloak over one arm. "I shall need these cleaned."

"We have an excellent laundress on staff. She's a seamstress as well. If you have anything that needs repairing or cleaning during your stay, she is quick and reliable." Lewis ushered them out of the parlor. "Mrs. Stannert, your room is on the second floor, not far from the DuChamps quarters. May I?" He made as if to escort the women up the stairs.

"No need." Inez took the key from him. "Thank you for your attention."

"We hope your stay here will only improve, after such a taxing beginning."

They mounted the stairs pausing on the landing before the looming statue of Hermes. The second-floor hallway branched to left and right, their lengths punctuated by widely spaced doors facing the front of the hotel. Harmony said, "Our rooms are to the right. Yours is a short way on the left."

She headed down the right branch, Inez close behind her. She stopped outside a room, extracted a key from her sleeve, and set a finger to her lips. "The nanny sleeps in the same room as William. I'll go in first, and wake her, so she doesn't startle."

Inez laced her hands together, willing the trembling to stop. William was just beyond the door. After all the waiting, the moment felt unreal.

Harmony opened the door, leaving it ajar, and moved inside. Moonlight from the far window cast deep shadows about the large and airy room. She leaned over a cot by the window and rocked the shoulder of the person sleeping there. A figure sat up, long hair, nightcap askew. Murmurs back and forth. Harmony turned and beckoned at Inez.

Inez slipped inside and walked toward the bed.

The nanny, Inez saw, was almost a child herself. Fifteen, she guessed, at the most.

Harmony pointed to one side of the room. Inez moved to the small bed and gazed, at last, upon her son.

For a horrible moment, it was as if she gazed upon an unknown child. When last she'd seen him, he had been an infant of eight months. Now, a few months shy of two years old, he lay on his back, arms thrown out, pudgy hands slightly curled. The face was at the same time familiar and not. Sorrow, guilt pulled at her, making it hard to breathe.

More than that, what struck her to her heart was the well-worn calico stuffed dog tucked under the blanket beside him. Faded, repaired with black thread, with only one shoe-button eye, it was the same dog Inez had placed in his arms the previous August. The small comfort, the one link to his life in Leadville that she had bestowed on him when she'd kissed him good-bye a year ago.

I have missed so much. First step. First word. Moments that photographs and letters cannot bring fully to life. Will he remember? Will he remember me?

She had not intended to touch him, but she couldn't stop herself. She laid an open hand lightly, as if cupping a fluffy dandelion, atop his head. His soft brown hair tickled, and she could feel his warmth against her palm. William stirred slightly, fingers of one hand clenching and relaxing. Inez heard the nanny hiss with an intake of breath behind her.

Inez tore herself away and returned to the nanny's bedside.

Harmony put an arm around Inez's waist. "You'll see him more tomorrow," she whispered. "When he's awake, you'll see what a wonderful, bright child he has become. Your son."

Inez nodded, unable to speak past the lump in her throat.

The sisters turned to the door, but not before Inez caught the nanny's expression. Inez would have expected to read annoyance in her features—annoyance at nearly awakening William, annoyance at disturbing her sleep.

But she did not expect the naked emotion, painted by moonlight with such clear intensity upon the nanny's face.

Hate.

Chapter Seven

Inez woke to the voice of the rushing creek and morning light fighting its way through the muslin curtains. She turned on her side, facing the window.

Maybe, she thought, she should have arranged to meet Harmony last winter or spring, so the time away from her son would have been shorter. Maybe she should have gone east to them, instead of waiting until they were able to come west.

She rolled to the other side, annoyed by the squeak of the inner-spring mattress. The latest, greatest in sleeping comfort, so said the advertisements. One night, and she was longing to return to her fainting couch in her room at the Silver Queen Saloon. She wondered if she had, perhaps, been played for a sucker in choosing the Mountain Springs House over, say, the Cliff House, which also touted that it had all the latest comforts of hotel and resort life in the Rockies.

Inez had read the articles, pamphlets, and advertisements about the various Manitou hotels while in Leadville and considered the options carefully. The enthusiastic flow of words about the Mountain Springs House and its elegant accommodations, first-class dining, stupendous gardens, and up-to-date accoutrements had swept her up and carried her along. Descriptions of its proximity to the medicinal springs and the natural wonders of Pike's Peak, the Garden of the Gods, Rainbow Falls, and various canyons had painted visions of peace and, well, harmony.

All of this and more had compelled her to suggest Manitou and the Mountain Springs House as the location for their meeting.

She turned onto her back, inducing another squeal from the springs, and laced her hands behind her head, staring up at white painted ceiling boards. The name of the creek that had pushed her from sleep finally surfaced in her mind, emerging from the welter of descriptive prose she had scanned: Fountain Creek.

A knock at her door brought her bolt up to sitting.

"Inez?" Harmony's voice came soft through the panels. "Are you awake?"

"Yes. Give me a moment." Inez hastened to the dressing screen, and grabbed the dressing gown she'd thrown over the top late last night before retiring. She threw it on and cracked open the door, revealing Harmony wearing a faint smile and a walking suit.

"We are scheduled for the last breakfast sitting," Harmony said. She glanced down the hall, somewhat nervously, then back at Inez. "Let's take a private stroll on the second floor veranda before going down."

"Is William awake?"

"Long since. The nannies and children dine early in The Ordinary. That's the dining room where the children and their nannies often take their meals. Lily and William are out on their morning constitutional with the other children."

"You should have awakened me then." Inez couldn't help it: disappointment sharpened her words into an accusation.

"Forgive me, dear sister." Harmony sounded sympathetic but not particularly contrite. "I know you're anxious to see your son, but there are things we need to talk about first. You will see him soon, I promise."

Inez tried to curb her impatience. An hour more or less was a small space of time compared to the months they had been apart. "Give me fifteen minutes," she said, calculating how fast she could slip into her day wear.

"I'll be in my room." Harmony shed her straw boater, and smoothed her hair, turning away.

Inez closed the door and hurried into her undergarments, muttering as she adjusted her chemise and did up the front fastenings of her corset. She struggled into the tight-fitting cuirass bodice of her gray and cream striped ensemble, an outfit that, she hoped, would take her through the day until the more formal evening dining hour.

With a sigh, she rummaged around in one of her trunks, extracting the silver hairbrush and a handful of pins, and did the best she could to fashion a simple French twist from her shoulder-length hair. With a further sigh, she tipped open one of the hatboxes, which disgorged a straw boater kin to the one her sister had sported. Throwing a lightweight shawl over her shoulders, she glanced at her soiled travel clothes, draped over the rocking chair. She hoped the laundress would be able to resurrect them.

Inez exited the room, locked the door, and moved down the hall, running a finger along the walnut wainscoting. Harmony answered after one knock. Hooking her arm through Inez's, she said, "We can take the air while I talk to you about a few things."

"I have much to discuss with you as well."

They went further down the hall and Harmony pushed open the door to the outside second-story veranda. "Nearly everyone's gone for whatever adventures and constitutionals they have planned for the morning," she explained. "I didn't want to wake you early, given what happened yesterday and last night. Poor Mr. Pace, may he rest in peace." She paused and added in a low voice, "I cannot imagine how it will be for Kirsten Pace, raising all those children without a father."

Inez had nearly forgotten, and wondered how she could have put the whole episode so completely out of mind. "Do you know the family?"

Harmony nodded. "Kirsten is a lovely woman and a devoted mother and wife. My husband Jonathan—you'll meet him at breakfast—became fast friends with Mr. Pace. They shared many of the same interests. Their nanny and our Lily spent much time together, so the children were frequently in your son's company. The little girl absolutely adores him."

"Speaking of William, will he be back soon?"

"Oh yes. After our breakfast."

Recalling the naked hostility in Lily's stare, Inez asked, "About Lily. Is she good with William? Where did she come from? She's not the woman you had in Denver last year, when you took William back with you."

"Oh, *that* woman." The three words dripped disapproval. "I walked into the nursery one day, and caught her drinking. With your son right there! I let her go on the spot, of course."

Inez hmmed, nonplussed by Harmony's intense reaction, then realized mere hmming wouldn't do at all under the circumstances. "Of course," she echoed. "You were very right to do so."

A memory of the taste of brandy from the previous night flashed across Inez's mind, firing a desire for more. The sharpness of the longing shocked her, until she recollected that it was now late in the morning and that her breakfast routine at the saloon consisted of a first cup of coffee, black, followed by a second augmented with a small splash of brandy or one of the finer whiskies she kept in her private reserve. Inez shook her head to banish the thought and brushed one hand along the porch railing as if checking for dust.

It was dusty.

"So," Inez continued, "you hired Lily to take her place? She seems young."

Harmony stopped midstep and faced to Inez. "Lily Harrigan has been in our employ for two years as a domestic." Her words speeded up, and then came out in a nervous rush. "First as a between maid, then as a nursery maid once your son came to live with us. When we let *that woman* go, well, Lily is wonderful with William, even though she is young. She's never given me any reason to disapprove of her conduct."

Harmony faced forward again and jerked back into rapid motion, her chin set with what Inez recognized as a stubborn jut uncomfortably reminiscent of their father. She continued, "Lily obeys, is agreeable, patient, takes her responsibilities seriously, and loves your son to a fault. She has no family to speak of, thus no distractions from her primary duty—taking care of William. I took her in as an act of charity, and it has worked out very well to date." Her tone had become increasingly aggrieved, as if she sensed Inez disapproved of her choice.

Inez hastened, "If Miss Harrigan has your trust, dear sister, then she has mine. I did not mean to gainsay you." *I will take this Lily's measure silently, since Harmony seems so intent on defending her.*

With a stifled sigh, Inez squinted out at the scenery. Beyond the hotel's gravel drive, the dusty red road fronted Fountain Creek, which was crowded on both banks by brush and scrub oak. A picturesque wooden bridge crossed the creek, and dirt paths beyond wound through dry grasses interrupted by large boulders and a rustic pavilion or two. People clustered about two rocky areas around what Inez surmised must be the vaunted springs. Raising her gaze across the little valley yielded a view of foothills, covered with yet more dry grass and scrub brush, with no Pike's Peak in sight.

Inez placed her hands on the railing and leaned to the left, to see past their hotel. Another grand establishment, twin of the Mountain Springs House, was situated some distance away beyond a small dirt road. From what she had read, Inez felt certain that it was the Cliff House. There was very little else to see, aside from the main road meandering away to the southeast. Her initial impressions of Manitou were not living up to its reputation.

To change the subject to something less charged than the nursemaid, she pulled the pamphlet out of her pocket that she had found in her room the previous night and read aloud to her sister. "Our magnificent lodgings are located within a few yards of those wonderful SPRINGS, the NAVAJO, MANITOU, COMMANCHE, AND SHOSHONE. The grandest scenery in the world surrounds it and the waters of the FOUNTAIN Creek flow nears its base." She glanced at Harmony's profile, still set in an uncompromising frown. "I hope you are not disappointed with Manitou, the scenery. It seems…"

Dry and dusty. Rather brown and withered.

"…a little less grand than all the writing made it out to be. It's most certainly not quite what I envisioned when I read it was called the 'Saratoga of the West.' I do apologize if I have brought you all the way here to something not quite as charming as you might have expected. Perhaps we should have picked a different place to meet. Somewhere more civilized. Chicago or St. Louis, perhaps."

Harmony's set jaw relaxed. A smile tugged a dimple into one cheek, and then she actually laughed, a full and unexpected sound of joy. "It's wonderful here, Inez. The air is clean, I can actually draw a breath without coughing." She set one hand on Inez's sleeve. "The hotel's physician, Dr. Prochazka, has me on a regimen of walking every morning and every evening. Our little party, William included, has explored some lovely canyons, and the waterfalls are magnificent."

A slight squeak of door-hinges and the clattering close of a screen door, followed by a rapid, heavy tread on the echoing veranda boards warned Inez that someone was behind and approaching rapidly.

Harmony's gaze skimmed past Inez to take in the approaching person. Her features settled into the sort of polite-but-distantly-annoyed expression that put Inez in mind of her mother when a servant would dare to interrupt.

Inez turned, fully expecting to see a male figure bearing down upon them. Her ears had long become attuned to the sound of steps on Leadville's boardwalks and the plank floors of the Silver Queen Saloon.

So, she was nonplussed to find the encroaching personage was a woman. A large woman, true. Nearly Inez's height, but with a touch more girth. Nondescript, in a gray, no-nonsense dress covered with an enveloping white apron. Eyes cast down as she rustled through what appeared to be a large picnic basket. Inez had an excellent view of the odd white cap, ruffles all around its edges, that sat atop dark hair shot through with gray. The faint, musical clink of small glass objects reached Inez as the woman carefully picked through the basket.

"Good morning, Mrs. DuChamps," she said in a low, mellifluous voice.

A voice on tiptoe: it was the first thing that sprang to Inez's mind. The voice, almost a whisper, was a sharp contrast to the heavy tread on the porch.

"Good morning, Nurse Crowson. Is something amiss?"

"When I didn't see you at the early breakfast sitting, I thought you might be feeling poorly. I came up to see how you were and to deliver these." She held out her large square hand. Two brown bottles, tiny kin to those that had featured in the previous night's catastrophe, nestled side-by-side across her palm.

Dismay jolted through Inez. She snatched the bottles from the nurse, exclaiming, "What are these?"

Harmony said quickly, "Nurse Crowson, this is my sister, Mrs. Stannert. She's joined us for our stay here at Manitou."

"I see." There was nothing servile in those two cold words.

Inez looked up, bristling at the tone, preparing for a verbal battle. Crowson stared at her with the calm of a grazing ruminant. Her eyes were the flat brown of pebbles, worn smooth and featureless by fast-moving waters. Like pebbles, they showed not a flicker of emotion, gave nothing away about what might lie beneath their surfaces.

Harmony reached for the bottles. "These are just the daily doses prescribed by Dr. Prochazka. One is for William, the other is for myself."

Inez turned the bottles over. There, written in a spidery hand on paper labels were the names Harmony DuChamps and William DuChamps.

William DuChamps?

The unexpected surname shot like an arrow through her heart.

Harmony took the bottles from Inez's unresisting hand. "Thank you, Nurse."

"What kind of tonic is William taking?" Inez's maternal fears roared to the forefront, stopping all other thoughts.

Harmony looked at the nurse for help.

"The doctor adjusts each prescription according to the patient's needs," that smooth, low voice rolled over them. "I believe, for William, the base is cod-liver oil. Very beneficial to a child his age. As for the rest, you would need to ask Dr. Prochazka yourself. I'm not privy to all of his prescriptions and mixtures."

"Thank you, nurse." From Harmony, it was a clear dismissal.

Nurse Crowson inclined her head. "Mrs. DuChamps, Mrs. Stannert." She made a swift departure from the veranda, the remaining tonic bottles tinkling lightly in the basket.

Inez reclaimed William's bottle. "You don't know what's in this?" She broke the wax seal with a small snap and held the open vial beneath her nose. A minty blast assaulted her olfactory senses. Lurking beneath was a slightly fishy undertone, and, below that, even fainter, a whiff of something faintly metallic.

"Inez, I don't ask. He is a physician, after all. I wouldn't presume to question him." Harmony gently removed the bottle from Inez and recapped it. "William takes a teaspoon of this after every meal. He thrives. You'll soon see for yourself."

Inez wasn't done. "William *DuChamps*?" She didn't add anything further. She didn't have to.

Harmony colored, but her expression stayed firm. "I was planning to tell you as soon as possible, but so much came up last night, and then this morning. Inez, it's easier this way and safer too. For traveling purposes and so on, there is less confusion with William having our surname. Surely you can see that."

She could. But still, it hurt. She took a deep breath, thinking that, if she truly held William's well-being uppermost, she could accept it, and set it aside for now.

But there was one issue left, unresolved.

Inez gently took her younger sister by the shoulders, and looked hard at her. Her pallor. Her thinness. "Harmony, is your health such that you must take this medicine?"

Inez easily identified the flash of surprise, followed by another emotion—fear, perhaps. It disappeared so quickly that Inez would have missed it entirely had she not been scrutinizing her sister at such close quarters. Harmony's expression settled into a surprised amusement, touched with affection. "Oh, everything is fine, Inez." She disengaged herself from Inez's grasp, looking down to secure the two bottles in her tote.

Tonics tucked away, she looked back up, earnestness painted across her features. "Please, don't alarm yourself unnecessarily. I would never, ever place William's health at risk. In fact, Jonathan and I wondered, at first, about the wisdom of bringing your son back to Colorado, even for a short visit."

She glanced down at her walking suit and plucked at the hem of the short jacket, then looked up at Inez. "But we received such glowing commendations about Manitou and particularly about Dr. Prochazka from the physicians back home. He is attached to the Manitou Springs House exclusively, you know. He had his training in Europe and is well-known among the New York and Newport set, although he didn't stay back East but a year or so before coming out here. Papa gave his blessing after hearing what Dr. Bell had to say."

Inez listened to Harmony's patter, looking for the deeper truth she sensed was lurking beneath the conciliatory words. The familiar name caught her off guard. "Dr. Bell? You are referring to Dr. William Bell? The physician who founded Manitou?"

A brief memory surfaced of Dr. William Bell, at her Leadville establishment, sitting in one evening for a round of cards in the company of Doc Cramer, one of her regulars.

It had not occurred to Inez that she might run into people in Manitou who knew of her association with the Silver Queen Saloon in Leadville. A chill settled over her.

Harmony nodded. "He's General Palmer's confidante. I gather he and General Palmer founded Manitou and Colorado Springs. Jonathan and I have been invited to a 'do' at the Bells' home next week. Mrs. Bell is quite a character I understand. Have you met General Palmer or Dr. Bell?"

"Colorado is a large state, Harmony. I haven't met everyone who lives here." It was discomfiting to think that her estranged father might actually have ties to her corner of the world. Determined not to get sidetracked, Inez continued, "I assume that with such credentials, you have talked to Dr. Prochazka about William's condition? What does he say about William's lungs?"

"He says William is the healthiest boy ever. A rambunctious tot, I believe were his words." Her expression sobered. "We broached the possibility of bringing William to Leadville, thinking we could send a telegram and come visit you. We actually discussed going to Leadville with the Paces, but in the end, decided against it. Dr. Prochazka didn't think it wise, given William's lung problems after his birth."

Inez suppressed a shudder at the thought of the DuChamps popping up to Leadville for an unannounced visit. Inez had a nightmare vision of Harmony stepping into the Silver Queen Saloon and coming face to face with Mark or Abe. New York may have fought for the Union, but her sister would probably not understand how a free Negro such as Abe could be an equal partner in anything, much less a business venture. On top of that, Inez had yet to tell Harmony about Mark. *She still thinks he's missing, most likely dead.*

Pushing the nightmare aside, Inez said, "Tell me about your husband. I haven't met him. Is he good to you? Are you happy, Harmony?"

"He's a good man. He's kind to me. We are happy." Harmony's eyes slid to the distant scrub-filled hills, then down to Fountain Creek. "Ah!" She broke away from Inez to lean over the rail, "There he is now! He walked with me this morning, but then went back out again. He has a very rugged constitution, does Jonathan." There was genuine fondness in her voice, and Inez's concern for her sister settled a little.

Harmony said, "We should be going inside. Jonathan is very punctual, and we shouldn't keep him waiting."

Without waiting for Inez, she started back to the door. Inez realized that her chance to tell Harmony about Mark was fast fading away. "Harmony, I have something to tell you."

"We can talk on our way down to the dining room," said Harmony as she pulled the door open. "I have something I need to tell you as well."

"I had best let you know now," said Inez as they walked through the door. "It's about Mark. My husband."

Harmony stopped, turned toward Inez, and waited.

"He's…" Inez gulped, then pushed the words out despite the sudden hammering in her temples. "He's alive."

Chapter Eight

Leadville

Mark is alive.

The words surfaced in Inez's mind as she was unwillingly pulled into wakefulness, propelled to consciousness by daylight pouring through the windowpane.

She turned and buried her face in the velvet pillow of her fainting couch. She wanted to just stay there, to hide in her small room in the upstairs of the saloon—her refuge from reality. But even though her eyes were stopped, her ears were not. A murmur of voices floated up from the kitchen below. Inez identified the Irish rise and fall of Bridgette's voice, followed by the muted clangs of heavy cookware. The deep monotonic tones of Abe Jackson, co-owner of the Silver Queen Saloon, threaded the culinary percussion. Lulled by the familiar back-and-forth orchestration of Bridgette and Abe, Inez began to hope that, perhaps, she'd dreamt it. A nightmare. None of it real.

Down in the kitchen, Mark laughed.

Inez bolted upright on the couch, illusion shattered.

Her muscles protested from the sudden movement and from sleeping curled up on the couch. She clutched at the small of her back and listened more closely, trying to make out what was being said.

Below, the three voices joined together in animated conversation, weaving in and out—Abe's bass, Mark's easy-going baritone, Bridgette's gliding mezzo-soprano. The harmony implicit in the unworded music caused a thunderous rage to build inside her, a rage fueled by the unfairness of it all. Not back for half a day, and he had already wormed his way into their graces.

She stormed off the couch and threw open the door of her wardrobe. Poking savagely through her clothing choices, she considered what impression she wanted to make on her wretched husband and traitorous friends downstairs.

First, she gripped and then dismissed a somber dark gray cuirass bodice. *Too severe. I don't want him to think I've been in mourning, pining for him all these months.* Then, her hand slid over a deep red, watered silk gown, low cut, spilling lace, smooth with promise. She thrust it aside. *Seductive? Absolutely not.* Finally, she pulled out and examined the basic components of a business-like outfit: a form-fitting dark-blue polonaise and an underskirt, enhanced by a row of shirring above a double-pleated flounce. The skirt was street length and would allow for sweeping haughtily down the stairs, into the kitchen, and, eventually, out the door without the mincing steps required by narrower skirts. Inez chose a cream-colored lace fichu to soften the neckline, added various required undergarments, and moved to the washbasin to begin her toilette.

As she scrubbed at her face and arms, bleakness shadowed her concentration. *I must see my lawyer today and tell him of this revolting development.* After drying off, she returned to her wardrobe, chose a hat with waves of feathers, and tossed it onto the couch next to her outfit.

She dressed, positioned the asymmetrical hat at a defiant slant, located a purse with decorative ruching that echoed the knife pleats of her skirt, and stuffed a pair of gloves into it. She paused to unhook a parasol wound about with a dark blue ribbon. Upon leaving her room, she heard Bridgette's muffled voice through the floorboards with the rising inflection of a question. Mark's muted response was short.

Bridgette's laughter vibrated up through the soles of Inez's stylish shoes.

Inez locked the door to her dressing room with a vicious twist and moved through the connecting office with a determined stride. She opened the office door just in time to see a calico streak—the saloon's cat—shoot down the hall and disappear down the stairs. Inez followed, her stomach tightening with every step. She marched through the main room of the empty saloon, frowning at the silent chairs and tables, the dust motes dancing in the late morning air.

She pushed on the passdoor to the kitchen. The cat brushed past her skirts and darted inside, leaving a smear of fur clinging to the lower tier of ruffles and doing nothing to improve Inez's mood. She gave the skirt a shake, saying testily to the room at large, "Why are the doors still barred? It's past opening time."

Three heads swiveled toward her voice. Three figures froze. It could have been a tableau from the past, except for the expressions on the faces.

Bridgette, hair pinned back smooth and tight into a bun, sleeves scrunched up over ample forearms, stood at her station by the massive cast-iron stove. One hand gripped an upraised ladle, dripping white sauce. The other, wrapped in a dishtowel for protection, held the lid of a large stew pot aloft. She stared at Inez with a guilty look on her face. "Why, ma'am. You're awake." Bridgette's eyes swiveled to Mark Stannert, sitting at one end of the long kitchen table, then swiveled back to Inez, apprehensive. It was almost as if she expected Inez to stalk up to Mark and commence beating him with the parasol.

Inez's grip on the parasol did tighten as she took a step through the doorway and into the kitchen.

Mark smiled and said, "Good mornin', darlin'. Hope our jawing down here didn't interrupt your beauty sleep." He rose from the chair at the far end of the table.

Her chair.

Then she remembered, through her flash of ire, that it had once been Mark's. She'd only jumped that claim after he'd disappeared.

Without responding, she switched her gaze to Abe Jackson, the Stannerts' long-time business partner, at the other end of the work-scarred and stained table. Abe was eased back in his chair, balancing on the two rear legs. Dark hands laced across his black waistcoat, he looked back at Inez with heavy-lidded eyes and an unreadable expression. It was as if he waited to see whether she would call or fold before deciding how to play his hand.

A beam of sunlight cast a sheen on Abe's steel-gray hair, the natural kink subdued with a copious application of brilliantine. His skin, normally the shade of the mahogany bar in the saloon's main room, appeared almost ashen in the bright light. The lines in his face were scratched deep by harsh shadows, the standup collar almost blinding in its whiteness. The glare slid from him as he leaned forward and brought the tilted chair upright, front legs hitting the floor with a *thunk.*

He picked up the spoon in the bowl before him. "Bridgette's got some mighty fine potato soup, Miz Stannert. Whyn't you set yourself down and have some."

Mark moved around the table and pulled out the vacant chair between the two men—Inez's spot in times before—saying, "Abe and I, we were just discussing when to open today. We thought to give you some time to rest up, being that it was a long night."

Mark's everyday, conversational tone—as if the previous fourteen months and fifteen, no, she corrected herself, *sixteen* days had been nothing more than one night's bad dream brought on by bad whiskey—made her shiver in fury.

"We can't go back," she said, deliberately shattering the illusion. "Don't even try to pretend that we can, Mr. Stannert. Too much has happened during your absence."

Mark stood by her unclaimed chair, thick fair hair combed into a smooth wave, mustache neatly trimmed and waxed, the face she had once loved, all so familiar, and yet not. The scar and more prominent cheekbones indicated that the missing months had stamped their hard passage upon him.

Inez was well aware that living in the high altitude of Leadville paired with the hard work of running the saloon had sharpened her own features and pared down her curves since they'd last been together as man and wife. *What does Mark see when he looks at me now?* She gave the unwanted question a mental shove.

"Inez." Mark's voice was soft, as if he understood her pain. "We can talk about this later." He glanced at Abe and Bridgette, his meaning obvious: let's not air our differences and dirty laundry in front of others. "Why don't you set a spell, have something to eat. Abe and I'll open the doors and put things to rights in the saloon."

"I've no time at present," she said, pulling her gloves out of her purse. "I have business to attend to, and I won't be here."

She bent her head, tugging on the gloves and straightening the seams, not looking at Mark. It was so damned disconcerting to see him standing there in the flesh. She said to the room at large, "We should set up a schedule for covering the saloon. There are four of us now working the bar, including the hired help."

Inez continued, still fussing with her seams, "An extra pair of hands should provide some added relief for you, Mr. Jackson, since your wife's time is so near."

She slid a glance at Mark, in time to see him nod and smooth his mustache. *Ah. He apparently knows about Abe's marriage. I wonder what else Abe has told him. I wonder if Abe has mentioned the Reverend Mister Sands. Or if Bridgette has. She could never keep a secret. The reverend's comings and goings here this summer were hardly much of a secret.*

Her stomach clutched with dread and betrayal.

"The Silver Queen is still closed on Sundays, as it has been from the beginning. That makes six days. Three for Mr. Stannert, three for me." She twiddled with one of the buttons and finally raised her eyes to Mark. Daring him to disagree with her. "I will lay claim to Saturdays, as I have a regular clientele for cards on Saturday evenings. Other than that, make what arrangements you will."

She expected Mark to protest that she was being a silly woman and to lay on the Southern charm. Instead, he simply asked, "Still the same table? Doc, that newspaperman, Elliston, right? He still losin' as much as he used to? Cooper, Evan, Hollingsworth, Gallagher?"

Inez interrupted, not wanting to hear the litany of names from their lives together. "There have been changes. Mr. Gallagher is seldom in town, and Mr. Hollingsworth met with an unfortunate accident last winter."

"May God save his soul," said Bridgette, crossing herself with the ladle. Drops of potato soup flew.

Inez jerked back into awareness that they had an audience in Bridgette and Abe.

Bridgette hastily turned away. She plunked the ladle back in the pot and dropped the lid on with a clang. Fussing with the dishcloth, she said, "The missus and Mr. Jackson have been busy as bees, Mr. Stannert. Why, you should see the gaming room upstairs. Quite the gentlemen's parlor, my lands, even though I don't approve of cards as a rule, but at least we keep the Sabbath, and that's a blessing."

Some of the tension leaked out of the room with Bridgette's commentary. Abe pushed the soup bowl away and stood. "I'll see to the doors. Folks are gonna think they're seein' a ghost when they spot you mixin' drinks."

Mark laughed an easy laugh, full of genuine affection. "Well, we'll just have to encourage them to keep drinking to clear their vision."

Inez had had enough. She turned to go, feeling like she would go crazy if she had to stay in the same room with her husband for a moment longer.

She pushed her way out the doors and into the cool, dark interior of the saloon. She was halfway across the floor, heading for the State Street entrance, when footsteps and the quick click of a cane behind warned her.

She whirled around, hissing through clenched teeth, "Do *not* talk to me right now, Mr. Stannert. And do *not* call me 'darling.'"

Mark held up a placating hand. "Dar…Inez. Hold your horses. I have something for you."

He reached into his pocket and pulled out a gun.

Inez gasped, then realized he held it out, grip first, not pointed at her.

He looked reproachful. "You said you lost your Smoot in the house fire. Can't let my wife walk down Leadville's streets without a bit of protection in her pocket. Picked this out special for you, this morning, first thing."

He opened his hand so she could see the gun, lying across his palm.

It was a perfect jewel of a pocket revolver.

Inez recognized it as a Smoot Number Three, offspring of her old protector. Its pearl grip shimmered in the diffuse light, begging to be held.

She looked up at Mark, and over his shoulder saw Abe, framed by the kitchen entryway, apparently not willing to walk into the main room and interrupt. Bridgette hovered behind him.

She realized, belatedly, that Mark had outmaneuvered her, again. If she took the gun, it would look as if she had accepted his gift and they were reconciling. *If I don't take it, I'll look like a hard-hearted harpy.*

"It's lovely, but there's no need," she said coolly. "One of my errands this morning is to pick up a replacement Smoot that I have ordered. Alas, you're too late."

With that, she spun on her heel, walked to the door leading out to State Street, and exited the saloon.

Chapter Nine

Harmony's hand covered her mouth. "Mark. Alive?"

"That's not all," Inez continued grimly. "He's not only alive, he's back. In Leadville. He will be coming to Manitou at the beginning of next week."

"Oh no," Harmony whispered from between her fingers. "That changes everything."

Inez frowned. "What do you mean, 'everything?'"

From behind Inez, a precise female voice drifted up the hall, saying, "Inez Marie Underwood. Now that you are here, we can finally stop all this ridiculous business and make arrangements to all return home to New York."

The voice hit Inez like a slap to the face.

In fact, she could almost feel the hand that accompanied that voice, the voice that had more than once delivered a sharp rebuke simultaneous with a flat-palmed physical blow.

Through her shock and disbelief, Inez kept her gaze on Harmony, trying to ascertain the truth before turning around. The widened eyes, the sudden flush accompanied by a guilt-stricken expression, and the previously confident, decisive young matron seemed to melt back into a child. Harmony's response confirmed what Inez already knew in her heart of hearts.

Harmony stepped forward. Her breath brushed Inez's cheek as she whispered, "I thought she would be waiting for us in the dining hall, that I could tell you before we went down so you would have a chance to prepare yourself."

"Harmony Elizabeth Underwood DuChamps," the voice was even closer. "You were not raised to whisper in front of others in such a rude manner. Nor, Inez Marie, were you raised to present your back to someone in their presence. Particularly if that someone is an elder. If I do not count as one of your elders, then you have forgotten more in this misbegotten corner of the country than your manners."

Inez arranged her features into a semblance of calm and agreeableness before obeying the implicit command and turning around.

Agnes Underwood, older sister to Inez's father, sailed forward, arms outstretched, beaming.

Willowy, of medium height, she was clothed in a loose flowing gown, quite unlike anything Inez remembered her aunt ever wearing in public. *Aunt Agnes, an aesthete? Well, she always did have a mind of her own.* Her hair was still abundant and black, her blue eyes still as piercing as a knife but nowhere near as sharp as the words she wielded to fearsome effect over every member of Inez's family for as far back as Inez could remember. As far as Inez could tell, Aunt Agnes hadn't changed an iota in ten years. She kept her age buried as deeply as her strategies, all deployed from behind the calculated smile.

Inez held out her arms in a returning embrace. "Dear, dear Aunt Agnes. Please excuse my rudeness. I must plead the shock of your unexpected appearance here in Manitou. You see, I was *also* not raised to present myself without notifying the host that I would be accompanying an invited party. Hence my momentary lapse of courtesy." As she pressed her long-lost aunt to her breast, Inez murmured, "I never use the name Marie, nor do I ever refer to my maiden name of Underwood, so please do not do so here. My last name is Stannert and has been for more than ten years. I am a married woman, as I'm certain you recall."

Agnes broke away and held Inez at arm's length. She smiled indulgently. "Of course I recall, silly girl. How could I forget, given the distress your untimely marriage caused the entire family. Why, Harmony cried for months and pined for years at your abandonment. Your father, as you probably know, refused to allow anyone to even speak your name, an order that stands to this day, I am sad to say. Your dear mother has never ever recovered from the neurasthenia resulting from your flouting of the family."

Agnes' gaze sliced Inez top to bottom, dissecting hair, face, costume. "My dear, I will never understand how you young women put up with the cuirass bodice and tight lacing. You cannot even draw a breath in such an outfit, much less walk at a healthy pace."

Inez cocked her head. "Aunt, when did you embrace the aesthetic philosophy?"

She waved an airy hand. "At my age, dear, I dress to please none but myself. However, that does not mean I stint on proper courtesy, deportment, manners, and conduct."

Inez could well imagine how Aunt Agnes enjoyed the bafflement of others as they strove to reconcile her devil-may-care outward appearance with her steely adherence to Hills' rules of etiquette. At least, when it suited her.

Agnes continued blithely, "As your sister knows, I decided long ago that your youthful error in marital judgment would not diminish my abiding affection for you, my eldest and most beloved niece, nor would it color our forever-looked-forward-to reunion. After all, the Stannert scoundrel is deceased, I understand. I would offer my condolences, but really, Inez, it is all for the best that he is gone." She turned to Harmony, who stood, arms crossed, as attentive as an audience witnessing a drama on the stage. "Let us repair to the dining hall. We must not keep Mr. Jonathan DuChamps waiting. The dear man does hate to be kept waiting, does he not, sweet Harmony?"

They moved down the hallway. As they approached the main staircase, Inez got a good look at Hermes in the daylight, watching over all who mounted or descended the stairs. He was impressively life size and did indeed sport a fig leaf. As she paused to examine the statue more closely, Agnes pulled her forward, remarking, "We shall take the ladies' entrance to the dining room. As is proper."

Inez could feel a pounding headache beginning somewhere behind her right temple. *I do hope the coffee is strong. It will have to be, if I am to survive this breakfast until I can excuse myself to see William.*

She shook her head, determined to settle one last thing before breakfast. "Aunt Agnes, you mentioned making plans to return 'home.' I assume you mean New York. However, the city is not my home and has not been for a very long time."

"My dear, there is absolutely no reason for you to stay here anymore, is there? I know you and your sister have been in correspondence for a long while. Indeed, I have been happy to accept the crumbs of information she has deigned to pass my way."

Inez could imagine the arm-twisting techniques Aunt Agnes had employed. Most likely, she had pestered Harmony nonstop on the train ride from New York to Denver until Harmony told all out of sheer exhaustion.

"I understand you have been attempting to obtain a divorce based on desertion. But your suspicions are that he is dead, correct?" Aunt Agnes didn't even glance at Inez to seek concurrence. "It is time you return to New York and your rightful family. Your son lives there, as does your only sister and the rest of the family. You can make amends with your father and tend to your mother. Return to New York, and there will be no censure in rejoining society as a grieving widow. Actually, your time of mourning would nearly be at a close, if we take into account the time that scoundrel's been gone. That way, you need not pursue this divorce nonsense."

Inez stopped. Aunt Agnes continued a couple steps to the head of the staircase, hand still in the air as if resting on the ghost of Inez's arm.

"Our lawyers will take over, they will have Mark Stannert declared legally dead, and…" As if just realizing Inez was no longer beside her, Aunt Agnes turned. At last, a frown broke through the perfect porcelain surface, lines of disapproval dipping between her eyebrows and pulling down on her mouth. "Yes? What is it, Inez?" Impatience bled through her tone.

Inez crossed her arms. "Declaring my husband legally dead may be difficult. Even for the family lawyers, Aunt Agnes, whom I am certain would find a way to declare the moon legally made of silver, spiderwebs, or green cheese, if Papa or you insisted it be done."

Staring down her aunt, Inez continued, "You see, Mark Stannert is very much alive. In fact, he will be here next week, so you will have the opportunity to meet him yourself."

Chapter Ten

Aunt Agnes, who had lowered her hand to the banister of the women's staircase, raised one eyebrow. "Is that so? Well, then. This situation will require a bit more labor to straighten out than I anticipated."

She sounded distantly disapproving, as if she were scolding a child for laying a dirty hand upon an expensive dress and leaving a smudge. She even glanced down at her flowing skirts and smoothed out a nonexistent wrinkle. "We can discuss this later. We shouldn't dillydally any longer." She started down the stairs, adding, "Come along."

Inez glanced at Harmony who had come up beside her during the exchange. "What does she mean by that?" Inez asked acidly.

Harmony lifted one shoulder. "Aunt Agnes is…impenetrable. We should talk further, when we can find a few moments alone. She usually rests for a spell in the afternoon. I can tell you what I know then. Come." She took Inez's hand, and gently tugged her to the staircase. "It's time you met my husband."

The dining hall for the Mountain Springs House was flooded with morning light from east-facing windows and the melodic hum of well-bred feminine voices, complemented here and there by a deeper harmonic line. White linen tablecloths blazed, and crystal-cut glassware, highly polished silverware, and fine china sparkled. Waiters in white jackets moved about with trays and silver coffee pots, prepared to pour or deliver on command. The corners of the room sported bronze statues that, like the one at the head of the main staircase, were mythical in nature, but far less massive. Inez readily identified Apollo and Athena, and spotted what she thought might be Hygeia, and Hermes yet again.

The room held mostly women, dressed in light colors and summer fabrics that almost sparkled in the wash of sun. Here and there, an ensemble was sliced with darker contrasting underskirts and trim. Lace spilled from necklines, and pleats and flounces and fringe graced long skirts. Few in the dining room seemed dressed for a long walk or a day of vigor. The combination of high society in a resort setting reminded Inez of Saratoga Springs and long-ago summer days as a child. In her mind's eye, she saw Aunt Agnes in hoop skirts, walking arm-in-arm with her father through the grounds of some nameless hotel, carefully circumnavigating other visitors wearing similarly wide skirts. Inez blinked her eyes to clear the vision.

Aunt Agnes in the here-and-now came back into focus. Inez could make out her aunt in her "pre-Raphaelite" artistic dress costume, moving with girlish grace through the room to a long table, nearly full, in the center of the room. The only figure she recognized was Susan, seated between an older and younger man.

"The dining room arrangement encourages guests to get to know each other," Harmony said, drawing Inez along. "Very quaint. Although, as you might have guessed, Aunt Agnes thinks it's quite barbaric that she must mix with the hoi polloi."

Both gentlemen stood at the women's approach. To Inez's surprise, Harmony bypassed the younger man and advanced to the older man on Susan's left. She bestowed a tender smile on him, before turning to Inez. "Dear sister, allow me to introduce to you my husband, Mr. DuChamps. Mr. DuChamps, my sister, Mrs. Stannert."

Inez smiled, trying to gauge the decade of the man who bowed far enough to reveal an endearingly bald spot on the crown of his head.

"It gives me great pleasure to form your acquaintance at last," he said.

An older gentleman sitting next to Mr. DuChamps had also popped up when Inez approached and now said, "Madam. You are a relation of the DuChamps? Allow me to introduce myself." He placed a hand to his chest, over a full salt-and-pepper beard of luxuriant and well-tended proportions, and bowed. "Dr. Zuckerman, a physician now practicing in Colorado Springs. I am also a colleague of Dr. Prochazka's, and a great admirer of the Mountain Springs House as a whole. Those at the helm of the house have a vision of the future that I embrace wholeheartedly, professionally, and personally, as I have explained to Mr. DuChamps in some detail these past days." He smiled. At least, Inez assumed that a smile lurked beneath the smooth waves of whiskers, given the sudden gathering of wrinkles at the corners of his eyes.

Inez inclined her head and murmured politely in reply.

"And this," Harmony turned to the younger man, whom Inez judged to be somewhere in his twenties, "is Mr. Calder."

Calder smiled, displaying brilliant teeth. He had the dark good looks of poet Robert Burns and the robust constitution of a man who reveled in the out of doors. In fact, Inez caught a whiff of the stables about him, as if he had spent the morning riding hard. Calder executed a deep bow and said with a soft Scottish burr, "Mrs. Stannert, charmed. Miss Carothers has told me much about you."

Inez raised speculative eyebrows at Susan.

Susan had the grace to blush. "Mr. Calder was inquiring as to how long we planned to stay here at the hotel. I was explaining the nature of my business, and that I'll be staying with Mrs. Galbreaith at Ohio House, after today."

Inez noticed that Calder, after his initial bow and smile, had immediately refocused his attention on Susan. He listened to her with great intensity as if her every comment held secrets he was eager to unravel.

"Perhaps we can plan a group outing to the Garden of the Gods to capture its wonders on plate and canvas," he said.

Two spots of color rose high on Susan's cheeks. She said quickly, "Mr. Calder is an artist specializing in *en plein air* painting. We've been talking about the extraordinary landscape around here, perfect for photographers and watercolorists. I'm particularly looking forward to the Garden of the Gods. Mr. Calder says he has explored the area extensively. They have the most interesting names for the various rock formations in the Garden—Montezuma's Temple, Tower of Babel, the Gateway, the Kissing Camels…"

Aunt Agnes, standing by Jonathan, tapped her fingers on the unclaimed dining chair next to his. Her expression made it clear that she was waiting for him to seat her, and that she was not happy at being ignored.

"It is wonderful for a young woman to have a hobby," she interjected. "Although I do confess, photography strikes me as a touch bohemian. Mr. DuChamps? If you would?"

Attention refocused, Jonathan DuChamps hastened to comply before escorting Harmony to the chair beside Calder. Aunt Agnes patted the empty seat to her left, with a meaningful look at Inez. "Come here, dear girl. It has been far too long, and we have much to discuss. Mr. DuChamps, please assist your sister-in-law?"

Much to Inez's amusement, Aunt Agnes batted her eyelashes.

Harmony's husband smiled indulgently at Aunt Agnes and pulled out the chair for Inez. Inez sat, preparing herself as best she could for the skirmish she was certain was coming.

Aunt Agnes wasted no time. Unfolding the fluted napkin pleat by pleat, she said, "Your son, Inez, is a handsome child." She made it sound as if he was a particularly unusual specimen of butterfly, pinned for display in an exhibit. "Your father is quite taken with him. The son he never had, you understand."

It was exactly what Inez feared most to hear.

"I don't think…" Aunt Agnes picked up her crystal water glass, turning it left and right. Sunlight flashed from the facets and shattered into rainbows on the blinding white linen tablecloth. "…given William's precarious constitution, the state of his lungs and so on, that he will allow your son to return to you here in Colorado."

"William is my son." Inez said. "Papa has no say in his future."

"So, what is your intention?" Agnes put the glass down and faced Inez. "Do you and this husband of yours—I don't even want to say his name—intend to spirit William away at the end of this visit? Are you and he in collusion? Would you really take your child back up to a place that could kill him?"

"Of course not!" snapped Inez.

"Of course not," Agnes agreed. "I'm glad to see we are in absolute agreement. I assured your father that we would be."

A polite cough to Inez's left drew her attention.

A waiter dressed all in white, reminding Inez of the ghostly figure from the previous evening, hovered with a silver coffee carafe.

"Please!" she said fervently. He filled her bone china cup. Inez inhaled the fragrant aroma of freshly ground coffee, and mourned the lack of any strong spirits to get her through what was proving to be one of Aunt Agnes' standard cat-and-mouse conversations.

Her thoughts turned to William and the worrisome development to his future as well as the increasingly complex present. *Perhaps I should excuse myself and wait out front, to be there when he and Lily return.* She glanced at the dining room entry, her grip on the cup tightening, her desire to see William so fierce it was almost as if she was willing him to materialize out of thin air.

The waiter approached Agnes, who nodded languorously. After he had vanished, Agnes continued in a matter-of-fact manner. "I have tickets for us all to return to New York in two weeks. If it were up to me, I would exchange them right now for tomorrow's train. We have been here a week, and honestly, that is a week too long for me. What passes for culture here is…" She waved dismissively. "Charades, chess, checkers, hops. I hear one of the nearby hotels, the Cliff House, proclaims it has a billiards hall for both men and women. Most unseemly. *Burro* rides to explore waterfalls, and the top of, what is it called, Pike Mountain?"

Inez lifted her coffee cup and sipped, to give herself time to calm down before answering. She was gratified to find the coffee tasted as good as it smelled. "Pike's Peak, Aunt Agnes. There was a gold rush in Colorado, twenty years ago. Don't you recall? I was only eleven, but even I remember the 'Pike's Peak or Bust' talk, and Papa's speculations about whether the gold was a true bonanza or simply the over-promotion of a few zealots."

Agnes shook her head. "I recall nothing of the sort. I always decried your father's inclinations to let you listen to all that folderol. He would insist on reading items in the newspaper to you, and even let you read it yourself. I warned him that it would not do, in the end. I was right. Look where you have ended up." She rolled her eyes toward the bank of picture windows, facing the hotel's back gardens and the landscape beyond.

"You might as well be on the moon," she continued. "This place. Saratoga of the West, indeed. I know Cara Bell finds this place enchanting. I wrote to her as soon as our plans were set, and we have been in communication since. She came to visit us when we first arrived and positively *filled* your sister and Jonathan's heads with nonsense about this place. On top of it all, what with doctor what's-his-name Pro-something-or-other and our hotelier Mr. Lewis, I do believe Harmony and Jonathan are bewitched and seriously considering summer residence. Yes?" This last was addressed in an irritable tone to the waiter, who had reappeared without the carafe.

He cleared his throat. "Pardon *mesdames*. Mrs. Stannert?" He directed this to Inez.

"Yes?" She set down the coffee cup.

"*Monsieur* Lewis wishes to speak with you." He looked to the dining room door. The hotelier, stood just inside, gazing in her direction.

"What is all this about?" Agnes demanded.

Inez recalled Lewis' parting words from the previous evening: the marshal will need to speak to you on the morrow.

A vision of Edward Pace's face, contorted in death, eyes empty of soul and life, crowded out the exasperation and vexation building inside of her. All of a sudden, Aunt Agnes' verbal maneuverings seemed very inconsequential.

"Excuse me, Aunt, this shouldn't take long." Inez cast a last look at her coffee, which would no doubt be cold by the time she returned, and rose, folding her napkin and dropping it on her chair.

Agnes heaved an irritated and theatrical sigh. "Your son will be back from his constitutional soon and be due for a nap, according to the schedule this Doctor Whosis has prescribed for him. Poor child, he tires in the morning so easily, despite all the cod liver oil foisted upon him. It is all the exercise, I expect." The implicit threat—*if you really care about your son, you'll not tarry*—was clear.

"I will return as soon as possible," Inez said shortly. Then, in passing by Harmony's chair, she leaned over and murmured, "This is no doubt about last night."

Harmony nodded. As Inez passed by Susan, Susan stood and said, "I'll walk with you." They wove their way around the tables, mostly empty now, while Susan added in an undertone, "The local marshal and the doctor. They just want information about last night. They spoke to me before breakfast."

Inez sighed. "To be expected. But the timing is not the best. Although I'm glad to escape from Aunt Agnes for now."

At the doorway, Mr. Lewis bowed again, and said, "So sorry to interrupt your breakfast, Mrs. Stannert. I will be sure to have a tray fixed special for your return."

"As long as the coffee is fresh and hot," said Inez.

Susan returned to the table. Mr. Lewis led Inez through a maze of hallways, left, right, then left again, and out a double door to the back of the hotel.

Inez paused on the veranda, which appeared to wrap around the hotel, and gazed at a garden bursting with green and abloom with late summer color. "We are well known for our gardens." Mr. Lewis sounded almost apologetic. "We're lucky to be close to a spring and a small creek. The water is diverted, allowing our visitors a small slice of Eden in this mountain paradise. I would be happy to see you are given a tour later, if you have any botanical interest."

He led Inez along a small gravel path toward a whitewashed, long single-story building at the end of the garden. "Where are we going?" Inez asked. "I assume this summons has to do with last night?"

His expression darkened, as if a shadow had passed even though the sun shown brightly. They rounded a corner of the winding path, passing a particularly fragrant tall puff of sage, dotted with small, cream-colored flowers. They nearly ran into a cavernous man hunched over in a cane-backed three-wheeled chair. The gray Nurse Crowson, piloting the chair from behind, brought it to a halt before it plowed into Lewis' shins.

Lewis stopped and greeted the invalid. "Mr. Travers, taking your morning constitutional, I see?" He inclined his head. "Nurse Crowson, splendid morning."

The man in the wheelchair nodded, then erupted into a wet-sounding cough that sounded as if it were tearing his lungs to shreds. He bent over, nearly doubled with the effort, head almost to his knees. Nurse Crowson hastily pulled out a gray handkerchief from her apron pocket and bent over, holding it over her patient's mouth. She looked up, pinning Inez with a disconcertingly opaque stare. Yet, when she spoke, it was not to Inez.

"Mr. Lewis, good morning. Lovely weather in the garden today. One can smell the mint and sage."

Without waiting for a response, she returned her attention to her patient. "Calm yourself, and breathe deep, Mr. Travers. When we return to your room, I'll bring you some of my tea." The coughing began to ease. The nurse folded the handkerchief, which Inez noticed was now tinged with a bright spot of blood, and slipped it into her apron pocket.

Lewis added, "Your nurse is right, Mr. Travers. The dry air cannot do anything but benefit, and the mint and sage will aid as well. Of course, Mrs. Crowson's tea is a marvelous aid for the breathing."

He and the nurse exchanged a glance shot through with some hidden significance. He turned to Inez. "Come, Mrs. Stannert. We shouldn't keep them waiting in the clinic."

Inez and Lewis circled the wheelchair, its patient and attendant, and continued to the building.

"We get many chasing the cure," said Lewis. "We are lucky to have Dr. Prochazka here. Since he joined our staff, we've seen truly miraculous recoveries, with many staying through the winter to benefit from his remedies and advice. Unfortunately," he shook his head, "there are still those who arrive too late, too far gone in their disease. Even the good doctor, trained as he is in some of the finest universities of Germany, cannot cure all cases of phthisis."

He glanced at Inez and caught her confusion. "Consumption," he amended. "My apologies. I am so surrounded by talk of illnesses and diseases here at the hotel and Manitou in general, listening to the good doctor discuss medical issues with his colleagues, that I often sound like I truly know what I'm talking about." His mouth twisted into a wry grimace. "But I would never presume to prescribe. Still, I was not overly surprised at Mr. Pace's passing."

"Is that what this is about?" Inez asked.

"Yes, ma'am. I would not have interrupted your meal, but you are the last, and the marshal is anxious to conclude this business. As we all are."

They were just short of the building when the door flew open. A woman's figure, in black from head to toe, burst through the opening and hurried in their direction.

Lewis stopped, as if his feet had turned into iron weights. "Mrs. Pace!"

Mrs. Pace, engulfed in a black veil, paused, then approached, full tilt. She took Inez's arm and said with force, "My husband was as strong as a man of twenty. He regularly walked for miles. The mountains and elevations here did not tax him at all, at least, not until Leadville. But even then, it was not until we were nearly back that it all happened. If it was the elevation, why did he not collapse until we were nearly returned? Why not while we were in Leadville, or going over that mountain pass? I don't know what brought him down, but it was not his heart. You were there, Mrs. Stannert. You saw him die. You saw as well as I!"

Chapter Eleven

Mr. Lewis finally lurched into motion. "Mrs. Pace, please, you are overwrought. You shouldn't be here. I was coming to escort you back to your room, to rest. I know this is a difficult time for you."

"*Difficult?* I have lost my husband. My children have lost their father. Our lives have changed forever. I wish I had never heard of this place."

Mr. Lewis attempted to take her arm. She evaded him and moved down a side path, heading toward what Inez intuited by the green verge was the aforementioned creek.

"A tragedy. A tragedy." Mr. Lewis gazed after her, visibly shaken. "The sooner this business is concluded, the better. Please, Mrs. Stannert, please come. I should see to Mrs. Pace."

Without further ceremony, he hurried her to the front of the building, saying, "This is Dr. Prochazka's clinic. The marshal, the doctor, and I decided it was best that any inquiry into Mr. Pace's demise be conducted away from the hotel, ears and walls and all. Talk of death is distressing to those who are fighting for recovery. Hope is what fuels the tonics, the cure." Lewis' distressed babbling made no sense to Inez, but she decided that it would do no good to pursue the conversation at that moment.

Lewis threw open the door, calling in a telegraphic introduction, "Marshal Robbins, Doctor Prochazka, Mrs. Stannert." He left Inez on the threshold and trotted back down the path after Mrs. Pace.

Inez entered the long, low-slung building. The walls opened onto a clinic setting, with a waiting area being primary. A number of empty chairs occupied the space, accompanied by yet another statue of Hermes on a corner pedestal. An entryway leading further into the building yielded an examination area, where two men sat. One was behind a desk, drumming fingers on the surface, the other leaned an elbow on a nearby table, idly turning a white tabletop statuette this way and that. Behind them, another door, half ajar, revealed an unlit slice of a room shrouded in shadows.

The man behind the desk saw her standing in the waiting area, rose, and moved around the desk to the table. He motioned her forward impatiently. She recognized the tall, almost emaciated form of the white-coated apparition from the night before. Today, he was dressed in a somber dark suit, watch chain and fob bridging one side of the plain black waistcoat to the other, a stand-up collar, higher than fashion might dictate, held closed with an untidy two-in-four knot. The wild mane of hair she recalled from the previous night had been fiercely tamed with a copious amount of grease, and combed straight back with nary a ripple or wave evident.

His companion stopped playing with the figurine and stood as well, well-brushed bowler hat in hand. Compact, non-prepossessing, and with a tidy Van Dyke beard, he was in stark contrast to the slouching rail of a man beside him.

The compact man stepped forward, "Mrs. Stannert? I'm Marshal Robbins, and this," he nodded at the scarecrow, "is Dr. Prochazka. This here is his clinic, which he's kindly offered so as to allow us to talk about yesterday's unfortunate events. Please." He gestured to a chair on the opposite side of the table.

Dr. Prochazka, Inez thought, did not look as if the takeover of his clinic was his idea, let alone his offer. He slouched back down into his chair, face drawn. The spectacles that he had pulled off upon standing, he now tapped idly on a black and red bound journal set askew on the table. Inez could just make out the upside-down gold gilt letters that spelled out *Physician's Day-Book & Journal.*

The marble statue standing guard over their meeting drew her eye. No fig leaf on this one, instead the statue sported a well-draped arm and lower torso, with the marble folds falling to sandals. He had a stone head of hair as tightly curled as Dr. Prochazka's the previous evening, only the statue's coiffure was considerably neater and shorter. Under his shoulder rested a long staff, with a snake coiled around it. Curious, she leaned over and touched the snake. The marble was cold, dense to the touch. "This is no Hermes or Mercury," she remarked.

Dr. Prochazka jerked as if smacked with a whip. "Hermes is an impostor! They insist on putting him up everywhere at the hotel, even in my waiting room. Everyone suffers the delusion that Hermes is the god of medicine. As you would say, poppycock!"

It would not be what Inez would choose to say, but she let it go.

"This is Asclepius." He picked up the statue, long fingers curling completely around the muscular stone midriff. "The proper god of healing and medicine. Few outside the medical profession seem to know or care. Do you know what Hermes is god of?"

Inez felt that she was being subjected to an impromptu oral exam on Greek and Roman mythology.

"Ah, well," she stuttered. "Hermes is the messenger of the gods, of course. He is also god of omens, and animal husbandry. And travel." She searched her memory, trying to dredge up some of her classical training.

"God of trade. *Commerce.*" Prochazka put special emphasis on the word, as if it were something unclean. "What has that to do with healing, hmmm? Or medicine? Although some think if you do not make money from an endeavor, well, why bother. He is also patron of cattle-rustlers, so appropriate to your West, as well as thieves and *trickery.*" The physician set Asclepius back down with a heavy thud. "You might say he is god of the charlatans that practice their medical quackery upon the simple and desperate. I find it infuriating that a resort dedicated to the healing arts would place statues of Hermes in every corner of every room."

Marshal Robbins cleared his throat. "Well, now, I think we'd best get down to business, so's the doctor can reclaim his clinic here. Thank you, Mrs. Stannert, for coming and speaking with us." He sounded as if she had not been summoned and it had been her idea to pop around and converse with them. "Mrs. Pace just left us, as you know, and was a bit wrathy."

"Hysterical," interrupted Prochazka. "With a touch of mania. Her mental capacity has been overextended. The woman needs bed rest, a proper diet to rebalance her, and a proper dose of restorative tuned to her needs. But I am not an expert in mental disorders."

The marshal shifted uncomfortably. "Yes, well, doctor, that may be. But her husband just died, so I expect she's pretty much a grieving widow. Mrs. Stannert, can you run through how you met the Paces and what transpired on the stagecoach during your trip?"

Inez scrunched her nose. "The trip is two days in length. Surely you do not want every detail of our journey."

"No, no," he assured her. "Talk about Mr. Pace, if you would. I gather he was ill when he boarded the stage out of Leadville?"

Inez tried to summarize her impressions of Mr. Pace and his health at the start and as the journey progressed. She noted his initial paleness and sweating and how his condition seemed to worsen the second day, even though they had descended a considerable amount by that time.

The marshal hunched over the wooden table, looking intently at her when not scratching notes in a small notebook. At this point, Inez, who had been focused on relating her story and her observations, became aware of Dr. Prochazka. He still slouched in his chair, an air of boredom surrounding him like a cloud. However, his foot was now jiggling under the table and he'd begun tapping his glasses again upon the bound journal.

Faced with these signals of impatience, Inez picked up the velocity of her narration. She described Mr. Pace's increased difficulty breathing, his near collapse at the stage stop in Florissant, and then, his insistence on taking his wife's tonic.

"That is immaterial," interrupted Dr. Prochazka. "The formulation was for Kirsten Pace, for her spasmodic asthma. It has nothing to do with Edward Pace. I examined him for cause of death. He died of *angina pectoris*." The physician stopped. His eyes moved back and forth, as if scanning a dictionary seen only by him. "Heart attack," he amended. "Possibly complicated by hydrocephalus. Or dropsy. Most certainly brought on by the altitude."

The marshal nodded in time to his words.

Perhaps it was the physician's abrupt dismissal of her observations. Perhaps it was simply that the two men seemed to be in such complete agreement. Or perhaps it was because Inez was acutely aware of Mrs. Pace's evident distress, as well as the fact that, as the minutes ticked by, her chance to see her son was slipping further away into afternoon. Whether it was one, more or all of the above, she felt her ire rise toward the two men facing her across the table.

"Still, the situation didn't turn deadly until he took the medication," she argued. "He nearly drained the bottle. His reaction was immediate."

Prochazka leaned forward, intent. "The bottle was sealed?"

Inez paused, searching her memory of that frantic space of time. The faint, audible crack of a wax seal being broken echoed in her mind. "Yes, yes it was. But even their child Mathilda said something about the medicine making her father ill."

Prochazka snorted with non-doctorly vehemence. "A child! What would she know? I would hope an education at University of Göttingen, study under Virchow in Berlin, being a physician in the *Krieg* would carry more weight that the babbling of a child!"

The marshal closed his notebook with a snap. "No one's denyin' your expertness in the matter of medicament, Dr. Prochazka."

Prochazka stood up abruptly and his chair almost fell backwards. The marshal caught it with one hand.

"If Mrs. Pace would allow an autopsy to be performed on her husband, we could lay this nonsense to rest," the doctor said. "I have no time for pandering to this woman, who makes accusations of me. I have patients, I am delayed in attending. Patients requiring attention, who have been…" he seemed to search for the word, "*denied* my treatment this morning and last night because of the fits of a hysterical female."

Inez frowned, thinking that Mrs. Pace had not acted hysterical during the previous night's moments of deep crisis. Rather, she had only appeared hysterical after her interview with the doctor and marshal.

"I know Mrs. Pace well," continued Prochazka. "Have treated her since the beginning of summer. She came here a frail woman, but is now much improved in the matter of her lungs. This mental stress, this maniacal behavior, it is merely a manifestation of her underlying weakness. I must see Mr. Travers now. Nurse Crowson said he is coughing blood again. She has been wheeling him about the garden for the past hour. Do you want a man's life on your hands for the sake of another who has already met his Maker, thanks to the vagaries of age and the unfortunate twists of circumstances?"

"Whoa, hold your horses, Doc," said the marshal. "Mrs. Stannert was the last person in the coach. We're done here. You can return to your patients, and sorry for the trouble."

While talking, the marshal had advanced around the table and was now motioning Inez to the door. She stood her ground, long enough to let Prochazka know she was not about to be run off, quaking in her boots, fearful of a display of temper.

"Perhaps," she said coldly. "Mrs. Pace's display of mental *mania* is no more due to her medical infirmities than this exhibit of rabid *spleen* is due to your poor manners, Doctor."

With that, she retreated in dignified haste, even as she heard him lapse back into the foreign tongue from the previous night. Strange mutterings followed her. "*Verrückte! Ztráta času! Idioti!*"

That last word, at least, was clear to her.

Marshal Robbins closed the door behind them, mopped his brow with a bright red kerchief, and set his bowler atop his head. "Well, Mrs. Stannert. I'd say you woke up the wrong passenger."

She was shaking with anger. "He's quite insufferable. What an absolute boor!"

Marshal Robbins squinted up at the back of the hotel, while he tucked his notepad inside his vest. "He's an odd stick, there's no doubt. But a powerful healer in these parts, so folks take his stand-offishness with a grain of salt. Too, the nurse, Mrs. Crowson, she's sound on the goose, real reliable with the sick and ailing. Keeps things on an even keel when the doctor gets wound up and is on the shoot."

Inez sniffed, and crossed her arms. The marshal started walking back to the hotel, and she matched his stride. "So, that is it?"

He looked at her, wary, a bit bemused. "What's it?"

"You're not asking more questions? You are not going to pursue the circumstances of Mr. Pace's death any further?"

"Now ma'am. I'm not one to pass the buck nor play to the gallery." He spoke slowly and deliberately, as if to a child. "At the same time, I'm not going to kick up a row where there's nothing to be gained. Gentleman comes a cropper on the stagecoach out of Leadville. Out of my jurisdiction, but Mr. Lewis says, real desperate-like, can I spare the morning to come down and give the matter some attention. So, I come. I ask questions. I listen to the answers."

He stopped speaking as Nurse Crowson approached with her charge, wheels clacking and squeaking. He stepped to one side on the gravel path to allow her to pass. Inez did the same. As the nurse headed toward the clinic, she nodded a greeting at the marshal. He ran a finger along the rim of his bowler in acknowledgment.

After nurse and patient had turned the corner, the marshal resumed. "For witnesses, we got a distraught widow, a passel of young'uns, a servant girl who won't say nothin' that doesn't sound like a quote from the Good Book, and that other gal, Miss

Carothers, who admits she doesn't remember what-all because she was too worried about the young'uns and tryin' to keep them from stampeding into panic. And then, there's you. I gotta say, Mrs. Stannert, I credit your testimony as observations of the first water, but I also respect Dr. Prochazka as being simon-pure when it comes to matters of doctoring."

Doctoring. Healing. Tonic.

A sudden thought struck Inez, and she slowed, trying to sort it out. "Marshal. Mr. Pace's troubles turned deadly right after he drank the bottled tonic. Is it possible, could there have been something more than or different from just the medicine in the bottle?" As she heard herself say the words, the natural conclusion loomed—a storm cloud in a darkening sky. "If that were the case, could the intended victim have been Mrs. Pace, and not her husband?" The thought sent a shiver through her. "Because that would mean she could still be in danger."

The marshal, who had stopped to hear her out, held up a hand to cut her off. "Whoa, whoa. That's a pretty wild idea you've roped there. No proof, for any of it, and no sense behind it. The bottle was sealed, you said so yourself. Besides, why would anyone want to strike at a woman like her? You're riding way out in front of the herd. I say it's time to wind up this business and move along."

She backpedaled. "Well, perhaps it wasn't intentional. Maybe it was a mistake. A miscalculation by the doctor or his assistant— too much of this, not enough of that—could be enough to turn a healing draught deadly."

The marshal, shaking his head, was already moving, putting distance between himself and Inez, as if her odd theories might be some infectious disease that he had no intention of catching. "The doctor does his own tonics. I know that for a fact."

Inez rolled her eyes. "Tonics, nostrums, sirups. Quackery and flimflammery. Probably all comes down to cheap whiskey and a touch of laudanum."

"It ain't like that, ma'am," he said stubbornly. "Dr. Prochazka's no quack or purveyor of patent medicines, and he doesn't make mistakes of the kind you're suggesting."

"What makes him such a saint? Did he breathe life back into your lungs and cure you of consumption?"

The marshal stopped again and pinned her with a steely eye. "No ma'am. But my wife was on the point of meetin' her Maker when we came to Manitou to take the waters out of sheer desperation. The doctor took her in as a charity case. I couldn't pay his fees on a lawman's salary. He saved her life. So sure, I suppose you could say he gave me my breath back. Without my Mary, you might as well ready my resting place in the bone orchard. Without her, I would've been a goner. My life, over."

Inez felt a flush rise to her cheeks, his rebuke stinging like a physical slap. "My apologies, Marshal. I didn't mean to pry. I should not have said all that."

"No ma'am. I guess you shouldn't've." He tugged on the brim of his hat, bringing it further down his forehead and shadowing the tightness that had appeared around his eyes. Without waiting for her, he moved briskly through the last of the winding garden path, up the porch stairs to the back veranda of the hotel, and disappeared inside.

Inez shook her head. The bitter scent of some strong herb and the drone of bees in a nearby rosebush filled her head as she tried to collect herself. Birds shrilled, and the temperature, she noticed, had climbed appreciably since her rising just a couple hours earlier.

She was without a hat, having left it in the dining room at the initial summons. The heat weighed heavily, like a clothes iron on a cotton drape, pressing her down. *I should have kept my suspicions to myself. Stepping on the toes of the local law, even inadvertently, was most unwise. I hope I don't have cause to regret my remarks any further than I do at this moment.*

Chapter Twelve

"Inez!"

Harmony's voice brought Inez out of her guilty reverie. Her sister was coming down the back steps, hurrying toward her. "The children are back! Come. Your son will need to rest soon." She took Inez's arm. "We try hard to keep him to the schedule the doctor recommended." She peered at Inez. "Is something wrong?"

"No, no. It's…" *I've been insulted by that pernicious quack. I've alienated the town's lawman. I'd give a small fortune for a stiff iced lemonade.* "It's just so warm," Inez finished, lamely. "In Leadville, the air isn't quite so oppressive. So where is William?"

Harmony guided her toward the hotel. "If you think the air here is oppressive, then you have forgotten what it's like back East in the summertime. Even in Newport, the air is so thick I can barely move when visiting Mama and Papa. The hotel's children just returned from their morning outing. The hotel is wonderful in keeping them entertained. This morning, Lily and William joined the others on an excursion on the little donkeys, the burros. The sweetest animals, so patient! They are all out in front."

While talking, Harmony and Inez had walked through the dim interior of the hotel, almost startling in its coolness after the trapped heat in the garden. They emerged onto the front porch. The rocking chairs on the ground-floor veranda were well occupied, and the squeaking of their gliders combined with the general confusion just beyond. The burros huddled, as if by sheer numbers they could prevail against the whistling and urgings of the stable staff to move them along. Inez gathered the stable boys were taking the burros to someplace other than the stables, because surely the pack animals would otherwise be stampeding toward home. *Sweet animals indeed.* Everyone in Leadville knew of the obstinate nature of the beasts, and their simple stubbornness in the face of switch or curse, if they were not inclined.

Mingling with the stable boys' shouts were the excited and tired voices of the children. Much like the donkeys, the children stood in a pack, with nursemaids, governesses, and nannies hovering, wiping a dusty face here, calming a sobbing girl in a smudged white smock dress there.

Inez cast an anxious eye over the swirling mass of knee-high urchins clinging to older children or adults as she and Harmony moved down the front steps. All of the very youngest children were half hidden in long skirts. She spotted Lily, just as Harmony lifted a hand, and Lily responded. Slowly, Lily, with William in tow, moved out of the crowd.

He was rubbing his eyes with a pudgy fist, leaving dirt smudges across his face as he did so. A straw hat dangled from his neck by a leather string. Inez's heart was pounding so hard and fast, the crash of blood through her veins seemed to cloud her vision. Unable to wait a moment longer, she rushed toward William and scooped him up in her arms. Inez buried her face in his hair, noticing, as she did so, how it had lightened, how it was now the same golden brown as Mark's hair. "William, it's me, your mama."

William reared back, smacking Inez's nose with the sudden movement, and screamed as if he was being scalped. Those nearby— adults, children, burros—hushed and stared at the spectacle. William's booted feet lashed out furiously against her skirts, and he twisted violently, trying to escape, howling the entire time.

Shocked, Inez nearly dropped the wiggling bundle of fury that was her son. Even as she attempted to grapple with his physical and verbal rejection, the observation flashed through her mind: There's certainly nothing wrong with his lungs right now!

Lily rushed forward, arms open wide. William screamed, snot running down toward his mouth, and held his arms out to her in return. He tilted dangerously, sliding from Inez's grasp. Inez felt as if she'd grabbed a wild cougar cub instead of the child of her own flesh and blood.

Lily snatched the toddler from Inez, saying with vehemence, "He doesn't know you! You scared him!" She turned away from Inez, as if shielding William with her body. "Shhh, shhh, little Wilkie," she cooed. "Lily's here. Lily's here."

Inez wrapped her empty arms around herself, in an unfilled hug, staring at Lily's back. Her snuffling offspring peered at her over Lily's shoulder. His eyes, lashes plastered together by tears, were suspicious, fearful replicas of the ones she saw in her mirrored reflection every day. She felt as if her heart had been ripped from its cage of bone and trampled in the dirt.

"Wilkie?" She sounded out the unfamiliar nickname. "His name is William!"

Harmony hurried up to her, saying, "What with Jonathan's brother William, his son Will, our stable boy Billy, and the D'Andelots next door with their little *Guillaume*, it just seemed prudent to give him a nickname."

"You might have told me."

William had turned his head away. One cheek now lay against Lily's shoulder, one arm dangling. The other was curled around her neck, the chubby fist gripping a long mousey strand of Lily's hair that had escaped her bonnet in back. Lily bounced him slightly, soothing him with a low murmur.

Harmony flushed. "It was an oversight. In our letters, you always referred to him as William, and I, I just followed suit without thinking."

"He doesn't remember me." Inez hardly could say the words.

"I show him your picture every night," Harmony insisted. "Inez, I'm sorry. I should have warned you that lately, Wilkie, that is, William, has been afraid of strangers."

"I'm not a stranger!" Inez snapped. "I'm his mother!"

"Of course you are." She closed her eyes, as if praying for patience, then opened them again, speaking slowly and carefully. "When you gave him into my care, he was eight months old. How much does a child that young remember? I don't know, but it has been that length of time and half as much again. I show him your photo, talk of you to him every day."

Harmony approached Lily and William. "Wilkie." Harmony gently stroked his back. He raised his head at her voice. Harmony guided Lily around, so William was facing Inez again. "This is your mama," she continued. "Remember the pictures of the pretty lady I show you every night? Mama, Wilkie. Mama."

For one heart-stopping second, William's hazel-eyed gaze touched Inez—a brief examination that burned to her soul. His scrutiny returned to Harmony, who was smiling and nodding encouragingly, as if willing him to say the word Inez had been longing to hear.

Lily's hair still clenched firmly with one hand, William reached for Harmony with the other, saying with triumph:

"Mama!"

Chapter Thirteen

Inez turned and blundered away into the crowd, fighting to control her distress.

"Inez!" Harmony hurried after her.

Inez scrubbed at her eyes, denying the tears that threatened to overwhelm, before taking a deep breath and facing her sister. She forced herself to speak calmly. "You were right. I should not have approached him like that. I'm certain he's tired, probably hungry. I need to be by myself for a while, Harmony. Please. I will join you later."

Harmony laid a detaining hand on Inez's sleeve. Inez fought the impulse to shake it off.

"He has never called me mama. That is, he did early on, but I and Lily have corrected him at every turn."

Inez didn't want to hear any more. "I need some time to myself. I will see you in a while. I will begin again with William after he is rested."

She began walking away, blindly, and nearly crashed into one of the small donkey carts.

"Whoa, ma'am!" The donkey wrangler leading the head burro hurried back to her. "Are you all right?"

Steadying herself on the lip of the cart, Inez looked up. The first thing that registered was the red kerchief tied around the wrangler's neck. Even so, it took a moment for Inez to see, through her misery, that the man in a much worn corduroy jacket and an equally worn short crown derby was Gene Morrow, the driver of the ill-fated stagecoach.

Morrow, who had taken her elbow to steady her, squinted at her, the dust caking up into the wrinkles around his eyes. He stepped closer, a concerned frown barely visible beneath his drooping mustache. "Mrs. Stannert? Are you feeling faint, ma'am?" Alarm was in his tone. He turned away, cupping his mouth, preparing, Inez was certain, to call for reinforcements to help her into the hotel. Seeing Lily mounting the steps, with William still in her arms, Inez knew that was the last place she wanted to be right then.

"Mr. Morrow, no," she said quickly. "I am fine, just a little overcome by the heat and dust. I was not watching where I was walking." She swiped at her eyes, grateful to have a reason to wipe the telltale tracks away. "I was just seeking some fresh air. Is there a place to walk, somewhere quiet and cooler?"

Morrow studied her for a moment longer. Apparently satisfied that she wouldn't keel over if he released her, he pointed around the far side of the house, toward a tangle of darker green. "There be a walking path over yonder, Lovers' Lane, with plenty of places to sit. It runs from here to the Cliff House, and beyond to the Manitou House."

With a murmur of thanks, Inez began to move away.

"Ma'am."

She turned.

He reached into the cart, saying, "Sun is pretty strong here. Addles the brain without a body even realizing." He pulled out a large-brimmed straw hat, adding, "Mr. Lewis insists I bringst extra headgear for the tykes and ladies who aren't prepared." He held the hat out to her.

She hesitated, then realizing that wandering outside without a hat would only serve to draw unwanted attention, accepted it from him. "Thank you."

He watched as she tied the ribbons under her chin before touching his hat brim and saying, "Anything else you need, just ask."

He stopped, as if contemplating saying something further, but in the end, simply touched his hat brim again and returned his attention to the lead donkey.

Inez headed around the far side of the house, toward the shadowed break in the wall of trees and bushes. She entered the cool dimness, and a sigh escaped. The light was softer, tinged with green, and the air carried a hint of moisture. Wild clematis and trees with peeling, scrubby bark hugged the path, shadowing it with their leaves and branches. Birds twittered and there was the muted plashing of a small creek or waterway, hidden beyond the green curtain.

It had been a long time since she was surrounded by so much green. In Leadville, trees were sparse, having been cut down early and reborn as buildings and boardwalks for the rapidly growing boomtown. Outside of town, evergreens of various types and size still existed, but nowhere was the growth as dense as what surrounded her at that moment.

Inez walked, eyes downcast, letting the sounds fill her and guide her thoughts. *I should not have assumed he would remember me. I was foolish to swoop down upon him like that.* Getting to know her son again was probably more than she could hope to accomplish in two weeks. Inez stopped in the path, realizing that she wouldn't even have William to herself for that long. Mark would arrive within the week and everything would change yet again. She had no doubt that she would then have an additional rival for William's limited attentions and affection: William's father, Mark.

As it is, we may both lose out to Lily.

A wave of jealousy, more intense than any she'd ever experienced, swept her from head to toe, leaving her shaking and shaken. She stood still, in the center of the path, until the wave subsided. With a clearer head, she decided that whatever was done would be done for William's sake.

Her attention returned to the world around her, and she became aware of another sound, weaving through that of birds and water. Somewhere, nearby, a woman was sobbing.

Inez followed the sound around a bend in the path. The path opened to allow room for a rustic bench with an intimate view of the previously unseen creek. The bench was occupied by Mrs. Pace in her somber, travel-worn black ensemble. An abandoned black travel hat with a puddle of net lay on the bench next to her. Head bowed, she gripped a pair of dark gloves in one bare hand, tight to her lap. With the other hand, she wiped her eyes with a lace handkerchief, then crunched the delicate cloth savagely into a wad.

Inez paused, uncertain whether to melt back around the corner without saying anything or to venture forward and disturb Mrs. Pace's solitude.

The decision was made for her when Mrs. Pace swung around, red-rimmed eyes wide, and said, "Oh, Mrs. Stannert, it's you." Her shoulders sagged.

"I'm, I'm so sorry for your loss," stammered Inez, falling back on courtesy. "I apologize for intruding. Excuse me." She started to back away.

"No, please, after that ghastly interview with the marshal and the doctor, I thought of trying to see you this afternoon." Kirsten Pace moved the hat to her lap. "If you would, just a moment of your time."

She looked down at the hat and bit her lip. As Inez approached, she burst out, "I don't even have proper mourning clothes. The children and I, our travel clothes are the closest things we have, to show our respect." Fresh tears glimmered in her eyes and spilled out over her cheeks.

Inez leaned forward. "Mrs. Pace, truly, none will fault you. Such an unexpected tragedy, and so far from home."

"And here we stay," she said through gritted teeth. "No sooner had I arranged for a telegram to be sent to Edward's brother, asking him to come to Colorado right away, than I was required to go talk to the doctor and the marshal. The marshal apologized for the intrusion, but Dr. Prochazka…he may be a brilliant physician, although I sometimes wonder, but the man has no human feelings."

She brought the damp linen back up to her eyes. "Excuse me, Mrs. Stannert, for this display of emotion."

"Please, call me Inez. It is I who should ask your forgiveness for disturbing you." Inez resisted the urge to put an arm around the sorrowing woman's shoulders. "So, is your brother-in-law coming to take you and your children home? Is that why you remain?"

Mrs. Pace shook her head. "Eric is, was, Edward's business partner. The hotelier, Mr. Lewis, actually had the gall to ask me this morning what would happen to the business negotiations my husband had initiated." She looked up, anger slicing through the tears. "I urged Edward not to get involved in something like this. We came for my health, but he was seduced by the visions Mr. Lewis and his cohorts painted of Manitou's future. What does, did, Edward know of health spas and such? Nothing!"

Inez held up a hand to stop her. "Your husband was forging a business agreement with Mr. Lewis?" Warning bells clanged loud in her mind. "You were against this?"

Mrs. Pace plucked at the net attached to her hat, then focused her eyes skyward, on the green canopy overhead. "I told Edward that the air and the exercise seemed to help. I don't believe in tonics. My father was a physician, and he claimed nostrums and such were nothing more than snake oil. But, Edward was so happy with the improvements in my health while we stayed here, and I thought, well, the tonic may not help, but it cannot hurt." She stopped. "Maybe," she said in a small voice, "I was wrong."

Inez leaned forward, intent, waiting for her to continue. When she didn't, Inez asked, "What do you mean?"

Mrs. Pace pressed her lips together until they whitened. Then, she burst out, "My husband did not have a weak heart! I refuse to believe the lies they told me about him."

"Who? What lies?"

"Dr. Prochazka insists that Edward died from some effect of the altitude that compromised his health drastically. He even suggested that being exposed to air of Leadville could have killed him."

"If that were the case," said Inez, "why didn't he improve when we came down from the mountains?"

"My question exactly," said the widow, twisting, and then smoothing the kid glove which now rested atop the hat. "Dr. Prochazka pooh-poohed my questions and said Edward was not a young man and that such things happen."

"Such *things?*" Inez was appalled at the physician's apparent insensitivity to the young widow's distress.

She nodded, then continued, "I don't believe for a moment that Edward died in such a way. I wondered about the tonic, although I have been taking it without side effects. Still, Edward was planning on signing the business agreement when he returned. Now, it's all quite a mess." She looked at Inez. "I know we have just met, but my hope is that you might help me. You were there when Edward died. You saw how he took the nostrum, and how it precipitated his collapse."

"Do you think your medicine killed your husband?" The small brown bottles for Harmony and William flashed through her mind's eye. "But, Mrs. Pace, that tonic was meant for you."

The women stared at each other.

"Are you still taking that elixir?" Inez asked.

Mrs. Pace's mouth set in a stubborn line. "This morning, I poured the day's dose into the potted plant in our room."

Inez sank back into the bench seat, thinking.

Neither woman said anything for a moment. Then, Mrs. Pace sighed, a sound pulled from her soul. She said abruptly, "I know your sister."

Inez blinked. "Ah! I heard. The DuChamps had thought to accompany you to Leadville, but changed their minds."

Mrs. Pace slipped on one glove, flexed her fingers into the slim pockets. "Edward was not the only one looking at investing in the hotel and the medical clinic."

Then, unexpectedly, she laid her hand atop Inez's.

Inez looked up to find the widow's piercing blue eyes boring into her. "My husband and Mr. DuChamps talked frequently late into the nights about how and where to invest in this area," she said. "Edward confided in me about some of their discussions, about how they dissected the pros and cons of one venture against the other, about what businesses they thought were poised to flourish and what ones seemed destined to fail. I know they were talking with General Palmer in Colorado Springs, Dr. Bell here in Manitou, Mr. Lewis here at the hotel, and with some of the physicians, including Dr. Prochazka and Dr. Zuckerman."

Surely, surely, this shadow does not fall on my sister and my son. Inez's insides curled in fear.

Mrs. Pace continued, "I must concentrate on the children and on what I'm going to tell my brother-in-law, and what I will do once he arrives. Would you, could you, please, just watch and inquire."

"Why do you think I could help?" Inez asked. "Truly, I'm here to spend time with family. I know nothing, or at least, very little, about this area, its businesses and its residents."

"On our trip down from Leadville, Miss Carothers and I spoke." She actually blushed. "It wasn't gossip, really. I was curious about Leadville, and the two of you. Two women, traveling alone, it seemed so brave and adventurous. In any case, Miss Carothers indicated that you are a most uncommon woman, that you have a courage and a way of seeing things, a propensity to action that is unusual, but welcome out here in the wilder parts of this frontier."

Inez shook her head, partly in frustration with Susan's vocal enthusiasms, partly at the idea that Manitou and Leadville could be considered a "frontier." "Miss Carothers has an artistic and creative nature, and is given to reading penny dreadfuls. She sometimes exaggerates."

Mrs. Pace persisted, "She said you have helped her and others who have been in desperate straits. I have no one to turn to here, Mrs. Stannert, no one but you and Miss Carothers. I believe there is something strange going on here. And it's not just me. Someone else is convinced as well." She stopped.

"Who?" Inez, despite her own woes, found herself being pulled into the vortex of the widow's pain and determination.

Mrs. Pace picked up the black hat, smoothed its voluminous veil, and settled it on her head, adjusting the brim. She turned to Inez, one hand ready to pull the veil down.

"Have you met Mr. Robert Calder?" she asked. "He is a guest at this hotel."

"We were introduced this morning," said Inez.

She nodded. "I will try to arrange for you to talk with him in some manner that will not draw suspicion nor breach propriety. When you are able, ask him about his brother, about his brother's stay in Manitou, and what became of him. You'll see. Not all is as simple as it seems. There is a poison here. Something unhealthy lurks, that needs to be drawn out and held to the light. Something that killed my husband."

Chapter Fourteen

Leadville

"Mr. Casey, I apologize for dropping in like this yet again." Inez stepped into her lawyer's entryway. "It appears I've interrupted your noonday meal."

"In my business, Mrs. Stannert, we are at our clients' disposal. Although I try to discourage the midnight visits, unless absolutely necessary." He held the door open with one hand, and a linen napkin with the other. "You know the way to my office," he added.

The scent of roast beef and onions followed Inez as she entered the office and slid into the chair opposite his desk. No sooner had Casey taken the upholstered chair on the other side than Inez bounded to her feet, as if they occupied opposite ends of a seesaw.

Casey, ever the gentleman, immediately rose as well. "Is something amiss?"

"There has been an unfortunate turn of events." She wanted to wring her hands, but balled them into fists and began to pace instead. "Regarding my husband."

Six steps carried her to the side window and a rectangular Wardian case, teaming with small green ferns. She placed two gloved fingers, tentatively, on one of the case's panes, staring at the imprisoned plants. Under her fingers, on the other side of the cool transparent surface, a spiky plant pushed its fronds against the glass, looking as panicked and trapped as she felt.

Gazing at the fern, Inez continued, "Mr. Stannert returned today. Out of a clear blue sky." She gestured toward the window, as if Mark might suddenly plummet down through the narrow gap between the two houses like an ill-timed meteorite.

"He's in town." She did an about-face. "It's insane!" she exploded. "Why now? More than a year, without a word, and then, just as I am about to be quit of him, he shows up?"

Casey still stood, observing her over the top of his glasses. He leaned over his desk with his fingertips resting on the surface as if it were a piano keyboard.

She added, "He seems to think we shall simply continue as we were before. As if his absence were nothing at all, as if he were never gone."

"Mrs. Stannert," he said. "Please, sit. We must work this through together." The gravity in his tone made her want to bolt. But there was no place to run.

She returned to the chair and sank into it. "Whatever shall I do?" she whispered. Then, she raised her voice. "This changes nothing. I still want a divorce."

He settled into his own chair, opposite. "Pardon me, Mrs. Stannert. But I must disagree. This changes a great deal."

She spoke her deepest fear. "Can he force me to stay married to him?"

The lawyer tipped his head to one side and then the other, neither yes nor no. "He was gone for the allotted time to prosecute for desertion. Laches is still a sound legal principle," Casey allowed. "Furthermore, am I correct that in that space of time he did not provide any support? Sent no monies?"

She purposely relaxed her clenched hands. "In the intervening time, there was no word from him, and certainly no funds."

He did another noncommittal head wag, and added, "Failure by husband to provide for wife for the period of one year entitles her to a divorce. But there is absolutely no guarantee. The exact wording stipulates a failure to make reasonable provision for the support of the family. One could argue *res ipsa loquitor*, the thing speaks for itself, that a husband who left a wife with a healthy bank account, a going business, a domicile and so on, did indeed support his wife, and that such provisions were made possible by the fruits of his labors. It's an approach I might take, should I be opposing counsel." His gaze sharpened. "Has he said what caused his absence? Where he has been in the interim?"

"No." She sank back into the leather seat, which sighed beneath her. "He wants to explain, but I would have none of it. The man lies as easily as you or I breathe. I would not trust a word he says." She raised her voice. "Surely, surely, he can't force me to stay married to him against my will. Can he?"

"The law is complicated in that regard." Casey looked out the window for a moment, then removed his glasses and looked back at Inez. Something had changed in his expression in that brief glance away. He was, she sensed, more distant.

"It is good that you came by, Mrs. Stannert. We need to talk, so now is as good a time as any." He folded his glasses, set them carefully to the right on a pad of legal paper, then laced his hands together and placed them in the exact center of the desk. "Mrs. Stannert, you have not been entirely truthful with me."

She reared back in her chair. "How dare you!" Even as she said the words with proper indignation, her thoughts skittered about, like birds trapped inside a room. She thought of the half-truths, the omissions, the outright falsehoods that had, somehow, tripped so easily off her tongue in their earlier conversations, back when she was certain Mark was dead, or at least good and gone.

"You have prevaricated not just once, but multiple times," he continued, as if she hadn't protested. "I grant you, spouses seeking divorce will often embroider a story. Bend the truth. Omit certain acts, events, and so on. As long as your husband was not in evidence, well, there was no one to demand an accounting, so I was willing to look the other way, in view of your evident distress and obvious wishes to proceed apace. Not a wise decision on my part, I suppose." He compressed his lips.

Inez sputtered. "I came to you, Mr. Casey, because you were well recommended. I am willing to pay whatever is needed to dissolve this sham of a marriage."

"Mrs. Stannert, if you want me to represent you, I promise I will do my best to get you a fair share of the property. I will do my best to gain you custody of your son. But I cannot do my job if you are not completely and absolutely honest and open with me. Particularly now."

She leaned forward in turn, gripping the edge of his desk. "What are you implying? This should be a straightforward matter. He was absent for more than a year. I want a divorce. How difficult can it be to get one, here in Leadville? I recall hearing about Elizabeth Johnson here in town. She divorced Mr. Johnson, married his brother a few months later, divorced him, and remarried the first Mr. Johnson, all in the space of a year."

Casey closed his eyes and pinched the bridge of his nose. Inez had the sense that he was holding his breath, perhaps even counting to ten. He finally said, with a sigh, "A vastly different case, Mrs. Stannert."

His hand went from nose to pocket, absently patted it, then wandered to the desk, finally coming to grips with his folded glasses. He settled them back on before directing his gaze and comments to her. "Were there children involved? Or sizable material holdings? Did either Mr. Johnson put up a fight against the charges filed? I assure you, the answer to the aforementioned questions is a resounding 'no.' Finally, do you truly want to compare yourself, put yourself at the same social footing as the aforesaid Mrs. Johnson, whose matrimonial miscalculations and missteps provided casual amusement for the elbow-benders lining the brass rails in town?"

"Of course not," snapped Inez.

"Then do not use her as an argument." Casey broke eye contact and picked up a pencil that lay to the left side of his blotter and transferred it to the right. He regarded it thoughtfully, then asked, "Do you indulge in checkers, whist, card games, the like?"

"On occasion," said Inez, wary of the change in conversation. "Why?"

"Any successful player of the gaming arts knows that it is important to think like the opponent, if one hopes to win. That is, if the game is one of skill and not simply luck. It is the same in the practice of the law. To succeed, one must think like the judge and the opposing counsel, know where his mind may lead, determine what paths are the ones of least resistance—that is, most likely to be taken in the case of an opponent who is either lazy or thinks to make an 'easy game' of it. It is also important to work out the more convoluted responses and tricks and snares that might be employed by an opponent determined to win at all costs. Everything is made easier by knowing the opponent, his strengths, weaknesses, and history."

"I told you, I know my husband. He clearly wants to patch things up and keep our marriage intact. I guarantee, he will be opposed to a divorce."

Casey picked up the pencil, and moved it back to its original position. "Mr. Stannert is not the opponent. I am talking about the opposing counsel, who will present the argument against our petition to divorce."

Casey leaned back, gazing at a spot over Inez's head. "I can think of three or four lawyers who would be more than happy to take up your husband's case. We shall see whom he chooses, assuming he takes that course and does not accede to our demands. But I will give you a taste of what may be facing us, should an agreement not be possible. I won't sugar the pill, Mrs. Stannert. This has the earmarks of a public spectacle, so you must prepare yourself for that possibility. We will be in a courtroom, facing a judge and a jury of peers."

"I...I thought," she stammered, "I thought you said it would be a more private proceeding."

"That was assuming the defendant would not be present. If, as you suggest, he appears and denies the alleged charges in our bill, the case shall be tried by a jury. A jury of men, much like your husband—businessmen, husbands, Leadville men of means. No doubt men who know both of you, or know of you."

Inez had a horrifying vision of a jury box populated with right-thinking men from her church, well-heeled customers of the Silver Queen, and local capitalists and entrepreneurs. Her blood ran as cold as ice water.

Casey continued. "Any jurist worth his salt will look to build a bridge to those men. Build sympathy for your husband's plight. Should I be representing a husband who was against the dissolution of his marriage, I would start by looking for someone to pin the responsibility on for the estrangement of affection of the *femme-covert*," his gaze switched to Inez, "the wife, that is. *Exempli gratia*," he began to twist idly to and fro in his chair, the spring squeaking like a tortured canary, "In an evil hour," he intoned, "a black shadow crept near, entwined around her and instilled into her breast the seeds of a discontent that he hoped would ripen into an alienation from her husband, and dissatisfaction with her lot in life."

Inez stared, feeling a guilty flush crawl up her face. *Could he be referring to my liaison with Reverend Sands?*

Casey glanced at Inez and said conversationally, "Never mind that, in this case, the husband has absented himself from hearth and home for many months. The point would be to feed into the fear that dwells in the heart of every married man or any man who hopes to someday marry. Yes, the lawyer for your husband would do well to paint you a weak woman, a woman who is easily influenced and led astray from matrimonial duties and convictions, but whom the husband hopes to reclaim with a firm and God-given right, to lead her back to wifely virtues and responsibilities."

Inez couldn't help it. She snorted in derision. "There are few I can think of who would believe me a weak woman," she said. "As for those wifely virtues and responsibilities, what about a husband's? Shouldn't he have been here for me? If there is to be blame, who has the greater share?"

He raised a hand and pointing upward said, as if speaking to a larger audience, "That man was made for God, and woman for man; and that the woman was the weaker vessel, is meant to be under the protection of the stronger vessel, man. The forfeiture of that supremacy is as much an infraction of the husband's right as though it was the infliction of violence upon her or him."

He paused in his oratory and added matter-of-factly, "From John Graham's closing of the McFarland-Richardson trial. He ended this part of his closing by summarizing 'the law of the Bible.' Needless to say, some of the strong-minded ladies present at the time were heard to hiss."

A bit of memory stirred at his mention of the trial. She thought she might have read something about it in newspapers, long ago.

"Was this a divorce case?" she asked.

"Abby Sage married, then left, Daniel McFarland. She was seeing a journalist, Albert Richardson."

"The *New York Tribune*," she said softly. "I remember some of the story."

He nodded. "McFarland sought out and shot Richardson. He began a *habeas corpus* action to recover the children. He also brought suit against Richardson for alienation of affections. Mrs. McFarland relocated to Indiana, obtained the divorce she sought on the grounds of failure to support, drunkenness, and extreme cruelty. She then returned to New York with the intent of marrying Mr. Richardson."

"Mr. McFarland shot Richardson," Inez whispered. "There was a deathbed marriage, and Richardson died. It was all over the newspapers." She sat back in the chair, remembering the lurid headlines that had fascinated her at nineteen, mere months before she met Mark. Once Mark had entered the picture, the fate of the doomed couple was no longer an item of interest to her as she lived out her own story of sudden passion and impulsive elopement. "I don't recall," she finally said. "What happened to Mr. McFarland and Mrs. Richardson?"

Casey settled back, hands clasped across his waiscoat. "The jury acquitted McFarland. Mrs. Richardson is still involved in literature and her dramatic pursuits. As to what became of McFarland…" He raised his shoulders in a shrug, then straightened up, returning to his more formal bearing. "All this, Mrs. Stannert, is by way of explaining what may lie ahead. For surely as the sun rises, if I were employed by Mr. Stannert to be his attorney in this matter, I would begin by looking for someone to blame for alienation of affections. For a wolf dressed in sheep's clothing. Or, to speak more bluntly…" He set his elbows on the desk and leaned forward. His chair emitted a warning squawk. "I would look most particularly for a seducer dressed in a clerical collar."

She found it hard to move, to breathe. For once, words failed her.

The grandfather clock in the entryway ticked loudly in the silence.

"You must," Casey continued in a gentle but firm tone, "be honest with me. I cannot prepare for a defense against tactics such as these unless I know about the circumstances."

The clock emitted a faint whir, the sound blunted by the closed office door, and struck one.

Casey pulled a pocket watch from his waistcoat, clicked it open. "I have appointments this afternoon and must take time to prepare for a court appearance as well. I'd like you to ponder my words. If you decide to move forward on this, with me as your legal representative, then you must gather the necessary papers. That includes any contracts regarding property and or other agreements of a legally binding nature signed before or during your husband's absence, any letters that can shed light on the current situation *vis-à-vis* your son. You must also begin a reckoning of personal and real property, any debts, and so on. I should add that this would *not* be a good time to dispose of or hide any assets, material goods, etcetera etcetera. We must keep everything crystal clear and on the up-and-up."

Inez felt as if the world, which had paused during the long conversation, was now beginning to spin again, but at a faster and more urgent speed.

"Is there any way to avoid a circus over this?" she implored.

"You could drop the suit."

She shook her head.

He held up a placating hand. "You did ask for choices. There is another possibility." He stood, came around the desk, and held his hand open to help her out of the chair. "Talk with your husband. Listen to his story, and report to me what he says. We will see if we can discover where the truth lies. We can then explore whether there is some way to fashion a dissolution without acrimony."

Chapter Fifteen

Inez sat on the bench alone in the quiet green of Lovers' Lane, willing the painful memory of the conversation with her Leadville lawyer to be washed away by birdsong and the dry rustle of leaves. She would have tried to outwalk the memory, but after she had helped Mrs. Pace, if she could, Mrs. Pace had extracted a further promise.

"If you could wait here by the bench for a while, so we are not seen leaving the lane together, that might be best," said the widow. "There's no reason for anyone to look askance at us, but it's best if we aren't seen talking together in situations that could be considered conspiring."

"Seen by whom?"

Mrs. Pace's expression had been next to invisible behind the dark veil. "I am not altogether certain, which is why we must be even more circumspect. I have pondered who would have anything against my husband or me. Dr. Prochazka, perhaps? But he seems so uninterested in anything not having to do with the medical realm. I was not in favor of some of Edward's plans, but although he listened to me, he was always a man to make up his own mind. I don't know," she concluded, her voice bleak. "But you should talk with Mr. Calder. I will also make a list for you of the people that my husband spoke of, in case there is some connection."

After Mrs. Pace had left and Inez had shaken off the memory of her ordeal in Casey's office, she sat a while longer and stared at the little creek, rolling over stones red, gray, and brown. "I cannot get involved in this," Inez whispered to herself.

She stood up, determined to deal with events one at a time. If she could help Kirsten Pace, she would, but not at the expense of her family. She vowed that, furthermore, she would not get involved in a wild-goose chase. Her own problems loomed large enough. Mark, William, and Aunt Agnes would all have to be dealt with in one way or another.

Her feet carried her out of the green tunnel, past the Cliff House, and to the back of the Mountain Springs House. She thought to head inside, to see if she could find a cup of coffee and something to tide her over until the next meal.

But her feet proved traitorous to that intention.

Instead, she skirted the winding paths of the garden and continued to the far side of the building complex. Straight ahead, some distance from the hotel—although, if the sounds of braying donkeys that morning had indicated, not far enough—was the hotel's stable and livery. On the near side sat the coach that had carried them all from Leadville to Manitou.

Why am I doing this? What can I possibly hope to find? Certainly nothing that will challenge the findings of a physician. Besides, the marshal isn't interested in hearing anything other than what he's already heard.

The argument she carried on with herself did nothing to stop her forward motion. As she approached, she saw the stagecoach driver come around the back of the buildings, buckets in hand. Behind him, a smaller figure carried a rolled-up canvas.

Inez hurried her steps until she was within hailing distance. "Mr. Morrow! A moment, if you please."

Morrow and the boy stopped by the open coach door. Inez approached, nearly at a trot. It was as if her body, and by extension, her feet, were afraid that, if she slowed down, she'd stop. And, with the cessation of movement, the mind with its ceaseless arguments and logical constructs would take over.

"Excuse me," she wheezed, setting a hand on the side stitch under her ribs and thinking that she should have worn something a little less constricting to accommodate the healthful precepts of hotel and clinic. "Mr. Morrow, have you done anything to the coach since we arrived last night?"

"No ma'am." He looked curiously at her. "Me and Billy here were just getting ready to sluice it out for tomorrow's run to Pueblo."

Billy. Yet another William. She pushed the mental whisper aside.

"Has anyone examined the compartment since Mr. Pace's death?" she continued.

Now his querying expression turned sober. "The marshal was here early this morning, but he mostly just poked his head in and gave a quick gander. Truth to tell, it needst a good scrubbing out."

Inez remembered the state of her traveling costume and the mess of vomit on the floorboards. The previous night, Morrow had given it the most cursory of wipes before wedging Mr. Pace's body into a sitting position on the coach seat.

She glanced at Billy. Stable boy though he was, no doubt used to shoveling manure and soiled bedding from horse stalls and burro pens, even his nose was screwed up in distaste.

"I'd like to take a look if you please. Particularly under the seats."

"Lose something last night?" Morrow asked. "Billy here can keep an eye out whilst he's scrubbing."

Billy looked none too thrilled by the idea.

"I'd like to look myself." *It certainly can't be any worse than the alley behind the Silver Queen on a Saturday night.*

Morrow took in her outfit. "Well, ma'am. It's not my place to say no." He turned to Billy. "Help me put this here canvas on the floor. Gives Mrs. Stannert something to kneel on."

Once the fabric was laid out, Inez clambered into the coach and set her knees on the coarse brown material. Placing her gloved hands gingerly on the tarp, she leaned down, holding her breath. The wide brim of the borrowed straw hat brushed the floor, keeping her from bending down any further. She straightened up, removed the hat and handed it to Mr. Morrow, who hovered outside the door to one side.

She looked first under the seat where the Paces sat. Nothing but normal detritus lurked in the darkness. Crumpled wax papers discarded from sandwiches and other victuals loitered in the shadows, along with an empty snuff tin or two, pages from newspapers or circulars, and what might be very old bread crusts and a couple of apple cores.

Turning her head, she checked under the other seat where she, Susan, and the nanny had sat. Mixed in with the common trash of travel, a faint gleam of a small shape—smooth, shiny, dark drew her eye. Reaching under the seat, she smiled as her fingers closed around the shape of a small bottle. Still on hands and knees, she held it in to the light filtering into the carriage. It was identical to the tonic bottles for Harmony and William. Turning the bottle over, Inez read the small, spidery script: Kirsten Pace.

Chapter Sixteen

"Eureka!" she said triumphantly.

"Ma'am?" Morrow's voice outside distracted her from her examination.

She tipped the bottle this way and that, delighted to see it still contained a few drops of some oily liquid. Careful to hold the small rectangular bottle upright, she reversed over the coach, setting an experimental foot out searching for solid ground. "I believe I have found something, which makes this exploration not in vain." Contact made, she backed out, trying to keep her skirts down around her ankles, which was a losing proposition. "I'm thinking it might make sense to do a more thorough exploration."

Inez straightened, turned, and stopped at Morrow and Billy's expressions. Morrow looked patient, but pained. Billy's thoughts were much more transparent. "Is she crazy?" was plainly stamped across his features.

She added hastily, "I know it sounds a little odd. But recall a man died in here yesterday. I believe it would be wise to examine all and anything that might have been dropped in the coach. I ask on behalf of the widow, Mrs. Pace. Anything we can do to help preserve her mental balance during these difficult times is, of course, important to her health."

Morrow said, "Sure, Mrs. Stannert, ma'am, if you think so. But, wouldn't you rather Billy or I be a-doin' that?"

Up on the second-story veranda, several couples lingered at the rail, staring in her direction. Warmth climbed up her face from the realization of what a spectacle she must have presented to viewers as she hunted under the seats, half in, half out of the coach.

"Perhaps your idea of having Billy pull out everything he finds in here and set it aside for me to look at is a good one," she acceded.

Billy looked less than thrilled at the prospect, but Morrow seemed relieved to have her out of the coach. He said, "It's powerful warm and just going to get warmer today. I can testify the rockers on the porch are right comfortable," he pointed with Inez's straw hat toward the hotel, "and the hotel's lemonade is first class." He held the straw hat out to her, adding, "I'll find you oncet we get the coach all cleaned out."

"Thank you," Inez said with all the dignity she could muster. She took the hat and tied the strings under her chin, hoping no one up on the second story recognized her.

Once she reached the shelter of the hotel, she examined the bottle more closely. It was unmarked, except for the paper label glued to the outside and a ring of wax still clinging to the rim. She tipped the vial this way and that, observing the liquid slide greasily along the inner surface and slowly puddle in one corner. *I should stopper it, so as to not lose any.* Her hand froze mid-tip. Where was the stopper?

Most likely, the cork had been swept out and into the road by the hem of a long dress or scuffed out by a shoe. A dark mood sifted over her, coloring her thoughts a deep sepia, like a scenic vista obscured by dust.

If something were amiss with the contents, how would I know? Even a skilled physician might not be able to tell. Who am I to think I can bring peace to Mrs. Pace and her children or justice to Mr. Pace if foul play was involved, and that is a sizable "if."

Perhaps it was the heat that pushed her thoughts into the dark. Indeed, the higher the temperature climbed, the more imprisoned she felt in the narrow Manitou valley, trapped between the foothills before her and the cliffs behind. Lemonade, she decided, would not do. A libation of a more definitive nature was needed.

She rounded the back of the hotel and mounted a wide set of stairs to the lower porch. The manager Epperley—neat in a summer suit, blond hair combed to a near-white silk—was holding the door open for a trio of ladies who were entering in front of Inez. He smiled, teeth gleaming beneath a mustache twisted and waxed to an uncompromising fare-thee-well. "Will you be joining the others in the dining room, Mrs. Stannert?" The sounds of diners at noon meal echoed to the left.

"In a while," she said evasively, sorely aware that she'd missed breakfast, but having no desire to plunge into what would no doubt be another painful encounter with Aunt Agnes and not yet ready to face her sister after the humiliating reunion with William. Instead she proceeded straight ahead, then turned to the right, seeking a moment's silence and liquid solace—if discreetly available.

Heading away from the music and dining rooms, she plunged into a hall from which the strong whiff of cigars blended with higher notes of alcohol. She hesitated at a partly closed door, then pushed it open and peered inside. Yes, it was the gentlemen's parlor, a wood and leather equivalent of the room she had been escorted to the previous night. It was vacant.

She spied a sideboard, with a number of bottles reflecting the subdued light that crept around the heavy velvet curtains over the one window. *I'm certain they offer the gentlemen something more than mineral water.* She entered the room, nudging the door back to its halfway position. Hurrying to the sideboard, she was gratified to find two bottles of scotch—one a decent brand, the other most definitely top drawer—and crystal glassware. Her hand had just closed on the preferred bottle when the parlor door swung open. Startled, she hid the bottle in her skirts and turned to find the manager standing at the entry, eyebrows raised.

"Pardon, Mrs. Stannert, are you lost?" It was a polite inquiry, providing her with an easy way to dissemble and demure.

She recalled the moment of collusion over the brandy the previous evening, the feeling that this Epperley fellow and she understood each other. She made a quick decision to take a chance on the truth.

"Not at all," she said. "I found what I was looking for." She displayed the bottle that she'd been concealing. "All I need, Mr. Epperley, is a few moments to prepare a glass, and I will retire to a more seemly location."

"Ah." A single syllable, which could have been a question or a statement, said it all. There was no condemnation in his tone, rather approval and understanding.

Still at the threshold, he looked up and down the hall, then added, "Most of our guests are dining at the moment, but there's always the chance that some gentleman, tiring of the company of wife, daughters, squalling babes, mother-in-law and so on, could appear seeking a moment of solace and a good cigar." He held the door open wider, and said, "Madam, if you would allow me, I believe I can mix you something that will meet with your approval."

Inez reluctantly set the bottle aside and followed him out of the room and down the hall. As he walked beside her, he pulled a cigarette from a case, and glanced at her, "Do you mind if I smoke?"

"Not at all."

He smiled. "Lovely. It's incumbent upon me to always ask the guests. Some of the ladies can be quite vociferous in their objections."

They passed the women's parlor, door ajar, equally quiet and deserted. Further down and nearly to the end of the hall, he paused outside a closed door where he pulled out a small carved box. He extracted a lucifer, struck the sulphurous head against the ribbed side of the box, and brought the small flame to the end of the cigarette, lighting it. Epperley inhaled deeply and exhaled, his sigh of pleasure curling up with the smoke. He sorted through a set of keys attached to his waistcoat by a silver chain, unlocked the door, and stood aside, offering Inez entrance with a languid wave.

The first thing she noticed about the room was the bank of windows, their drapes pulled back to allow views of the garden and clinic behind the hotel. The room itself seemed to be set up as a game room. Several tables had checkerboards inlaid on their tops in exotic woods, decks of cards neatly stacked in open cases, and a glass-fronted base that displayed a magnificent array of silver and gold chessmen. However, there was also a bar, although no bottles to advertise whether it served merely ice creams and phosphates or something more to her taste.

Epperley gestured to Inez to take a chair facing the gardens and began to rummage beneath the bar. Things began to look more positive as he set a tall glass on the bar, remarking, "Alcohol and tobacco are the two purest evils, according to Dr. P. Don't let him catch you cozying up to the scotch. He's liable to ring out the leeches and proclaim your humours dangerously unbalanced."

"Dr. P?" For a moment, she was lost.

"Dr. Aurelius Pro-whatcha. I never could keep his bloody name straight. It was better before he arrived and the original hotel physician slunk off to hang his shingle in Colorado Springs. 'Zuckerman' rolls off the tongue with no problem." He paused, squinting at Kirsten Pace's bottle, which Inez had set on the table before her. "Don't tell me Dr. P already has you taking some remedy or other. Pardon me for saying so, Mrs. Stannert, but you hardly appear the invalid."

"It's not mine," she said, then searching for a plausible target, added, "It's for my sister, Mrs. DuChamps."

He pulled out two unmarked bottles from below the bar and deposited a scoop of fine ice into the tall glass. "Ah yes, the lovely Mrs. DuChamps. Charming woman. The climate here seems to suit her. Even more than that, she seems to thrive on the scenery and doesn't mind the dust or heat."

Turning, he selected a cutting board and knife before reaching into a jar on the shelf and extracting two lemons.

Epperley glanced around at Inez's exclamation of disgust.

"I abhor lemonade," she said. "If either of those bottles are mineral water from the local springs…"

"Never fear, Mrs. Stannert. I believe I have your measure, so to speak." He prepared a plain lemonade as he talked. "Along with being the manager of this fine hotel, I'm the resident mixologist. You Americans are so inventive with your various concoctions, never afraid to toss this and that into a glass, top it with a bit of fruit, and see where it goes, even to the point where the talk devolves into nonsense and the barking irons are employed. But that's the West for you. Endless entertainment and fascination for a remittance man as myself."

"A displaced son from Britannia's shores? You have plenty of company here in Colorado," Inez commented. "The state is crawling with remittance men."

The lemons good and truly squeezed of every last drop, Epperley added a judicious tot of sugar and mixed it all with a long spoon.

Inez fervently hoped there was more to his recipe.

He nodded. "There's truth to that, indeed. Especially here, in Manitou and Colorado Springs. I'd heard of 'Little London' years ago and devoured Ruxton's *Life in the Far West* as a lad, which pretty much convinced me that my future lay in the mountains and plains of the States. In any case, I just had to give it all a try. Banking wasn't my interest, the homestead went to brother Harris, and then, I met this lovely lady." He paused in his narrative and shook his head.

Inez found her interest piqued. *He came West for a woman? But Lewis said Epperley chased the cure to Manitou.*

Epperley continued, "For any number of reasons, it was time to 'vamoose,' as our local gendarme might say. I decided, well, why not make an adventure of it? So off to the land of buffalo, bubbling springs, and red savages came I."

Apparently satisfied with the lemonade, he extracted a shot glass from beneath the bar and opened the first bottle. "Imagine my disappointment to find most of the savages and nearly all the buffalo gone. Ah, well. Wandered around a bit, and pulled up here. As for the liquid part of my employment, it all started as a hobby, then became a bit of an obsession. Can't say I mind tweaking the good doctor, what with the small portion of notoriety I've brought to the Mountain Springs House as a result."

"By the 'good doctor' you mean Dr. Prochazka?"

He pointed the stirring spoon at her. "World-famous physician Dr. P, got it in one. 'Life is short, and Art long; the crisis fleeting; experience perilous, and decision difficult. The physician must not only be prepared to do what is right himself, but also to make the patient, the attendants, and externals cooperate.'"

He added a measure from each bottle, stirred again, and placed the glass on a saucer alongside a spoon and a sprig of mint. "First aphorism of Hippocrates. I tinkered with the field of medical arts at one point, but it all just seemed like too much effort and not enough fun."

He came around the bar and brought the glass to Inez. "Now tell me if this doesn't meet with your approval and if it isn't a jot more refreshing than whiskey neat at noon."

She took a spoonful and tasted sweet lemon overlaid with…

She looked up. "Is that gin and bourbon?"

He grinned, all teeth below his ferociously pointed mustache. "Bulls-eye, as they say. You have, Mrs. Stannert, most excellent taste."

She took another spoonful and allowed the iced concoction to melt in her mouth. "I shall have to remember this."

Resting his back against the bar, he had picked up the cigarette again and was staring idly out the window as he inhaled, then exhaled. The word "yes" hissed out like steam from a mineral spring. "You are welcome to add it to the repertoire you offer up at the Silver Queen," he said, knocking ash onto the floor with the flick of a finger. "Say, you could even name it after me. The 'Epperley' has a nice ring, don't you think?"

The frozen ice dripped from her spoon. "How did you know?"

His gaze switched to her and his lips twisted into the shadow of a smile. "You obviously knew a high-class brandy when presented with one and held your liquor admirably well for a lady. I was curious, so made a few discreet inquiries this morning. It's a small and well-connected group of displaced, disowned, and dissolute Brits in Manitou, any number of whom pilgrimage religiously to Leadville every month with their allowances, returning with empty pockets and 'barrel fever' from over-imbibing. The Silver Queen is well known, as is her proprietress, Mrs. Stannert."

Her eyes narrowed as she contemplated that her efforts at keeping a low profile amongst the guests might all shatter like a mirror whose nail had given way. "Well known, you say?"

"A slight exaggeration, sorry. Well known among my colleagues who are wastrels and wretches. You needn't fear that I'll say anything to our guests and so on."

She tapped the table with her spoon, lemonade forgotten for the moment, as she regarded him. "So all this bonhomie, chit chat, airing of personal stories is professional courtesy?"

"Quite. I have nothing but admiration for another practitioner of the art of mixology."

"I see." She stirred the half-consumed icy slush, thinking. "I'm curious. You've been here in Manitou, how long?"

"Three years."

"What do you think of the hotel's prospects? Would you advise me to invest?"

He laughed heartily and unexpectedly. "Oh ho. Don't even think of bringing it up to Lewis. If you are interested, you'd best get your husband, your father, or your uncle to front for you."

"What do you mean?"

"Oh dear, Mrs. Stannert, are you going to force me to spell it out? Here I thought you were so perceptive." He waved the nearly consumed cigarette around in a vague figure eight. A good inch's worth of ash fluttered to the linoleum. "I personally have no problem with the thought of you joining our merry band and making buckets of money when the area takes off. But Lewis runs it pretty much as a gentlemen's club, if you get my drift."

"How unfortunate," said Inez. "I've a bit of pin money of my own, and I'm not averse to investing where I can see an excellent return." She sighed theatrically. "But it's true that I'm not that well-versed in the hotel or spa business. Since Mr. Stannert will be joining us later, perhaps you might give me some information I could pass along to him."

Epperley shook his head, mouth thinned as if restraining unspoken words. He drew on his cigarette one more time, before putting it out in the shot glass, and extracting a second from his cigarette case. "The prospects for an excellent return are there." He spoke cautiously, without looking at her. "I've invested myself, so I've got my hopes, to say the least."

"You're invested in the hotel?"

"A part owner, actually. One-third in." He lit the cigarette and inhaled with vehemence. The smoke uncurled as he spoke. "I'm not one to play at games of chance, but I do see a likely future for Manitou in general and the Mountain Springs House in particular. After all, the consumptives have been flocking this past year, clamoring for Dr. P's miracle cures."

She regarded him, thinking that there was more than a tinge of distaste in his mentions of the doctor. "Mr. Lewis said you came to Manitou to take the waters for consumption."

"Stuff and nonsense." He managed to sound irritated and amused at the same time. "A little fable he likes to trot out to encourage and comfort the tourists and invalids. I don't know why he insists on saying that. There are many who have improved during their stay here, without having to resort to tall tales."

Inez thought back to Harmony's comment that her husband was considering investing. Too, there was Mrs. Pace's statement that not all was as it seemed at Mountain Springs House.

Slowly, as if approaching a half-wild animal, she said, "So, you are saying the hotel has a solid future. But you are also saying don't trust Lewis. You're even suggesting I not trust the doctor. However, you seem to indicate I should trust you."

"That is correct." There was a studied indifference to his tone, a "take it or leave it" air.

Looking for a way to pierce the artifice and see the truth in him, she said, "So, why did you really leave England? A second son seeking adventure or a lothario breaking one too many hearts?"

She meant to shock him. To see if she could freeze the shifting mercurial façades he kept pulling up before her.

Something tightened in his demeanor, and for a moment she glimpsed anger, flickering like a dark flame. "Oh, I didn't break her heart. She broke mine. Utterly. I could have turned to the law, I suppose. Sued for divorce, thrown my family into total shame and humiliation." He drew hard on the cigarette before exhaling and releasing another long plume. Finally he said, "I caught her *in flagrante delicto*, and even had my pistol in my hand. I could have saved myself much grief by pulling the trigger and ending it all."

Chapter Seventeen

Leadville

After leaving her lawyer's office, Inez set out for Evan's Mercantile. Striding down the Harrison Avenue boardwalk toward Chestnut Street, Inez clutched her parasol in a furious fist, as tight as if she had Mark's neck instead of the handle in her grip.

One of the fringed tips of her open parasol brushed against the top hat of a passing gentleman. He caught the tumbling topper with an exclamation of annoyance before it hit the dirt and tobacco-juice-splattered boards.

"My apologies," said Inez unapologetically.

Coming to the corner of Harrison and Chestnut, she closed the parasol, hoisted her hems an added inch, stepped nimbly off the boards and into the street. Parasol at the ready, she started to run the gauntlet of Harrison's wide rutted street, dodging wagons, carts, horses, scattered bits of dried or steaming manure, and other pedestrians. As she whacked the rump of a too-slow burro with her parasol so she could lunge through the moving gap between two ore carts, Inez was glad that the streets were at least dry and not knee-deep in mud and offal. Of course, there was always the danger of twisting an ankle and going down—a dangerous prospect and all too real, especially for those unused to navigating the busy thoroughfares of Leadville.

Safely on the other side, she used her closed parasol as a cane to steady herself on the steep stairs up to the boardwalk level of Chestnut. After tapping the parasol on the boards to loosen the burro dust that clung to it, she walked a half-block before making a hard left into Evan's Mercantile or, as it announced on its windows, "Leadville's Lead Purveyor of Fine Goods, Firearms, and General Merchandise—Anywhere."

She'd often thought, on entering the store, that the "Anywhere" might be a tad over the top, but she was not about to correct the grammar of one of the most steadfast and loyal players at her Saturday night poker games.

Bob Evan himself was behind a counter in the dry goods section, talking to one of the earnest young clerks who seemed to come and go with the Leadville seasons: here in the brilliant summers, gone in the brutal winters. Inez heard Evan say, "When Mrs. Warner returns, tell her of course we can obtain the Valenciennes lace she is looking for. Never send her to another store. We can always get what the customers want. Especially now that we have the railway to town, it's a simple matter of..." Evan broke off his earnest dissertation when Inez laid her parasol on the countertop, and his square face broke into a smile.

"Mrs. Stannert! What a pleasure to see you." He adjusted his wire-rim glasses and turned his full attention to her. The silent clerk took advantage of the storeowner's change in focus and slipped away to help a woman dithering among the bolts of calico.

"Good morning—oh my, it's afternoon, isn't it—Mr. Evan. I'm here to replace my pocket pistol. Alas, it didn't survive the house fire, and I've been slow about getting a new one." She glanced toward the gun case, which was a judicious distance from the fabrics and laces portion of the store.

Evan came from behind the counter. "I heard about the fire. I'm glad that you managed to escape. Anything you need to start anew, let me know. I'll provide a first-rate discount on house goods."

She murmured her thanks as they walked to the firearms portion of the store.

Evan continued, "I said the same to Mr. Stannert when he came by this morning and bought that little Smooth Number

Three. In fact, he just returned it not an hour ago, saying you had something else in mind." He referenced Mark as neutrally as if he were discussing the expected arrival of a wagonload of flour.

Inez stopped by the gun case, and gripped the wood-bound edge of the glass top, attempting to tamp down her irritation at Mark and reply in equally neutral tones. "I'd prefer the model I had before—Remington Number Two, Smoot's Patent."

Evan slipped behind the case saying, "Certainly, if that's what you want. But the Smoot Number Three is a beaut, chambered for .38 caliber. Thought you'd like the pearl grip on the one I sold to Mr. Stannert. Anyhow, there's also the Smoot Number Four. I have a dandy specimen, if you're interested."

Inez held up her gloved hand, fingers spread wide to stop his enthusiastic patter. "I want a Smoot Number Two, as close to my original as possible. For sentimental reasons, you understand."

"Oh sure, sure." His head bobbed, and he smoothed his brown hair absently, running his hand over the top of his head as he turned his back to the case and looked at the shelves.

"Here we go." He reached high and retrieved a small hard-leather case. He set it on the glass top and opened it, remarking, "I guess this was just waiting for you, Mrs. Stannert. Took it from a fellow who needed the money for a ticket out of town. Guess he thought he'd come to Leadville and become a bonanza king just picking the silver up off the ground. Told him he was way too late, that most of the mining district was all staked out and he ought to test his luck elsewhere."

Her heart gladdened at the sight of the pocket pistol, sister to the one that had been lost in the flames. She extracted the gun from its resting place, pulled out the cylinder pin, and removed the cylinder to examine the chambers and the barrel.

Evan leaned one elbow on the counter. "Clean as a whistle. No rust or corrosion. She was well taken care of, Mrs. Stannert."

Inez nodded her approval and placed the revolver back in its red-velvet lined case.

"Excellent. I'll take her and a box of the appropriate cartridges, please."

As Evan set the box of bullets beside the leather case, Inez opened her purse asking, "How much will that be?"

"Oh, no problem. I'll put it on Mr. Stannert's line of credit."

Hand frozen in the purse, she fixed him with an iron gaze. "What?"

Evan retreated a step, bumping into the shelves. "Oh. Well. When Mr. Stannert came in and we talked about the fire and all, and how he wants to rebuild. We discussed it, and like I told you, I'll give you a first-rate discount on goods and so on. So, of course, he wanted to have a line of credit sufficient to...Well, the saloon is going gangbusters, I know he's quite impressed with how you and Mr. Jackson handled all the business while he was gone..."

She withdrew her money purse and smacked it on the glass. "I'll pay cash."

He looked startled, and a bit shocked, as if she'd offered to do a dance on the gun cabinet. "Really, Mrs. Stannert, that's not necessary."

"Then I would like to start a line of credit that is separate from Mr. Stannert's."

Evan glanced left and right, as if seeking an escape. "Well, this is most irregular." He finally looked at her, a bit piteously, and said, "It can be arranged. Where should I send the bill?"

"Send it to me at the Silver Queen Saloon." She swept gun and cartridges into the sizable purse. "Will you still be attending the Saturday poker games, Mr. Evan?"

"Oh, sure. Nothing has changed." His tone indicated that he didn't think that was the case at all, but before she could challenge him further, he hurried on. "Mr. Stannert told me that the Saturday games would continue. I was glad to hear that, Mrs. Stannert. I look forward to them, you know. I am a fellow of habit. He explained that he'd be running a game on Fridays, extending special invitation to out-of-towners. I told him I thought it was an excellent idea."

"You did, did you." She could hardly speak around her mounting anger.

"Well, sure. With the trains bringing folks up on Fridays, makes sense to get 'em when their pockets are full." He chuckled. "Gives them the weekend to repent of their sins, so to speak. But oh yes, you can count on me for Saturday evenings, Mrs. Stannert."

She smiled through gritted teeth. "So pleased I can count on you, Mr. Evan. Thank you for providing me with replacement firepower."

She exited the store and stood in the blinding late July sunlight, wavering a bit.

Mark was against a divorce. He had re-established a line of credit at Evan's. He was starting an "exclusive" game for out-of-towners on Fridays. He planned to rebuild the house. *Her* house.

Her feet began walking of their own accord. If her skirts were looser, she'd have broken into a run. As it was, she remembered nothing of the trip from Evan's store on Chestnut to the lot that held the charred remains of her home on Fourth Street.

Blessedly, there was no one there. Inez stepped up on the creaking fire-blackened wood of the front porch, and waded into the ashes and charred, melted, broken remains of her life. At the spot where she estimated baby William's room had been, she sank to her knees, oblivious of the soiling to her skirts. She pulled up half-consumed pieces of wood and plaster, and found a shard of decorated wood from William's cradle, varnish blistered, wood discolored, the ornate bit of design that lined the headboard barely visible. Tears fell onto the piece of molding, where they vanished, soaking into the porous, heat-seared wood.

"Inez." Susan Carothers' voice sounded soft and urgent behind her. A gloved hand settled on her shoulder, and Inez heard the soft crackle of burnt debris as Susan circled around to kneel before her. "Mr. Evan came to my studio and said I should find you. He was concerned. We guessed you might be here. Tell me what you need. I'll do whatever I can."

Unable to speak, Inez reached up and gripped Susan's hand. Motionless, they knelt among the ashes together, holding hands.

"I need," Inez finally said, "to see my son. I will be meeting him and my sister in Manitou, in less than two weeks." She looked at Susan. "Will you come with me?"

Chapter Eighteen

Epperley's bitterness at betrayal mixed with her own memories. Inez eased back in her chair and studied the manager of the Mountain Springs House with a closer eye.

Epperley averted his face, as if to avoid her scrutiny, and ground out the cigarette in one of the shells of lemon rind. Inez noted the hunched set in his shoulders, the sudden tightness in his jaw, and the slight tremor in the hand that snuffed the cigarette. He might as well have shouted out his regret at having been so glib as to have inadvertently spilled so much to her.

A muffled rap at the window caused them both to jump. Epperley looked up, and his face smoothed into a welcoming smile. "It's your sister, Mrs. DuChamps, and her son."

Inez resisted the impulse to blurt, "*My* son." Instead, she turned toward the window. Sure enough, Harmony was smiling on the other side, William's hand clutched in hers.

William— washed, brushed, dressed afresh, and presumably fed and rested—peered about the veranda. One chubby finger shot out, pointing at a nearby rocking chair. Inez could just discern the opening and closing wings of a butterfly resting on the back of the rocker. The nanny, Lily, stood behind Harmony, arms crossed, a sullen glower under her white cap. Harmony gave the window one more little tap and pointed to the door, eyebrows raised. Inez nodded and gestured for her to come inside.

"Here she comes. The little boy—your nephew?—has quite a bit of the devil in him." Epperley absently straightened his cuffs, touched his collar and tie. "I can see the family resemblance. He has your eyes, Mrs. Stannert."

Another fashionably dressed young woman, promenading past the window with two young boys in tow, stopped, shaded her eyes with a hand and leaned to see past the window's reflection. A wide, dimpled smile spread across her face, and turned the young matron into a slip of a girl.

"Mrs. McLaughlin has found us out as well. Her two boys will be clamoring for ices, mark my words. I suppose I shall have to open the room for afternoon business," said Epperley.

He leaned over the counter, stashed the liquor bottles out of sight, and then straightened up, brushing at his waistcoat and remarking, "Well, that was probably far more than you wanted to know about the hotel and so forth. Of course, if you have any questions about the medical side of the business, I'd say talk to Dr. P or perhaps Nurse Crowson. She's quite conversant on most matters, and easier to track down than the doctor. When he's locked in his back room, it's best not to attempt conversation."

"The back room? Do you mean his study?" She remembered spotting a shadowy room beyond a half-open door, indistinct glassware glinting on counters, during her inquisition with Dr. Prochazka and the marshal.

"Not quite. He's conducting 'research' back there. Very important, will-change-the-world experiments. So he says." Epperley made it sound as if he suspected the physician of engaging in acts of sexual perversion rather than intellectual advancement.

As Epperley approached, pulling out the key to the door, Inez popped the sprig of mint into her mouth and chewed, hoping it would mask the flavor of the spiked lemonade. The mint blasted into her throat and sinuses. She hated mint.

Swallowing hastily, she held up the tonic bottle. "Have you something I can cap this with?"

"Of course. The corks litter the place. You find them in every room and every potted plant." Epperley paused by a knick knack shelf, out of reach of curious little fingers but eye-level for adults, and fished out a cork from a delicate china bowl. "Should you ever need one, we collect them here, and the good nurse gathers them up periodically and trots them back to the doctor."

He handed her a cork, which she used to stop the small bottle before slipping it into her pocket.

Epperley reached the door just in time to hold it open for Harmony, who breezed in, William in her arms, Lily following in her wake. "Inez, we missed you at lunch! I see you have found the ice cream parlor. You have had something to eat, I hope? You've been treated to one of Mr. Epperley's famous lemonades, I see."

"Absolutely delightful lemonade," agreed Inez. "Just the way I like it, not too sweet."

"Should I prepare one for you and the young sir?" Epperley made a movement toward the counter.

"No, thank you, we have just finished luncheon." Harmony's gaze switched back to Inez. "I'm so glad we found you. The doctor likes us to walk after midday meals. He says it is good for the constitution. So we are going on a small walking excursion. Do say you'll come with us!"

Inez pushed the empty lemonade glass aside and stood. "Certainly." She cast a glance at William and caught him gazing at her with an expression that reminded her of Mark sizing up a new opponent at the poker table. William immediately hid his eyes on Harmony's shoulder.

The lemonade-gin concoction in Inez's stomach churned and turned sour.

How could he forget me, his own mother? The more time I spend with him, the better the chance that he will remember.

"I shall need to fetch a hat and a parasol, but I shall be quick about it," said Inez. "Where will this excursion take us? To the mineral springs across the road?"

Harmony gave a small laugh, laced with sisterly fondness. "Oh, that is hardly more than a few minutes stroll, unless we were to go up to Ute Iron spring. We should save that for a cooler day. I thought perhaps to show you some of the marvelous rock formations nearby. This area is so different from the East, it takes my breath away. Truly a natural wonder." She tickled William, saying, "I thought we would visit Williams' Canyon. Wilkie! We are going to walk through the canyon that bears your name!"

William wiggled as she tickled him. At the sound of his nickname, he lifted his face off her shoulder and bestowed a delighted grin on Harmony. That smile felt like a stab of a knife to Inez.

"I'll see you on the front porch, then." Unable to stop herself, Inez reached out and stroked a little stripe-stockinged calf peeking out from under William's dress. He kicked once, half-heartedly.

Inez nodded her thanks to Epperley, who was juggling lemons for the young McLaughlin boys, who alternately clapped and demanded lemons of their own. She headed for the door, thinking that, yes, she definitely needed to spend every minute she could in William's presence. *No matter how long it takes, I won't rest until he finally smiles and holds his arms out to me.*

Twenty minutes up the path that led into Williams' Canyon, Inez was puffing. The glove that held her parasol aloft was soaked with sweat as was the back of her neck. Gravel crunched beneath her walking shoes at every step. With every inhalation, the sharp scent of dust made her want to cough or sneeze. She longed for another glass of Epperley's powerful lemonade to quiet the tickle in her throat.

It was hard for Inez to understand how Harmony could remain so cheerful and fresh-looking as she walked along, pointing and exclaiming over the striated canyon walls, banded with red and gray rock. As least, Inez reflected, it was mostly shady in the canyon, and they seemed to have it to themselves. It was also wide enough for them all to walk abreast. William had toddled manfully up the approach, but once the canyon was reached, he fussed and tugged at Lily's skirts until she took him up. Lily trudged beside Inez, seeming impervious to William's weight. Her oversized straw hat provided additional shade for William, who snoozed and drooled on her thin, stoic shoulder.

At least, with Lily beside her, Inez was able to lightly rest one hand on William's back as they walked. He slept on. Lily didn't pull away, but she also refused to look at Inez. She simply matched her stride to Inez's, and Inez felt absurdly grateful for that.

Harmony chatted on. "Did you know that the canyon is named after one of New York's own?"

When Inez shook her head, she elaborated, "Mr. Henry Truman Williams, the New York editor and journalist? Well, perhaps you haven't heard of him. He wrote a guidebook about the San Juan Mines a decade or more ago. Jonathan read it and was quite impressed. Isn't it lovely here? All the rocks, their colors and the way they are layered, like a fancy torte." She smiled at Inez. "Do you have canyons like this in Leadville?"

"Heavens no." Inez flashed on the wide-open spaces of the Arkansas Valley, Leadville nestled at the head of the Arkansas River, the tallest peaks of the Rockies five miles distant. She felt the walls of Williams' Canyon close in, squeezing the breath out of her. "In Leadville, it is more wide open. It's a mining city, of course, so there is plenty of industry—smelters, mines, stamping mills, and what have you. Still, there are some lovely meadows outside of town and the wildflowers are extraordinary."

Harmony tipped back her parasol to gaze at the cliffs looming overhead. "Well, then, this must be a treat for you. Ah, The Narrows are just ahead. Let's go through and then decide how much farther we want to walk."

"The Narrows? You mean, it becomes narrower?" Inez wondered how she'd be able to manage.

"Why, you can almost reach from one side to another as you pass through. It's quite the adventure."

"I had no idea you were the adventurous type."

Harmony glanced at her. Inez thought she saw a shadow of… anger? Impatience? It flitted across her features so quickly, Inez couldn't be sure she read it right.

Harmony lifted one shoulder. "When you left home, I was ten years old. We did not begin our correspondence until much later. Even now, I have to be careful in writing to you. Should

Papa discover we are in constant communication, he would be most unhappy. When you and I were finally together again, last year in Denver, it was only briefly."

She didn't have to say: When I came across the country a year ago, at your urgent request. When you entrusted William to my care.

"I suppose we don't know each other very well," Harmony's voice had a forced lightness to it. "But we can begin to remedy that in our holiday together, here in Manitou."

"Of course," Inez assured her. "I just wish the time we have together could be longer. A couple of weeks is really such a short time."

"We shall make the best of it. Ah! Here it is. The Narrows."

It was, indeed, narrow. More than that, the sides of the slim defile were not parallel. One side of the cliff bulged out, overhanging the path, while the other side seemed to lean back as if to escape, much as Inez wanted to do.

"We'll go through, shall we?" Harmony closed her parasol and walked through first.

Inez closed her parasol as well and trotted through the opening. There was room for two people to walk abreast, yet Inez couldn't help but feel that if she were to inhale, she might get stuck between the two walls. Lily shifted the toddler's weight, repositioned a satchel hanging on one arm, and followed.

"Good!" Harmony clapped her hands once. "There is a good place to rest just a few steps farther on. We can then decide whether to continue or return. I have heard that the trail ends at a waterfall. I've not been able to walk so far as to see it. I hope to do so, before the end of our holiday."

On the other side of The Narrows, Inez put her parasol back up and looked around. The walls of the canyon drew back, taking their proper place some distance from the path and leaving a small open area. Dusty green bushes and small gnarled trees, interspersed with grasses and tumbled rock of various sizes, dotted the canyon landscape.

William woke and began to grumble the way small children do.

"Lily, why don't you take him up the path a bit and change him," Harmony said.

Lily set William down on unsteady feet. "C'mon, Wilkie, let's get you fresh nappies."

He grabbed one of her fingers, and she led him up the path.

"He's still in diapers?" Inez asked. "Shouldn't he be past that?"

"He was, but the traveling has made all that difficult." Harmony watched them until they disappeared around a bend. "It's just easier this way. And really, what does it hurt?" Holding the parasol tipped against the breeze, she began pacing the width of the narrow trail. Inez watched her bite her lower lip and worry it with her teeth.

"Is there something that concerns you, sister?" Inez asked.

Harmony stopped. "Does it show so easily?" The parasol dipped. She crossed her free arm across her body, supporting her elbow.

Inez waited.

Finally, her sister said, "Yes. I am concerned." Harmony's voice, which had been cheery and full of confidence on the hike up the canyon now sounded small and uncertain. "What do you think of the Mountain Springs House?"

"The hotel?" Inez tried to discern what lay behind the thread of fear that laced Harmony's words. "It seems a perfectly reasonable establishment. Pleasant staff, well run. Don't you like it?"

"No, that's not what I meant. I meant, what do you think of its business prospects?" Harmony looked at her, face taut with the struggle to hold some strong emotion at bay. "I ask, because I know you essentially ran the family business up in Leadville, during your husband's absence. I could tell from your letters that it prospered. You even engaged in some business contracts and agreements on your own, didn't you? So you must be able to assess a business situation. Certainly better than I can. What do you think of the Mountain Springs House's possibilities?"

It was as if a dark cloud had appeared out of nowhere, covering the intense blue summer sky. Inez recalled snatches of conversation with Mr. Pace on the stagecoach ride, Kirsten Pace's "all is not right" assertion by the creek, Epperley's sideways comments about the hotel. A shiver went down her back that had nothing to do with the breeze tunneling through The Narrows, setting the dusty leaves quaking.

"I am more familiar with mining prospects, truly, than resort areas such as Manitou and Colorado Springs," Inez hedged.

"Still. What do you think of its prospects? Be honest."

Inez was quiet a moment, gathering what she knew, turning the information this way and that, trying to pin down her uneasiness about the place.

Finally, she spoke. "Manitou has been tooting its horn for some years now, as has Colorado Springs. However, this area is still a bit in the back of beyond, in my opinion. Its time may be coming, but it certainly hasn't arrived. At least, not to the extent that all the advertisements and promotional hoopla suggest. Manitou is no Saratoga Springs. At any rate, not yet," she amended. "It is hard to know when that time will come, or if it ever will. I get the impression that there is plenty of talk, that people are trying to create the anticipation of a coming 'boom' or bonanza in tourist trade and invalid care. The Mountain Springs House seems no different in that regard, in hatching plans for the future."

"Plans. Yes, well, that is part of what worries me." Harmony took a deep breath. "Please, don't tell anyone what I am about to tell you. I fear Jonathan is getting in over his head and will bring ruin on us all."

Alarmed, Inez asked, "What do you mean?"

"I told you, didn't I, that he and Mr. Pace had been conferring, looking about for investments, before Mr. Pace went to Leadville? Apparently things have progressed beyond just talk." Harmony's mouth set in a thin line. "This morning, Jonathan showed me an agreement he intends to sign. It promises that he will invest... well, a great deal of money...to become part owner of the hotel. I was shocked at the sum spelled out. It is far more than what he had talked about previously. Perhaps, with Mr. Pace's death, all the hotel's hopes for the future are pinned on us."

"Oh, Harmony." It was all Inez could think to say.

Harmony hastened, "I don't mean to sound hard-hearted. My heart aches for Mrs. Pace. But I'm worried. No, more than that, I'm frantic." She twisted the handle of her parasol, and it began to rotate, sending pulsing shadows over her face. "Jonathan knows nothing about the business of health resorts, spas, mineral waters, cures, and the like. He has always been so cautious before, and now it is as if he has some sort of fever, as if he has lost his mind. He's thrown all caution to the wind."

Inez shook her head, mute. Inside, she damned the folly of men who jumped into deep waters at the siren call of easy money, when they had no knowledge of the currents.

"That's not like my Jonathan," Harmony continued. "Why, just this morning, he was saying we would get rich, that it would be so simple. We invest a little money now and we make that amount ten, a hundred, a thousand times over, in less than a year. A year!" Her eyes looked dark and fearful in the shadow of the parasol. "He doesn't seem to see this is a huge gamble, one where we could lose nearly everything. He's playing a game and, and I don't believe he knows the rules. We could be ruined!"

Inez thought how familiar this all sounded. The belief in the "sure thing." The talk of getting rich overnight by betting the whole pot, because the returns looked so good and the deal was such a sure bet. The risks, the odds, the repercussions of losing—all seemed as insubstantial as smoke when Lady Luck smiled and gestured with her fan.

Inez asked urgently, "Has he signed anything yet?"

"Not yet. I begged him to wait. What could a couple more days matter, I said. I pointed out it would give him time to think this over, gather more opinions, more information, because, no matter what he said, it *is* a great deal of money. He finally agreed to wait when he saw how upset I was becoming. But this morning he left, right after breakfast, with Mr. Lewis and that Dr. Zuckerman. I don't quite know who Dr. Zuckerman is, really. He says he is a local physician. I'm guessing he may be involved in the hotel in some way. When he joins us for meals, he always hovers around Jonathan. Oh, Inez. I know Jonathan chafes at home. He runs the business for Papa and does a wonderful job, but I don't think Papa gives him enough credit nor the responsibility nor the due that Jonathan feels he should have. I believe he sees this opportunity as a way to make his own fortune, apart from Papa. He even said, with what he would make from investing in the Mountain Springs House and its future, we would be free. That was his word, free."

Inez couldn't stand seeing Harmony so distressed. She walked over to her sister and took Harmony in her arms. Harmony remained stiff, her arm still crossed in front of her, hand locked tight on her elbow, a barrier between them.

"I won't let that happen," said Inez. "I have seen this behavior before, in Leadville. Only up in the mountains, it's silver, not soda springs, that drives men mad."

"There is something going on here, Inez."

"I'll find out what it is. Only, be careful, Harmony. Go along with what people say. Be agreeable, and don't argue. But don't let your husband sign anything. Point out the other opportunities in Colorado, in the San Juans, in Leadville. I could talk to him about silver mines up there, what the word is on the street for good investment. Maybe we can distract him enough to at least make him pause and weigh other possibilities. Still, he probably wouldn't countenance business advice from me, a woman." She felt her throat go tight with panic. "Surely, surely you can keep him from inking on the dotted line, for just a few days."

"What will you do?"

"I'll talk further with Mrs. Pace and Mr. Calder. I'll ask around. Discreetly, of course, and see what I can find out about the Mountain Springs House and how it stands, financially."

Harmony put her forehead on Inez's shoulder. "When we first made arrangements to come out here, Jonathan said, if I liked it, we could buy a small summer home." Inez felt her tremble. "That way, we could be close by you. We could be a…a family."

She pulled away, wiping her eyes, and walked over to a small group of flat-topped rocks while Inez followed. "I didn't mean to talk about all that, it just spilled out. But I'm glad I did, and I'm grateful that you'll help. I've been feeling so at sea about this. Too, I'm glad we finally have some time to ourselves."

Harmony approached a table rock just the right height for sitting. A boulder perched atop one edge, leaving just enough room for them to sit side-by-side. Harmony dusted off the flat surface, and spread out a linen cloth to sit on, indicating to Inez to join her. Inez sat, shifting away from Harmony so as to not crush her skirts. Inez's elbow barked against the rough surface of the boulder and she exclaimed in annoyance as a sharp pain radiated up her arm. She set her hand on a dark stripe in the middle of the rock and nudged it, experimentally. The boulder rocked, just a little. Inez hastily removed her hand, thinking that someone should give the massive rock a good shove and send it to the ground, where it would be less of a nuisance and a danger. She wished she'd had more to eat that day than a few sips of coffee and ersatz lemonade. With all that Harmony had told her, she felt her stomach roil with nausea and dread.

Harmony closed her parasol and set it, like a line of demarcation, between herself and Inez. She then untied her wide-brimmed straw hat, removed it, and flapped it like a fan, stirring the tendrils of dark brown hair curling at her temples.

"I actually had a different question that I wanted to ask you, Inez. I do hope you won't take offense at what I'm going to ask."

Inez covered Harmony's gloved hand with her own. "Nothing you could ask will offend me. What do you want to know?"

"Now that your husband has returned," she cleared her throat, and continued with a tremor to her words, "is it your intention to take William back?"

Inez slid her hand away and fisted it in her lap. "I won't lie to you. I've thought about it, hoped it would be possible. But it is a complicated situation between Mr. Stannert and me. I believe he is anxious we regain William and become a family again. I've discussed William's health with our doctor in Leadville. He thinks that, with William now a year older, he might be able to handle Leadville's weather and altitude."

"You can't!"

Inez flinched. It wasn't Harmony who spoke, but Lily.

Inez twisted around to find Lily standing in the path, a soiled nappy in one hand, William's fingers clasped tight in the other.

"You can't take Wilkie," Lily repeated. Her face was blotched red with anger. "We're his family, not you! He belongs with us. The missus and mister and me."

"Lily!" Harmony sounded horrified. "That's enough!"

Inez rose slowly, retorts in a turmoil. Possible responses battled for speech, including, "How dare you presume!" and "I most certainly can take him," and "I am his mother. No matter what happens, no matter how long we are apart—a day, a year, a lifetime—nothing will change that."

Before Inez could settle on one or the other or something entirely different, Harmony marched forward, took William's hand from Lily's, and said, "Go back to the hotel. Now. I will speak to you later."

Lily looked down at William, whose face was beginning to scrunch up, preparatory to crying.

"I, I'm sorry, ma'am. I just said what I know's the truth. You and the mister, you're the only family he knows."

"These are not matters for you to decide or remark upon. I hired you to take care of Wilkie, and that is all."

Lily's shoulders crumpled in, and she looked as if she might start crying as well. Without a word, she turned and threaded her way back through The Narrows.

Inez remembered her last glimpse of William when she left him with Harmony at the Denver train station. His little face had peered at her over the shoulder of the nursemaid Harmony had hired, features squeezing together in puzzlement as Harmony and the nursemaid boarded with him on the train.

William was now crying and calling out, "Eee-eee" at Lily's departing back. He looked up at Harmony, and said, "Want Eee-eee."

Harmony crouched down and said, "There, there. Lily will be waiting for us at the hotel. Now, show me. Where is your nose?"

He stopped crying and touched his nose.

"Where are your eyes?"

He blinked his eyes rapidly, then covered them with both hands.

"Good, Wilkie! Now, where is my nose?"

He reached out and touched Harmony's nose.

"Good!" She picked him up and walked over to Inez. "Wilkie, look at the pretty lady here." She directed William's gaze to Inez. "This pretty lady is your *maman*."

Inez smiled in what she hoped was an encouraging manner.

William stared at her as if she'd suddenly sprouted an extra head. "No."

William's dismissal of what, to him, was clearly a lie was unambiguous. Not just in the single syllable, but in his posture, in the incredulity that bloomed in his eyes as he regarded Inez. The cold gaze made Inez sick at heart.

Harmony pushed on. "Where is *maman's* nose?"

He turned back to Harmony and touched Harmony's nose.

She pushed his hand away and said, "No." She sounded desperate. "I am not *maman*. Wilkie, look, here she is. This is your—"

Inez interrupted. "You will only confuse him, Harmony." With a sudden inspiration, she said, "I have it." She leaned down and looked into William's eyes. "William, I am *Mutti*. Can you say that? *Mutti*."

The doubt and suspicion in his face lingered for a moment, then cleared. He ventured, "Mutti?"

"That's right." Inez nodded encouragingly. "Where is Mutti's nose, William?"

Slowly, he reached out, touched the tip of her nose with one finger and said, "Mutti nose." A fleeting look of puzzlement, something half-remembered, seemed to flit through his eyes. Then, it was gone.

Relieved and hopeful at last, Inez captured his finger and kissed it. "Yes, William. Yes."

Chapter Nineteen

"I am sorry, Inez." Harmony sounded subdued. "When he first began calling me Mama, I tried to correct him. I should have insisted he call me differently. *Tante*, for instance."

Inez nodded, thinking that yes, she should have, but it was too late for that now. Then, she had a sudden thought. "Does William call Jonathan…"

"Papa," Harmony stopped, and covered her eyes with one hand. With a shaking voice she said, "Inez, I never thought twice about it, after a while."

"When Mr. Stannert arrives, it would be politic to let him know what's what before he sees William again," Inez said grimly. "So he's not caught off guard."

A rhythmic squeak-crunch-squeak-crunch of approaching wheels on the other side of The Narrows stopped their conversation.

The squeaking and crunching grew louder, reverberating in the rock passageway ahead. Through some odd trick of acoustics, Inez also heard a strangely familiar but as yet disembodied voice ratcheting through the passageway ahead of its owner. A voice, soothing as the water shushing in a stream, but not clearly male or female, said, "…has treated many such as you with remarkable results. He practiced all through The War of the Great Rebellion and has impeccable credentials."

The amplification cut off as an invalid chair emerged from The Narrows, propelled by Nurse Crowson. Inez now recognized the voice as hers. The hunched figure in the chair, heavily swathed as it was, was clearly Mr. Travers from that morning's meeting in the garden. Nurse Crowson, slightly bent over, was murmuring into her patient's ear as she pushed. Harmony called, "Good day, Mr. Travers, Nurse Crowson."

The nurse halted and straightened. Her expression, at first surprised, passed to a frown, and then a soft smile to fit the words, "Good afternoon, Mrs. DuChamps, Mrs. Stannert. How was your constitutional?" Her gaze switched to William. "How is your son today?"

Inez's instinct was to clutch William close, to hide him and any lingering infirmities from the nurse's critical, cool gaze. Her response, "He's fine" was overrun by Harmony's "He is breathing well, no coughing, plenty of stamina. Good appetite and sleeping soundly."

Nurse Crowson's smile widened fractionally. "Excellent. I'm glad to hear the tonic and the climate are having the desired effect. The combination of Dr. Prochazka's medicines and the inherent healthfulness of the springs and air are quite miraculous. Take one or the other away, and the results could, indeed, be quite different. Of course, the specifics of his condition must be carefully monitored. Not all respond to the same regimens in the same way."

Mr. Travers wheezed, his chest heaved, and he fell into an escalation of wet-sounding coughs. Inez, who was no stranger to consumptives—Leadville also had its share of "lungers" looking for the right combination of dry air and altitude to affect their cures—nonetheless winced at the racking noise. His fit passed, and Travers sucked in a tortured breath to wheeze, "Must… see…the doctor."

Nurse Crowson resumed pushing the chair. "We will arrange it." She nodded to Harmony and Inez as she and her patient passed by.

William regarded the chair and its turning wheels, then looked at The Narrows and up at Harmony.

She nodded encouragingly. "Go ahead, Wilkie."

Wilkie ran into the passageway. He stopped, still within sight of Harmony and Inez, tipped his head to look up at the overhanging cliffs, then hopped up and down and began shouting. His delighted hoots and shrieks echoed back to Inez and her sister.

Harmony lowered her parasol in the shade of the strait. "We should probably walk a little faster so we can have time to rest and dress for dinner. There is usually a musical concert afterwards, although the musicians vary. I believe they rotate amongst the various Manitou hotels, and I don't recall who is playing tonight. Tomorrow, it's games in the parlor. Charades, *tableaux vivants*, and so on."

Inez inwardly groaned at the prospect of having to endure endless parlor games and halting musicians of uncertain talent, but said, "If you will be there, so will I."

She lowered her parasol to follow her sister. Before passing through The Narrows, she glanced back up the path to where they had stopped. Nurse Crowson and her charge had paused at the same point, as if to take in the view further up the canyon. Only the nurse, instead of facing the scenery like her patient, was gazing toward Inez and The Narrows, with a barely discernible frown.

No sooner had they turned off the path to town and headed to the back of the hotel than the stable boy Billy darted up to them, remembering at the last moment to snatch off his cap. "Mrs. Stannert, Mr. Morrow says he has the trash ready for you to look at."

Harmony looked at Inez, mystified. "Trash?"

"In the confusion last night something fell from my valise," Inez improvised hastily. "Mr. Morrow was kind enough to clean out the stagecoach so I could see if I can find..." Find what? Her imagination failed her. She finished lamely, "...it."

"Well, then, we shall see you at dinner." Harmony leaned over and whispered, "I'll try to arrange it so that you don't have to sit next to Aunt Agnes again. Once a day is quite enough."

Inez smiled her gratitude to her sister, kissed the top of William's head, then hurried after Billy. He led her to an area inside the stables that was, Inez happily noted, out of sight of guests strolling the back gardens and the verandas.

The tarp was stretched out, the refuse and debris displayed such that she could see each piece separately. Inez was grateful she wouldn't have to root around through a mish-mashed pile of garbage.

Morrow was standing by a table consisting of a plank supported by two sawhorses, examining what looked like a worn girth strap. He looked up as Billy and Inez approached.

"Afternoon, ma'am. Glad the boy found you. Here's all we found in the coach. Floor's clean as a whistle now. I set Billy to scrubbin' it down with lye and ashes. You couldst probably eat your dinner from it and be satisfied."

A memory of Mr. Pace retching on her skirts and the floor rose before her. Inez quickly suppressed it. "Thank you, Mr. Morrow, Billy." She strolled before the tarp, examining the contents.

A couple of empty whiskey bottles. Moldy bits of bread that looked hard as rocks. A lady's glove. The odd bits of newspaper, waxed papers, empty snuff tins, and apple cores that she had glimpsed before. Then…

"There!" she exclaimed, triumphant, and pointed. "Billy, could you bring me that small cork? It's by the apple cores."

Billy, looked at her, doubtful, then at Morrow, who nodded.

He stepped onto the canvas, picked up the small, elongated, stopper, and handed it to her.

She fished Mrs. Pace's tonic bottle from her pocket, pulled out the replacement cork, and compared it to the one Billy had given her. They looked the same, except that the one from the coach still had wax adhering to the top and sides. She plugged the bottle with it, just to be sure.

It fit.

Chapter Twenty

Up in her room, Inez shed her dusty clothes and set them aside for the hotel maid to freshen. Wearing her satin wrapper, she set the small tonic bottle and its stopper on the polished wood table in the center of the room. She toyed with the coiled tubing that fed the table's gas lamp, thinking back on the death of Mr. Pace, and the various things she'd learned about the Paces' visit and about Manitou in general and the Mountain Springs House in particular since her arrival.

First, there was the fact that Mrs. Pace was here for her health. Inez picked up the tonic bottle, turning it this way and that. It was brown, not as small as the ones Harmony had received that morning for her and William, more of a mid-size. The label identified it as belonging to Kirsten Pace. According to the conversation on the stagecoach, it had held at least a day's worth of tonic. Mr. Pace had taken it all in a single gulp. How many doses did it hold? Four? Five? Could it be that simply taking that much in one swig was enough to kill him? *I shall have to ask Mrs. Pace how often she takes it and how far apart the doses should be. If she is at the concert tonight, perhaps I can talk with her.*

Could he have simply died of some sudden heart ailment? In Leadville, it certainly happened. Young men and old, the rarefied air could send an otherwise healthy man keeling over with nary a peep. It seemed the luck of the draw, sometimes, that did it.

Inez tipped the top of the bottle toward her. The wax on the top of the cork was a bit darker than that on the side, perhaps, she thought, due to dirt. Or bootblack of some kind. She thought back on the valise it had been pulled from. Perhaps some of Ayer's Cherry Pectoral had dripped onto it. She rubbed the top of the cork with her thumb, but the color seemed to be in the wax itself. She set the bottle aside to consider what else she knew.

Assuming for a moment that the fatal dose was for Mrs. Pace, what reason could anyone want to have her sicken and die?

She was against her husband investing in Manitou. Investing in the Mountain Springs House. Would someone take offense at that? And if so, who?

Who was "invested" in the Mountain Springs House's success?

As far as she knew, there were three: owner Franklin Lewis, physician Aurelius Prochazka, and manager Terrance Epperley.

Could there be others?

Inez thought of her own business dealings. There was the backroom deal she'd crafted with Madam Flo. The grubstakes she'd invested with various Leadville prospectors, in hopes of sharing the wealth of a lucky strike. Some of these deals were public, others she chose to play close to the vest. It could be the same at the Mountain Springs House, she decided. There could be public investors and private investors. Men who, behind the scenes, were gambling on the rise of the hotel's fame and fortune. It made sense, given Dr. Prochazka's reputation and the region's claim on health through its mineral waters and various treatments.

Of course, having the hotel's patients die as a result of partaking of its medicinal cures would be very bad for business and for the physician's reputation. So, if Mrs. Pace's tonic was poisoned, could it have been with the aim of casting the hotel and its attendant physician into disgrace? In which case, any competing hotel or physician who harbored murderous tendencies could have bribed someone at the Mountain Springs House.

Inez shook her head, realizing that her Machiavellian thinking was taking her in circles. She wished that she could put out that she was interested in investing in the hotel and generate some interest. But, as Epperley had pointed out, no one in Manitou, where she was not well known—except by ex-pat British wastrels and drunks, apparently—would take her, a woman, seriously.

Ah, if only I were a man!

What she needed, she thought, was a male shill. Someone who would be willing, or who she could persuade, to play the part of a potential investor in Mountain Springs House. Someone wealthy, or at least able to convincingly portray a wealthy nob. Someone people would instinctively trust, someone good at getting people to confide. Someone who was skilled at reading people and their motives. Someone who could charm men and women alike. Someone a tad deceitful. Someone who could bluff with the best, and improvise when necessary. Someone like...

Mark.

Chapter Twenty-one

Damnation!

Inez slammed the small bottle down in frustration, then hastily picked it up again and examined the glass bottom closely, to be sure the force hadn't cracked it. Satisfied the vial was intact, she set it down gently to one side.

Elbow on the table, chin in palm, she tried to come up with other possible confederates. It had to be a man, one she could trust to be "on her side." Casting an inward eye over the ranks of men from Leadville, she plucked first one and then another from the lineup for consideration.

Abe?

Abe Jackson, part owner of the Silver Queen Saloon, along with the Stannerts, was more than a business partner. He and Mark had met during the Civil War and teamed up at war's end with the common aim of "making a fortune" in the war-torn Eastern seaboard. Once Mark and Inez eloped, they had traveled together, eventually settling in Leadville at the beginning of its silver rush. Inez regarded Abe as a friend and a confidante, although they had their moments when they were at odds. But she would trust him with her life. He could be as wily as Mark, given the right circumstances.

But these were not the right circumstances. Much as she would like to obtain Abe's help, she knew it would be impossible, for several reasons. His wife was about to give birth any day. Even more to the point, a colored man—no matter that he was born free and came with a fat bank account—would not be welcome to sit at this particular table.

Jed Elliston?

He was a newspaperman, and hint of a local business scandal could bring him on the run. He had helped her in the past. However, a "local" angle was necessary to gaining Elliston's interest and compliance. As far as Inez could ascertain, the current situation in Manitou had no Leadville ties. Too, Elliston was understaffed at the newspaper and had his hands full just keeping up with Leadville's doings.

Doc?

Doc Cramer had several variables in his favor. He was a physician, so could perhaps worm his way into the closed medical establishment in Manitou. He was familiar with Dr. William Bell and General William Palmer from the War, so that was another plus. He was her family physician and had not only seen William into the world, but had brought all his medical skills to bear on keeping William alive and breathing through the first harrowing winter of his small life. If Doc thought she or William were in danger, he'd come in a heartbeat. But. Doc was, to put it bluntly, a lousy liar, and too fond of good brandy and friendly conversation to be trusted with an underhanded scheme such as the one she was planning. One glass of brandy too many, and he'd invariably say something that would tip their hand.

It was no use. Mentally riffling through the cards she'd been dealt, Inez realized she only had one on which to pin her hopes: Mark.

If it was a poker hand, she would have folded and walked away. But there was far more at stake in this game than mere money.

She sighed. Resigned. Turning to the small bedside stand, she extracted a pencil and stationery embossed with The Mountain Springs House at the top, and began drafting a telegram.

◇◇◇

At dinner, Harmony, true to her word, arranged for Inez to sit apart from Aunt Agnes. Agnes and Inez shared Dr. Zuckerman as a dining companion, who all in all was more interested in conversing with Harmony's husband, Jonathan, across the table than with either of his dining companions. Rebuffed in her attempts to flirt with the physician, Agnes turned her attentions to young Robert Calder on her left, taking occasion to shoot an occasional pointed and disapproving glance at Inez.

Inez cast back over the day, trying to come up with something she might have done that would put Agnes in a tiff. Several events came to mind, but none that her aunt could conceivably have known about. Inez resigned herself, certain that Agnes would eventually reveal what displeased her, and probably sooner rather than later.

Partway through the stultifying dinner—oyster soup, baked pickerel, boiled tongue, roast leg of mutton, banana fritters, stewed tomatoes, chicken salad en mayonnaise, and blackberry pie—Inez became aware of the conversation between the Dr. Zuckerman and Jonathan DuChamps. It was an eerie echo of the "hard sell" she had often overheard between a huckster and a possible investor. Only, whereas in Leadville the talk focused on silver, mines, and assays, here in Manitou it was of consumption, mineral waters, and cures.

"What of the Duket cure? The Salisbury Plan?" Jonathan inquired, leaning intently over the table. "I've heard they both show great promise."

"Oh, cures abound," Zuckerman pronounced. "Duket is nothing but flimflam and humbuggery. 'Relentless greed sets the trap and death is partner in the enterprise.' That was said by some observant fellow or other. I'd not give the Duket so-called cure a second glance. As for Salisbury plans, Dr. Salisbury believes that food is the agent of tremendous power that causes consumption." Zuckerman leaned forward in emphasis. Inez feared for his pampered beard should it stray into the stewed tomatoes.

He continued, "The treatment, in a nutshell, is based on the idea of removing the cause by ridding the blood and tissues of the presence of the yeast by starving it out. He also advocates wearing flannel and daily riding. Salisbury states if the directions are followed faithfully, consumption in all its stages *becomes* a curable disease." He raised a finger. "Note that he does not say he cures, but the disease *becomes* amenable to treatment."

Harmony, sitting across from Inez and listening with anxious eyes, laid a hand on Jonathan's sleeve. "Perhaps," she said sweetly, "this is not conversation for the dinner table."

"Oh, sorry, my dear, of course," said Jonathan hastily.

"Actually," said Inez, "I find the conversation fascinating." She turned to the doctor. "I would be curious to know, since you are obviously a man eminent in the field," she could have sworn his chest beneath the carpet of beard puffed like a pigeon, "just how is one to tell the truth from the lies?"

He smoothed the beard down over his dinner jacket and said, "An excellent question. The simple answer is, 'Find a reputable physician and accept his guidance in the matter.' Aside from that, I would add that nostrums, in particular, can be dangerous. I had heard of one containing a large proportion of kerosene and a smaller proportion of turpentine, and a small amount of aromatic oil. It would make a better furniture polish than a remedy."

"So, you are saying that nostrums, tonics," Inez cast a glance at Nurse Crowson, who was off to one side of the room arranging her array of small bottles, "are useless?"

"Not at all, not at all. Excellent progress is being made with the use of injections of medications, most primarily mercury salts, Lugol's Solution, and carbolic acid. Why, Dr. Prochazka's work is an excellent example of current day thinking. He has combined the healthful mineral waters of the springs here in Manitou with various elements to produce what I believe is a tonic of unparalleled medicinal virtues. Dr. Prochazka is a visionary, a scientist. Consider the success of his prescriptions, his medicines, his regimens, and the work he is doing on phthsis. It is absolutely extraordinary. Look to the numbers, dear lady, look to the cures! I myself have made the study of tuberculosis my life's work. I have examined the results here at the Mountain Springs House and am completely committed to Dr. Prochazka's methods."

After copious amounts of coffee to offset the heavy food and conversation, Inez rose with the rest of the party and said her goodnight to the physician. As she started toward the door, Aunt Agnes caught up with her and said, *sotto voce*, "Inez. I understand you were pawing through stable debris this afternoon. Perhaps this is an activity in which ladies indulge in Leadville, but I assure you, it does not reflect well on you or us here in Manitou. Please be mindful that some of these guests are of the first water. Any idiosyncrasy could find its way into the general milieu, and who knows how far it could travel."

"Aunt Agnes, I believe the event you speak of has been misconstrued. I merely went to the livery to see if something I had dropped in the stagecoach had turned up. That is all."

For all the good her explanation did, Inez might have whistled into the wind. Agnes merely plunged on. "Where were you this afternoon? You all came back from your walk, and you disappeared. I was rounding up players for my *tableaux vivants* for tomorrow evening. I had thought you would be perfect for a particular part I had in mind, but it's too late now. Too bad, for it would have been an excellent opportunity for you to redeem yourself."

They were well out the dining room now. Some of the diners drifted toward the porch, while others moved to the stairs or the music room. As the music room entrance loomed before them, Agnes' grip on Inez's elbow became more vise-like and she inquired, in a louder, honeyed voice, "You *will* be joining us for the concert, will you not, dear niece?"

Inez took hold of Agnes' hand and removed it from her arm. "Of course, dear aunt. I wouldn't miss it for the world. But first, I have business at the front desk. I shall be there presently."

Inez moved to the reception desk, resisting the urge to rub her aching elbow. Mr. Lewis was behind the counter. While he retrieved a room key for a nanny and her fussy charge, Inez stared at the two bucks mounted on the back wall, either side of a wall clock. She counted twelve points on the one to the left; thirteen on the one to the right. The clock ticked. The baby whimpered in the nanny's arms. The taxidermied deer stared back at Inez, glassy-eyed.

She tapped idly on the counter with the folded paper she had labored over before dinner, and considered what she was about to set into motion. Like the mechanism of gears and springs in the wall clock, once the telegram was out of her hands, she would have no choice but to move forward until events wound down to their conclusion, whatever that may be.

The nanny sent on her way, Lewis finally directed his attention to Inez. She asked, "Is it possible to send a telegram tonight to Leadville?"

"Why, of course, madam. We have blanks here. Would you like to fill one out now?"

"Please."

He pulled out a blank form and handed it to her, pushing the pen and ink bottle toward her. She unfolded the paper that held her carefully crafted words and copied them onto the form. After waving the form in the air to dry the ink, she handed it to Lewis.

"I'll see to this personally." Lewis took the paper from her with a small bow.

It could not have played out better if she'd planned it. "Thank you *so* much," she gushed. "I would hate to miss the concert." She then added, as if in afterthought, "Would you please cast an eye over the message and make certain it's readable?"

Lewis stopped in the act of folding the form and said, "Why of course." His gaze lowered to the paper.

She knew all the words there by heart, having chosen them carefully, deliberately. They unrolled in her mind as she watched him scan the message:

> *Dearest Husband,*
>   *Make haste to the Mountain Springs House soonest. The weather is perfect, the investment opportunities unparalleled. I eagerly await your arrival.*
>
>   *Fondest regards, Your Loving Wife*

She was pleased to see his eyebrows rise fractionally and a shadow of a smile tug at one corner of his mouth. "All perfectly legible. You have lovely penmanship, Mrs. Stannert." He folded the form, tucked it into his coat jacket and turned to an idle doorman, motioning him to stand behind the counter. "I shall take this to the Manitou House myself, where they have a telegraph office, and have it sent *immédiatement.*" He cleared his throat. "Forgive me if I am being forward, but is Mr. Stannert looking for business opportunities in Manitou?"

She beamed, having no need to invent her delight with his question. "Indeed he is, Mr. Lewis. Mr. Stannert has been keen on this region for a while now. He asked me to let him know if I thought it worth his while to explore the possibilities here." She batted her eyes. "I'm honored that he would trust me with such a weighty task. I suppose I flatter myself that he values my feminine opinion in such things."

She detected a new spark of interest in Lewis' eyes. Encouraged, she added, "I immediately saw what an absolutely first-class establishment you have here in the Mountain Springs House. I have also been hearing wonderful things about Dr. Prochazka and his clinic. I would not be fulfilling my duty as a good helpmeet if I did not encourage him to come as soon as possible."

Lewis was nodding solemnly, head moving up and down in rhythm to the tick-tick-tick of the small pendulum in the wall clock behind him. "You are a most astute woman, Mrs. Stannert. Thank you so much for your kind words. We shall be very happy to show Mr. Stannert around and answer any and all questions he may have. I, too, believe the Mountain Springs House has a bright, bright future."

Inez beamed some more and fluttered her fan to relieve the warmth rising to her cheeks. *Mr. Lewis has taken the bait—hook, line, and sinker. Mark will be able to reel him in without trouble, and we shall see if he has any secrets worth knowing.*

She just hoped that Mark would recognize and remember their old code, from years past. Words ending with "–est" indicated a situation existed that had the opportunity for financial gain, if they played their cards right. Repeated three times meant that the opportunity required moving in the highest circles of society—In essence, "Bring your best clothes and manners." Remarks about the weather provided the time frame and urgency. "Perfect weather" indicated that the opportunity existed *now*, and there was no time to waste. She just hoped that he did not take "dearest husband," "fondest regards" and "loving wife" at face value. *If he does, I'll straighten him out once he arrives.*

Chapter Twenty-two

The music had already begun. Indeed, while standing at the reception desk, Inez had been partly aware of an enthusiastic rendition of the overture to Herold's *Zampa* swelling from the music room. After concluding her business with Lewis, she hurried into the room. She surveyed the backs of the audience for Mrs. Pace. The young widow sat at the far end of the last row, accompanied by an open chair. Behind her, Mrs. Crowson stood attentively, hands folded on top of an invalid chair holding a young woman, wraithlike in her thinness and wrapped in a heavy shawl. Inez wondered briefly at the absence of Mr. Travers. Inez spotted Susan Carothers, dressed in a rose-colored summer gown she'd not seen before, sitting next to Robert Calder in the front row. Inez suppressed a smile as their heads leaned together over a shared program.

She became aware that Aunt Agnes on the other side of the room was leaning forward in her seat, trying to catch Inez's attention. Turning away from her aunt, Inez picked up a concert program from the podium next to the door and sidled along the back wall toward Mrs. Pace and Nurse Crowson. The trio of musicians, bent over cello, violin and piano, entered the coda. Inez sidled faster. She edged into the chair by the widow just at the final triumphant notes. Applause followed, muted by evening gloves and sounding like bird wings in flight. The musicians shifted and exchanged quick words in hushed undertones. The audience leaned forward as one, as if in anticipation.

The small noises of a summer's evening in the country stole in through the French doors opened to the front porch: crickets, frogs, the whisper of a breeze through foliage. Inside, women's fans made a soft shushing as their owners took advantage of the sudden stir of fresh air, redolent with the smell of roses.

Inez nodded at Mrs. Pace, who turned a pale face toward her, black ribbon wound through her smooth blonde French twist. Inez glanced down at the program. The evening's musical offerings included Goldmark's "Serenade" from "Rustic Wedding Symphony," Wagner's "Tannhauser March," and an unfamiliar piece composed by the violinist. Standard musical fare for such a venue, she thought, then brightened at the finale: Schubert's "Serenade," one of her favorites.

She flicked open her fan and allowed it to waft desultorily to the sliding melody of Goldmark while she pondered what she was going to say to Mrs. Pace. She decided that it was best, in the public venue, to simply keep her company and make small talk.

At a break between numbers, Inez leaned toward the widow and asked, "Are you a musician, Mrs. Pace?"

"Not really, Mrs. Stannert." She plucked at her skirt, the color of sorrow, then said, "I know that some would consider it improper for me to be here. Particularly so soon after."

There was no need for her to say after what.

She continued. "But my rooms are so confining, and I find music soothing. At this time, so far from home, I need comfort wherever I can find it."

Inez nodded sympathetically. The musicians began again, and one number flowed into the next. It wasn't until just before the finale that there was another appreciable pause.

As the audience shifted, throats cleared, and the pianist pulled out sheet music, there was sudden movement from the front row. Robert Calder approached the musicians, spoke to the pianist, who turned and held a whispered conversation with his compatriots. They all bowed briefly toward Calder, who settled himself to one side of the piano, hands clasped in a military style behind him. The musicians took their positions.

Mrs. Pace raised her black fan and murmured behind it to Inez. "This happened at the last concert."

With the first notes, Calder belted out in a strong and energetic tenor, "*Leise flehen meine Lieder, Durch die Nacht zu dir.*"

Inwardly, Inez winced. Technically, the vocal performance was flawless, but Calder's voice was so...enormous. Enthusiasm aside, it carried no subtle emotions, no overtones, simply hit the notes directly and decisively as a gandy dancer would drive a railroad spike with a maul. She did notice, however, that his gaze, when not directed over the audience's heads, returned again and again to Susan.

At the end of the performance, Inez joined the polite applause. Behind her, she heard a dismissive masculine snort. She twisted around to find Dr. Prochazka, slouched against the wall with a pained expression. His evening jacket was rumpled and dusty, as if he had picked it up off the floor and hurriedly donned it minutes ago. Amid the rustling of the audience and rising voices, Inez asked, "Dr. Prochazka, you did not enjoy the performance? Are you perchance a music critic as well as a physician?"

She meant it as a barely concealed jibe. A little parry and thrust in response to the morning's meeting, which still stung her memory.

But instead, he seemed to take her words at face value. He flicked a bit of lint from the lapel of his jacket and said, "I know enough to know that one should not perform a piece when one does not know what one sings. Or plays."

Despite her own misgivings, Inez found herself coming to Calder's defense. "I thought he sang proficiently. And certainly with a great deal of bravura."

The tall physician looked down his nose at her. His expression was civil, as befit the venue, but Inez detected disdain trying hard to shove the polite façade aside. "Mrs....Stannert. Yes? I have your name correct?"

She nodded.

He continued, "*Sprechen sie Deutsch*, German?"

"Do I speak German? No." Inez's language proficiencies extended to the French and Latin forced into her by a long-ago tutor, a smattering of Louisiana Creole from Abe, and a bit of Spanish from wanderings through Texas with Mark and Abe.

"Neither does Herr Calder. Of that I am certain," said Prochazka. "In Schubert's *Ständchen*, the singer exhorts, pleads with his lover to make him happy. It is hope in the face of hopelessness. Mr. Calder knows none of this. He sings as if calling to his sheep, lost on the far side of a hill."

Inez couldn't, in honesty, argue. It was a perfect description of Calder's rendition.

Prochazka continued. "As for the musicians, they were, perhaps, carried away with Mr. Calder's eagerness. But there are so many subtleties to the *Ständchen* they did not even try to catch, such as the rise and fall of the opening line through the tonic minor chord. The yearning leaps of the central phrase to the minor sixth of the dominant. The supple turns of the closing line around the tonic."

Inez was impressed with his sudden virtuosity. "You play the piano, then?"

"*Nein.*"

"There you are. And keeping company with the very man I was looking for." Agnes' voice rang in Inez's ear. "You are coming to the ladies' parlor, are you not, dear niece? It is a chance to discuss the evening's performance away from the gentlemen, who, if truth be told, are usually somnolent by the time it is all done, and dying for their cigars and brandy."

She spoke to Inez but stared at Dr. Prochazka, as if to trap him in place with her gaze. "I shall be there shortly myself and expect to see you. But first, I must have a few words with the good doctor about tomorrow night's festivities."

Prochazka frowned. "What is this about?"

"I need you for a very important, shall I say, pivotal part in my *tableaux vivants* tomorrow." Aunt Agnes waved a hand dismissively. "Nothing elaborate, not like my arrangements in New York. But, when out in the wilds, one must make do with what one has." She laid a hand upon his arm, drawing him away from Inez. "As the physician of this resort, it is important that you have a primary role in our little event."

Inez turned to comment on Aunt Agnes' powerful powers of persuasion to Mrs. Pace, but the young widow had slipped away, leaving only a faint, lingering scent of lavender behind.

Inez caught up with Susan in the reception area of the hotel. The area was clogged with guests. Some retreated up the grand staircase to their rooms, many women moved down the corridor toward the ladies' parlor, while the men retreated toward the gentlemen's smoking room or to the outside porch. Through the open front doors, the night appeared black as pitch. Once again, Inez was struck by the difference between Leadville, where gas lights illuminated the business district and round-the-clock entertainments on State Street and Harrison Avenue lent their own flickering lights to the crowded boardwalks. Here in Manitou, one could step down the porch stairs, walk a few steps, and be swallowed into nothingness.

Inez suppressed a shudder and turned to Susan, whose arm was linked through Robert Calder's. Inez noted a particularly rosy glow to Susan's cheeks and an unusually bright sparkle in her eye. Susan, practical, level-headed Susan, could she be smitten and so quickly?

"Wasn't that a lovely concert, Inez?" Susan gushed. "Doesn't Robert...Mr. Calder...have a wonderful voice? He told me he offers to sing at every concert and everyone looks forward to it."

She gazed up at Calder as she said this. His eyes fixed upon her with admiration clearly stamped across his face. Inez realized that the attraction was, indeed, mutual. An unexpected wave of protectiveness rose in Inez, making her almost want to step between them and halt things lest her friend be hurt.

Susan is an adult, not a child. Granted, she is not savvy in the ways of the world...but still...how is one to learn about love and infatuation if one does not experience it in all its ups and downs? What matters if she has a bit of a summer romance here, in Manitou,

*where few know her and, even if they disapprove, what of it? Besides,
Calder is only here for a while, looking into the death of his brother.*

Susan turned back to Inez. "Mr. Calder is going to meet me
and Mrs. Galbreaith at the Garden of the Gods tomorrow. Mrs.
Galbreaith and I are going to take some stereoscopic images; the
landscape is perfect for the technique, and she knows the best
places and the best times of day. Mr. Calder had already planned
to be in the Garden painting, fancy that!"

"Tomorrow appears to be a popular day in the Garden," said
Inez. "My sister has arranged for a family outing there as well,
so we shall look for you."

"It is," Calder said, "a very large area. The chances of 'running
into each other' are not high. However, we shall be taking a noon
meal at the Gateway, if you would care to join us."

"I shall let her know," said Inez, making mental note of the
'us' designation. She turned to Susan. "How are accommodations
at Mrs. Galbreaith's?"

"Very nice. Her boarding house is just across the valley and
up toward the Ute Iron spring. Mr. Calder is going to walk me
back this evening." Her cheeks flamed brighter.

Inez said her farewell to the couple, then turned to gaze at
the broad staircase, with Hermes waiting at the top. She was
contemplating sneaking upstairs, pleading tiredness in the
morning for her nonappearance in the women's parlor, when
Aunt Agnes emerged from the music room, looking like the cat
that caught the mouse.

"I'm so glad you waited for me, dear niece. Now that I am
through with Dr. Prochazka, we can walk into the drawing room
together." She took Inez's arm with an iron grip, and leaned on
her with a sigh. "I am not as spry as I used to be. More's the
pity. The greater pity is that I must do these *tableaux vivants*
with so few people."

"I don't suppose you had to put yourself through the bother if
you didn't want to," said Inez. "There is plenty of entertainment.
Our hosts seem intent on keeping everyone busy."

Agnes waved this away with an irritated flip of her fan. "Everyone is always galumphing about, up this canyon or that. Going off to see the waterfalls or the rocks. Rocks, I ask you, what is so special about *rocks?* Give me the British Museum, the Metropolitan, or the Parthenon in Greece. How strange that with all there is to see elsewhere in the world so many people from the Eastern seaboard and abroad would be here. Yet they all disappear during the day, leaving me limited resources to draw on for my visions. But an artist must persevere through all the travails and tribulations. Wait until tomorrow night, when you see what I have managed to accomplish."

They turned and entered the women's parlor, and Inez almost beat a hasty retreat, hit with claustrophobic panic.

It had been a long time since she'd been closeted with so many ladies in so small a room. In the music room, she hadn't registered the number of women, dotted as they were amongst the gentlemen. But here, they filled the space with their rich, rustling fabrics, the high registers of their voices, the whisk of fans and the slight, musky feminine smell.

Agnes drummed her fingers on Inez's arm. "See the woman with red hair standing by the fire screen, in the lime and violet poplin? That is Mrs. Banscombe. Absolutely disfigured with summer freckles, poor dear, that's what comes of being out in this wretched sun. Honey mixed with lukewarm water works wonders to fade them."

Inez looked with surprise at Aunt Agnes' blemish-free face. Agnes raised one well-shaped eyebrow. "You don't remember, silly girl? You were all a-freckle in the summers. We could never get you to wear a bonnet out of doors. I tried every concoction under the sun to repair your complexion, without much success. Perhaps that's why you are so dark now." Her gaze swept past Inez. "Ah! There is your sister. We should urge her to retire so she doesn't overdo."

Agnes steamed ahead like an ocean liner toward Harmony, bringing Inez with her.

Harmony looked up. The blush Inez had noted in her face early that day had faded. Her thin hands were clasped in her lap.

"My dear, I've brought your sister to you," said Agnes to Harmony, as if she had caught Inez in the act of skulking away. "I do believe you may have had a surfeit of the outdoors today." Agnes cast a suspicious eye over her. "You look exhausted."

"I am fine, Aunt Agnes. I'm just resting a bit before heading upstairs." Harmony looked past them. "Nurse Crowson's arrived with the evening's draughts and her famous mint tea. I suppose Mr. Epperley will be along shortly with the mineral water. We shall be able to drink to each other's health before retiring."

Inez turned to see Nurse Crowson at the parlor entrance with her basket in hand. Inez fancied she could almost hear the light tinkling of glass bottles, knocking gently against each other. A dining room waiter followed the nurse, rolling a tea cart, its little brass wheels squeaking. The cart was laden with tea cups, tea caddy, and several tea pots. Inez's throat began to close as the scent of mint assaulted her. Epperley brought up the rear bearing a large tray of cut crystal glasses holding the odious springs water.

Inez also spied Mrs. Pace, sitting in a chair almost behind the door. She excused herself and made her way through the mash of feminine forms to Mrs. Pace, just as Nurse Crowson handed her a small tonic bottle and moved away.

"How many doses does your bottle hold?" Inez asked without preamble.

Mrs. Pace looked up in surprise. Her hand opened.

Inez saw that the container was much smaller than the one she had found in the stagecoach.

"This is one night's worth. Not," Mrs. Pace added in an undertone, "that I will take it. I will empty it out the window as soon as I return to my room."

"I was more interested in the one your husband drank from in the stagecoach. It was larger, was it not?"

"It held a day and night's worth." Her voice faltered. "I should have taken the cursed bottle away from him. Knocked it out of his hand…"

"No thank you. You may return it to the dispensary." Harmony's words rose above the general babble of women's voices.

The chatter in the room died to a few surprised whispers. Everyone turned to look at Harmony.

Nurse Crowson stood by Inez's sister, the nearby light from the table lamp glinting off the dark brown glass of a small tonic bottle she held by the neck. Harmony sat, ramrod straight, hands folded in her lap, making no attempt to take the bottle.

"You can tell Dr. Prochazka that fresh air and exercise are the only tonics I need." Inez was shocked by Harmony's adamant tone, more reminiscent of Aunt Agnes or her father than her little sister.

"I will not be needing this *restorative.*" The way she said it made it sound as if she were referring to a pile of fresh horse dung.

Aunt Agnes tapped Harmony on the arm with her closed fan and hissed, loud enough for all to hear, "Please, Harmony, don't make a scene."

Nurse Crowson's mild-mannered expression didn't change. The only signs that she had heard was a slight tremor in her hand, causing the light to shiver on the glass, and a vertical frown line marring her smooth forehead. She finally said soothingly, "Mrs. DuChamps, it is encouraging that you feel so invigorated. But, if I may speak from my position as one allied with the medical profession, how could you possibly know what it is that led to your recovery? I recall when you first came here, you could hardly walk the length of the veranda without needing to sit and rest. It's wonderful to see how your stay at the Mountain Springs House has brought your strength back. But speaking as one who has seen this tale played out a hundred-fold here at this house, how can *you,*" the word curdled with a barely discernible twist of scorn, "be the authority on what has made your recovery so complete? Have you any idea how fortunate we are at the Mountain Springs House to have Dr. Prochazka with us? The doctor, with his years of experience abroad, his skills, and his training, understands and knows the manifestations, the treatments, and the cures, for respiratory and pulmonary ailments. He knows best, absolutely. How sad it would be for you and your family, if by going against Dr. Prochazka's prescriptions, you were to relapse into your former state or…" she held the bottle closer to Harmony, nearly under her nose, "Worse."

Harmony lifted a hand.

Inez held her breath, willing her sister to not argue, to take the bottle and, like Mrs. Pace, dump it later in solitude.

Harmony pushed the tonic away. "No, thank you," she repeated.

The scene froze, like one of Aunt Agnes' beloved *tableaux*. Agnes sat next to Harmony, looking at her niece as if she had grown fangs and sprouted fur. The women nearby stared, fans opened flat against the bosoms of their gowns as if to ward off any evil that might creep within and weaken their lungs or beating hearts.

Movements by the parlor door drew Inez's gaze. Epperley must have withdrawn at the first sign of an altercation—Inez spotted the tray with mineral waters on an occasional table in the hall—and returned with Lewis. The two men stood at the threshold, shoulder to shoulder or rather shoulder to ear, for Epperley was by far the taller of the two. Epperley leaned against the doorjamb, arms crossed, a slightly bored expression as if he were watching a not particularly well performed amateur play. But Inez noticed that his crossed arms shielded hands knotted into angry fists. Lewis looked pale, as pale as a victim of the wasting disease. His fingers fluttered on the front of his waistcoat, helpless.

With a chill, Inez realized that, of all the people who had a stake in the Mountain Springs House's reputation and its miracle medical wonders, most of them were in the room and had heard Harmony's every defiant word.

Chapter Twenty-three

Inez unstuck herself from the wall and tried to maneuver through the crowded room, anxious to reach her sister's side and stop her from saying anything further.

But Lewis moved faster. Vibrating with managerial concern, he interposed himself between Harmony and Nurse Crowson. "Of course, Mrs. DuChamps. Of course. If you do not wish to take whatever draught Dr. Prochazka has prepared for you, I'm certain that no harm will occur from missing a dose."

Squeezing past a cluster of women barring her trajectory to the loveseat where Harmony sat, Inez thought it uncanny—not to add annoying—that Lewis' calm attitude and slightly patronizing tone so exactly matched Nurse Crowson's. It was like hearing the same note played again, only an octave lower.

Lewis continued, "I am pleased that you had such a splendid, invigorating day today. Up Williams' Canyon, wasn't it?"

Inez finally reached the loveseat. She fluttered her fan to draw Lewis' attention and said, "Mrs. DuChamp and I had the most marvelous time. Goodness gracious, I'm so impressed with her endurance. Why, I have lived in Colorado for years, and she outpaced me the entire distance!"

The deflection worked. Lewis' gaze switched to Inez. She could swear he was viewing her with suspicion, as if the rapidly fluttering fan didn't stop him from seeing straight through her machinations. He said with a surprising authority, "When vitality returns, it's easy to take on too much too soon, which can be dangerous to a delicate constitution." He broke off and glanced around the room, as if realizing there were many avid ears listening to what he said.

Looking around as well, Inez noticed that Crowson had stepped away, and the scorned restorative had vanished back into the basket. She continued her rounds, unobtrusively handing out other doses to various women.

Whatever he saw in the room seemed to bring Lewis back to his role as hotelier. "It's easy," he began again, retreating to a smooth, obsequious tone, "to let the beauty of the mountains and the landscape in Manitou carry us away, make us forget our limitations. Why, I myself have had the humbling experience of attempting Pike's Peak, only to be done in by the exertion and forced to spend the night on its rocky slopes. I was woefully ill-prepared for that particular adventure." He laughed a little, shaking his head at his own folly.

A woman in a sky-blue gown that, to Inez's eye, would be better placed in a New York drawing room than in a Western hopeful with scrub oak for forests, said coyly, "That is why you have the little burros to do the walking for us, is it not, Mr. Lewis?"

Some of the other women tittered behind their fans, and the tension in the room eased.

Lewis smiled and bowed slightly. "Exactly, Mrs. Wentworth. That way we can allow you lovely ladies to enjoy your excursions in the mountains with no danger of being overcome by the experience or the altitude."

Inez sensed the unspoken words hovering in the air: overcome like the impetuous Mrs. DuChamps, who took on more than she should have.

Harmony must have sensed it as well, for she stiffened as if preparing a retort. Inez placed a warning hand on her sister's shoulder, squeezing slightly. She willed Harmony not to say anything more, surrounded as they were by people with a penchant for gossip and conjecture.

Harmony twisted around, anger tight across her wan features. "We should go up now, don't you think, dear sister?" Inez said to Harmony, adding to Lewis, "We have another lovely excursion planned tomorrow. Off to the Garden of the Gods, for a bit of a picnic. I've never seen it and am looking forward to the trip."

Lewis nodded approvingly. "You'll find it most agreeable I'm sure, Mrs. Stannert. A pleasant drive and a pleasant destination. "

A woman on the nearby settee, whose fan was slowly wafting back and forth, almost as if it were too heavy to hold, volunteered, "The Garden of the Gods is aptly named, and Williams' Canyon is quite scenic. Why, I walked all the way up to The Narrows yesterday. I credit the good doctor's prescriptive directions." She smiled up at Nurse Crowson.

Nurse Crowson nodded approvingly, as if to acknowledge a student who had completed her recitation satisfactorily.

"Keep to the plan he set forth for you, and you shall make it all the way to the Cave of the Winds before you leave," said Nurse Crowson. She fished through the basket and handed the woman a small brown bottle.

The woman brightened. "Thank you, Mrs. Crowson. I'm looking forward to that day." She took the bottle and tucked it away into the small satin purse dangling from her wrist.

The sound level in the room returned to normal. Aunt Agnes stood. "Well, I think we have all had enough excitement for one night."

Despite her annoyance with Agnes' presumption, Inez found that she had to agree. The room was stuffy, the crowding nearly impossible, and, it would be best to get Harmony out of the room and away from measured gazes. Let her words be forgotten by whatever flow of conversation continued.

Inez's gaze wandered over to Mrs. Pace's chair. A different woman, dressed in pink satin, sat there now. She would have to find another time to talk with the widow.

Harmony rose, and did not object when Inez took one of her arms and Aunt Agnes the other. But Inez could tell from her compressed lips that she was not happy. Even so, Inez could feel her lean on their support as they headed toward the door.

No sooner had they reached the stairs to the upper floor than Jonathan DuChamps hurried from the direction of the men's smoking room, wrapped in an anxious expression and the scent of cigar smoke. Epperley followed, at a more leisurely pace.

So, the wife acts out and the husband is called?

"Harmony!" He said her name with intensity, as if he were afraid that if he didn't stay tightly controlled, he might shout it out. "Mr. Epperley told me that you are not feeling well."

"You were misinformed," Harmony said with dignity, then Inez felt her suddenly sag, her full weight dragging down.

Jonathan leapt forward to add support to his fainting wife. Inez gasped once, holding her up. Jonathan's gaze met hers, and for the first time, Inez realized that he was frightened. Frightened for her sister.

Harmony recovered almost immediately. "It's nothing, Jonathan. I must have stood up too quickly. Truly, it was a good day, the best in a long time. I had plenty of fresh air, ate well, enjoyed the music and the company. Don't spoil it by fussing at me."

"Well," said Aunt Agnes. "*He* may not fuss at you, but *I* shall. I shall take you straight up and no argument. If you won't take your tonic, then I insist you have a restorative brandy."

Jonathan said, "The doctor has said that alcoholic stimulants have no therapeutic value whatsoever, that they do nothing to sustain the vital forces. That, indeed they can be dangerous to recovery."

Agnes rounded on him. "*Mr.* DuChamps. I am not advocating your wife guzzle it by the pints. She has had a faint, and a small glass of brandy will restore her flagging energies. Please arrange for the brandy and some hot compresses."

Jonathan took a step back, obviously not about to cross Agnes, who now held Harmony up with one protective arm about her waist.

Inez, who felt as if she could use a little restorative brandy herself, didn't blame Jonathan one whit for retreating. She had seen Aunt Agnes take on bankers, magnates, railroad barons, and titans of industry, including: Inez and Harmony's father. None stood against her. Or if they tried, they did not do so for long.

Her protective ferocity seemed to breathe some life back into Harmony, who said, "Aunt, I can walk. You do not need to drag me up the stairs."

Inez stepped forward, intending to help them, but Agnes snapped, "Good night, Inez." It was as if going up Williams' Canyon and Harmony's subsequent collapse were all Inez's fault.

Stung, Inez fell back to stand by Jonathan, watching as Agnes clucked and fussed over Harmony all the way up the stairs, across the landing, and out of sight down the hallway.

Jonathan removed his glasses with a sigh, pulled a handkerchief from his breast pocket, and polished them.

"What is ailing Harmony?" Inez asked.

"Ailing is a little strongly said, Mrs. Stannert." He put his glasses back on, along with some of his composure. "Most likely Mrs. Underwood, your aunt, is right. Mrs. DuChamps is probably just overtired, and a stimulant, a little brandy, might invigorate her, if she will take it. Although so late in the evening, I believe I would prefer she were given a sedative to help her sleep." He glanced around. Epperley, who was leaning on the nearby reception desk, straightened. "I shall happily prepare a brandy for the lady. A hot toddy, perhaps? I'll arrange for one of the maids to prepare the compresses."

Just as Epperley disappeared down the hall, Lewis hurried up. He held out a small brown tonic bottle and said, "Perhaps you might persuade Mrs. DuChamps to take this."

Inez wanted to snatch the bottle from him and dash it to the floor.

Jonathan took it and tucked it into his pocket.

Lewis continued, "I would even suggest tipping the dose into the brandy. I assure you, she'll probably not even taste it."

Outraged, Inez burst out, "She was very clear in the parlor room that she didn't want it."

Lewis closed his eyes for a moment, pained, then opened them and addressed Jonathan. "Who is to decide what is best for Mrs. DuChamps? True, she refused her evening dose. Certainly humoring the request seemed trivial at the time, but that was before her collapse. I think..." he stopped, then qualified with, "I am no physician, of course, but I think it would be wise to follow Dr. Prochazka's prescriptions for Mrs. DuChamps, given the circumstances. But, you are her husband, so of course, the decision is yours."

What of her *decision?*

Inez didn't have to ask. She knew, to her own detriment, the way the game was played.

Men decided, and women deferred.

Jonathan nodded without comment, then glanced at Inez. "We will see you at breakfast, I assume? Good evening, Mrs. Stannert, until the morrow." He turned and climbed the stairs to the second floor.

Inez tried to regain her composure. This was nothing new, she told herself. The world had always been thus. It was simply that, over the past year, she had become accustomed to reigning in her own realm, the Silver Queen, in Mark's absence. With his return and her submersion into the resort world of Manitou, she was receiving reminder after painful reminder that life outside her little kingdom ran by a very different set of rules, with other people in charge.

But if I cannot best them in direct combat, I shall use subterfuge. I mustn't show how much this galls me. I must appear to give way, for now. And I must find a time to meet with Kirsten Pace tomorrow.

She heaved a theatrical sigh, for Lewis' benefit. "Apologies for my outburst. It is just so upsetting to see my sister so frail. I will concede that my overprotective feelings got the better of me."

"Quite naturally so, Mrs. Stannert," the hotelier assured her. "No offense taken."

"Have you paper and pen?" she asked. "I must write a note to one of the guests."

"But of course."

They went to the reception desk, and Mr. Lewis handed her a creamy sheet with the The Mountain Springs House printed along the top, and a pen and ink bottle. Inez crafted a short note:

I must speak with you at some time convenient to you. May I pay you a call in your room tomorrow? You may leave me a note with whatever time is best for you. Signing it with her name and room number, Inez fanned the paper to dry the ink, and folded it twice. "Could you tell me which room Mrs. Pace is staying in?"

"Oh, we would be happy to hold the note and deliver it to her tomorrow," said Lewis.

"No trouble," Inez hastened. Even in an envelope, the note, she feared, would not escape from determined prying eyes. "It's a note of…a sensitive female nature." Let him imagine what he may. "I shall simply slide it under her door so as not to disturb her at this hour."

Lewis looked doubtful, then said, "Of course. If you prefer."

He hefted the registration book, and turned back a page. "Mrs. Pace is in room 211."

Just down the hall from Harmony and William. "Thank you, Mr. Lewis."

Once upstairs, Inez looked both ways. The hallway was quiet, deserted. Down the long arm of the hall, just before the the women's staircase to dining room, a single gas lamp guttered in a sconce. She hastened in that direction, past Aunt Agnes' lair, Harmony and Jonathan's rooms, William and Lily's dark door, and two more rooms, finally halting before Room 211. Inez paused, put her ear to the door, thinking that if she heard anyone stirring, she'd venture to knock.

Nothing.

Feeling somewhat foolish and oddly vulnerable in the light of the hissing lamp, Inez knelt and slid the folded paper under the door. Straightening up, she looked around. No shadows or shapes indicated that someone was watching. Then, somewhere off in the dark, she heard a soft click.

A door shutting?

It was impossible to know.

Moving out of the pool of light, Inez hurried back to her own room, unlocked the door, hastened inside, and locked it behind her with a sigh.

She turned and looked at the window. She'd neglected to draw the sash before leaving for dinner, and the night air blew in softly through the half-drawn up window. The blind tick-ticked as it swung against the glass. She moved to the window, to pull the sash down and draw the shade. Instead, she leaned upon the sill and allowed her eyes to adjust.

What had been a blank, unremitting blackness outside began to resolve—a night sky pricked with icy pinpoints. The gravel driveway in front of the hotel, joining with the dusty road called Manitou Avenue, and the silhouetted shapes of the rustic pavilions by the mineral springs. The dim path winding from the hotel cut across the road to a small bridge that led to the springs, and beyond.

She closed her eyes, breathing in the sweet scent of night-blooming roses and under that, sharp mint and the gunmetal scent of water over stones. *I hope these events that seem so impenetrable now will also become clear tomorrow.*

Chapter Twenty-four

Leadville

The shots on State Street, ringing through the early morning air, didn't wake her. Nor did the drunken shouts of a fancy man and his I'm-not-going-to-take-it-anymore whore, having it out at last, in the rutted hard-packed dirt of Stillborn Alley.

The whistle of the night wind, bitter to a fault, screamed down from Mosquito Range and prowled through the red-light district. The merciless breeze snapped up refuse and tumbled it through the streets, and embraced the helpless men, women, and dogs, caught outdoors, all shivering to their bones. Through it all—shots, shouts, sighs of air—Inez slept soundly.

It was the slight rattle of the doorknob, the hitch of locked latch, that brought her fully awake.

The same sounds in the same order had disturbed her sleep each of the previous few nights, always around four in the morning.

Just as she had done for every one of those nights, she reached over to the secondhand nightstand. Her hand curled around the comforting grip of her husband's Navy Colt revolver, his prized possession from his days in the Civil War. She sat up in bed and steadied the gun with her other hand, using a two-handed grip that guaranteed accuracy. Or at least, accuracy enough to get the job done.

Eyes no longer shrouded by sleep or dreams, Inez narrowed her gaze on the doorknob. In the pre-dawn light, leaking in through a windowpane bordered by heavy velvet and filmed with lace, the crystal facets of the knob winked at her with a subdued gleam. The knob turned one way, then the other, going only to the limit of its lock before forced to a halt.

Inez's world shrank to the knob and to the familiar heft of the gun in her hand. The barrel pointed unwaveringly at a spot about one foot to the right of the keyhole. She wondered, just as she'd wondered the previous times, if tonight would be the night she'd have to pull the trigger.

She didn't speak.

Words were no longer necessary.

Inez cocked the gun. The metallic click was loud, louder in that small universe than the escalating argument of whore and pimp down the street. Louder than the steady thump, thump, thump of stamp mills echoing up California Gulch, deep into the heart of Leadville's city limits, and up into the mining district. Louder than her own breathing or her own pulse thudding in her ears.

Loud enough to be heard on the other side of the door.

The knob stopped its tentative rotation.

Inez knew that, just as her own exhalations and heart's blood took up all the space in the room and in her head, so it probably was for the man on the other side of the door: her husband, Mark.

The stillness stretched on for perhaps half a minute. Neither stirred on either side of the door—entrance and exit, barrier and breach. Finally, finally, she heard the squeak of footsteps as he turned and walked away. Inez counted the footsteps as they descended the stairs to the ground floor of the saloon, then lost them as they faded across the wide expanse of the silent, closed saloon. She heard the faint sound of the heavy Harrison Avenue door scrape open and shut. Inez would have sworn she could even hear the key turn in the lock, so attuned was she to this nighttime ritual of husband and wife.

Even though she was tired, exhausted with a weariness that was only partly due to having closed the saloon less than a handful of hours previous, she completed the ritual, rising and peering through the break in the curtain. The unmistakable form of her husband on the boardwalk below. He would have been instantly recognizable to her, even if he walked among a hundred other similarly clad gentlemen through Leadville's business district. With a slight limp, he crossed the wide Harrison Avenue boulevard—wide enough to turn a team of twenty mules hauling a full load of silver carbonate of lead ore. She watched until he entered the Clairmont Hotel, before breaking the silence in her room.

"Bastard!"

She no longer flung that epithet or any others at him through the closed door. Saying anything at all just seemed to open the door to escalated screaming on her part and shouting or endearments, or entreaties, or explanations on his part. All of which, she had finally come to realize, only led to a hobbling fatigue, an inability to arise at the appointed time, burning eyes, aching head, and a churning stomach that refused the breakfast meals prepared by the saloon's cook, Bridgette. The refusal of meals increased Bridgette's hovering, concern, and offers of advice—none of which Inez had the patience to bear.

For the first three nights, that had been the pattern. Inez, locked in behind her barricaded door. Mark, locked out on the other side. Inez yelling, Mark placating.

"You were gone for over a year!" she'd shout. "Not a word, a note, nothing! How dare you come back now!"

Over and over, in murmuring counterpoint to her staccato accusations, he said, "Darlin', I was bushwhacked, hauled out of the back alley, not even conscious, thrown in the back of a wagon and hauled out of town like a load of dirty laundry. I'd never leave you on my own. You and William are my world. The only thing that kept me going all this time was the hope I'd see you both again. It took months for me to even come to my senses. By the time I finally realized I was far away, in a different town, almost a prisoner."

"If you had cared, *really* cared, you would have found a way to get word to me. I waited, and waited, until there was nothing left but despair. I was certain you'd died."

"I wrote letters," the disembodied voice on the other side of the door insisted. "You never answered. I thought you'd turned your back on me. Wouldn't've been the first time. I thought you'd gone back East, to your family."

"Oh, you always have a story ready, don't you," she sneered.

"I was ready to head to New York," he insisted, "but then I saw the divorce notice in the *Rocky Mountain News*. You were still here, in Leadville, wanting a divorce, saying I'd deserted you. I hadn't deserted you, I'd written, but you didn't write back. Why didn't you try to find me?"

"How was I supposed to do that when I had no idea where you were?"

The words went on and on until dawn, back and forth through the wooden barrier. On the third night, Inez realized that it wasn't going to end until Mark wore her down and finally got his way and she opened the door. That third night, she'd cocked and pointed the revolver at the door, saying in a tone both deliberate and cold:

"Mr. Stannert. If you do not go away from this door tonight, this minute, I shall shoot. You always said I was no good with a knife, but with guns and words, I excelled. Do you remember? Since words do not seem to reach you, I shall shoot if I must. So listen, and listen well. Do not talk to me again, unless it is daylight, during business hours and about business and business only. Do not expect that you can waltz back into my life, just as you please, and take your place by my side. At first, I thought you were dead. And then, I thought you had deserted me."

"But Inez, our son—"

"I have told you, I sent William back East to live with my sister. He is there now. Here in Leadville, I have rebuilt a life for myself after all the heartache and hell I went through after you left. There is nothing between us any more except the business. As you told me after you won the saloon in that card game, you, I and Abe own the saloon together: A third and a third and a third."

"Darlin', I—"

She fired the bullet into the doorframe.

With her ears ringing from the shot, her hands stinging from the recoil, she said, "That was a warning, Mr. Stannert. Next time, I aim three feet to the right." The splintered wood showed where the projectile had entered. It lay buried in the heavier wood of the frame, a mute and leaden reminder of her final words to him that night.

After that, there was no talking, but the nightly visits continued. Only the stealthy twist of the knob, the silent testing, to see if she'd relented, rethought, forgiven, and forgotten.

But she swore she'd never forgive.

Or forget.

Chapter Twenty-five

Inez awoke in her Manitou hotel room, addled by sleep and utter darkness. Her hand flailed through the air, searching for a nonexistent night table holding Mark's Navy Colt revolver. Wisps of her interrupted dream thinned and vanished.

She relaxed, dropped her hand over the edge of the bed, and tried to still her galloping pulse.

A sound.

She'd heard something, she was certain.

Inez rolled over, toward the window. The shade was drawn and still. No breath of air moved it. The moon had set, plunging the room into deepest night.

She rolled back in the other direction, then sat up slowly.

Listening.

The inner-spring mattress creaked beneath her, and Fountain Creek sounded in a pulsing, unceasing roar outside. Otherwise it was as if the entire world—all its creatures, the elements, the very earth itself—slept.

Or perhaps, like her, it was all awake, and holding its collective breath.

Then...

There!

A faint scratching at the door, like someone trying to wake her up, but too timid or cautious to knock.

"Inez?"

It was the smallest of whispers, hardly more than an exhalation. No clue to whether the speaker was male or female came through in that one faint word.

"Who is there?" Inez clutched her covers.

The scratching stopped. The whisper became incrementally louder. "Come quickly! It's William!"

Oh no! William!

Bounding from the bed, heart skittering, Inez raced to the door in her nightgown. Throwing caution aside, she yanked it open, and peered down the long hallway of rooms. The wall lamp at the end of the hall was out, allowing no access into the gloom. She thought one of the doors might be the slightest bit ajar, which one she couldn't be certain, the dark flattened all perspective. Was that a dampened light shining from underneath? Was it William's room?

She started down the hall, hastening toward the ghost of a partly open door.

Inez pulled even with the grand staircase leading to the ground floor, all of her attention focused on the tunnel ahead of her. A shadow detached itself from the niche at the top of the staircase. It was as if the statue of Hermes had suddenly come to life. Startled, Inez only glimpsed a shape entirely cloaked, hood pulled low, before she received a violent shove that sent her reeling toward the staircase.

A misstep as she tried to regain her balance, and her foot met empty air.

The dark shadow fled down the hall, away from Inez.

Inez clutched in vain for the staircase's banister, beyond her reach, and fell.

Jarring pain rocketed through her elbows, ribs, knees, and back as she tumbled down stairs. She yelped as the back of her head smacked a stair's edge, and a burst of light tore through her vision. Inez grabbed frantically, trying to stop her downward plunge. Her hand whacked into one of the vertical balusters, and she grabbed hold. She felt, more than heard, a pop in her shoulder as her arm twisted and took her full weight. The pain was instantaneous, intense, deep. For an agonizing moment, she thought her arm would rip from her body.

Unable to hold on through the pain, she let go. Her tailbone bumped down one more stair, adding a second jolt of pain. She finally stopped, sitting upright, short of the floor by about six steps.

Up above, doors slammed, indistinct voices exclaimed. Even through the unbearable throb of her shoulder, she made a point of tugging down the hem of her nightdress, which had rucked up about her knees in the tumble.

The wooden staircase vibrated with footsteps, clattering down to her. A flickering light grew brighter, casting her shadow long and wavering across the reception area to the hotel's front door.

"Mrs. Stannert! Good Heavens, what happened?" Jonathan DuChamps knelt beside her and set the candle lamp on a nearby tread. He peered at her, looking strangely vulnerable with no glasses and a jacket thrown hastily over a nightshirt with buttons askew. His expression turned grave. "Your shoulder," he said.

Inez spared a glance at her left shoulder, which radiated pain. Beneath the flannel nightgown, it sloped grotesquely and unnaturally down and forward. Looking at it seemed to make it hurt even worse, if that were possible. She took a hissing breath between her teeth and looked away, pain filling her mind like a red mist.

"Inez!" Harmony's worried face appeared in the mist beside her husband's. She clutched her shawl with one hand, and covered her mouth with the other. "Your shoulder," she whispered between her fingers.

Aunt Agnes' voice floated down from the stairs above. "What on earth were you doing on the stairs?"

"Did…you come to my door?" Inez gingerly cradled her arm, trying to take the weight off her shoulder, her mind fuzzy with pain.

"This time of night?" Agnes moved past Jonathan and Harmony, stopping at the stair below Inez. She set down her own candleholder on the tread. "Who would have reason to be out and about right now?"

"I don't know," said Inez faintly.

"Were you sleepwalking, Inez?" Agnes inquired. "I recall, you had an unfortunate habit of wandering about your room, still asleep. Your mother was worried sick you would wander out into the halls and who knows where, so she locked you in at night. Do you remember? You were no more than seven or eight."

Inez opened her mouth to say she hadn't been sleepwalking, someone had shoved her down the stairs, but then snapped it shut. *Perhaps it's wisest to keep that to myself.* "I thought I heard someone calling. I went out to see who it might be and, next thing I knew, I was falling."

Agnes nodded, vindicated. "Sleepwalking. I have heard that a copper wire, wrapped around the limb of a sleep-walker on going to bed and extending to the floor prevents sleepwalking. Has something to do with electricity, I believe."

"Mrs. Underwood, she's had a bad fall and injured her shoulder," said Jonathan sharply. "Mrs. Stannert needs medical assistance, not advice on sleepwalking."

Inez mentally gave Jonathan points for explaining the obvious to Aunt Agnes and stopping her blather. Other visitors clustered about now, up on the second floor. Inez could only imagine the racket she'd made, crashing down the staircase. Nearly the entire floor seemed to be either up on the landing in their nightwear and hastily thrown on shawls and jackets.

Jonathan looked up at the gathering crowd, made a gesture as if to push nonexistent glasses up the bridge of his nose, and addressed the watchers. "Can someone bring a physician? Dr. Prochazka, or Dr. Zuckerman or...there's another one I met just this evening in the smoking room, can't recall his name." Under his breath, Jonathan muttered, "The place is crawling with damned doctors, surely one of them could be found at this hour to do what he's paid to do."

Jonathan DuChamps rose another notch in Inez's estimation, even as Harmony whispered, "Jonathan! Language!"

The front door squeaked open and Nurse Crowson entered, covered neck to toe in a voluminous cape and carrying a black leather bag. She froze as she took in the scene on the crowded stairs, but when she spoke, her voice revealed no surprise, only mild curiosity. "Is something amiss? Mrs. Stannert, did you fall?"

"She was sleepwalking and fell down the stairs," explained Agnes. "Her arm bothers her."

Nurse Crowson set the bag by the newel post at the bottom of the staircase, and knelt by Inez. "Let's see, then." She reached out.

Jonathan DuChamps snapped, "We need a *real* physician, Mrs. Crowson."

Inez held her breath and through a haze of pain, watched to see how Nurse Crowson would take this inadvertent slap to her vocation. All she said was "Dr. Prochazka is often up late. I'll see if he is still in the clinic."

She rose, retreated down the stairs, picked up her bag, and vanished toward the back of the hotel.

Inez closed her eyes just as Harmony said, "What was Mrs. Crowson doing out this time of night?"

"Maybe taking a walk. Who knows?" Jonathan sounded tired.

"He, or she, knew my given name," Inez said.

"What?"

Inez shook her head, hurting too much to repeat it.

Whoever came to my door, whoever drew me out, called me by my first name.

Chapter Twenty-six

People had begun to drift back to their rooms when Dr. Prochazka hurried up, not a handful of minutes later. He still wore his rumpled evening clothes from that night's concert, but now had a half-buttoned laboratory coat over them.

Without preamble, he said, "Nurse Crowson said you fell down the stairs. That you have an injured shoulder."

"She was sleepwalking," said Aunt Agnes promptly. "What a rude awakening, I'm sure. She certainly woke most of us on the second floor with her crashing down the staircase."

Prochazka didn't seem to be listening. He set one surprisingly gentle hand on the misshapen shoulder area. Inez winced.

"A humeral dislocation. Or, as often said, your shoulder is out of joint. It is a simple procedure to correct. Although it can be painful." He looked around. "Where is Mrs. Crowson? It would be best to give you laudanum beforehand. It will help with the pain and allow you to relax. This goes faster, easier, if the muscles are relaxed."

"No laudanum," Inez said through gritted teeth.

Dr. Prochazka adjusted his wire-rim glasses and peered closely at her. "You are obviously in pain. The laudanum is my own formulation. You will taste cinnamon, honey. It will work quickly, make my task easier, allow you to recover more efficiently. I use only the minimum amount of alcohol, if that is what concerns you."

She shook her head. Inez didn't trust laudanum in its various forms and concoctions. She had seen too many women—and men—fall under its power and fade into shadows of their former selves, as enslaved to its call as an infatuated lover is to an indifferent mate. "I'd rather take the alcohol. Brandy. Whiskey. scotch whiskey is best."

The physician looked exasperated. "This is ridiculous."

A sound at the bottom of the stairs, like a half-swallowed exclamation. Franklin Lewis, elegant hotelier, clothed in wrapper with the hem of a nightshirt doing nothing to cover an expanse of spindly white shins, knobby ankles, and feet stoppered by slippers. Nurse Crowson stood at his side, hands folded into her voluminous cloak. Lewis held a candle in another of the hotel's brass holders aloft for light. The flickering of the flame bounced off their twinned, square-set faces.

"Mr. Lewis," said Prochazka. "Please bring a large dose of scotch whiskey, as the lady requests. Quickly. Mrs. Crowson, please measure out two doses of my laudanum. You know which cabinet." He fished in the pocket of his white cotton coat and tossed her a ring of keys. "Mrs. Stannert insists on arguing she does not want it. However, she may change her mind later."

He looked at Jonathan DuChamps. "It would be far easier if she were lying down."

"Take her back up to her room, then," Agnes suggested.

Prochazka looked up at the long staircase, and came to a decision. "The bottom of the stairs are closer. A hard surface is better than a mattress. She should, however, have a blanket to lie on."

Jonathan promptly disappeared up the stairs.

Lewis reappeared carrying an alarmingly full glass of whiskey. "Mrs. Stannert, I advise you sip this slowly, as it is a very powerful spirit."

Inez took the glass and held it to her teeth, which were chattering in pain. Normally, she would have worked her way slowly to the first sip, but this was not the time to savor the liquor's complexities and nuances. The first sharp swallow brought tears to her eyes and anesthetized her throat. The next three slid down easier, creating a path of fire to her stomach.

She gasped slightly, feeling the fire burrow out to her limbs and down to fingers and toes. Cradling the half-empty glass, she said, "I believe I'm ready."

"I can reduce—that is, repair—your shoulder very easily," Prochazka said. "It is not a complicated procedure. It will take but a moment, and the intense pain will be gone. Like this." He snapped his long fingers.

The sound put Inez in mind of a bone breaking. She shivered.

Jonathan reappeared with a blanket and a shawl draped over his arm.

Dr. Prochazka helped her to her feet and supported her around the waist, much as Aunt Agnes had done with Harmony hours previously. Jonathan spread the blanket on the polished wood entryway. The doctor lowered her to the blanket with Jonathan's help, and said, "Wait." He looked at Jonathan. "It would be best if you kneel by her as well. Hold her right arm, help her stay still."

The physician positioned himself next to Inez's injured shoulder. Inez looked from one kneeling man to the other, suddenly put in the mind of a *tableau vivant*.

But if it were a real tableau I wouldn't have the urge to scream. I do hope screaming won't be part of this scenario.

She wondered if she needed more whiskey, but decided that she'd best save the rest of the glass for a celebratory knockout once the worst was over.

Dr. Prochazka firmly grasped her wrist and elbow, and said to Inez, "I have done this many times. It will be quickly over." He gave Jonathan a nod. Jonathan placed hands on the upper portion of her right arm, holding her steady. The physician pulled her left arm down and out, away from her torso, then rotated her forearm up and out. Something in her shoulder shifted with a bone-deep pain. She clenched her jaws to keep from crying out loud. An agonizing stretch on her shoulder, and something slid, popping into place.

She couldn't help it. A squeak escaped. But at least, it wasn't a scream.

The pain, indeed, had miraculously disappeared, leaving only a deep ache, camouflaged by woozy warmth. How her shoulder would feel once the whiskey wore off, she couldn't guess, and frankly, didn't want to know.

"Done," said Prochazka. "Now, to retire and rest." He turned to Nurse Crowson, who had suddenly appeared, back from her errand for the physician. She handed him a small tonic bottle along with the ring of keys. Prochazka gave the bottle to Jonathan, instructing, "A teaspoonful now, before she sleeps. Another tomorrow, should she need it."

Inez sat up slowly, and eyed the quantity of whiskey left in the glass on the floor by Jonathan. It would be more than enough, she decided, to ensure she wouldn't need any of what was in the small brown bottle.

Harmony, who was hovering by the stairs, said, "Mrs. Stannert was going to join us in a trip to the Garden of the Gods tomorrow. Is that still wise or should she stay here and rest?"

Prochazka shrugged. "As long as she is not at the reins or climbing the rocks, I see no harm in that."

Inez raised her arm—to her surprise, it obeyed her—and rubbed her eyes. She said, "Thank you, doctor."

He stood, helped her to her feet, and said, "You are lucky I was here. The sooner the shoulder is put back in place, the easier it is. Too much time passes, and it becomes more painful, more difficult." He looked at the grandfather clock. "I must get back to work."

To work? When does he sleep?

"Let us help you to your room," said Jonathan. He picked up her glass, and Harmony came across the floor to join them.

Aunt Agnes added, "We'll all walk you up the stairs, Inez, and make sure you are well in your room for the night, or what's left of it. Goodness, what a fright you gave us all."

Inez turned to accept the glass from Jonathan and caught a glimpse of Lewis and the nurse, conversing in low tones by the reception desk. The intensity of their whispers caught her attention as well as something about their stances. They bent toward each other. Lewis was doing most of the talking and he looked…angry? worried?

Mrs. Crowson was shaking her head slightly. She suddenly laid a hand on Lewis' sleeve with a single word. They both turned to look at Inez, similar expressions of suspicion, doubt and…

Could it be fear?

What have they to fear from me?

Jonathan on one side of her said, "Slowly up the stairs, Mrs. Stannert," while Agnes on the other side said, "Just how much of that liquor did you drink, dear niece?" Harmony placed an extra shawl gingerly over her shoulders. It occurred to Inez that maybe it wasn't her they were scrutinizing.

It gave Inez something to mull over as she carefully climbed what now seemed a very long set of stairs to the second floor.

Chapter Twenty-seven

"Are you certain you are feeling well enough to do this?" Harmony asked for the umpteenth time. She had the reins of the buggy and was focused on the curve in the road ahead, so didn't see Inez roll her eyes.

"Harmony, I am fine. Dr. Prochazka was correct. Once he settled my shoulder in place, the pain went away, and I slept like a baby." Although Inez thought that the remaining scotch probably had as much to do with her recovery as the doctor's magic hands. "Are you certain you don't want me to drive?" she added. It made her nervous to see Harmony, who still struck Inez as being on the frail side, in control of the buggy and horse. From the toss of her head and the prance in her gait, the mare in the traces was more than happy to be out of the livery.

"I shall echo your sentiments, dear sister, and say really, I am also fine." She flipped the reins lightly, urging the horse up the incline. The four wheels squeaked faster. "Everyone treats me like an invalid, and yet I've never felt better since coming to Manitou. I'm stronger than I've been in quite a while. Wouldn't you agree, Lily?"

Lily, face bowed and hidden, nodded, the motion intensified by the large straw sunhat she wore. "Yes'm," she said, nearly inaudible.

"Now, as I was saying," Harmony continued. "We passed Balanced Rock on Buena Vista Drive, just as we left Manitou. But oh, wait until you see the Gateway! It's magnificent."

"So have you been this way before?" Inez asked.

"Oh, yes. Mr. DuChamps took us and Aunt Agnes to see everything when we first arrived. It's nice that the Garden is only a couple of miles from the hotel."

Inez gazed at the evergreens on one side of the road and the red sandstone formations on the other. "Where is Mr. DuChamps today?"

Harmony's hands tightened inside their buckskin gloves. "More business to attend to."

Inez turned to William, who sat trapped between Inez and Lily. "So William, you've seen the rocks before?"

No verbal answer, but a prompt arm shot out, finger pointed at a particularly spindly formation by the side of the road. He looked up at her from under a round-brimmed sailor-style hat, hazel eyes questioning. Inez smiled, "That's right, William. Those rocks are red. And I hear there are more magnificent ones ahead."

"He's seen 'em before," muttered Lily in an undertone that Inez could barely discern. "You like climbing on rocks, right Wilkie? We'll climb another mountain sometime." She hugged him fiercely to her.

He wiggled out of her grasp, shouting, "Rock!"

"Oh, he's quite the little mountain goat," said Harmony.

Inez was alarmed. "You let him wander around on these?" Visions of William clambering about under Balanced Rock—a huge cubical boulder teetering on a single apex—flashed through her mind.

Harmony smiled indulgently, a single dimple appearing, then gone. "Only small ones, Inez, and only when he's holding tight to Lily or Jonathan's hand."

Inez thought back to William's stiff-legged and determined race down Williams' Canyon the previous day, and wasn't certain she liked the sound of that at all. But she decided to let it pass.

She glanced over at Lily. Lily had been very quiet, and had spent most of the ride with her head tilted down, not looking at the sights as they passed. In fact, when she'd met them for breakfast, William in her arms, she had given Inez only one guilty glance, murmuring, "G'morning, ma'am," before busying herself with making sure he at least ate, as opposed to wore, the majority of his oatmeal.

"The Gateway is up ahead." Harmony pointed at an immense wall of red sandstone, broken in the middle. A road wound between the two monolithic walls of rock. Inez gasped.

Harmony glanced at her. "So, this is new to you? Leadville doesn't have scenery like this?"

"Not at all."

Inez had to admit, the rock entrance to the Garden of the Gods was imposing. Then, through the clop-clop of the horse and the squeaking of the wheels, Inez heard something else. "Stop a minute."

Harmony brought the buggy to a halt.

"Do you hear that?" Inez asked.

Everyone, except William, listened intently. The wind shifted bringing the plaintive skirl of...

"Is that bagpipes?" Inez said.

"It seems to be coming from over there," said Harmony.

Inez squinted up at another formation, which looked very much like someone lying at ease, nose pointed to the sky. They listened to the lonely music for a bit. "Who would be up there, piping away?" Inez wondered aloud. "It doesn't look easy to climb."

Harmony shook her head, and said, "We are almost to our picnic spot beyond the Gateway. Maybe we'll discover the musician on the other side."

A short while later, they passed through the gateway of giants. Inez gazed up. "Impressive."

"When Jonathan brought us here, he said something about the gate not being one of human workmanship. There is an air of the artificial about it, because the massive portals seem to have been carved; but the workmanship is all divine.'" She smiled. "Jonathan told us a bit about it: The pillars of the gate to either side are red sandstone, and three hundred and eighty feet high, too high for any but the Great Architect to think of rearing."

Once they reached the other side of the Gateway and were a comfortable distance into the valley itself, they stopped for lunch. Lily spread out a blanket and set out the baskets. Inez and Harmony trailed after William, who seemed intent on picking up every single rock and examining it, before carefully setting it back down in its resting place.

"Harmony, can you tell me what, exactly, Jonathan mentioned about the hotel and its current situation?" Inez asked in a low voice, glancing over her shoulder at Lily. They were far enough away that she felt certain Lily would not be privy to their conversation.

"Well," Harmony passed a hand over her eyes in thought. "I know that the major hotels in Manitou are vying for guests and prominence. It is apparently quite a coup to have Dr. Prochazka with the Mountain Springs House. But I believe he came at a price. Something about supporting his research into consumption and so on. They built the clinic for him, you know."

Inez shook her head. "I really don't know anything about it."

"Well, this is Dr. Prochazka's second summer here. Lewis told Jonathan that the Mountain Springs House had the highest winter occupancy rate of any of the hotels in the area. He made quite a to-do about it and credits the physician."

"I'm surprised that some of the other hotels haven't tried to steal him away," Inez observed.

"It goes beyond Dr. Prochazka and his physicks," Harmony said. "Jonathan told me a few of their plans. They are going to add a bowling alley, for instance, and a billiard room, and another story to the hotel."

Inez raised her eyebrows.

"They also have plans to add cabins to accommodate more guests," Harmony continued. "You've seen the Cliff House, nearby? I gather they are one of the Mountain Springs House's fiercest rivals. You've seen the tents dotted all around their hotel? It's from the overflow. Well, the Mountain Springs House wants to enlarge its own property, and build cabins on the extra land."

Inez shook her head. "All that will not come cheap."

"That is what Jonathan told me." Harmony paused. "I was so alarmed that I interrupted him, told him he couldn't be thinking of sinking our life's savings and our future into such a perilous scheme. We began arguing at that point. I don't know if there might have been more he'd been planning to tell me about their schemes."

Inez frowned. "What you have said is enough. They sound as if they have grand plans. It will cost a great deal to accomplish all that and to hold onto Dr. Prochazka as well, particularly if he is perceived as an asset."

Harmony and Inez paused, watching William. He was examining with great interest an iridescent beetle that had been hiding under the most recent rock. He bent down and picked it up.

"No!" Inez said sharply. "Put it down, William!"

He looked up at her. His small fingers squinched down on the beetle's carapace. The beetle waved its legs desperately. "No!" he said, just as sharply.

Inez bent down and slapped his hand. With a cry, he let go of the beetle, which hit the ground and scuttled off to a new hiding place.

"Inez." Harmony sounded reproachful, as if she wanted to scold Inez but didn't dare.

Inez brusquely brushed off his dirty, sweaty palm with her gloved hand as he squirmed and tugged. She said, "Harmony, you don't know the creatures in these areas. A harmless insect this time, a poisonous spider the next."

William was crying now. Inez gripped his hand and said, "Let's get some lunch. Are you hungry, William? Bread and butter?"

"Hunng-gy," he muttered, rubbing his eyes.

"And sleepy too," said Harmony.

They started back.

Harmony said, "I've been meaning to ask you about last night." She lowered her voice. "You weren't sleepwalking, were you."

"No," she said shortly.

"What happened?"

"Someone tapped on my door and whispered, 'Come quickly. It's William.' I could not even tell whether it was a man or woman. It could have been anyone." She shook her head. "I bolted out of the room without looking behind me or to either side. Sheer stupidity on my part, to be so impetuous."

Harmony set a hand on her wrist. "You were driven by instinct, Inez. You thought your son was in distress. Any mother would have done the same."

"I just can't work out who it was," Inez continued. "I let on to Lewis that Mr. Stannert might be interested in investing, so what good would have come of him or one of his allies shoving me down the stairs? I must admit, this morning I considered Mr. Epperley. He and I exchanged words yesterday. I think he tried to present himself as a confidante and overplayed his hand. Mayhap Mr. Lewis hadn't had time to talk to Epperley about my telegram to Mark."

Harmony stopped walking. "Telegram?"

"I sent a telegram to Leadville last night," Inez explained. "I asked Mark to come as soon as possible. I know him: he will be able to worm his way into these affairs of men in ways that I cannot."

Harmony's troubled stare fixed on William, who was gazing longingly at a large black crow hopping about, pecking the dusty ground. "But I thought Mr. Stannert wasn't coming until next week. That you wanted this time alone with William."

Inez sighed. William tugged on her hand, leaning with all his body weight in the direction of the crow. "Bird!" he shouted.

William's pulling made her recently injured shoulder ache, so she let him go. Together, Inez and Harmony watched as he ran full tilt at the bird, which took off with a startled squawk.

"I feel the situation here is too volatile," Inez said shortly. "We need someone who would be sympathetic to our reasoning, and…" She dusted her gloved palms together, stopping herself. She had almost said, "And Reverend Sands is out of town."

I must stop thinking of him. He's not due back in Leadville until General Grant has finished with his Colorado trip and heads East. That will be much too late to help me here. I wish I could write to Justice, reach him in some way. But I'm not even certain where he is right now.

Instead, Inez finished with, "And Mr. Stannert, for all his faults, and he has many, would not want to see you or me or William exposed to any danger. He will help." *I will make certain that he does.*

Harmony crossed her arms. "Do you think we are in danger?" She looked as though a sudden chill had swept over her.

"I think," Inez said soberly, "we must be very careful. Careful of what we say. Careful of who is around when we talk. For instance, last night, when you refused the tonic from Mrs. Crowson, that probably wasn't wise."

"I was tired," Harmony said. "I suppose I shouldn't have said anything, but it all just slipped out. Nurse Crowson can be irritating, sometimes. Since Mrs. Pace's return, I've just been taking the bottles and tipping them out when no one is looking."

Inez gazed at her offspring, now busy kicking the ground where the bird had been, sending puffs of red dust and grit up with each jab of a booted toe. "What about William's doses?"

"He still takes them." She looked shaken. "He *does* have a lung condition, that has long been the case. Your physician in Leadville said so, as did our doctors in New York, and Dr. Prochazka in Manitou. William is doing well here, so I didn't see the harm. I thought maybe it was helping. Do you think he's in danger?" Her voice quavered.

"In danger? Why harm a child? Who would do such a thing, and to what purpose? It would only discredit the hotel and its doctor." Inez paused. "Unless, that is exactly what someone is trying to do."

Chapter Twenty-eight

Inez felt caught, trapped as surely as if the huge monoliths of the Gateway were grinding together, mashing her between tons of sandstone. She felt as if she was startling at shadows, but that these shadows had substance and were reaching out with poisoned fingers to touch those she loved.

Licking her lips, she tried to calm the sudden upwelling of fear. "We mustn't panic," she said. "After all, how many people have actually been stricken by taking medicine that originates from the Mountain Springs House and its clinic? Only Mr. Pace, that we know for certain."

William had returned and grabbed a fistful of Harmony's skirt. He was tugging her toward the picnic blanket, where Lily sat slicing yellow cheese to go with the bread.

"However, we must be circumspect," Inez added. "I will talk further with Mrs. Pace, as soon as possible. Please, Harmony, don't do or say anything that will draw attention to you in any way."

They had no sooner finished their meal and were still lazing on the blanket when they heard the rattle of an approaching wagon and a cheery "halloo." Susan waved from the passenger seat. The woman at the reins, however, was a stranger to Inez. Trotting along beside them on a magnificent roan was Robert Calder. The wagon clanked and rattled like a tinker's caravan.

"I'm so glad we caught up with you before you left," said Susan as they drew up and stopped by the horse and buggy. Inez rose and walked over to them. In the back of the wagon, Inez glimpsed stacked metal boxes, some of which she recognized as holding Susan's photographic equipment and cases of photographic plates. "I wasn't certain you'd still be here," Susan continued, "and I wanted to introduce Mrs. Galbreaith."

Calder slid out of the saddle and helped both women down from the wagon.

Mrs. Galbreaith turned out to be a pleasantly no-nonsense woman with a firm handshake. "Please, call me Anna," she insisted.

"Anna and I have been roaming about the Garden since early morning," said Susan. "Sunrise here is magnificent. The colors in the rock and the sky, you cannot imagine. If only one could capture those colors on the plates. Black and white is such a pale imitation of reality. Anna has photographed the entire Garden at one time or another, and has done a marvelous job of showing me around. As has Robert…Mr. Calder."

"I was explaining to Miss Carothers how the Garden changes with weather and time of day," said Calder. "Right after a rain, its hues are deeper, and it becomes so vividly red that if I were to paint it true to life, none would believe my vision real. In the soft light of evening, a sagy green suffuses the vegetation. At sunset, the last rays of the sun cause the enormous tablets of stone to flash out with surpassing grandeur."

Inez glanced around at the strange rock shapes, silent as monuments to forgotten deities. "The Garden brings out the poet in you."

He grinned. "I am more skilled with a brush than with words, so imagine how a writer feels, surrounded by such glory." He added, "Seeing the Garden by moonlight should not be missed. I would be more than happy to be personal guide to you ladies one of these evenings."

Susan clasped her hands together. "That would be lovely!"

Mrs. Galbreaith cleared her throat. "Thank you for the invitation. However, I have seen the Garden aplenty by moonlight and have a full house for the next few weeks, so must regretfully decline."

Inez said, "I cannot speak for my sister, but I would certainly enjoy that."

Calder smiled. "'Tis decided, then. We shall make a jolly outing of it." The mare hitched to the buggy whickered, as if volunteering for the expedition. He turned to her, still smiling, and scratched her nose. She whuffled into his glove, ostensibly looking for a treat. "I know this one," he remarked. "She's full sibling to my own."

Inez looked at both horses, and realized that they indeed shared the same coloring and conformation.

He continued, "Did Mr. Morrow warn you of her wretched eating habits? Both of them, they eat anything and everything. You must watch her on the trails and during your stops that she not get into the thistles and locoweed."

"That's right, he told us, and I forgot," Inez felt guilty. The pretty little roan snuffled at the bare dirt as if she might seriously consider eating the few scattered red pebbles. "Mr. Morrow even gave us a nosebag, saying we should feed her when we stopped. Poor thing, she's probably quite hungry."

"No matter," said Calder. "Mine had more than his fill of grass by a stream while I painted earlier." He opened one of his saddlebags and pulled out a full nosebag. "Shall I?" He hefted the nosebag in the air with raised eyebrows.

"That would be wonderful," said Inez.

"Did you see Balanced Rock?" Susan asked. "We are going to stop there on the way back, and Mrs. Galbreaith has promised to take my picture while I stand by it. I shall have to send a cabinet card home to my parents. They shall be most impressed!"

Calder's horse, already burdened down with two canvases, a small easel, and a paintbox snorted as if in agreement. After checking that both the wagon's horse and his own mount were properly tied off, Calder took the grain-filled bag to the buggy's mare and slipped the strap over her ears. Inez went to introduce herself to the huge roan, who after a suspicious sniff, accepted her touch. In the process of admiring the horse, which was, she decided, a truly magnificent animal, she glimpsed in the open saddlebag an odd-shaped bundle wrapped in a green, blue, and black tartan with a thin red thread running through. A partially collapsed bladder, covered with the same pattern, bulged alongside the wrapped objects.

Calder returned to his horse, and strapped the saddlebag closed. "Shall we join the others?" he suggested.

Susan had already joined Harmony, Lily, and William on the blanket. As the three of them—Inez, Calder, and Mrs. Galbreaith—moved to the picnic blanket, Inez ventured, "Were you, by chance, playing bagpipes a while ago atop a ridge?"

"Indeed I was."

"It was quite haunting. Lovely music. But bagpipes?"

He sobered. "'Twas in honor of my brother, who came to Manitou to find health but found death instead. He was eldest and has left me head of the family. Part of my responsibilities, as I saw it, was to come here and determine what brought him down."

Mrs. Galbreaith said, "I am so sorry to hear of your loss. I will say, however, that so many people come here, hoping to find a cure or at least treatment for their illness. Some do recover, but many do not."

Inez pondered the almost complete lack of accent and the ease with which Calder fit into the general high-class milieu of Manitou, before asking, "Have you spent much time abroad?"

He paused, removed his hat, and, with a forearm, pushed back a tangle of black curls. Mrs. Galbreaith moved on to the party on blanket, and Inez lingered behind, curious as to his answer.

"Schooling in England, then more time in New York. As younger brother, I was encouraged to create my own future. I had hoped to be a painter. I was making some small name for myself in New York circles when I learned of Alec's death." He sighed. "If I'm required to return to the 'auld hame' and give up the life I've planned, I want answers as to what happened to my brother first."

He glanced toward Susan, who was playing peek-a-boo with a delighted William. He started to move toward her. Inez stepped to block him and lowered her voice to say, "Mrs. Pace said I should talk to you. I have my concerns about the Mountain Springs House and she said you did as well. Can you tell me, what happened to your brother?"

"Mrs. Pace, is it?" He stared hard at her, then, seemed to come to a decision. He took her arm and steered her away from the blanket, saying in a louder voice, "One of the formations you must observe is Cathedral Spires, Mrs. Stannert. Do you see? Over there?" He pointed to a grouping of sharp, sheer formations. Standing so close, his hand clasped on her elbow, Inez was aware of the pleasant smell of horse, paint, and sweat that emanated from him.

"Very much like spires of churches," Calder added, "but much grander than any made by the mere hand of man." He then lowered his voice. "Alec arrived late last summer, drawn to this cursed place by word of Dr. Prochazka's successes with victims of consumption and the wasting disease. My parents were all for him going to Spain for his health, some place closer to home and warm year-round, but he'd not hear of it. Still, after he arrived in Manitou and all through winter and into the spring, we heard good reports. In fact, he began talking of the place as a business opportunity." He paused, staring out at the spires, which to Inez looked for all the world like red rock knives threatening the cloudless sky.

"I assume this all changed at some point?" Inez asked.

"His symptoms suddenly took a turn for the worse," said Calder. "Gone were the hopeful missives. He began to write that Prochazka was a sham. That his cures were no better than the charms hawked from gypsy carts. All talk of a possible business connection vanished." He shook his head. "I believe he put too much faith in an imperfect science. But what happened next shocked us all."

"What was that?"

"He was turned out of the Mountain Springs House, without so much as a by-your-leave. Not the hospitality he'd been greeted with initially, I assure you."

Inez was shocked as well. "Why?"

"I do nae know." Distress slipped through into his speech. He heard it himself, gave her an apologetic smile, and shook his head. "After careful observation and thought, I've decided that the Mountain Springs House is eager to only have successes and no failures. Someone dying while 'on the plan' brings down the cure rate, you see? No longer can they boast without reservation, 'Carried in on a mattress, walked out on his own!' That's one of their claims they make to those who are ill. With Alec, it was the opposite. He walked in on his own, and was then carried out in the dead of night."

"Why didn't he say something? Surely he must have protested. If it happened to him and others, well, I would imagine the reputation of the House would be a shambles."

"He'd found another savior," said Calder. He pivoted about to eye the happily chatting company on the picnic blanket. "In his last letters, he told us he was comfortably settled in Colorado Springs, at the Colorado Springs Hotel. A different physician was attending him, one who promised the impossible yet again. A total cure." Calder's mouth twisted bitterly. "*Another* total cure, based on a different regimen. He was content to let sleeping dogs lie."

"A different physician? Who?"

"Ah, he was cagey about that. But something turned up that I can explain more thoroughly later. I'll tell you this now, however. From some things he wrote, I believe that introductions must have been brokered from someone at the Mountain Springs House," his eyes narrowed. "That is the person I am seeking. For whoever it was led him down the road to his death. He should have come home, where he could have been treated by the family physician. Where he could, at least, have died surrounded by family who loved him."

"He died in Colorado Springs? How can you blame someone in Manitou for that?"

"I believe my brother was silenced to keep him from revealing that the treatments were a sham. Silenced, to keep from discussing whatever business plans and overtures were made."

"You think he was killed?"

"Easy enough," Calder said with a shrug. "He was weak and racked with the fevers and pains of the wasting disease. Alone, far from home, would nae take much, a gentle push, too much of this and that in a bottle of 'restorative' or a medicinal inhalant to topple him into the grave, him and whatever he knew."

Inez took a step back, aghast, then recovered. *Really, how different is it from those who kill to secure a mining claim in the mountains or a handful of gold in the alleys?*

"So, you think someone at the Mountain Springs House put your brother in touch with this other physician, who killed him either purposely or through medical ineptness?"

"I've no doubt of it."

"Who?"

"I suspect Lewis. Prochazka would nae do so, and my brother would nae trust him, after all that. Prochazka aside, Lewis stands to lose the most and would have been happy to ease my brother out of the hotel. He has an oily way about him, of ingratiating himself into people's good will. Plus he seems to have some medical knowledge and has the pulse of the medical community."

"There's also Mr. Epperley," she said.

Now it was his turn to be surprised. "The hotel's manager?"

"Also part owner, and apparently heavily invested in the hotel. You didn't know?"

"Nae, I didn't. This puts a different light on things." He sounded grim. "I thought I'd figured it out, but now…"

"Mr. Calder." Susan's voice wafted from the picnic blanket. She was smiling at them. "Are you giving Mrs. Stannert the entire geological history of the Garden?"

He waved and called back, "Not at all, Miss Carothers. I'm saving that lecture for our moonlight adventure."

Gazing at Susan's beaming face, shadowed by the flapping straw brim of her summer hat, he said softly, almost to himself, "Ah, Miss Carothers. The bright star in this whole dark and sorry business of mine. Who would have guessed I would meet such an enchanting creature here, so far from, well, nearly everywhere. If it were up to me, I'd conduct the family business from Colorado. Who knows? I may yet find a way. We have many connections in New York and Boston. Colorado is not that distant, by train and telegraph."

"Miss Carothers is my dearest friend. I would not take kindly to anyone trifling with her affections." Inez bit her lower lip, sorry for having spoken so bluntly to one who was, by all appearances, kind and open. "Forgive me, I was out of turn."

He slanted a glance at Inez. "Never fear, Mrs. Stannert. I may wear my heart on my sleeve, but I am, above all, a gentleman, one who appreciates outspoken, creative, intelligent women. I very much admire and salute Miss Carothers, and would do nothing to hurt her, in any way."

Calder offered his arm to Inez, and she took it. They began walking toward the group. He added, "I will be picking up Miss Carothers and her photographic paraphernalia tonight so she can join us for dinner and take photos of the *tableaux* afterwards, at Mrs. Underwood's request." He sobered. "Why don't you and I take a stroll around the hotel's garden later this afternoon. Perhaps about four, when most are resting before dinner and the evening's activities. We can talk more, and there is something I'd like to show you as well."

"Four o'clock, it is then." They reached the picnickers, and Inez met Harmony's questioning gaze with a forced smile. *I do hope whatever Mr. Calder has to share will shed more light on this mystery.*

Chapter Twenty-nine

After an "après meal" of leftovers, taken together, everyone prepared for the return drive to Manitou.

"We'll make quite a merry wagon train, coming into town," remarked Susan, as she tightened the ribbons of her straw hat under her chin.

Inez held the buggy steady as Harmony climbed in, slid to the right side, and picked up the reins. Lily helped William up into the seat before getting in herself. Their horse tossed her head with an odd whinny and sidestepped first one way then the other. The shafts of the buggy shuddered, causing the buggy to sway.

Inez stopped, one foot on the buggy step. "Goodness, what has gotten into her?"

Harmony tightened the reins to stop the horse's dancing. "Perhaps she's eager to get home. Mr. Morrow assured me she was gentle, but had a great deal of enthusiasm."

"Well, then, since we should get back quickly so that you and William can take your afternoon rest, we shall accommodate her," said Inez. She stepped up, and settled in next to William, putting an arm about him. Lily, who also had her arm around William, glared sullenly at Inez, and withdrew her own hold.

"Everyone ready?" Calder asked. He'd helped Mrs. Galbreaith and Susan into their wagon after picking up the picnic things for them all, had retrieved the nosebag, and was mounted ahead of them. He trotted up to their buggy, frowning slightly. "Your little mare seems agitated."

"The sooner we are on the move, the easier it will be, I'm certain," said Harmony.

"Would you like me to drive?" Inez asked.

"No, thank you!" snapped Harmony. "I'm quite capable of handling a horse and buggy. I'm not an invalid."

Inez bit her tongue, and glanced at Calder. He raised one eyebrow, but only said, "Why don't I go ahead of you. That'll give her a horse to follow, and she might settle a bit." He guided his horse to the head of the party and they moved up the incline, through the Gateway, and out of the Garden.

Inez twisted around in her seat, catching a last look of the Gateway, with Sentinel Rock guarding the entrance.

She'd no sooner twisted back when their horse gave a loud, nervous snort, jumped as if she'd seen a snake, and bolted. Harmony gave a cry of warning as the buggy streaked past Calder and his mount. Inez had a flashing impression of a bucking horse, ears pinned, and Calder yanking his horse's head away from the runaway carriage.

William let out a sharp, scared cry. Inez hugged him. Harmony fought to hold the reins, feet braced on the dash. Inez sensed she was using all her strength to keep the horse from zigzagging.

Inez shouted at Lily, "Help her!"

Then, seeing Lily's scared eyes and frozen face, Inez instead pushed William roughly toward her. "I'll do it! Hold him tight!"

Lily wrapped her arms tight around William.

Inez leaned over, glad that she wasn't using her injured shoulder, and shouted at Harmony, "Hand me a rein."

The horse began to weave. The buggy tipped dangerously from one side to the other. William was crying. Lily let out a terrified squawk. Inez tried not to see the sharp rocks lining one side of the road and the ditch off to the other. She said to Harmony, calmly as she could, "Give me the other rein, then you pull on the brake."

Harmony moved so Inez could grab her rein. Now she held both, but the pull on the reins was crosswise. The carriage began to drift toward the ditch, the horse fighting to continue running.

Inez scooted right on the seat, nearly squashing William, and said, without taking her eyes from the road, the lathering horse, and its pinned ears, "Lily. Hold William on your lap."

With William off the bench, she was able to sit more to the center and keep the reins straight. "Harmony, pull slowly on the brake. Slowly. We don't want it to snap and fail."

Sweat ran into Inez's eyes, and her hair whipped across her face, stinging and blinding her. Somewhere along the way, her hat ribbons had come loose and the hat had disappeared. Into the back of the buggy, she hoped. It was a nice hat. She didn't want to lose it.

She tried to concentrate on controlling the horse and keeping the buggy upright and on the road.

With William's sobs ringing in her ears, she said, "Lily. You must make him stop. The noise will only scare the horse more."

The crying was immediately muffled. Inez didn't dare look over, but she imagined that Lily's hand was involved. She vaguely heard Lily murmuring softly to soothe William. She took the same tone, only slightly louder, for the horse. "Whoa, girl, whoa."

She could feel the drag of the brake as Harmony engaged it ever so slowly. Inez's right arm was beginning to burn and she couldn't hold the rein as tautly as she wanted. The horse and buggy began pulling to one side. She struggled to bring the two reins together so she could hold them mostly with her good hand. The curve looming ahead looked nearly impossible to make.

The carriage slowed further. One front wheel dipped over the lip of the ditch, throwing Harmony hard against the arm rail, then righted again.

Hooves pounding up behind them. The pounding decelerated to a pace just slightly faster than the buggy. Calder trotted by, swung his horse in front of theirs, and slowed down further. Suddenly, without warning, the buggy horse stumbled, and stopped. Head hanging low, sides heaving, the beast let out a piteous groan. Inez hopped out of the buggy. Lily took her hand from William's mouth, and he let out a hearty scream as if he'd stored it up special for this moment.

"Get him out!" snapped Inez. "Take him to the wagon!"

Lily squeezed past Inez and almost stumbled in her haste to disembark. Clutching William close, she ran back to where Susan and Mrs. Galbreaith had stopped.

Calder was by the mare's head. He looked up at Inez, sweat-plastered hair hanging about his face. "Can ye take my horse? I must get her free of the traces."

Inez slipped from the carriage and ran to grab the reins and lead Calder's horse out of the way. Calder unharnessed the distressed horse. He led her away, off the path, and behind a low outcropping, talking to her low and soft the whole time. Inez held her breath, watching them go. Calder's mount jerked his head, as if wanting to follow, and Inez had to switch her focus to calming him down. She glanced back, just in time to see the mare's head weave up and down in a strange twitchy motion, and then she collapsed, out of sight behind the rocks. Calder immediately knelt and disappeared as well. Inez started in distress, wanting to go help, but needing to stay with Calder's horse, who was becoming increasing agitated. The women's voices, rising in horrified exclamations, and William's loud wails did nothing to improve the situation.

Harmony finally hurried back to comfort William. Mrs. Galbreaith turned the reins over to Susan and hurried behind the outcroppings. She, too, knelt and disappeared from sight. Long minutes ticked by, until Calder and Mrs. Galbreaith rose and, sober-faced, returned to the road.

"What happened?" Inez said anxiously. "Should we fetch her some water? Is she unable to move?"

"She's dead," said Calder. He ran a sleeve across his sweating face.

Disbelief rolled over Inez. "But how?"

"What on earth just happened?" Harmony asked. She was approaching, carrying William and looking shaken. "She just bolted, as if she'd seen a snake."

"There was no snake, nothing to upset or frighten her," said Inez. "She was agitated before we even departed from the picnic spot, remember? She was so restless, we could hardly set foot in the buggy."

Mrs. Galbreaith added, "That was not a natural death. The poor sweet mare. Perhaps she ate something along the way? Didn't you say, Mrs. DuChamps, that Mr. Morrow had said she was indiscriminate in her tastes? Perhaps she took a mouthful of something bad. But it would have to have been something dreadful for her to die as she did, and so quickly."

Calder looked at Mrs. Galbreaith, an awful light growing behind his eyes. Without a word, he came over to his own horse. Inez held the horse still while Calder rummaged through one of his saddlebags. He pulled out the nearly empty nosebag, opened it, and sifted among the remaining contents.

Inez asked, "Could the grain have gone bad? I've seen horses react to spoilt grain, but not so rapidly."

A whispered curse, said low so none but Inez could hear. He pulled something out of the bag and held out a clenched hand to Inez, saying, "This is nae spoilt oats." He opened his fist. Sprinkled amongst the expected oats, corn, and barley, several small, smooth, blue-black berries glinted dully.

Chapter Thirty

"I don't recognize those berries. What are they?" Inez asked as Calder slipped them into his jacket pocket.

With a face full of thunder, he said, "I know what they look like. But, if I am correct, they are a far way from home."

"Well, what do you think they are?"

"*Paris quadrifolia.* Herb Paris."

She frowned, shook her head.

"I'm not surprised the name is unfamiliar to you. I've only seen the plant in the old forests of Britain and on the Continent. Another name for it is Truelove." His lip curled. "Herb Paris is poisonous, fatal to human and horse alike. The plant itself smells beastly when in bloom. Like a plant of the devil himself."

"What is it doing here, in Colorado? And why? Was it an accident that it ended up in the feedbag?"

"I intend to find out. That an innocent animal would die sets my blood aboil."

"Who would want to kill a horse?" She glanced involuntarily at the rock outcrop that hid the mare's body.

"Not just any horse. My horse. The feed was meant for the horse I rode."

Inez stared. "But, anyone could have taken him out."

He shook his head. "I bought that horse from Morrow when I arrived early this summer. It's mine and mine alone. No one else rides him."

"Someone meant to do you harm?" Although it was a blazing hot afternoon and Inez had nothing to shield her head from the heat, she felt suddenly cold, as if winter had descended. She couldn't help but glance around at the foreign landscape of red rocks, dead grasses, and gray-green brush.

His mouth twisted. "I always ride on less traveled paths. Had I not found the stream with ready grazing nearby, I would have fed the horse the grain prepared, without a second thought. Who is to say what would have happened on some of the steep rock slopes we traversed, if he had…" Calder didn't finish.

He didn't have to.

After a short conversation by the side of the road, the group decided that nothing could be done but to leave the dead mare where she had fallen. They lashed the buggy to the back of the wagon, such that it could trail behind.

It was a very subdued wagon full of people who finally arrived back at the Mountain Springs House. Mrs. Galbreaith had managed to fit everyone in her wagon, by shifting photographic boxes and equipment about. William had sobbed himself to sleep in Lily's arms, one dirty thumb plugging his mouth. Calder followed behind, keeping his horse at a sedate pace. Inez's recently injured shoulder ached, but at least it did not seem re-damaged. She ignored the muted pain, preferring to focus on the odd findings in the feedbag and the sobering demise of the horse.

Billy came from the livery and stared at the buggy behind the wagon. "Ain't thet one a' ours?" he asked. "Whar's the horse?"

Calder dismounted and said, "I'll explain to Mr. Morrow, lad. Is he in the livery?"

Billy nodded.

"Help the ladies with their baskets and unfasten the buggy and wheel it around to the back, then," said Calder. He leaned over to Susan, still in the carriage, and said, "I shall arrive for you about five, as we planned? I'll bring a carriage for you and all your boxes, cases, and camera, for the *tableaux* tonight. Will you still be my guest for dinner and the evening, despite these unfortunate circumstances? You must come, or face my profound distress and Mrs. Underwood's wrath. She's counting on you to take photographs of her scenes, you know."

Susan's smile was but a ghost of its usual self. "Yes, of course, Mr. Calder. I said I would, and I will."

At the porch stairs, Harmony placed a hand on Lily's shoulder, stopping her before they went up. Harmony addressed Inez saying, "I don't know how we—I and Lily—can thank you, Inez. I remember, even as a young child, that you always had a way of staying calm, even under the most stressful of situations. If you hadn't been there today, I don't know what might have happened."

"Harmony, you are the one who was brave," countered Inez gently. "Dealing with a runaway horse is something that I've done over the years. You were the one who had to face it for the first time, with the unknown and the fear that comes with such an experience. You stayed the course. You didn't panic nor fall into hysteria. You were the heroine of the piece, dear sister." She hugged her briefly, then released her. "Go and rest. I will see you at dinner."

She ruffled William's sweat-curled locks, then watched sister, son, and nanny ascend the stairs to the hotel. Sighing, Inez ran fingers through her own dust-filled hair and followed them, thinking she would have to take some time before dinner herself to tend to her appearance. She approached the reception desk, where Epperley was sorting out a tangle of guest keys. "Any telegrams or messages for me?" she inquired.

"Good afternoon, Mrs. Stannert. Indeed there is one." Epperley reached below the desk and handed her an envelope. "Came while you were out. Did you have a pleasant journey to the Garden of the Gods?"

"More excitement than expected. Mr. Calder can provide the full story." She watched him to see how he would respond to the mention of Calder's name.

Epperley merely raised one nearly invisible blond eyebrow and said, "Well, he is the sort of chap who causes a stir wherever he goes." He returned to sorting keys.

She leaned her elbows on the reception desk. "Would you care to expound upon that?"

He seemed wholly intent on unhooking two keys whose metal rings had become entangled. "I spoke out of turn. Mr. Calder hasn't made many friends in Manitou, what with his constant questions."

She drew the envelope between her fingers. "You mean the business of his brother."

He gave up on the keys, and directed his gaze at her. "Yes, Mrs. Stannert, I mean the very sorry business of his brother. I was here when the elder Mr. Calder was staying at the hotel. He was the sort of chap who liked to burn the candle brightly, so to speak. He came for treatment but was not willing to rein in any of his less-than-healthful habits in the process. So, of course his condition worsened. He eventually had it out with Dr. P., and consequently left."

"What happened to him after he left?" She flapped the envelope against her palm, curious to see what more she could glean from the hotel manager.

Epperley shrugged. "I didn't hear much else about him after that until the news of his death."

"Did he take on another physician for treatment after he left here?"

"Can't say." Epperley leaned forward over the mound of keys. "I have no doubt Mr. Calder has presented his side of the story. I can assure you, whatever tale he told you is not true by half. After all, Mr. Calder the younger was not here and what consumptive heir is going to write home to his family, saying, 'Came here to recover in the country air but have sunk into dissipation and spend my time gambling and eating opium as the spirit moves me'? Not bloody likely, if you will pardon my frankness."

She straightened up, watching him narrowly. "Can you tell me why should I believe you over Mr. Calder? After all, you have pinned your hopes and fortunes on the future of this hotel, while he is heir to a successful business. Seems it would be your word against his, with you having the greater reason to prevaricate."

Epperley set the keys down. If she hadn't been watching him so closely, she might have missed the slightly more-than-necessary force applied to metal keys as they met the wood of the reception desk and the barely perceptible downward turn of his mouth.

I have touched a nerve, it seems.

But when he glanced up at her, all she saw was a professional concern, colored with distant chagrin. "Word gets around, Mrs. Stannert. I understand your husband is due into town, and that he is looking for the wisest position for his money, a good bet for the long haul. Right now, betting in Manitou is like betting in roulette—the best position, is to be with the house." He pushed the keys aside. "Mr. Stannert will no doubt hear from those who wish to discredit the Mountain Springs House and her doctor of medicine. We are, truth to say, the only hotel here with an in-house physician of such repute."

"I find it interesting that he remains," said Inez. "Not that this isn't an outstanding establishment, but with all the other hotels around trying to woo invalids and vacationers, it seems you must be on your guard against competitors anxious to snatch him away from the Mountain Springs House."

Epperley patted his waistcoat and extracted his cigarette case. Three women came in the entrance and lingered, chatting. He returned the case to his waistcoat with a sigh. "Some have tried to lure Dr. P. away from us. Other hotel owners and operators, and even visiting families who fancy having their own physician at their beck and call. He'll have none of it, and there are ill feelings. Lies are spread, rumors fed." He turned an unreadable gaze on Inez. "If your husband expresses doubts over some half-baked story, you might remind him that Manitou isn't so different from Leadville, in some respects. Only in Leadville, if one hasn't yet staked a claim, it's too late. In Manitou, the boom is just beginning. Now is an excellent time to make one's move and put one's money on the table. A year or two from now, who knows?"

"So, you'd like me to counsel my husband on the excellent management of the Mountain Springs House and tout Dr. Prochazka's medical wonders?"

"We can show your husband numbers and provide names and introductions to patients who have benefited from Dr. P's treatments." He swung a key by its leather fob. She saw it was the one to her room. Epperley continued, "You have proof yourself, close to home: your sister and her little boy. They are absolutely ship-shape, wouldn't you say?" He handed her the key with a smile. "Such a pleasure to have you here, Mrs. Stannert, an absolute pleasure."

Up in her room, Inez tore open the envelope, pulled out the form and read the words painstakingly printed out by the telegraph operator: "Dearest Wife, I shall be on the next train, prepared for any and all weather and the best of opportunities. Fondest Regards, Your beloved Husband."

Three words ending with –est meant he'd understood her message. "Next train" meant he would be here tonight, tomorrow at the latest. Mention of weather and opportunities—he would come ready to deal with any and all situations, any and all social classes. Good enough.

But, "Beloved Husband"?

In the past, they had always closed such coded missives with "Loving Husband" and "Loving Wife." The word "beloved" was not part of their system and seemed entirely inappropriate, given the circumstances.

She flipped the telegram onto the bed.

Surely he isn't hoping that I have changed my mind about resurrecting our marriage. If so, I shall cure him of that, in short order.

After her ablutions, Inez checked her lapel watch. Time to meet Mr. Calder.

She took one more look in the mirror: Hair fiercely brushed until it was gleaming again, scented lightly with rosewater. An outfit appropriate to taking a "turn around the garden," and a parasol and hat to match.

There was little she could do about her sun-kissed face. A parasol borrowed from Mrs. Galbreaith for the ride back to the hotel had been better than nothing, but had been no replacement for her hat, lost in the mad carriage dash down the winding road from the Garden of the Gods. Now, a rosy flush from sunburn was the result. She knew from experience that, by morning, the flush would fade leaving her olive complexion another shade darker. *If I were home in Leadville, Bridgette would be tut-tutting and insisting I apply her concoction of borax, alum, camphor, sugar candy and ox-gall. Well, I shall just have to manage without.*

A pang of homesickness swept through her. Right about now, Abe and the hired help would be at the Silver Queen Saloon, getting ready for the evening rush—polishing the glasses, refilling the bottles, sweeping the floors. Bridgette would be giving the evening's offering of stew a last adjustment, adding a spoonful of salt, grinding a bit more pepper, or preparing a last batch of biscuits. If Inez were home and the reverend were in town, perhaps the two of them would both be sitting in the saloon's kitchen, talking about the local politics, or perhaps he'd be engaging Bridgette in a bit of theological banter. Indeed, Bridgette was so enamored of the good "Reverend Mister" that she was willing to forgive him almost anything he said about the Fall, the Trinity, and the Hereafter. Inez swallowed the ache rising in her throat.

Those times were gone. With Mark's return to Leadville, her world had capsized. Putting it to rights looked to be long and tangled process.

She wished that Reverend Sands could be the one traveling to her side instead of Mark. But the reverend was far away, unreachable, unaware of Mark's return and the events in Manitou. Inez squared her shoulders and buried the longing in her heart, determined to put Justice Sands out of mind. *Right now, Harmony and William must be my main concern. To keep them safe, I'd make a pact with the devil. And with Mark coming, that may just be what I'll have to do.*

◇◇◇

"So, what have you to show me?" Inez inquired. The sound of gravel crunching underfoot, the green leaves and colorful blooms of the late summer garden were like a balm to her soul.

Robert Calder, however, did not appear to find the turn around the garden as soothing an activity as she did. "Presently, Mrs. Stannert. First, I'll tell you of my conversation with Mr. Morrow. He was as disbelieving of the death of the little mare as I was. I showed him the feedbag contents. He, like you, had never seen the fruit of Herb Paris and had no idea how it came to be there. I described the plant to him, and he swore he'd not seen it growing in Manitou."

"What does it look like?"

"A single stalk, two hands high. At the top, four leaves are arranged in a single whorl around the stem. The very center of the whorl bears a solitary, arrow-petaled, star-like green flower with golden stamens. The fruit was as you saw."

"You said it grows wild in Britain and in the Continent. How did it come here?"

"Ah, that's the question. To grow the plant from a seed is a long process, two years from seed to fruit."

Inez gazed about the garden, the overwhelming profusion of plants.

"There is none here," Calder assured her. "I looked carefully upon my return, and have regarded this garden with great interest all summer. I know it well. So, there is no Herb Paris lurking among the mint, but there is plenty else. Stroll with me, Mrs. Stannert, and I shall educate you on the ways of herbs, and their flowers, leaves, and roots. But before we do that," he glanced about, "while we still have the place to ourselves, I'd like to show you this." He reached into his waistcoat pocket, extracted a small pasteboard, and offered it to Inez, adding, "When Alec's possessions were sent home along with his body for burial, we found this in one of his books."

Inez took the small rectangle, which she recognized as a calling card. On the front, in simple type, was set:

Dr. Galloway

She turned it over. The back was blank.

She looked up at him. "And?"

"That is all."

"You, of course, inquired about this Dr. Galloway around town and at the hotel where he last stayed?"

"Of course." He shook his head. "However, I probably went about it all wrong, asking as I did with the heat of accusation."

"You spoke to Dr. Prochazka?"

"Indeed. He initially claimed no knowledge of the man."

"Initially?"

"He will not talk to me now. I admit I unwisely voiced my skepticism regarding his methods and treatments. After that, we stopped conversing altogether, and he's given me the cold shoulder ever since." His expression tightened. "It will be interesting at tonight's *tableaux*. I suspect he would call down heaven's own lightning to strike me dead, if he could."

Inez played with the tassel on her parasol as she pondered. Bees buzzed sonorously about the garden. One blundered into her gloved hand, and she shook him off. "I shall tell you something as well, in case it proves useful in your endeavors." She related the small bit of conversation she had overhead in The Narrows between Nurse Crowson and Mr. Travers. "He indicated he wanted to meet the physician she spoke of, and she said she would arrange it," she finished. "Then, the next day, poof! Mr. Travers is gone from the Mountain Springs House. At the time, I thought that Mr. Travers was demanding to see Dr. Prochazka, but now, I wonder. Perhaps they were speaking of a different physician. Could Nurse Crowson be the link to this mysterious Dr. Galloway? Perhaps she takes the invalids who are doing poorly and arranges to have them transported away and treated by him?"

He cocked his head. "I'd not considered the nurse. She is like Prochazka's shadow, does his bidding. I could imagine her wishing to keep his good reputation intact. So perhaps her loyalty to him is a key."

He offered his arm. "Meanwhile, allow me to show you the garden."

She placed her hand on his jacket sleeve. "I shall be delighted, Mr. Calder. I know little about plants, besides the usual 'language of flowers' that I was taught at my mother's side."

He nodded, "My love of painting led to an interest in botany that became an obsession. That obsession has served me well here." He began, "Many plants that have healing powers can also be deadly. I was astounded, upon coming to the Mountain Springs House, to find such a wealth of them here. Someone is a careful gardener for so many of these to not only take root, but to thrive as well. The question is: to what purpose?"

With this introduction completed, he walked, pointed, and explained. "*Achillea millefolium* or yarrow is esteemed as a vulnerary, used to heal wounds and stop bleeding. Also has a reputation in Orkney for dispelling melancholy." He smiled at mention of the outpost islands of his homeland. "Over here is *Arenaria montana* or sandwort. It relieves cough, purifies and cleanses the blood, and reduces fever. Clematis is everywhere around Manitou. Unusual to see it in flower so late. It is used as a diuretic and diaphoretic, and useful locally and internally in—pardon me for being so blunt—syphilitic, cancerous, and other foul ulcers."

He walked on. "Ah yes. I thought of Mr. Pace, when I contemplated this one: *Digitalis Purpurea* or foxglove. Foxglove is used for dropsy, to strengthen a weak heart, yet in the improper proportions, can be used to stop one as well. I haven't mentioned it to the widow. I have my suspicions, that is all."

Inez stared at the clusters of tubular flowers. They were the most delicate shade of purple-pink, speckled within with darker purple. She could imagine a summer frock of those hues, perhaps in dotted swiss. "Do the flowers provide the poison?"

"The leaves. Tincture or an infusion in strength could have done it. With the other elements tossed into a tonic, who is to say if it would taste or smell much different?"

Inez swallowed hard. "I would imagine it easy enough to poison the entire hotel-full of guests, if one wished to, with none the wiser."

"Someone would catch on. But one by one, with people carefully chosen, that's a different story. Particularly when many are invalids to begin with. As you know, there is always a danger that the wrong person may take the dose."

The wrong person or the wrong horse, she thought.

He stopped and stared at a tall plant, with star-shaped, green-centered flowers in a long cluster. "Death camas," he said. "Nothing good about it. Every part is poisonous, with the seeds particularly so. Ingest, and you will experience difficulty breathing, coma, and death. Can't imagine what it's doing here, in a physician's domain. But then, this is a strange place, wouldn't you say, Mrs. Stannert?"

People began to drift out the back door, spilling onto the piazza, where the women opened their parasols and the gentlemen settled their straw boaters.

Calder said, "Our private time together is coming to an end, I fear. I must get to the livery and hurry off to collect Miss Carothers. Don't want to keep her waiting. I'll just add that I've identified all the plants in the garden, and there are others that I wonder at their cultivation. Lily of the Valley, for instance."

"Is Mr. Calder giving you a lesson on botany, Mrs. Stannert?"

They turned around. Behind them, Nurse Crowson smiled, a questioning tilt to her head. Inez couldn't imagine how she'd crept up behind them: the nurse was pushing an empty invalid chair, which certainly would have made some noise on the walkway.

"I'm just on my way to gather up a patient for an afternoon airing and couldn't help but overhear," said the nurse. "If you have any questions about the garden, I'd be happy to answer them."

"I have a question," said Calder, "perhaps you could direct me to where I could find this." He pulled out a folded handkerchief, and opened it, revealing three dull blue-black berries nestled inside. Mrs. Crowson had abandoned the chair, circling around it to see what Calder held. The berries revealed, she took a hasty step back. "How unusual. I don't believe I've seen the like. Where did you find them?"

Calder's face tightened. "It's Herb Paris."

She looked around the garden, as if lost. "Herb Paris? Well, I have heard of it. But we have none in the garden."

Mr. Lewis, who had been chatting with a couple further down the path, came hurrying their way. "Is something wrong, Nurse Crowson? Mrs. Stannert?" He ignored Calder.

But Calder wasn't the type to be ignored. "Yes, quite wrong, Mr. Lewis. Someone tried to poison my horse today."

"Your horse?" His gaze bounced between Calder and Inez. "I heard of your unfortunate ride today. Runaway buggies and carriages, an all too common occurrence here. That is why we encourage the ladies to hire drivers, or make use of Mr. Morrow, when he's not busy. It's very lucky that you escaped harm."

"But the horse was nae so lucky." Calder stepped toward Lewis, who shrank back and placed an arm around Mrs. Crowson, as if to protect her from Calder's ire as well.

"Someone put Herb Paris in my horse's feed," said Calder darkly. "It was no accident, but deliberate."

"Mr. Calder," Lewis said with dignity. "I cannot imagine why you would make such an accusation. I understand you are still overwrought from your brother's death. We did everything we could for him, while he was here. As I told you, he would not follow the regimens set forth. He would not listen to the doctor. What more could we do?"

"He withered and worsened, and ye threw him out into the snow." Calder closed the berries into a fist.

"Mr. Calder, I believe that you would be happier at some other venue," Lewis said. "We have extended hospitality to you all summer, only to have you conduct the most villainous campaign against us. We have been the best hosts possible, yet you persist in slandering us left and right. Mr. Calder, I suggest that you find other lodgings on the morrow or the day after at the latest."

Inez caught her breath. But Calder didn't explode. Instead, he refolded the berries into his handkerchief and pocketed them. "So am I to be approached next by the helpful Dr. Galloway who will provide miracle cures for my bunions?"

Lewis' stern expression faded into startlement. "Dr. Galloway? I, I've not heard of him."

Nurse Crowson stood mute by Lewis' side, hands clasped together, staring at Calder as if he were mad.

"No. Of course not," said Calder in disgust. He turned to Inez with a quizzical raised eyebrow. "D'ye think Mrs. Galbreaith might take me in, in her pleasant boarding house? Or perhaps I should seek out lodgings at the Colorado Springs Hotel?" He turned back to Lewis and said, "I'll be out by end of tomorrow, I promise you that. But I'll not be far, and I'll not stop searching for the truth behind my brother's death."

He turned on his heel and headed to the livery.

Chapter Thirty-one

"Herb Paris?" Dr. Zuckerman pursed his lips and patted them delicately with his napkin.

Inez tried not to look at the small dribblets of crème fraiche from dessert trapped in his beard.

"Well, Mrs. Stannert, it's not part of my usual pharmacopoeia. Let me think. I can recall this: It's narcotic. When ingested, it would be most upsetting, perhaps causing delirium and convulsions, depending on the dose. Yes, a poison, most definitely." He squinched up his eyes. "If I recall correctly, Linnaeus, the naturalist, asserted that the root operates as a gentle emetic, like ipecacuanha. But you'll not find it growing here in Colorado, nor anywhere in the Americas, I believe."

"Is it deadly to people? Animals?" Inez persisted. It had taken the full eight courses of the dinner to finally wind the conversation around to this topic. Zuckerman, once again her dinner companion, had waxed enthusiastic about the area's hunting and fishing, the new dairy concern down the road, and General Palmer's efforts to promote Colorado Springs back east. Talk about herbs, plants, and their medical uses, had proved difficult to interject into the flow of his monologue.

"I cannot say, given that I cannot precisely recall just how poisonous the various plant constituents are." The scrape of chairs echoed through the dining room as diners rose. Zuckerman set his napkin down, creaked to his feet, and pulled out Inez's chair so she could stand. "Perhaps Dr. Prochazka, since he is a native of Europe and trained on the Continent, might have a familiarity about it."

She stifled a sigh. Asking Dr. Prochazka any medical-related question was something she wanted to avoid, if possible. Besides finding him a tad intimidating, she was afraid that asking questions about poisonous plants and materials would, in return, unleash a crescendo of questions that she would have to sidestep and dance around. All she wanted was information as to whether Herb Paris could, indeed, have been what sent the mare to her doom.

She cast an eye about the room. Neither Harmony nor Aunt Agnes had been present at that seating. They had taken an early dinner to prepare for the *tableaux*. No Calder, either, and she'd not seen Epperley doing his usual rounds about the tables. Instead, Lewis had been host, and Inez had watched him as he chatted, presented bottles of wine, and directed the waiters. She observed him blundering into several chairs, and once nearly colliding with a waiter carrying a full tray of plated boiled tongue and chili sauce. His smile wavered, and she thought she detected a tremor in his hands.

Nurse Crowson had been there, too, with her usual basket of bottles and her equanimous demeanor.

As Inez took Dr. Zuckerman's arm and allowed him to escort her from the dining area, she noted a paucity of young women and men and began to wonder just how many of the missing were participating in her aunt's *tableaux*.

"I understand your aunt, Mrs. Underwood, has been very busy with her artistically-inspired scenes," said Dr. Zuckerman. "She even persuaded Dr. Prochazka to participate. That, in itself, is a major feat, for he is not one to socialize, as a rule, preferring as he does to focus on his research into pthisis and his patients."

She turned down Dr. Zuckerman's offer of a stroll around the front veranda, pleading for a moment alone before the doors to the music room opened to display Agnes' flesh-and-blood masterpieces.

Seeking solitude, Inez slipped out the back door and stepped to the edge of the garden. The unseasonably warm evening had pushed the plants into aromatic hysteria. She inhaled. Herbal and floral fragrances assaulted her—sharp, soft, bitter, sweet, cloying—and over all rested the blanket scent of freshly turned earth. Crickets chirred, a temperate breeze rustled leaves, stirred branches, caressed her face. Inez glanced over at the livery: a single flickering light lay a dim path out the partially opened door, probably Morrow or the boy Billy, she guessed, giving the animals their evening feed.

Then, she heard voices, low, intense, a different tenor from the social babble that wafted ever so faintly from the front veranda of the hotel. The voices seemed to come from the far side of the hotel. She walked toward the conversation, curious, keeping her steps light.

As she approached the corner, she heard Lewis saying, "Galloway. Galloway, he asked about a Dr. Galloway."

Crowson's soothing voice replied, "A coincidence. A common name."

"But I've not heard of a Dr. Galloway around here, and I know nearly every practitioner from one end of Colorado Springs and Manitou to the other."

"Perhaps a physician passing through town? You know the area draws them, like honey draws flies. Please, Victor, do not agitate yourself."

His voice rose in pitch, tinged with panic, "Don't call me that! Not here. Remember where we are."

Victor? Inez cocked her head, intrigued. She leaned dangerously close to the corner, wondering if the nurse's response might shed light on Lewis' odd exclamation.

After a long pause, Nurse Crowson continued, her words and tone a balm to ease a troubled spirit. "Franklin, look at your hands, they are shaking. Let's go back inside and I'll fix you some tea to calm you down. You must be there when the doors open. You need only make one circuit of the *tableaux* and say something pleasant to Mrs. Underwood. She will be expecting praise, and you should give it to her. Then, no one will mind if you resume your post at the desk."

There was the click of a latch, an elongated rectangle of light illuminated a bare patch of ground and then narrowed with the closing of the door.

Now why would mention of a Dr. Galloway send Mr. Lewis into such a state? Obviously, the name is familiar to him, and upsetting as well. And why did the nurse call him "Victor" and why did he respond so strongly to it?

Inez waited a moment, then circled around the corner to where Lewis and Nurse Crowson had stood. On this far side, facing away from the livery, the ground fell away in a gentle slope. There was, she now realized, not only a door tucked under the veranda, but several small, unassuming windows as well, shuttered tight. The lower floor extended that length of the hotel. Thinking of the stairs leading up to the hotel entrance proper, she realized that there would certainly be room underneath the main floor for storage and such.

But a door?

An entrance and exit tucked away where most guests would not even notice. She wondered if it was used by all the hotel staff or if it was private. She was tempted to examine it, perhaps turn the knob, but decided that that would probably be unwise. *For all I know they are standing on the other side, even now.* Retreating back to the garden area, she gauged that the door and whatever lay behind it was under the kitchen and dining area of the hotel.

Noticing the lack of voices outside, she picked up her skirts to hurry up the stairs, and made her way to the reception area.

The foyer and entry hall were crammed with guests and visitors, all jostling, waiting for the doors to open to the music room. Some parents had their older children with them, and she heard one mother instruct her son, "*Tableaux vivants* are 'living pictures.' The people in the scenes are like statues. They are posed and supposed to hold especially still so we may view the scene, just like we would at a museum. Do not talk to any of them, not even your sister, or try to make her laugh or respond in any way."

"How come they picked her and not me?" he groused.

The mother smoothed down his cowlick. "When you can hold still without wiggling, sneezing, or sticking out your tongue for ten minutes at a time, perhaps they will."

The doors were flung open by a radiant Aunt Agnes, dressed in a startling rose and purple ensemble that frothed with lace and flounces. Inez's first thought was how it was a dress appropriate for a younger woman. Her second thought was that it didn't matter what fashion might dictate: the cut and color suited Aunt Agnes perfectly. The audience streamed into the room at last, Inez pulled into the wake. The room had been transformed, emptied of chairs, the grand piano pushed to one side. Different tableau groupings were staged around the walls. Behind each posed scene, someone had tacked muslin over the wallpaper, providing in some cases a plain backdrop, and in others, a painted one.

The next thing Inez noticed was that the displays had a decidedly classical theme. The posed players, for the most part, wore what looked like classical Grecian-style draperies that covered the limbs from ankle to elbow. Inez wondered, briefly, how many Mountain Springs House sheets and tablecloths had died so that Aunt Agnes' *tableaux* might live.

Aunt Agnes was happily occupied with greeting various people and accepting the exclamations of amazement and admiration, leaving Inez free to wander as she wished. She circled through the room, taking in each scene and looking for Harmony, Jonathan, Calder, and any others she might recognize. Harmony was posed as Diana, readily identifiable by the quiver of arrows on her back, and a small moon crown holding back her dark hair, which had been powdered white. Her other hand rested on a small stuffed deer with antlers lashed to its head. A woman in front of Inez exclaimed, "*Diane de Versailles!* The very likeness!" She added in a lower tone to her female companion,

"Although thankfully she's clad in a longer gown than the actual statue."

Jonathan posed nearby with a painted wooden replica of a lyre and a stuffed snake curled about a wooden stump. Inez thought he made a rather solemn and pale Apollo. If she had been choosing players, Inez supposed she would have chosen Epperley, with his white-blonde hair and Anglo-Saxon good looks. *Aunt Agnes probably assigned Jonathan the role to complement Harmony's role as Diana.* An amateur painting of a vibrant yellow sun resting in a chariot splashed the muslin behind him.

The next *tableau* featured three young girls, obviously enjoying themselves and having a hard time not whispering and giggling. Their arms twined around each others' shoulders, and Inez guessed they were the three graces. "Aglaia?" said Inez, testing them. One twitched a smile. Another teetered in her carefully draped sheet and said in a stage whisper, "I'm Euphrosyne, and this is Thalia!"

She finally stopped before a puzzling scene that included Calder, Epperley, Dr. Prochazka, and three female guests, including the red-haired and befreckled Mrs. Banscombe. Inez cocked her head and tried to make sense of the grouping. Epperley wore a silver bowl on his head like a helmet and held a brass caduceus that Inez recognized from the statue of Hermes at the top of the entrance staircase. He stood behind Calder, who knelt on one knee, in a beseeching pose, arms outstretched to Prochazka. Prochazka seemed to be basically playing himself, frowning darkly at Epperley and Calder. The physician leaned on a rough-hewn tree limb with a stuffed snake twined up the length. The three women, arms entwined like the young Graces at the other end of the room, stood to the far right. All except Epperley had clematis wreaths around their brows. It looked all the world to Inez as if Dr. Prochazka was a disapproving father, denying two suitors access to his three daughters. One of the suitors was clearly Hermes. But the rest?

That was when Susan said at her elbow, "What do you think?"

Inez turned in surprise. "I thought you were to take photographs. I must say, it's quite a production that Aunt Agnes put together. I'm impressed. This had to come together quickly. I'm not certain how she did it."

Susan smiled, eyes on Calder. "She is a wonder, your aunt. I took all the photographs before the doors opened. I thought it best to do so before everyone arrived. It took a little longer than I'd planned, as the room kept getting smoky from the flash powder. My part is done now, so I can just enjoy it."

"Do you know what this scene is?" Inez asked.

"I can explain it to you. Let's move on a bit so others can take their turn to see."

They wandered over to the French doors, where a table had been set up with a punch bowl and cups. Susan said, "You're not alone in your confusion. I had no idea myself what it was supposed to be. It was apparently Dr. Prochazka's idea and is taken from a scene in the Museum Pio Clemens in Rome. Not Greek, but Roman, which is close enough for a tableau, I suppose. It features Mercury and a merchant approaching Asclepius. The three women are the graces Meditrine, Hygeia, and Panacea."

The light went on. "Asclepius, ah yes. I heard Dr. Prochazka rail on about him."

Harmony nodded. "Dr. Prochazka wouldn't pose for a photograph until he had explained it all fully to me. He evidently doesn't like all the little statues of Hermes scattered about the hotel. He said that if they won't honor the real god of medicine, Asclepius, they could at least choose one of his three daughters, who symbolize medicine, hygiene, and healing. Anyway, he told Mrs. Underwood that if she wanted him in a tableau, it would have to be a scene of his choosing. She agreed, saying that as long as it was classical in nature, she would go along with it."

"I just had no idea he would pick something so obscure." Aunt Agnes' voice sounded nearly in Inez's ear. She moved between Susan and Inez, threading her arms through both of theirs. "I had hoped Dr. Prochazka would pose as Zeus or Poseidon. I thought he'd be perfect as a god with a thunderbolt or trident." She sighed. "People have no idea what the tableau is supposed to be, it confuses everyone. I should simply stand there and explain to anyone who passes by. Well, at least it *is* classical." She beamed at Inez. "So, dear niece, what do you think?"

"Extraordinary," conceded Inez. "I don't know how you managed it."

Aunt Agnes looked satisfied. "I must circulate so as to not neglecting my duties as a hostess." She sailed off into the crowd, a pillar of rose and violet energy.

No sooner had Agnes moved on than Inez heard Mr. Lewis say behind her, "Pardon me, Mrs. Stannert?"

Without taking her eyes from her aunt, who had snared Dr. Zuckerman and was gesticulating at the medically-themed tableau, she responded, "Yes, Mr. Lewis?"

She turned, almost expecting to see Nurse Crowson hovering at Lewis' side.

But the person who stood next to Lewis wasn't the nurse.

Lewis said, unnecessarily, "Madam, your husband has arrived."

Chapter Thirty-two

Inez's limbs were as immobile as the living statues around her.

Mark stood by Mr. Lewis, smiling, top hat in hand, travel coat draped over one arm.

In their early years together, it had astonished her how Mark Stannert could spend hours in a rattling train—ashes, cinders, and dust sifting through windows and down onto everything—or an equally arduous amount of time in a stagecoach or on horseback, and yet, upon arrival, look as elegant and dapper as if he'd strolled out from an elegant resort. She had finally come to accept that as a given, after many years of marriage.

What astonished her *this* particular time was her immediate, nearly overwhelming impulse to throw herself at him in sheer relief at his arrival.

That impulse, however, quickly died.

Mr. Lewis was addressing Mark. "We have put you in one of the suites that recently opened up. I do hope you will find it to your liking. It's one of our best, with a perfect view of the creek, the bridge, the springs, and across the valley to the foothills of Pike's Peak. We are in the process of moving Mrs. Stannert's trunks and boxes into the suite, as well."

That unstuck her feet from the floor. "You're moving my *things* into the *suite?*"

He retreated under the pressure of her incredulity and anger. "Well, not me personally, of course. The hotel staff is doing the packing and moving. Is there something wrong?"

Inez knew she had to bring her roiling emotions under control. Sharing a suite with Mark had not been part of her plan, but she realized now that it was, of course, a logical response on the part of the hotel.

Mark moved forward and took her elbow, saying amiably to Mr. Lewis, "We are most appreciative of your hospitality. Mrs. Stannert and I approve of a hotel that puts its customers' comforts, needs, and desires first, and foresees them, when possible. Isn't that true, darlin'?" He squeezed her arm, a reminder to be civil, hold her tongue, play her part.

Steaming inside, Inez managed a smile at Mr. Lewis, even while she envisioned ripping the brass caduceus from Epperley's posed hand and skewering the hotelier with it. "But of course, dear husband. That's certainly one of the many virtues I've had the pleasure of experiencing here at the Mountain Springs House, and one of the primary reasons I urged you to cut short your other business obligations and come, posthaste, to Manitou."

"We believe in catering to our clientele." Lewis' radiant expression could put Apollo in the shade. "Please, relax and enjoy the pageantry here, while we put your rooms to rights. Shall I take your coat, Mr. Stannert? We shall have it brushed and ready for you, bright and early on the morrow."

Mark handed him the overcoat, and let go of Inez, offering her his arm instead. Inez took it, and he said, "Why don't we look around, and you can tell me what this is all about." He then leaned toward her and said in her ear, "I had nothing to do with the room arrangements, darlin'. Just so you know."

His warm breath tickled her ear, and she drew back a bit and fluttered her fan. "If you say so. *Dearest.*" The emphasis left no doubt as to how she felt about the whole affair. "I imagine we shall manage. We always do, don't we? Now, I have several people to whom I should introduce you. Some are family, whom you've not met or whom you haven't seen in a long time. Oh, you knew Miss Carothers was here in Manitou, didn't you? I believe I told you that much."

Susan stood stock-still by the punch bowl, crystal cup in hand. "Hello, Mr. Stannert," she said. Her eyes flashed to Inez, searching for clues on how to act.

Inez nodded encouragingly and said, "Miss Carothers has been a godsend to me here. How lucky we are to be friends."

Mark bowed to Susan. "It's good to see you again, Miss Carothers. Our paths haven't crossed since I returned to Leadville. I am glad that you and my wife have continued your strong friendship."

Susan bobbed her head uncertainly. "It's good to see you again, Mr. Stannert, and in good health." Inez saw her gaze linger on the scar on Mark's face, before flicking to the silver-headed cane he leaned upon.

"What brings you to Manitou, Miss Carothers?" Mark asked. "My lovely wife told me you were accompanying her, but not the reason. Looking for new vistas for your considerable talents?"

"I'm here to learn some techniques from Mrs. Anna Galbreaith, who does marvelous photography in and around Manitou and the Garden of the Gods." Susan colored. Her hands jumped a bit, sending the punch cup splashing. She looked down at it in surprise, as if she'd forgotten she held it, and then added hastily, "Mr. Stannert, you should try the punch! It's made with the local soda waters. There's lemon, sugar, a touch of mint. I'm not certain of all the ingredients, but it's quite good."

Mark moved to the bowl and looked at Inez, eyebrows raised.

"No, thank you. I find the local waters do not agree with me." Inez snapped the fan through the air in vicious little swipes.

"Dear niece, surely you are going to introduce me to this elegant gentleman?" Aunt Agnes had abandoned Dr. Zuckerman and swooped back.

"Of course, dear aunt. Mrs. Underwood, allow me to introduce to you my husband, Mr. Stannert. Mr. Stannert, Mrs. Underwood, my aunt."

"Your husband?" Her blue eyes went wide. "I thought you weren't arriving until next week, Mr. Stannert. Such a pleasure." She offered him her hand.

Mark abandoned the punch and took Aunt Agnes' hand. "The pleasure is all mine." He bowed over it like a courtier.

Aunt Agnes looked Mark up and down, taking in his impeccable grooming, the expensive cut of his hand-tailored suit, and the silver-headed cane with obvious delight. "Why, niece, I had no idea you married such a model gentleman. All the stories I've heard make him out to be such a *rascal*," She said the word as if it was a charming trait. "Of course, I never met him while he was in New York courting you." Inez could translate that as well: Mark had dropped into her life, wooed her in a whirlwind, and two weeks later, they had eloped. Hardly a proper length of time for a courtship.

Agnes continued, "It's high time that he be properly brought into the family."

The family that disinherited me for marrying him a decade ago. Inez wanted to spit.

After offering up the punch to Aunt Agnes, which she accepted, Mark turned to Inez and said, "Why don't you tell me about these *tableaux,* darlin'?"

Aunt Agnes set down the punch and attached herself to his other arm. "Didn't your wife tell you? I am the master creator of this event. I can tell you everything you want to know, probably *more* than you want to know."

"There could never be too much, Mrs. Underwood, should the explanation come from such a charming, well-learned, and intelligent woman as yourself."

Inez wanted to roll her eyes, but forbore. She knew, from growing up around Aunt Agnes, that her flamboyant, determined aunt harbored the belief that she soared miles above most mere humans in acumen and intelligence. Including above most men. Mark, with his easy, apparently inborn ability to read people, had managed to worm his way into Aunt Agnes' approval, without hardly lifting a finger.

Inez took as deep a breath as her stays allowed and tried to tamp her rising irritation at Mark's dead-on flattery. She pasted a smile on her face and held his arm close, in case eyes should swivel their way. And there were plenty of calculating eyes upon the three of them as they made the circuit of the room, with Aunt Agnes talking and gesticulating at every station.

Toward the end of the circuit, Aunt Agnes, with apologies, moved to the center of the room, clapped her hands, and said, "Thank you, all. I believe we should give our actors their due and allow them to stand down and approach the punch bowl, at will."

Applause rippled around the room as each of the statues relaxed and stepped away from their stations. Inez watched as Calder and Epperley bounded apart as if driven by opposite energies. Calder glared at Epperley with open dislike. Inez gripped Mark's arm tighter and said under her breath, "The dark fellow over there is Robert Calder, from New York and Scotland. His brother met an unfortunate end here. I'll explain later. Epperley is the hotel's manager. A remittance man, you know the sort. He has staked a lot on the success of the hotel."

"Hmm. Who is the tall fellow who looks like he'd rather be anywhere than here?"

"That's the hotel's physician, Dr. Prochazka. He's the main draw for this resort. People come from all over the world to be treated by him. Dr. Prochazka is widely respected in such circles and trained at the University of Göttingen. He may be brilliant, but he's not particularly sociable."

"Immune to your charms?" murmured Mark.

She smiled brilliantly at him. "I haven't made a serious effort. Ah! Here come my sister and brother-in-law. Be on your best behavior."

After introductions and small talk, Mark said, "You must pardon me, it's been a long journey, and I would like to spend time with my wife." Inez pinched the inside of his arm through his jacket, hard. "I'm most desirous of seeing my son after all this time. Would it be possible?"

"Of course!" Harmony was perfectly kind, sweet, but Inez detected a wary distance. "Inez, do you want me to go with you to William's room?"

"I know the way," she assured her sister.

Calder and Susan approached as well, and Susan introduced Calder to Mark, then turned to Inez. "Mr. Calder is going to help load my photographic equipment up in the buggy and take me back to Mrs. Galbreaith's," she said. "Mrs. Galbreaith and I are planning to wander around town tomorrow and see what images we might capture close to town. And then..." She looked at Calder.

Calder said, "After an early morning stroll, I shall relocate to one of the other Manitou hotels, perhaps the Beebe or Manitou House. Once I am settled, I will collect Miss Carothers and we shall waltz the night away at the Cliff House tomorrow evening." He smiled down at Susan. "It will be my reward for all that I must do on the morrow."

It took some time for the Stannerts to make their way out the room, what with the introductions, nods and bows, and exchanges of pleasantries. Once they reached the reception desk, Mr. Lewis handed Mark a key, saying, "You'll find the suite on the second floor, all the way down to your right."

Inez paused at the directions and asked, "Isn't that Mrs. Pace's room?"

"It was."

"Where did she go?"

Lewis looked distinctly uncomfortable. "I believe she found lodging at the Cliff House. She decided she needed a place where she could have a little more quiet and seclusion."

"That does not sound like Kirsten Pace," Inez said under her breath as they went up the stairs.

"You know her?"

"She is one of the reasons I called you to come early. I'll explain in a minute. Ah, here is William's room. He has a nanny that stays with him."

She knocked softly on the door and called out, "Lily? It's me, Mrs. Stannert."

After a short while, the door opened a slice. "He's asleep, ma'am," she looked to be half-asleep herself.

"I've brought Mr. Stannert with me. He would like to see William for a moment."

Lily was suddenly wide awake. She stared at Mark, as if he were a nightmare that had, somehow, crept out of the shadow world of dreams and stood now before her. "You're Wilkie's pa?" she asked faintly.

Mark nodded. "That I am."

"Oh." Her eyes slid sideways, a tremulous quiver in her chin. "Are you, are you taking him tonight?"

"No, no," Inez said hastily. "Mr. Stannert just wants to see his son."

After a pause, Lily slowly opened the door wider and let them into the bedroom.

Inez led him to the bed by the window. The little calico dog of his infancy was crumpled in one fist, the thumb from the other hand secured in the mouth. It was an odd sensation for Inez to stand with Mark, side by side, watching William sleep.

After a moment, Mark pulled off one glove and gently, very gently, laid a hand on top of William's head, like a benediction. William stirred, but didn't wake.

"He's grown so much," Mark said softly.

Inez crossed her arms. *All this wouldn't have happened if you hadn't left the way you did. Left us alone. We would have seen him grow together.* The hurt of abandonment flooded through her, shaking her with the power of the early days. She bit her tongue against accusations that no longer mattered.

It's over. I've vowed to only go forward and not look back, and that's what I will do.

Chapter Thirty-three

Once they entered the suite, Mark lit the gas lamp on the table in the sitting room while Inez did a quick reconnaissance. She was happy to find there were two bedrooms, with doors, separated by a sitting room. The trunks had been shuffled into the larger of the two bedrooms. She opened her trunk and was relieved to find her pocket revolver resting atop her neatly folded stockings. *I should be carrying this, not leaving it packed away. This place has lulled me with its high society and manners.*

She turned to Mark, standing in the doorway. "I will take this room, and you can have the other. We will get your trunks moved tomorrow."

"As you wish," was his only response. He strolled over to a carpet bag, opened it, and pulled out two goblets from the Silver Queen and a familiar bottle.

"Brandy!" Inez exclaimed.

"I thought, this being a hotel dedicated to the recovery of health and the balancing of the humors, I should bring a little *aqua vitae*. For medicinal purposes, of course." He held the bottle so she could see it. "Your favorite, I believe?"

"My favorite, as you well know." She moved past him to the table and chairs in the sitting room, saying, "We must talk. Now."

Mark poured a measure of brandy into each glass, picked one up, and swirled the liquid around. "Yes, we must. But first," he handed her the glass and picked up the other, "to a truce."

She narrowed her eyes. "A truce? What kind of truce?"

He set his glass down. "Now, darlin'. You sent for me, remember, and reading between the lines, I gathered you were in some distress, so dropped everything and came right away. I'm here to help. But in return, I want something from you." He looked at her, his blue eyes colorless, taking light from the table lamp.

She drew back. "How *dare* you presume!"

"Darlin', don't *you* presume." He sat down at the table, and indicated the chair opposite. "Here's the deal. You tell me what the trouble is, and what you want me to do. In return, we set our differences aside and act the happy family, and present a solid front. To your family. To William. No washing dirty linen in public. You remain civil to me, and I to you."

Inez cradled the warming glass, watching him closely. "That's all?"

"That's all. I only ask that you hear me out without shooting at me."

"Ha!" She set the glass down with a *tink*. "I knew it. You want me to halt divorce proceedings. That's what you're really after."

Mark rolled his glass between his hands. "I'd be lying if I said no. I'm hoping once I tell you my side of the story, explain what happened after I left our house that day, that you'll give it due consideration and eventually take me back."

"So. You want me to sit here while you spin out your tale."

"I want you to listen without interrupting. To hear me out to the end."

Rather than answer right away, Inez brought the glass to her mouth and let the brandy slide in. The spirits-filled heat in her mouth hinted of apples and recalled a hot summer evening, long ago. She and Mark lay on a grassy hill, brandy close at hand, the night heat having sapped all their energy. Her head rested on Mark's chest, riding the rise and fall of his breath. All her senses had been captive to the act of inhalation and exhalation, and by the panorama of a dark sky invaded by stars.

Inez set the glass and her memories aside. "Very well. Since this involves my sister and her husband, I will listen. And I won't interrupt."

She crossed her arms. Mark raised one eyebrow.

Inez shrugged. "The deal didn't include that I believe you. Only that I listen."

"Fair enough. I know you can sniff out a lie quicker'n a coon dog can pick up the scent of a ring-tailed bandit. I'd be a fool to lie to you, Inez."

Mark tipped another inch of brandy into her glass, and an equal measure into his own.

He began. "Last year, May ninth. Our boy just turned five months old. We'd been talking about selling the saloon, moving on for his health. Going to Denver or maybe making our big move to San Francisco."

Inez kept her arms crossed, her back rigid. *Would he really think I need reminding? The day is branded on my mind and heart forever.* She said, "You said you were going to talk to some possible buyers for the saloon. You thought you could play one off another, see who would offer the most."

He held up a finger, like a teacher gently remonstrating a truculent student. "My time to talk, Inez. That's our deal." He continued, "I made all the arrangements, signed the papers. Had money in my pocket from a handshake deal backed by cash."

He stopped, took a deep breath, and said, "I was on my way to the Silver Queen, bringing the papers for you and Abe to sign and put the cash in the safe, when I did something stupid." He swirled the brandy in his glass, took another taste, set it down and said, "I stopped for a drink at the Comique. Just a quick one, you understand. I was trying to settle my mind on our next steps, thinking about how long it'd take to complete the transactions and when we might be able to leave Leadville."

He had been leaning forward, over the table. He now settled back and looked directly at Inez. "I said I wouldn't lie and I won't. I was talking to one of the actresses who had finished up a two-night show. She was saying good-bye to the folks she knew, and I offered to buy her a drink. We talked."

Inez squinched her eyes shut, as if that would make his words disappear. *Actresses. Always, it was actresses.*

"Darlin', I swear. We only talked."

"Go on," she said through gritted teeth.

"Anyhow, I suppose I must've been a little careless and someone got a look at the roll I was carryin'. Because when I went out back to Stillborn Alley to relieve myself, he must've followed me." He stopped and passed a hand over his eyes. "Going through the door to the alley is the last thing I remember."

The Comique. He was just halfway down the block, other side of the street from the Silver Queen. Inez picked up her brandy with shaking hands and took a larger mouthful than was prudent, ignoring the burn as it raced down her throat.

"As to what happened then," Mark said, "I only know what I was told. When I didn't come back after a while, the actress sent some Johnny-boy out to look for me. He found me bleeding in the mud, head stove in, stripped of near everything except what God gave me at birth, and damn near dead. The actress, Josephine's her name, had me bundled in a blanket, carried to her wagon, and she took me with her out of town."

Inez leaned forward, incredulous. "You bought her one drink. You talked. You were beaten, and she *took* you with her? Like you were some homeless mongrel she found on a street corner?"

"I know, I know." He sounded tired. "Later, I heard I wasn't the only one who was unlucky that night. I heard the papers called it the bloodiest night in Leadville's calendar. Garrotings, robberies, assaults, killings on State Street, Harrison Avenue, up on Capitol Hill, on the road to Malta…But I didn't find all that out until much later."

"I remember that night." She looked away, so he couldn't see her pain. "Later, when we could not find you anywhere, I thought you had been killed in the melee. That you had been robbed, killed, tossed down some abandoned mine shaft."

He didn't remonstrate her for interrupting, simply tipped more brandy into her glass. "Josephine tells me she thought I'd died six times over the following two days. She finally found a doctor, only to have him tell her she'd do better to set aside money for a coffin rather than spend it on bandages, ointments, and restoratives. Josephine's not a woman to believe anything she doesn't want to hear. I gather she threw him out, swearing he was a charlatan and a carpetbagger. Still, it was months before I recovered my senses."

"How many?" Inez asked.

Mark frowned. "How many what?"

"Months."

He looked at the gas flame in the lamp, brow furrowed. "Six, maybe seven. And my leg didn't heal for a long while. It still isn't right, even now. All that time, we kept moving. She had to go where the work was, so we crisscrossed Kansas, Colorado, Wyoming, New Mexico territory…never did come back to Leadville."

I'll bet she made sure of that. Inez bit her tongue to keep the words from escaping.

"When I was finally well enough," he said, "I told her everything. That I was married. That I'd left you waiting in Leadville that night. That I had a son, and would have to go back. And I started writing letters, to you and Abe."

"We never got them," Inez said tersely. "Not a single one. Did you give them to Josephine to mail?"

He looked at her in honest surprise.

Inez sighed and looked away. *How can a man be so smart about the ways of men yet so stupid about women? He gave her letters to mail, and she probably threw them away, first chance she got.*

"In every letter I sent," he continued, "I asked that you reply to me care of General Delivery, Denver. We crossed through Denver every few months, and I'd check. But I never got a reply from you or Abe. So, I thought, maybe you'd both just given me up for dead and sold the saloon. Maybe Abe had headed to New Orleans or San Francisco, and maybe you'd gone back East, home to your family, with William. It took a while, but I finally remembered your family's address in New York. I sent letters there, to you, to your father, your mother." He shook his head. "No one answered. But I was certain that was where you'd gone. I figured maybe your father wasn't giving you the letters…after all, he'd been against our marriage from the start, and would probably be glad to have you think I was dead and gone. So, I thought, well, I'd start all over again. Go back to gambling, since we were traveling so much, and make enough to bring you and William back. When I had enough, I figure'd head east, knock on your daddy's door, and win you back."

Inez shook her head at the impossibility of it all, the upside-down nature of what she was hearing. She picked up her snifter, deciding that, yes, she needed another sip, or two, or more, to get through the rest of the evening.

Mark said, "It was sheer luck that I happened on the divorce notice in the *Rocky Mountain News*. I had to read it several times to accept what I was seeing: You were still in Leadville. We were in Denver at the time. Josephine had to head to Kansas City, and I told her I would be returning to Leadville." He stopped and looked steadily at Inez. "I took the first train up I could get. You know the rest."

I don't know "the rest" by half. She had questions, so many questions demanding to be asked. Things that didn't make sense about his story, questions about Josephine and their relationship during his time away. But the expression on his face couldn't have said it plainer if he'd shouted: he was done talking about his life during those missing months. Done for now.

Still…

She leaned forward, having to ask, needing to read his face when he answered, to see if he was telling the whole truth, a half truth, or an outright lie. "Did you really write letters while you were recovering and afterwards? You wrote to Leadville, and back to New York?"

He lifted one hand wearily and dropped it. "What shall I swear on that will convince you I'm telling the truth? On my mother's grave? The Bible? How about on our son, since the blood that runs through his veins belongs to both of us." He gave her a level stare. "I swear on our son that I tried to reach you, in every way I could."

She waited. "Are you done? Have I performed 'adequately' to fulfill my side of the bargain?"

He shifted in his chair. "I'm done. Now, what's the real story here at the Mountain Springs House."

Inez drank deeply and waited for the liquor to warm her limbs and soften her words. Then, she started from the beginning, with the terrifying trip from Leadville and Mr. Pace's death.

She finished with the Herb Paris, Calder's near-miss, the wild buggy ride and unfortunate demise of the livery horse. At that point, her glass was empty and the bottle nearly so. "I realized that I wasn't making much headway," she said slowly. "If this were Leadville, it would be different. But I'm too bound here. Too confined by rules and society expectations, too concerned for family." She shook her head. "I realized I needed help. I thought that if anyone could help me get to the bottom of the doings here, it would be you." The words were bitter and difficult to say, but she said them.

Inez added, "They are obviously hungry for investors at the hotel. I understand they are planning to expand and grow their operations. Everyone is expecting a boom in Manitou. When will it come? Hard to say. But the sick, the dying, they arrive in ever-increasing numbers, looking for a miracle. Right now, many seem to believe that miracle will arise from Dr. Prochazka. I suppose those who are behind the Mountain Springs House are eager to keep that belief alive and fan the flame. On the other hand, the people who do not recover, who falter and fail despite the best treatments…well, how convenient for all if they just go away in some way or another, wouldn't you think?"

Mark nodded somberly. "You still have Mrs. Pace's medicine bottle from the stagecoach?"

The bottle was safely tucked away in one of her hat boxes. Inez brought it to Mark. He looked it over carefully, rubbed his thumb along the stopper, and removed it to sniff at the vapors trapped inside. "Can't tell anything through the mint," he said, and restoppered it. "Why would they want to kill Mrs. Pace?"

"Because she was working to convince her husband to back off from investing here? Because she was outspoken about the efficacy of the medical treatments?"

"But why kill the man's wife? Seems that would halt any chance of gaining an investor. Particularly if the tonic was to blame."

"She has a weak heart," Inez explained. "If she had taken her dose and died in Leadville, it would have been put down to the altitude and her condition. None would consider a tonic she had been taking all summer without ill effects."

Mark looked away, deep in thought. The gas-fed flame inside the glass lampshade hissed and flared.

"Strange," he said finally.

"What is strange?"

He glanced at her, smoothed his mustache, and then said, "You recall I've started a Friday night poker game for out-of-towners."

"Of course," she said stiffly.

He continued. "The night before you left, I had a couple of wealthy greenhorns from back East show up. They were taking in the town, looking over the mines, weighing where best to put their money. The desk clerk from the Clairmont directed them my way, saying if they wanted to take part in a friendly game of the better sort, to go to the Silver Queen and tell Mark Stannert that he'd sent them over." A brief smile flashed over his face. "That boy has a lot of horse-sense. He only sends the ones primed to have a good time and with money to spend." Then he sobered. "One of the men was named Pace."

Inez sat up straighter, dread welling up inside. "Mark. You didn't."

Mark sighed and splayed one hand on the table. The light winked off his wedding ring. "I was sociable and hospitable as always, but this Pace fellow was a constant complainer. Going on about Leadville being washed up, no opportunities, on its way to being a ghost town once the silver disappeared. Ended up driving most of the other players away, until it was just him, me, and another greenhorn from Tabor's hotel." He drummed his fingers on the table. "Pace made some bad moves at the table, and I wasn't inclined to be lenient. He got under my skin, so I decided it would be an opportune time to provide him with a different kind of 'investment opportunity' and add to our bank account, courtesy of his funds."

"Oh no, Mark." She rested her head in her hands.

"Well, darlin', how was I to know what would happen and that you'd take up with his widow, of all people? Anyhow, I relieved him of all he carried and then some. Although I won't press the widow with the script he signed. Didn't plan to push it any further, as it was."

"Oh, Mark." She couldn't come up with anything else to say.

The drumming ceased. "I regret the loss of self-control. It's possible, you know, that it *was* his heart that gave out, just as the doctor said. I'd bet my bottom dollar he didn't tell his wife of his night at the Silver Queen. Probably weighed heavily upon him."

Inez looked up. "Then, there is all the more reason to resolve this. If it's all a coincidence, although someone pushing me down the stairs and trying to poison Calder's horse doesn't seem very coincidental, you can at least advise Harmony's husband on the validity of this possible investment he is poised to make. So, are you talking to Lewis tomorrow? Is he planning to show you the sights and give you his pitch?"

"It'll be a regular party. *Messieurs* Lewis, Epperley, and DuChamps, along with a Dr. Zuckerman. Early breakfast, a walk around the grounds, then meet the hotel's physician. I guess he's the star of the show."

"Listen well to what they say, ask appropriate questions, and wave your bankbook under their noses if they seem suspicious. While you do that, I shall go talk to the widow Pace, and do some looking around for myself."

Mark stood. "Just be sure to be back by ten in the morning, and dressed for a drive. I've made arrangements for a family excursion tomorrow. You, me, William. Horse and buggy."

Inez narrowed her eyes. "Why didn't you mention this sooner?"

"I'm mentioning it now, which is the first chance I've had." He rubbed his face. "It's been a long day on the train. Meeting all your relatives on top of it took me by surprise. That aunt of yours seems smart as a steel trap and able to whip her weight in wild cats. Anyway, I thought it would be a good idea for us to take William and go for a ride. Give us a chance to get to know our son again."

I know my own son. The retort died unuttered, as she realized the few days of awkward and intermittent contact with William had only proved that she really *didn't* know him. Not that well, not yet.

She said instead, "I should warn you, William did not remember me." The memory of their initial meeting was still too fresh and painful to elaborate on. "Even now, he approaches me almost as if I were a stranger. And they call him Wilkie."

"Wilkie." He looked bemused. "Not a bad handle. Sounds like an actor."

"My son will never go on the stage." Inez rose abruptly. "Let's not let our talk veer in that direction. I believe it's time to bring the evening to a close." She hesitated, and then said, "Thank you for coming, Mark. I would not have asked for your help, if I could have thought of anyone else who could do this."

"Then I'm all the more honored that you would turn to me, despite your misgivings," said Mark.

"Just don't let me down. As you have so often in the past." She walked to her bedroom.

Mark followed. "'You wound, like Parthians, while you fly, and kill with a retreating eye.' Haven't changed a bit, have you. Always with the last word, on the way out the door."

Inez turned by the foot of the bed, cold as steel. "Don't quote Samuel Butler at me, and let's not even begin discussing 'last words out the door.' Why are you following me into *my* room?"

He held up a placating hand, went to his trunk, opened it, and pulled out his leather collar box and a black silk waistcoat. He then grabbed his carpetbag. "Just gathering what I need for tonight and tomorrow morning. Good-night, darlin'. Sweet dreams."

Chapter Thirty-four

After Mark left her room, Inez twisted the night latch, tugged to be sure the door was secure, and paced the floor, trying to calm down. *I hope I haven't erred in asking Mark for help.* She finally prepared for bed and blew out the candle in the Mountain Springs House brass candleholder.

But she couldn't sleep.

Tossing about on the unfamiliar spring bed and listening to the creek's constant babble and the symphony of frogs, Inez thought of the Paces and Calder and Susan. Of tonic bottles, poisons, and handkerchiefs soaked with bloody sputum. Of Mark and the Reverend Justice Sands.

She drifted off into uneasy sleep, only to be awakened by the loud crunch of carriage wheels over gravel. She got up, thinking it would be a reasonable time to use the chamber pot. Before pulling it out from its cabinet, she went to the window and lifted one side of the drawn roller blind. She saw a cloaked figure climb out of the buggy and disappear under the hotel veranda. The driver, invisible under the dark top, waited. The harnessed horse stamped and shook its head. Inez couldn't be certain in the night, but given its size and its stance, she thought the horse might be Calder's.

Through her open window, Inez heard the front door open and close. The driver slapped the reins, and the horse and buggy proceeded around the building toward the hotel livery. Inez leaned close to the glass, watching the buggy disappear from view. *If I'd taken the other bedroom, I'd have a window on that side and perhaps even see who exits the livery after dropping off horse and buggy!*

There was nothing to be done but complete her business and return to bed. Now, she had something else to think about. *If the driver was Robert Calder, then who was the passenger? He took Susan back to the Ohio House. Surely, he didn't bring her back here.*

Inez banished the scandalous thought from her mind. She knew Susan as well as anyone and could not believe that, even in the heat of a whirlwind summer romance, she would risk her reputation in such a flagrant manner.

With a troubled sigh, Inez turned on her side, wrapped the feather pillow about her ears, and finally drifted off to sleep.

Inez waited in the lobby of the Cliff House while the bellboy took her calling card up to Mrs. Pace. As was proper, she had written "To Inquire" at the top of card. She hoped Mrs. Pace would agree to see her, despite being in seclusion, and that the formal inquiry would be enough of an entry for the widow to accept a visitor without comment from hotel staff.

The bellhop reappeared and said, "Mrs. Pace said to bring you up to her rooms."

Inez followed him up a flight of stairs and onto a second floor much like the one at the Manitou Springs House. The wallpaper was different, a different carpet covered the wood floor, the gaslights had different shades, and the niche at the top of the stairs held a stand with a vase of cut flowers instead of a statue of Hermes. Like the Mountain Springs House, the Cliff House also had a double veranda. When Inez remarked on the similarities, the bellhop, who was a nephew of the owner, gleefully noted that unlike the Mountain Springs House, the Cliff House had a billiards hall, a third floor, and even a telescope on the rooftop for stargazing. "You should stay here on your next visit," the earnest young man said. "We are ever so much better than the Mountain Springs House."

"But you haven't a resident physician," remarked Inez.

He looked sly. "Not yet. But my uncle swears that before the year is out, he'll either have convinced the doctor there to join up with us or he'll find someone just as good, if not better."

Inez tucked that intriguing bit of gossip away for further mulling.

Upon being announced and entering, Inez looked around the sitting room, and decided that the Cliff House and the Mountain Springs House must have shared the same architect and decorator for the rooms as well.

"Thank you for seeing me," Inez said.

Kirsten Pace sat by the window, her heavy crape veil and hat on the nearby window seat, a silver tea service ready and waiting on a low table. "Mrs. Stannert, I am glad you came. I meant to leave you a note, but I left the Mountain Springs House on short notice, and there was much to gather up and organize." She indicated a nearby empty chair aslant of her own. "Please, sit and tell me if you have any news. The children and Miss Warren are on a day excursion to Cheyenne Canyon, and I have only myself and my memories for company. I took the liberty of ordering tea for us."

"Most kind of you." Inez sat and began cautiously, "You asked for my help a few days ago. I agreed, but I had no idea how difficult it would be to gather information. However, my husband arrived last night, and we have put out that he is interested in exploring business opportunities. We shall see how it evolves. Meanwhile, I have some questions for you."

"Please ask. Anything to lift the mystery of my husband's death."

"Do you know, were any papers signed, agreements sealed?"

"None, as far as I know. I think they would have said something, even given the circumstances, if it were otherwise. Too, my husband was unusual in that, if he was going to sign an agreement, he would have included me in the room. Even if we disagreed about a particular venture, if it wasn't directly related to his day-to-day business, he always asked that I be present." Mrs. Pace shook her head. "I am certain. No papers were signed."

Another question popped into Inez's mind as a result of Mrs. Pace's comment. It hadn't been on her list to ask, but it was something she'd wondered about. "Do you happen to know where Mr. Lewis conducts hotel business? Surely not at the reception desk or in the gentlemen's parlor."

Mrs. Pace lifted her hat and smoothed the veil, before setting it back down. "There is a small room just past the gentlemen's parlor. The children and I accompanied my husband there once. They wanted to see where he spent his days doing 'business,' while we went out on picnics and excursions." She smiled sadly. "Mr. Lewis graciously allowed Mathilda and Atticus to come in and look around. It was clearly just a room for signing papers or discussion. No bookcases, no safe, a minimal amount of papers and furniture."

"Hmm. There must be a working office elsewhere. Too, the hotel seems full to capacity. There are no other buildings on the grounds, besides the livery and the clinic. Where do Mr. Lewis, Mr. Epperley, Mrs. Crowson, and the rest of the staff reside?"

"I can't speak for the regular staff. Mr. Epperley once made a remark that indicated he and a few other men from 'across the pond' set up housekeeping elsewhere in town."

Inez tapped a finger on the handle of her closed parasol. "What of Mr. Lewis and Mrs. Crowson?"

Mrs. Pace hesitated and then said, "Did you know there is a lower level to the hotel?"

A tickle of excitement ran down Inez's back. "As a matter of fact, I recently discovered a door under the far side of the veranda."

Mrs. Pace nodded. "The children—Mathilda and Atticus—were playing hide and seek in the hotel one day, and they somehow gave Miss Warren the slip. She and I were searching, and I found a staircase that led downstairs."

"Where?" Inez interrupted.

"Continue down the hall between the music room and the dining room, all the way to the end. There are no rooms in that direction, so no reason a guest would ever come across it. I took the stairs. A mother has a sixth sense, I just felt certain they were probably playing their game down there. It was quite a revelation, there is an entire lower story to the hotel. At the bottom of the stairs to the left, there is an enormous storage area. To the right was a hallway. My children were in the corridor, peering through a keyhole and whispering. Of course I spoke sharply to them. I've taught them better manners than that! They jumped back, the door flew open, and there was Mr. Lewis! I think he was as surprised as I was. The area behind him was considerably illuminated, so the room had either windows or lighting fixtures of some sort, I suppose."

"You think he lives down there?" Inez was intrigued.

"That is my thought," she said. "He closed the door quickly behind him, so I saw nothing of the inside. He told us, 'This is a private area. Off-limits to guests.'" She paused. "He was very firm when he said it. Not angry. I don't think I ever saw him truly angry during our entire stay, but he was definitely disturbed to see us."

"If he toils down there, most likely the working papers of the hotel are there as well," said Inez, thinking aloud. "Particularly since there is not a proper office upstairs."

"That would make sense." Mrs. Pace agreed.

"Do you think Mrs. Crowson also resides in that nether world? Unless she rooms somewhere in town."

"Well, here is the thing." Mrs. Pace lifted the lid, and satisfied at last, poured the steaming liquid into porcelain cups. The fragrant scent of English breakfast tea wafted over Inez. "While we stood in the hallway, I detected the strong scent of mint. I immediately thought of my tonic, of course, but my very next thought was—"

"Nurse Crowson's tea," finished Inez.

"Too, there was a door across the hall from Lewis'," added Mrs. Pace. "Another set of rooms, perhaps, for Mrs. Crowson? It makes sense for her to live on the grounds, since she works so closely with the physician and helps the invalid guests. In any case, that was that. Mr. Lewis locked the door behind himself, escorted us up to the lobby, and went on his way. Miss Warren was nearly beside herself with worry. I gave the children a good scolding and told them not to go down there again. Cream? Sugar?"

"Sugar, please. One lump."

Mrs. Pace complied and handed Inez the porcelain cup and saucer.

"Thank you," said Inez. "Your perceptions are very helpful."

"Are they? Do they provide insight into my husband's death?"

"Perhaps. I need to puzzle it out. But I do have a sense about these things. If I could just get into those rooms…" She realized she was speaking aloud, and stopped. "I do have a couple of questions about your trip to Leadville." She hated to ask, but felt she must. "What happened the night before you left?"

Kirsten lifted her teacup to her lips and pondered. Then, she lowered the cup, without tasting, and said, "It had been a long day. I had hoped to go to some of the mines with my husband, but the altitude was difficult for me, so I returned to the hotel to rest instead. The children, Miss Warren, and I ate dinner in the hotel's dining room and retired early. Mr. Pace came in late that night. He seemed agitated. He woke me and Miss Warren, and told us we would all be leaving Leadville in the morning. Luckily, we had not unpacked much, as it was only to be a short trip. We left before dawn to catch the stagecoach."

"Do you know where he went that evening?" Inez persisted. She held her breath, awaiting Mrs. Pace's answer, waiting to hear if she mentioned the Silver Queen or a wild night of gambling.

Mrs. Pace shook her head. "I supposed he was taking dinner with some of the promoters he had met that day. Given his attitude upon returning, I assumed that talks had not gone well at all. He was most anxious to leave town." She sighed. "It was so strange. We had embarked on the journey to Leadville with high hopes and optimism. Something must have happened for him to turn so completely on the town and its prospects."

Inez set her mouth in a grim line. Clearly, Mr. Pace did not confide in his wife over the debacle at the gaming table. *So like a man to crow about his wins but stay mum on his losses.*

She weighed saying something to the widow about what had happened at the saloon, decided against it, and said gently instead, "Sometimes that happens in Leadville. I have lived there long enough to see many arrive full of hope and optimism, only to be dashed by the harsh realities. Perhaps your husband saw the truth sooner than most and wisely decided there was no reason to stay. But now, I have something I want to ask you."

She pulled the small tonic bottle from her purse. Mrs. Pace's eyes went wide.

"I found it on the floor of the stagecoach," Inez said. "The stopper, too."

Mrs. Pace took it gingerly, as if its very surface could contaminate.

Inez leaned forward. "How many bottles did you take to Leadville?"

The widow rubbed her finger down the side of the smooth brown glass. "We were to be up there five days, so it was five bottles."

"How many did you consume?"

"One for the day we took the train up," she said aloud. "One for the day there, another for our first day back on the stagecoach." She looked down. "And this one, on the second day on the coach."

"So you had one left over?"

She nodded.

"Do you still have it?"

"When Miss Warren unpacked the carpet bag, I took the bottle and emptied its contents."

"I understand," Inez said gently. "Do you still have the bottle?"

"I turned it back to the formulary. They always collect the bottles afterwards. Perhaps it is a way of keeping track of the doses." Mrs. Pace ran a thumb over the top of the bottle, frowning.

"Is something wrong?" Inez asked.

"The stopper, it's just darker than I recall. Perhaps from being on the floor of the stagecoach."

"Would you open the bottle and tell me if it smells different from what you had before?"

Mrs. Pace took out the cork and handed it to Inez. She held the bottle tentatively up to her nose, and inhaled. "Mint," she said. "The bottle is empty, but there is still a strong mint smell. I think this is stronger than usual, but I can't be certain."

Inez was examining the cork, frowning. The top surface was indeed darker compared to the rest of the wax, down the sides to the point where the cork would seal.

"May I see the bottle a moment?"

Mrs. Pace handed it back.

Inez examined the ragged ring of wax around the bottle's neck: It was a cloudy white, like the wax that still clung to the sides of the cork. Removing a glove, she picked at the dark wax on the top surface with a fingernail.

Bits flaked off, revealing the paler layer below. She lifted one large fragment, and the dark wax fell away in a single chunk.

"Someone resealed the bottle top?" she said aloud. "But not the entire bottle. So the cork wasn't removed, else the new wax would have covered the old seal. So why only the top?"

With a sheepish glance at Mrs. Pace, Inez fished her oft-ignored reading glasses out of her reticule and hooked them over her ears.

This is no time for vanity, but for clear and sharpened vision.

Even then, it was hard to see—given the rougher surface where the added layer of wax had attached—what the original wax surface had looked like and if it had been disturbed in some way.

But if one surface tells half the story, then perhaps the other will tell me the rest.

With excitement and dread building insider her, Inez turned the cork over to examine the bottom. She tipped it, to send a slanting light over the smooth cork surface.

There, in the center, a dark dot displaced the brown finish. A hole.

Chapter Thirty-five

"When I stripped all the wax off, there it was: a hole in the top. Someone punctured the cork with something thin and sharp, like a needle," Inez finished.

"Hmm." Mark kept his eyes on the road ahead, but Inez could almost imagine him running through her story of her meeting with Mrs. Pace, from beginning to end. "Anything else about the bottle strike you or the widow as odd?"

"She thought the mint smell was stronger than usual. Of course, it's hard to tell, from vapors several days old. It's a miracle any of the liquid remained at all."

"Maybe the tonic has some oil mixed in. The coach was left untouched overnight, you went hunting under the seat the very next day. Lady Luck was smiling on you, Inez."

"I hope she smiles a little longer so this whole business can be resolved. William!" she said sharply to their offspring, who was squirming between them on the buggy seat. "Sit still!"

Their family outing had started on a low note for Inez. After his morning tour of the hotel and grounds, Mark had met Harmony, Lily, Inez, and William in the garden to prepare for the ride. Lily had handed off a large drawstring bag to Inez, saying, "For Wilkie. Fresh nappies and pilches, extra frock 'n stockings, mashed-potatoes-gravy to eat." She said all of this very fast, without looking at Inez.

Meanwhile, Mark had crouched down to William's level and said, "Wilkie, look what I've brought for you," and held out a toy. This was not a simple ball or hoop, but a small tin horse with a bell around its neck, mounted on a miniature wood boat with four elegantly turned tin wheels. William's eyes widened. Mark set the toy on the ground and pulled the string attached to it. The bell around the horse gave a series of small, sharp *pings*. Mark held the string out to his son. William released Lily's apron hem, and grasped the string. He tugged it, the wheels lurched forward, and the bell chimed once.

William had looked up at Mark and smiled, open-mouthed with delight.

Jealousy had stabbed Inez through and through, sharper than any needle.

The wheeled toy, of course, had to come with them on the drive. When Mark asked if Inez had a preference as a place to go, she promptly said "Cheyenne Canyon," with the half-formed idea that they might run into the Pace children and nanny, and perhaps form a party. The thought of spending time alone with Mark—with only William for buffer—made her nervous. The drive, it turned out, was one recommended to Mark by Morrow, so he was agreeable to the proposition. It also was taking longer than she'd anticipated, so she took her time detailing the conversation with Mrs. Pace.

The road wound up and up, the horse plodded, slowly, methodically. Inez wanted to grab the reins from Mark and urge the horse to at least a trot.

"So, that was my morning," she finished. "Did you learn anything about the Mountain Springs House or the clinic that might be useful?"

"Well, I'd say if there's humbug going on, Dr. Zuckerman is part of it, but not Dr. Prochazka," said Mark. "Dr. Prochazka is all tied up in his clinic, and his work on consumption and wasting diseases. I'd say he doesn't give a hoot about the hotel itself, just as long as he can stay king of his own castle and clinic. Dr. Zuckerman, though, he comes on considerable strong about the future of the area. He swears he's locked up a fortune in Manitou and Colorado Springs and says the area will 'make money rain.'"

"What's your take on Zuckerman? He apparently has a physician's credentials."

His lip curled. "I've been in the game long enough to recognize a bunko steerer. Doesn't matter if they be pedigreed or half-breed, dressed in silk or shoddy. It's the same hook and line."

"Exactly what I thought," Inez said, feeling vindicated. "So, are you allowing him to reel you in?"

"I'll allow him to believe he's landing a sucker with a large bank account. For now."

Inez couldn't help it. She threw back her head and laughed. It was such a relief to have someone on her side who understood the game and who could so expertly identify a con in play and turn it back on itself. *Until Mark arrived, there was no one here in Manitou I could talk to openly about this.*

A sudden image of Reverend Sands blew across her mind. She choked off the laugh, feeling a traitor.

They'd reached the top of a sloping mesa, and Mark halted the carriage. He pointed to a colony a few miles away and below, commenting, "General Palmer's town, Colorado Springs. That's where I got off the train last evening. Didn't have much opportunity to look around. The hotel's carriage was waiting when I arrived." Tiny buildings and structures were sprinkled along a grid of platted streets. Small trees showing as a line of faint green dots at distance, courageously guarded the main boulevard. The town appeared very isolated against the open plains to the east. The wide space, which seemed to rush on forever without boundary to the end of the earth, made Inez feel very small.

"Shouldn't be long before we're in the canyon, according to the hotel's driver, that Morrow fellow. Then we can stop somewhere along the water."

"What about Lewis and Epperley? Are they players as well?"

William's toy was becoming a major annoyance, as he turned it this way and that, rolling it on his lap and shaking it to make it ring. The corner of the toy's platform seemed to bump the same spot on Inez's leg at every jounce along the way. She covered the corner with her hand, to cushion the sharp edge.

"Didn't hear much from them today. Zuckerman did all the talking, when Prochazka wasn't. I'll spend more time with them tomorrow." He glanced sideways at Inez, then back at the road. "One thing I noticed though, that was passing strange."

"What is that?"

"Well, the talk turned to the War, as it inevitably does among men of a certain age. Between Mr. DuChamps and myself, we stood up for the blue and the grey. No hard feelings, we agreed, as the time's long past now. Dr. Zuckerman declaimed that he'd been part of the forces out here in the Far West, and saw not much in the way of action besides an almighty lot of cholera, typhoid, and French pox. Even Epperley spoke up, offering his English opinion on the War Between the States."

"So?"

"So, Franklin Lewis said not a word."

Inez squinted in thought. William struggled to remove her hand from the boat, prying her fingers back. She ignored him. "Did Mr. Lewis perhaps not fight at all, then?"

Mark shrugged. "He shifted the conversation back to money, so of course everyone jumped like hounds offered a fresh-killed rabbit. But as we talked about this battle and that, where we were when word of surrender came down—none of us in the War will ever forget that momemt—he looked for all the world like someone had backed him up to a wall and shoved a pistol in his face. I pegged him as a deserter or something of the like. I'd bet a dollar to a dime that he's hiding something that happened during the War that's beyond the usual horrors. Something he's ashamed of."

She nodded. *Men and the War. Even if they don't talk about it, you can see in their eyes that they are remembering. Just as with Reverend Sands: the War is with him always, like a shadow. Even when the shadow's invisible—at high noon, or the darkest midnight —it's there. Inescapable.*

Thinking of the reverend induced a muddle of longing, guilt, and an overwhelming sense of loss. "Will you meet more with them tomorrow?" she asked.

He nodded. "Your brother-in-law and I will be sampling soda waters from the various springs and hearing of all the plans for the future—no doubt with an eye as to how much they're hoping to slide from our pockets. Later, we're scheduled to dine in Colorado Springs with local movers and shakers. It'll be a long day away."

"See if you can't get both Epperley and Lewis to go with you. I'm going to do a little looking around the hotel, and it will be easier if neither of them remain behind."

"Just where do you have in mind, Inez?"

She hesitated. "Well, there's a lower floor to the hotel. Mrs. Pace went down there once, looking for her children. She said that, in addition to a storage area, there are rooms, which may include Lewis' private office and some living quarters. I'd like to see if I can find any papers that might provide an indication of the current financial health of the hotel. If I don't have to worry about Lewis and Epperley, I'm certain I can fast-talk my way past any other hotel staff."

"I'm sure you can." He was quiet a moment, and then added, "Be careful, Inez."

"Of course. And you be careful they don't fast-talk our hard-earned silver right out of your pocket." It was only after the words were out, that she realized she had said *our* silver. She clamped her mouth shut, annoyed with herself.

The road had narrowed as it entered the canyon, and the air cooled. Fir, spruce, yellow pine rose high above while birds squawked, cawed, and sang liquid songs. A stream of frothy water rushed by, roaring as if demanding to be set free from its banks.

A widening in the canyon appeared as they rounded a generous turn. A buggy with "The Cliff House" lettered on the back was pulled to one side, the horse standing patiently and the driver settled on the ground nearby, back to a large boulder, hat pulled down over his eyes. "This looks like a good place," Inez said.

Mark pulled to a stop, gazing into the mountains. "Heard tell there's seven falls tucked further back."

"We've gone far enough." She pulled the satchel Lily had provided for William from the back seat of the buggy, hopped down, and stretched out her free arm. "Come, William."

Still clutching the toy, he hesitated, then stepped into her embrace. She staggered a little under his sudden weight. The toy banged into her still aching shoulder. Stifling a curse, she set him on his feet and took his hand.

"Will you get the picnic basket?" she called over her shoulder, and approached the snoozing driver.

"Pardon me," she said. "Is this the buggy for the Pace party?"

He lifted his hat, looking a little bleary-eyed from his nap. "Yup. Chillun and their nanny's down by the water."

"Thank you," she said, and started down the trail, tugging on William's hand to encourage him along. "Come along, William. You have some friends down here who will no doubt be happy to see you."

William had a death grip on the string of his pull toy, it jounced and bounced down the trail, the bell on the horse tinkling fast and violent. The approach was blessedly short, ending in a long, winding bench of gravel by the stream. Inez was happy to see two small figures, dominated by a larger one cradling a baby, about fifty feet away.

"Look, William, it's Mathilda, Atticus, and Edison." She waved to get their attention.

The two older children ceased poking sticks in the gravel and bounded toward Inez and William.

"Wilkie!" screeched Mathilda.

Inez let go of his hand, and Mathilda heaved him up off his feet a few inches. "Eeeuw," she said. "You need your nappies changed, Wilkie."

She promptly set him back down, saying, "Where's your mum and da, Wilkie?"

Inez started to say "Right here," but stopped short.

Atticus had circled around to examine William's toy. He experimentally tapped the bell. Wilkie shouted, "No! Mine!"

He yanked the string, causing the horse to flip over. The bell gave up a muffled *thunk.*

Glad for the distraction, Inez said, "I'd better hold this for now."

She picked up the toy, ignoring an indignant wail from William, just as the nanny puffed up with Edison.

"Hello ma'am, Mrs. Stannert. Imagine seeing you here. We're all getting a little fresh air while the missus rests. It's lovely here, but careful about the water. I'm keeping the children back because it's quite fast."

She set Edison down in the gravel on his cushioned bottom and bent over to view William.

"Well now, if it isn't the little mister," she cooed, and chucked William under the chin. Addressing Inez, she said, "We've moved to the Cliff House, you know. Expecting that we'll be there for a few days yet. You should bring Wilkie by; the children would love to play." Then, under her breath she said, "Ma'am, he needs his nappies changed, just thought I'd say."

"Uncle Eric is coming on the train," said Mathilda. "He's going to take us home, now that papa's gone to heaven." She stopped, touched one of the black mourning bows attached to the shoulder of her dress, and looked down as if she'd let slip a secret she wasn't supposed to tell. "I have to wear these on my frocks now," she said to Inez. "It's to show respect for my papa. Mama has to wear all black, all the time."

Mark came up, picnic basket and blanket over one arm, and Inez performed introductions. He spoke as seriously to Mathilda and Atticus as if they were adults, and bowed to Miss Warren. Miss Warren batted her eyes at him; the children stood taller, as if he had conferred some dignity upon them. Inez was glad there wasn't a family dog or he, too, would have been eating out of Mark's hand.

"Can we come to your picnic?" asked Mathilda. "We had ours hours ago, and I'm hungry."

Miss Warren let out a scandalized "Hush! Manners!"

Mark smiled at Mathilda and said, "Give us a little time to recover from the ride. Perhaps you'll all join us later for dessert? I spied cookies in the packed victuals."

Thus mollified, the two Pace children allowed themselves to be hustled by Miss Warren to their end of the stream bank.

William began walking after them, apparently ready to abandon his new toy for the children's company. Mark took his hand and said, "Let's find rocks to throw at the water."

"Rocks!" he said, and obediently trotted alongside his father.

Inez followed, rooting around in the satchel for clean things for William. Once Mark had claimed a picnic spot with the blanket, Inez took William off into the bushes to change his diapers. It was an entirely different procedure, she discovered, to change an uncompliant toddler compared to the infant she'd last labored over.

Much messier, for one thing.

Not willing to lie down, for another. William insisted on being changed standing up.

"Have it your way," she muttered, and pulled off his frock, which would have to be washed in any case, and stripped the soiled pilche and linen diaper from him. He seemed to believe that, freed from clothes, he was also free to return to a pre-civilized state of being, and made an attempt to run back to the beach *au naturel*.

Inez grabbed his arm. "No," she said sternly. She searched around, and handed him a stick, saying, "Here. Hit that rock, William."

Whacking a handy red rock with the stick kept him occupied long enough for Inez to wipe him clean and dress him in clean clothes.

She considered the soiled diaperings, muttered, "We are *not* carrying these back with us," rolled them up, and stuffed them under the rock savaged by William's stick.

By the time she returned to the picnic spot, she was feeling the approach of a foul mood. She deposited William on the blanket beside Mark, pulled a damask napkin from one of the picnic baskets, and went to the stream. She plunged her hands into the icy water, scrubbing vigorously.

The low rumble of continuously moving water filled the space between the canyon walls and washed out all other sound. The stream flowed in a series of small waterfall leaps down to their relatively level area. Inez rested her hands on a submerged rock at the edge, where it was shallow. The racing water made the rock look like rippling silk, but the hard surface beneath her fingers was smooth and slick.

Inez stood and wiped her hands, tingling with the cold, on the napkin. She heard Mark say behind her, "Cold roast chicken, hard-boiled eggs, buttered rolls, jam, strawberries, cookies, and lemonade. I brought a little something that might make the lemonade more to your taste."

She turned slowly.

Mark was opening a bottle of sherry; two cut-glass tumblers waited next to the lemonade jug. "Ended up smuggling the sherry out from the men's parlor this morning," he continued. "Once we return to Leadville, I'll prepare you a Saratoga Brace Up with bitters, sugar, lemon and lime juice, anisette, one egg, brandy, mineral water. I think you might like it. Best way to imbibe mineral water, which I understand you're not overly fond of."

Mark crouched by the tablecloth looking up at her, the blue of his eyes softened by what appeared to be affection. The crinkle around his eyes, the odd dimple that punctuated his lopsided smile, it was all just as she remembered. He had removed his hat, and the water-scented breeze lifted his light brown hair on one side, sending a strand across his forehead. William sat on a corner of the blanket, trying to feed his toy horse a strawberry.

The picture of a perfect family.

It could be us. It could be.

For a moment, she felt dizzy. Dizzy with longing. Dizzy with regret. Dizzy with a sudden lurch in her stomach, as if she'd slipped into deep water and was tumbling away, heading toward the rapids and out of control.

"So did you do to Josephine what you did to us?" The question came out cold, colder than water straight from the high mountain snows.

He looked up, his smile fading. Confusion replaced the smile, followed by a wary cautiousness. "What do you mean?"

"Did you just up and disappear? One day you were there, the next morning, you were gone. As you did to William and me."

"Inez, we aren't going to talk about this now." The caution was gone, replaced by iron determination.

He stood and limped toward her, wiping his hands on one of the napkins. She moved back, away from the blanket and the stream, closer to the trees. "So, it's up to you to decide what we talk about and when? How very convenient. For you."

"What do you expect me to do?" He said in exasperation.

"Tell me the truth! The whole truth, even if it hurts, not some abbreviated version. You left me, Mark. As far as I can tell, you left me for another woman. You have been gone for months. Not for a night, or a week or two. This is nothing like what happened in *Dodge*." Even as she said it, she realized that the reference to the stormy events in Dodge City, where their marriage had very nearly ended, was a low blow.

Mark jerked back, his face tightening. "I said I'd explain later."

"Later." She sneered the word. "It's always later with you. Don't bother, Mark, I can read between the lines. You said yourself that after you recovered, you stayed with her. You never even considered coming up to Leadville after that, did you? You could have come up to see, to see…" *See if I was there. If we could rebuild our life together.*

"Inez, I told you. It was months before I could move about on my own. By that time, I thought you'd have left Leadville, given William's health."

There it was, the accusation: *You abandoned our son. You gave him away.*

"I was *waiting* for you," she said. "Waiting for word, any word. You could have written and posted a letter yourself, after you were better. You could have sent a telegram. But you didn't, and all I could think was that you were dead, after all that time with no word. But you weren't. You'd simply decided to set up house with this other woman, this Josephine." She was throwing the words at him as if they were rocks, pounding him with all the hurt and fury she'd held inside for so long. "You didn't come back because you didn't want to, you unfaithful, two-timing son-of-a-bitch!"

Mark closed the distance between them, reaching out for her. She stepped back again, out of his grasp, into the sheltering tree line. He moved with her, finally capturing her arm, forcing her to stop her retreat.

"Are you going to tell me, darlin', that you were waiting for me from last summer to this—the faithful wife, pining in an empty bedroom, watching out the window with a candle lit for my return?" His voice returned her anger tenfold.

The roaring that filled her ears was no longer the stream, but the hammering of her heart.

Mark continued, "I hope you aren't thinking of lying to me and saying yes. Because I know about Gallagher last summer. About Masterson—good almighty God, Bat Masterson of all people—last winter. And I know about Justice Sands."

She gasped, and then demanded, "Who said all this?"

"Well, Inez, I've had some time to catch up with old friends since you left Leadville and came down here. It's not always what people say, it's more what they don't say, and how they don't say it. How they move their eyes when you ask a particular question. How and when they change the subject. You know, darlin', there are always those who do talk. It's just a matter of, as you said, readin' between the lines."

"Don't you *dare* accuse me. You, of all people."

He shook his head. "Inez, this time, you've outdone yourself. Yes, I stayed with Josephine. I told you straight out, and explained why. But while I was with her, how many men did *you* have climbing in and out of our marriage bed, after you sent our son back east? I'm wondering now, did you send him away so you could be free to—"

She slapped him.

They froze, staring at each other. He didn't touch his face, didn't look away. It was as if her blow had no effect whatsoever, except for the narrowing of his eyes and an ever-tightening grip on her arm.

"You don't know what I went through." Inez whispered. She pulled her arm out of his grasp. He let her go.

"That's true, Inez, I don't. But you don't know what I went through either." He took another step forward, she took another step back: a choreographed dance of discord. A dance they'd executed so frequently in their life together, Inez knew the moves by heart. This time, though, she had no idea how it would end.

Mark's expression turned rueful. "I know you won't believe this, but I want us to have a chance, see if we can't resurrect the life we had before, or make something better. I'll do anything, walk through fire, if you'll agree to one more try. And Inez," his voice became ominously gentle, an overlay of menace tempering the soft Southern drawl, "I advise you to give my request some serious consideration. When we get back to Leadville, if you take up where you left off, trying to get a divorce, I won't lie down and let you roll over me. I talked to a lawyer after I pieced together what was going on in my absence. I'll tell you, darlin', if we were runnin' a race, I wouldn't put a plugged nickel on your chances of winning."

"Mr. Stannert?" A small voice piped up behind Mark. "'Scuse me, sir? Ma'am?"

Startled, Inez and Mark turned to see who spoke.

Standing a respectful distance away, Mathilda Pace was holding her little brother Atticus by one hand, and William's sleeve with the other.

Still burning with the heat of emotional battle, Inez dumbly registered that William was drenched, that he was crying and rubbing his eyes with one soaked sleeve. Miss Warner was coming up behind Mathilda. She lugged Edison in one arm and held her long wet skirts up and away from the ground, her mouth pursed in disapproval.

"What happened?" Inez hurried forward, grabbed up William and hugged him to her, ignoring the sudden soaking of her dress.

Miss Warren answered in a long rush, "We were coming up to see if you were done with your picnic, so the children could play together, and saw him, little Wilkie, heading into the stream, you see, because we could see his toy in the water, the fast part toward the middle it was, and he was just starting after it, I didn't see either of you anywhere, so I had to run pretty fast, and me carrying Edison like this, I only had one hand free, so I waded in and grabbed him by his collar just as he lost his balance, lucky for him I did, for if I'd been just a little slower..." She ran out of breath and stopped, hitching Edison up higher on one hip.

Inez began to shake. The tremor started deep inside and spread out in a growing wave to her limbs. Soon, she was trembling so hard she could barely hold William. "Thank you, Miss Warren," she whispered. Then, "William, William." She buried her face in his wet hair.

Through William's indignant cries, she could hear Mark say, "Miss Warren, we owe you a debt of gratitude we can never begin to repay. If you hadn't been so vigilant and quick on your feet..." At that point, the words ceased having any meaning to her, becoming just a babble of voices.

There was Miss Warren's partially mollified tone, Mathilda's rising inflection of a question, and Mark's soothing response. Inez heard a chorus of "good-byes!" followed by the chattering of the Pace children and their nanny, fading with distance. Only then was Inez aware that Mark had, at some point, put his arm around her and William.

Inez whispered, "Mark, William almost, he almost..."

"He's all right, Inez. He lost a toy, which can be replaced, that's all. He's fine, without a scratch."

"But everything could have so easily turned out differently. He could have...oh god, I can't say it. And it was our fault. We weren't watching, we were so caught up in our silly squabbling. It's all just like before, like it's always been. Things go well for

a while and then, something happens, and we are at it again."
She finally looked at him.

His face, so close to hers, was serious, somber, the light of
anger gone.

"We can't do this anymore, Mark. We can't."

He pulled them both into a comforting embrace. She shut
her eyes, breathing in the reassurance of his familiarity and his
voice as he said, "We won't, Inez. It'll be different this time. I
promise."

Chapter Thirty-six

The drive back was mostly a silent one. Inez changed William into his last set of dry clothes and held him on her lap the entire journey. He didn't protest much, apparently too tired to squirm or fuss. After a short while, between the rhythmical clop-clop of the horse and the swaying of the buggy, he fell asleep. Inez was then free to hold him as tight as she wished. She felt that if she loosened her hold on him for even one moment, he'd disappear, vanishing as surely as if he'd been carried away by the icy waters in Cheyenne Canyon.

"Let's not tell my sister about this," she finally said to Mark. "It will only distress her. She is distressed too much as is, what with everything that has happened."

"I believe Mrs. DuChamps is not the only one bearing the burden of worry," Mark said. "Have you seen how her husband watches her on the sly?"

Inez rested her chin on top of William's head, thinking. Finally she said, "I don't believe I have."

"He looks at her as if she might just vanish in a puff of smoke at any time."

Inez clutched William's warm weight even closer.

"Is she here for treatments?" Mark asked.

"Harmony is taking a tonic and is on a regimen prescribed by Dr. Prochazka," Inez said. "But I gather it's for her nerves, for a mild case of neurasthenia. She won't discuss it, but it can't be too serious. Why, she outpaced me on an excursion up Williams' Canyon the other day. She insists that the Colorado air and locale suits her and that she has never felt better."

"No coughing?" he persisted. "Does she eat well? Mrs. DuChamps is very thin, very pale."

"Harmony does not have consumption!" Inez said it louder than she'd intended. On her lap, William stirred. She quieted her voice, trying to inject the same certainty in a whisper. "She would have told me, if so. If she was hiding that fact, I would know."

"Well, darlin'. Maybe her husband and the doctor decided it's best not to tell her."

At her exclamation of disbelief, he said quickly, "Didn't mean to stir up a hornet's nest, Inez. Just letting you know what I observed, that's all."

"She's fine," whispered Inez. She lightly ran the back of her hand down William's cheek, wrapped one of his curls around her finger. "Nothing that sunshine, fresh air, and a release from worry won't cure."

"If you say so."

She glanced at Mark. It wasn't like him to back down so quickly, to give in to her insistence without at least a further question or two. But he had stopped, and was now gazing at the view before them. They were almost down the winding road and about to enter the main road between Colorado Springs and Manitou. Late afternoon shadows from the westering foothills lay long across the valley to Manitou. "We'll probably be there in time for dinner," said Mark. He slapped the reins, and the horse moved forward. "If you don't want to tell your sister about today, I'll leave it to you. We can just tell everyone we had a pleasant excursion and that William's toy did not float after all. We needn't make it sound as if anything occurred, other than a lost plaything."

Upon arriving at the front of the hotel, Inez accepted the reins from Mark. She waited for Mark to come around and take William from her, so she could turn over the care of horse and carriage to the livery boy, Billy.

The hotel's front door flew open, revealing Aunt Agnes. Inez blinked. Today, Agnes had apparently eschewed the artistic, and was clad in the latest and most restrictive fashion. Even at that distance, Inez managed to register a stunning outfit in gray and white—silver cuirass with plastron over a darker gray revers with a deep, white, pie-crust frill encircling her neck. Agnes hurried across the veranda and down the steps as fast as her fashionably slim skirts would allow. Long black fringe edging the slate-gray V-shaped overskirt shimmied as she covered the ground with tiny, quick steps...*sans* hat.

Inez tensed. "Aunt Agnes would never venture out of doors in such a proper ensemble without a hat, unless something was seriously amiss."

Jonathan DuChamps appeared at the still open door, following hard in Aunt Agnes' footsteps.

Inez thought it would be a close call to see who won the race to the carriage—Agnes, who had a head start, or Jonathan, who was catching up with his long stride.

It was Agnes by a nose.

Inez handed William down to Mark. "Aunt Agnes, what's wrong?"

Agnes put a hand over her bosom, saying, "The most horrible thing, Inez. The most horrible thing. I will never set foot out of New York again. This place, they can return it to the Indians."

"Harmony?" Inez's blood ran cold.

"Your sister's fine," Jonathan assured her. "Truly, something very unfortunate has happened, but not unusual. I don't want you to be unduly alarmed..."

"That marvelous Mr. Calder!" Agnes burst out. "He's dead!"

Chapter Thirty-seven

Inez felt as if someone had thrown a blanket over her head, muffling all sight and sound, taking away all sense.

"Mr. Calder, dead?" she stammered. "What happened? When?"

"*Dread*ful," said Agnes. "He was so young, so vibrant, so talented, in the prime of his life. I could understand if he were an invalid and had passed away in his sleep, but this…"

"What happened?" Inez demanded in a stronger voice.

Jonathan cut in before Agnes could continue. "He had an unfortunate accident up Williams' Canyon. Fellow must have had no warning at all, no time to move out of the way."

"*Crushed*," said Agnes with dismay and an underlying relish that Inez found positively ghoulish. "A ton of rocks loosened from The Narrows wall and…"

"Mrs. Underwood, you are letting your imagination run away to no good whatsoever. This is not a situation that requires added drama, in that it is tragic enough in the truth," said Jonathan. He turned back to Mark and Inez. "As I understand, Calder was prone to going out for an early constitutional, walking or riding often before sunrise. He apparently was on his way up the canyon, and had just exited The Narrows when the rocks fell. The most common deaths around Manitou, I've been told, are runaway buggies and rocks falling off the cliffs and walls. As far as anyone can tell, it was mercifully quick."

"His head was *crushed,*" Agnes added emphatically. "Jonathan, you must not allow Harmony or William to go up there again. It's dangerous. In fact, we should arrange for the first train home."

"I'm sorry, Mrs. Stannert," said Jonathan. "I understand you and your young friend had made his acquaintance soon after you arrived."

It was as if someone had suddenly ripped the blanket off her muddled sensibilities, leaving her staring into the sun. "Miss Carothers! Has anyone told her?" She looked from Jonathan to Agnes. Seeing their blank expressions, she said, "I am going. Immediately. She is staying in Mrs. Galbreaith's boarding house, so that is where I'll be." She gripped the reins tighter, moved across the buggy seat, and took the whip from its socket. "Mark, will you please take William back to his room? I shall return later this evening. Do not wait up for me."

She nodded at Billy, who immediately let go of the horse's head. She commanded, "Trot!"

The horse started trotting down the drive. At the fork that led back to the road, the horse hesitated at the pressure of the reins, as if any direction other than toward the livery must be a mistake. She increased the pull of the rein and said again, "Trot!"

Training took over, and the horse obeyed the command, moving out of the drive and back onto the main road, rising to a trot.

Dusk was closing in under the shadow of Pike's Peak when Inez knocked on the door of Ohio House and was greeted by a solemn Mrs. Galbreaith. "We heard early today about Mr. Calder," Mrs. Galbreaith said. "Susan insisted we go to the canyon and see where it happened. Neither of us could quite believe it. She was quite distraught, but determined to take photographs of the area where he died." Mrs. Galbreaith shook her head. "Susan developed them this afternoon and is looking at them now."

She escorted Inez into the parlor, where Susan stood by a podium, one arm braced, as she examined a handful of images with a magnifying glass. When Mrs. Galbreaith announced Inez, Susan put down the glass and said, "Hello, Inez," very subdued.

Inez wanted to run to her and give her a hug. But she held back, instead walking up to her friend, putting a hand on her shoulder.

Susan covered her face with both hands. Inez was afraid she was crying, or in danger of bursting into tears. Instead, Susan very slowly rubbed her face, as if trying to bring life back into a countenance too weary and sad. She dropped her hands at last. "They say it was an accident."

"I heard."

"It wasn't," Susan's mouth, usually so quick to smile, curved downward. "It couldn't be. Not from what I've found here." She gazed down at the images on the flat top—two cabinet cards, two unmounted photographs, all of The Narrows.

Inez moved closer. "Show me."

Susan slid the two cabinet cards toward Inez and handed her the magnifying glass. "These were taken by Mrs. Galbreaith just a handful of days ago. It's The Narrows, from both sides."

A familiar male figure stood just visible beyond the looming overhand in both images, hands in pockets, a carefree smile beneath the hat. Inez lowered the glass. "Is that Mr. Calder?"

"Yes, that's Robert." Her voice caught. "Now, look at the ones I took early this afternoon. He's gone, of course, having been taken back to town, but the rocks remain."

Dread pushing through her, Inez picked up the glass and looked at the two unmounted pictures. A fair-sized boulder and a number of smaller, fist-sized pieces lay in the path.

"Do you see any difference in the rock walls? Either direction?" Susan's voice was intense. She stood so close to Inez, looking at the photos, that Inez could feel her breath on the back of the hand holding the glass.

Inez looked at the both sets, the old and the new. "No, they look the same to me."

"That is because they are. I took the cabinet cards with me, so I could be sure to take my photographs from the same angles and distances. There are no fresh scars, no difference in the rock walls before or after the incident."

Inez slowly lowered the glass and gazed at Susan, absorbing what that meant. "Those rocks on the ground, the ones that crushed him…"

"Did not fall from the wall, as everyone says they did." Susan's hands, resting on the podium, curled into fists. "It was not an act of nature."

"Then what happened?" Inez pondered a bit. "Did someone kill him and try to make it look like nature's handiwork? If so, where did these rocks come from? That one to the side, it's too large for even a very strong man to pick up and move. And moved from where and how? Could it have been hauled in by cart? How awkward that would be. Even at an early morning hour, a horse and cart, or a handcart might be noticed. That rock had to be from the canyon, somewhere close by."

Her time by The Narrows with Harmony slowly came into focus. "Wait," said Inez. She picked up the glass and looked more closely at the two images taken on the far side, where Inez and Harmony had talked. In the older image, she could plainly see the flat-topped rock where they had sat, side by side. Where Harmony had placed the closed parasol between them before asking about William, and where Inez had smacked her elbow on the sharp edged chunk of limestone, balanced to the side.

There, in the newer image, was the same bench-sized rock. Only…

"It's gone," said Inez.

"What's gone?" Susan bent over the photographs.

Inez handed Susan the magnifying glass and tapped lightly on the recent image. "This bench-like rock is set back from the trail, but not much. Look at the far end of it. What do you see?"

Susan examined the image. "Nothing."

"Yes. Now, look at Mrs. Galbreaith's photograph."

Susan did. Inez heard her suck in a breath. "The boulder on top. It's gone."

"Now, look at the other photo you took today with the rock in the road."

Susan was silent for a moment, then lowered the glass, staring at Inez. "They are shaped the same and have that dark streak down the middle. It must be the same stone."

Inez nodded. "Someone moved the boulder. They created a scene, a tableau set up to look like rockfall. It's a common occurrence, so when he was found, people saw what they wanted to see, what they expected to see. But you're right, Susan. It was no accident. Someone killed Robert Calder."

◇◇◇

Inez stayed long enough to share a cup of tea with Mrs. Galbreaith and Susan. "Mrs. Crowson's mint tea," said Mrs. Galbreaith. "Nothing better during stressful times."

By now, Inez hated the very smell of mint, but she sipped to be sociable and out of respect for Susan's sorrow. Inez herself was still stunned by the revelation that Calder was dead. He had seemed larger than life, with so much energy and with fortune smiling on him. How could he be gone? *The world is not a just place. I know that. Some wrongs, one must simply shoulder and go on. But others, one must fight to right them. This is one of those times.*

"I will take the photographs to the marshal tomorrow," said Susan.

Mrs. Galbreaith lay a hand over hers. "My dear, do as you must, but I'll warn you that he is not likely to give much consideration to a misplaced stone and missing marks on the canyon walls. Accidents such as these frequently happen, and, in this case, without clear evidence of foul play—his wallet was still in his pocket, no thievery, no evidence of a fight—why would anyone look any further? Too, this is the summer season. Visitors and tourists are the lifeblood here, the marshal will probably want to treat it as a simple accident, an unfortunate matter of timing, and make as little of it as possible."

"I owe it to Robert to try," Susan said fiercely.

Inez said, "I will go with you."

"It may not be easy to reach Marshal Robbins. He will probably be at Henry Colby's saloon in Colorado City," Mrs. Galbreaith commented.

"A saloon?" Inez raised her eyebrows in interest, thinking of the thin line of buildings staggered along the road between Colorado Springs and Manitou that was the sum total of the "city."

"Indeed. One of the very few in the area," said Mrs. Galbreaith with distaste, obviously misinterpreting Inez's curiosity. "Since Colorado Springs is dry, and Manitou has no such establishments within its city limits, it is up to Colorado City to supply spirits to the dissolute. Pardon, I did not mean to disparage the town or our marshal, of course. In any case, it would be best if I send one of my boys to find him and bring him here. I shall invite the marshal to join us for lunch, and that should bring him round most promptly. Mrs. Stannert, would you join us as well?"

With this plan in place, Inez said her farewells, and gave Susan a hug at the door.

"Thank you, Inez," Susan whispered in the embrace. "I only knew him a few days. But I felt that we were kindred spirits, even so."

"Never apologize for mourning those who have gone," said Inez. "We will find out what happened. I promise."

On her way back to Manitou Springs House, Inez reflected bleakly that with all the promises she had been making—to Mrs. Pace, to Harmony, and now to Susan—she seemed no closer to finding the truth. She gave herself a little mental shake. *That is not so. We now know that Dr. Prochazka appears to turn away the hopeless cases, perhaps to protect his reputation as a bringer of medical miracles. Lewis is hiding something to do with the War and has probably varnished the truth about the hotel's financial future and current status. We know that Lewis and Epperley cannot abide anything that throws a shadow over the Mountain Springs House's vaunted prospects, and that at least some of the hotel's investors seem desperate for others to join them. Drowning men will grab at each other and their rescuers, pulling them under with them into Poseidon's watery realm.*

She drove the horse and buggy around the hotel, directly to the livery. As she'd hoped, Mr. Morrow was there. After stepping out of the buggy, Inez followed Morrow through the double doors. She caught sight of a separate room to the side with a bunk, and a kerosene lantern next to an open book on a simple table.

"I'm impressed that the hotel staffs the livery at all hours," she said conversationally.

"Well, with the hops, balls, dances, and entertainment at the various hotels, we have people arrivin' all hours of the night and sometimest into the morning," said Morrow.

"So, you live here?"

He shifted his hat back a bit, and selected a halter from the tack hanging on the wall. "During the summer season, there's always someone here. Billy's old enough, he takes the nights wherest we don't expect much in the way of coming and going. I do the rest."

"Mr. Calder took a buggy out last night."

He released the horse from the harness before replying. "Yep. Heard about him. Real sad."

"Tragic." Inez agreed. "Were you here when he brought the buggy back?"

"That I was." He looked at her, straight on. Not offering anything, but not holding back either.

"How did he seem to you?"

"Well, I knowst he's been sparkin' that young lady who came down from Leadville with you. Seen them a couple times out walkin' and such. He seemed in high spirits." He shook his head.

"What?"

"Well, just thinkin' of the crazy business in the Garden of the Gods yesterday. Good horses, both. They were bred from the same sire and dam." He looked toward the stalls, in the back of the livery. "Guess that boy is without a rider now. I know he looked forward to getting out for a good run every day, just like the gentleman. They were two of a kind, full of high spirits and not afraid of next to nothing."

"After the incident in the Garden, did Mr. Calder ask you about the nosebag?"

Morrow glanced at her. "That he did. He knowst I had nothing to do with it. I was as sorrowed as he was. We had a considerable confabulation about it all."

Inez stepped to the side as Morrow began to brush down the horse and clean her coat. "Any idea how that happened? How the poison berries got mixed into the feed?"

"Nope. It's not even a plant fromst around here, he told me."

"Do you have your suspicions?"

"You do ask a lot of questions, Mrs. Stannert."

She set a gentle hand on the horse's withers. The equine flesh was warm and comforting to the touch. "There's a lot here that needs to be brought out into the open, Mr. Morrow. I can understand you have loyalty to the people here, but look at what has happened. Calder's brother, early this year. Mr. Pace, on that ride down from Leadville. That poor mare in the Garden of the Gods, an innocent victim if ever there was one. And now, Mr. Calder. Taken one by one, there seems to be a logical explanation for each. Calder's brother? Simply his time, he was killed by consumption. Mr. Pace? Heart attack, brought on by age and his trip into the high mountains. Mr. Calder? Rockfall, which is nothing unusual, I've been told. But the horse, that is where explanations fail. If things had progressed differently, Calder and his horse would probably have been far away from everyone. Everyone knew he liked to venture out into wild and unreachable territory and he'd planned to ride into rocky, steep terrain that day. What would have happened if Calder's horse had eaten Herb Paris under such circumstances? Going up or coming down a steep slope, a fatal misstep, a sudden spook, horse and rider would have been broken, most likely dead. It would have been chalked up as another 'accident.' But it didn't happen that way."

She watched Morrow closely as she laid it out, stepped him through the story. It was like guiding a horse from the buggy seat with a barely perceptible wave of the whip. She saw how his face, so expressive in its weathered lines, closed up in sorrow, how an unseen burden bent his shoulders.

Inez continued, "Not to cast aspersions upon the people who have died, but one could say, well, each of us has our sins to bear, perhaps these deaths reflect some hidden sins we have no knowledge of. But a horse? A horse, an innocent animal, has no sin. Someone decided to kill one of God's own creatures and make it suffer. I have my own sweet mare, and the thought of someone wishing her harm is intolerable." She paused, sensing she had touched him where his deepest beliefs were held. "Mr. Morrow, if you know anything that might help work this out, please tell me. For instance, who comes and goes regularly, late at night? Who would have access to the horses, such that Billy, or you, would not give it a second thought? Mr. Epperley, perhaps? Mr. Lewis? What about the medical personnel?"

He turned his back, focused on finishing the currying. "Epperley goes circulatin', sometimes. He came back late the night afore Calder went up to the Garden. Nurse Crowson, she tends to some of the invalids 'round here when she's not workin' with the physiker. She walks around town, but sometimest takes a buggy to outlyin' areas. She came in late that night as well. Lewis, well, he owns the whole shebang and comes and goes whensoever he wants. He'll wander in, make like he's giving the place the eye to be sure all is proper. My take is, I believe he sometimes prefers the simple company of horseflesh. Life's uncomplicated out here in the stables, not like in the hotel. The horses don't complain and jump all over you if the victuals are too warm or too cold."

Despite herself, Inez smiled. Then she asked, "What about the physicians, Zuckerman and Prochazka?"

"They've naught interest in the animals." He dismissed them with a shrug. "Only as they carry them from here to there. Dr. Prochazka's up all hours—you can see light in the windows, almost all night—but he doesn't leave his clinic."

At least, not when you're awake.

Still, that seemed to lift suspicion from the two physicians. Too, she couldn't imagine a doctor purposely taking a life. It ran so counter to the philosophy of the healing arts. She sighed. *My bet is on Lewis. That is where I'll start tomorrow.*

Chapter Thirty-eight

"Remember to take your key with you. Don't hand it in to the front desk," Inez said. It was after breakfast the next morning, and Inez and Mark were in their suite, preparing to go their separate ways for the day.

"Just what do you have in mind?" Mark gave his top hat a last pass with the hat brush.

"I plan to gain a key to the kingdom of the Mountain Springs House," she said, setting her own key on a side table in the sitting room. "Have you heard any more talk about Robert Calder's passing?"

"Just what little I gathered last night when I got in. Lewis said they have packed his belongings, and between him and the marshal, they are sending notification to his family. Guess since his brother stayed here last season for a while, and since Calder was here most of the summer, they know how to reach his kin." He glanced at Inez as he settled the hat on his head. "How is Miss Carothers holdin' up?"

"Very saddened. She liked him a great deal. Makes me all the more determined to find out who is at the bottom of his death." She picked up a lightweight summer shawl draped over a nearby chair. "I will be meeting her and the marshal today, although I hardly expect him to change his tune based on a couple of photographs. Still, we shall see what he says." She glanced out the window, calculating the light. "We should head downstairs. I'm certain your companions are champing at the bit, eager to take you around and have you sample each of Manitou's wondrous mineral springs while they expound on how many grains of carbonate of soda in a pint here, how many grains of lithia there. I cannot abide the stuff, and I'm nearly as weary hearing about the health benefits of the water as I am about Nurse Crowson's mint tea. Epperley is going on this day-long jaunt as well?"

"I'll have all the bigwigs with me."

"Good. Then we shall see what we shall see. Just don't let Jonathan DuChamps sign anything, if you can."

"I'll play to the gallery so they leave him alone," Mark held the door open for her.

As he locked the door behind them, she said, "Be sure to pocket your key."

"You told me that once already, darlin'." He slid it into his jacket, and with the silver-headed cane tucked under one arm, offered her the other.

Downstairs, she watched him leave with Lewis, Epperley, Zuckerman, and Harmony's husband. She took a casual turn around the veranda to give them time, watching the children at play, shadowed by nursemaids and nannies. The staying-in adults—mostly the frail, and the elderly—moved in a slow cadence on rockers. She smiled at Nurse Crowson, who approached her, wheeling her patient in a rattan-backed invalid chair.

"Good morning, Mrs. Stannert," she said.

"It would be better if not for the sad business of yesterday."

"Ah, poor Mr. Calder. That was a sad business indeed. He did love his early-morning constitutionals. Going out alone, though, certainly has its dangers, if one doesn't know the area."

"He was here for the entire summer," Inez pointed out. She reversed direction to walk with the nurse and her charge.

"Still," said Nurse Crowson, pushing the chair smoothly over the boards, the little squeak, squeak, squeak of the wheels announcing its progression. "Visitors become so charmed by the natural wonders, they sometimes forget that this is still a wild place."

"Yet," said Inez, thinking of what Morrow had said the previous evening, "you walk alone at night."

The wheels did a little stutter, and Nurse Crowson paused to tuck a blanket more closely around her patient. "Are you cold?" she asked. "We can go inside now, if you'd like. We've had the fifteen minutes the doctor recommends."

A claw-like hand ventured out and a voice made thready by coughing said, "A little longer, Mrs. Crowson. Such a pleasant morning." The nurse commenced pushing again.

"You were out the night before last," Inez continued. "I saw you getting out of Calder's buggy, out front of the hotel, from my window."

That brought Nurse Crowson's eyes full upon her. For a moment, Inez felt as chilled as when she had plunged her hands into the stream up in Cheyenne Canyon.

"I couldn't sleep," added Inez, somewhat belatedly, realizing that it sounded as if she was spying out the window, perhaps looking for her return. "I heard the buggy arrive when I was sitting by the window, getting some air."

Nurse Crowson looked away. "I was out walking. Mr. Calder was kind enough to offer me a ride back to the hotel. You are having trouble sleeping, Mrs. Stannert? You should have told me or the doctor earlier. I shall prepare you some of my tea for tonight. I promise, it will help you sleep."

Inez suppressed a wince at the thought of more mint. "Most kind. But I wondered, are you not afraid being out alone so late at night? It seems it would be dangerous. I have heard there are catamounts that roam about the area."

Nurse Crowson laughed. An unexpected sound. There was a merry tinkle to her voice that hinted at the young girl she had once been. "I know this area well and know how to take care of myself. I tend to some of the invalids in the various boarding houses as I have time in the evenings and at night. There are so many suffering. I do what I can to bring relief to those who ask."

Inez's gaze fell back upon the patient in the invalid chair. "Your dedication is admirable and appreciated by many, I can tell."

Mrs. Crowson seemed to warm to the praise, a faint smile growing on her face.

"For instance, Mr. Travers," Inez continued. "Is he still at the hotel? I've not seen him of late."

The smile vanished. "He no longer is here."

"Do any of your patients reside at the Colorado Springs Hotel?" Inez asked, thinking that, no matter what the nurse had told Lewis, she might know of the mysterious Dr. Galloway, given her connections to the invalid community.

"No." The response was abrupt. "There are plenty needing assistance here in Manitou and nearby without my venturing to Colorado Springs. Good day, Mrs. Stannert. We have been outside long enough, and I must prepare my patient here for the baths. You should try them, the mineral baths. Very healthful."

Inez looked out at the long ramshackle building sulking next to Fountain Creek, a walking distance away. "I shall keep it in mind."

Nurse Crowson spun the chair in a half circle and headed back to the main door.

After dallying a minute or two longer, Inez returned to the reception desk. The morning clerk was smooth-cheeked and sported an ambitious line of peach fuzz, struggling to become a mustache.

"Oh, I'm so sorry," she told the young earnest-faced clerk behind the desk. "But my husband locked my key in our rooms, and he's out for the day. Quite silly of me, I know, to forget it."

"No problem at all," he assured her.

Inez watched as he opened a small drawer at belly level behind the desk and pulled out a skeleton key on a large ring. She suppressed a smile of satisfaction. They went upstairs, and he opened the door with a flourish. "Madam."

"Thank you."

Once he left, Inez retrieved her key, made sure she had what she needed for the next step in her plans, went to DuChamps' suite and knocked.

A moment later, Harmony opened the door and invited her in. Lily and William were already there, rolling a ball back and forth across the floor of the central sitting room. Aunt Agnes sat close to the door, looking for all the world like Cerberus guarding the gate to the underworld.

"Aren't you going out for your morning constitutional?" Inez inquired.

Harmony sighed, and glanced at Aunt Agnes. "Dear aunt has decided we are not to leave the hotel unless we are accompanied by either Jonathan or a guide. Honestly, Aunt Agnes, what danger could possibly befall us by walking up to the spring for a cup of mineral water and then back again? Dr. Prochazka instructed us to take the air, at least twice a day. You were so insistent that I follow his prescriptions to the letter."

"We can have someone deliver the water here," said Agnes, snapping her fan open as if it were a weapon. "Stampeding horses. Falling rocks. Wild animals. No, we stay here. A little later, we shall stroll around the veranda. That will provide fresh air enough."

"Perhaps Inez could come with us to the springs," said Harmony. "Why, the Manitou Soda spring is only a few steps over the bridge, and the Navajo is just a little farther."

"Certainly she is invited, but we will not go out until Jonathan returns or we can take one of the hotel staff with us. Preferably someone who is armed with a pistol and knows how to use it in case we are attacked by a bear. Or a snake."

Harmony rolled her eyes at Inez and said, "In that case, I suppose we shall have a quiet day inside today, because Jonathan is not due back until nearly dinnertime."

"Oh dear," said Inez. She added, "Do you perchance have any empty bottles of tonic about?"

Harmony's eyebrows drew together. "One from yesterday. Why?"

Inez held out her hand. "I shall be happy to return it for you." She wiggled her fingers in a give-it-to-me gesture. In a low voice, she said, "Please. It's important. I'll explain later, if you wish."

Without a word, Harmony disappeared into the bedroom and returned, handing Inez a small brown bottle. Inez tucked it into her reticule with a smile. She turned to Aunt Agnes, saying, "I will be going to Ohio House to visit Miss Carothers today, so shall be on the lookout for rattlesnakes, dear aunt. But before I go, I have something I must discuss with you." She located a wooden chair that had been moved aside to make room for Lily, William, and the ball, and arranged it so she could sit facing Aunt Agnes.

Aunt Agnes pulled her head back, like a turtle that didn't appreciate the sudden intrusion. "Well, then, what is it, Inez. Goodness, you can move back a bit. I can hardly breathe."

"I know you have lived with Mama and Papa these past few years, since Harmony married," said Inez, staying where she was.

"Of course." The fan moved faster. "*Some*one had to be there for your mother. Your father is my brother, and none knows better than I how little he is around these days. Too, someone needs to keep an eye on things. And run the household, since she has been so weak. Harmony has her own household and your son to consider, so one can hardly expect her to take up the additional burden."

Inez didn't miss the accusation, but chose to dodge that battle.

"I understand that Papa threw away all the letters I wrote home." Inez watched closely, to gauge her aunt's reaction to this simple fact.

Agnes sniffed. "He did not toss them. He burned them. Except for a few I was able to smuggle to your sister after her marriage, so you could re-establish your relationship."

Inez nodded. That was true. Harmony had told her as much. "I understand that Papa did the same with Mark's letters. The ones he sent to New York, addressed to me, this past year."

She saw Aunt Agnes' eyes widen, then dart furtively left and right, as if looking for an escape route. Finally, that penetrating blue gaze fastened on Inez with unblinking intensity. "He wrote to you? In New York? I don't believe so. I never saw letters to that effect. If he told you so, he was lying."

Inez raised an eyebrow, without comment. *No, dear aunt. He wasn't lying. You are.*

Agnes continued, picking up steam, "He is probably just trying to worm his way back into your good graces."

"I thought you liked him, Aunt Agnes."

Her fan ceased its frantic fluttering, snapped closed, and Agnes tapped Inez's gloved hand with it condescendingly. "Oh nonsense, dear child. How could I like a man who *deserted* you and your wonderful little boy, only to turn up now, as you are finally ready to return to your family? I'm doing my utmost to be polite, but really. I don't trust him, and you shouldn't either."

Inez smiled thinly and stood. "Well, I hope you have a pleasant morning. I shall be back later today, after the noon meal. I do hope you get out for that turn around the veranda. I suspect if all the consumptive guests are safe sitting on the piazza, you will survive as well."

◇◇◇

As for lunch at the Ohio House, it went about as Inez expected. Marshal Robbins was more than happy to devour Mrs. Galbreaith's fried chicken, potatoes and gravy, and blackberry pie, and consume quarts of lemonade, but was not inclined to listen to Inez's and Susan's theories on Calder's death.

"Ladies," he finally said, pushing empty plates and the four photographs to one side. "Mr. Calder was an ace-high fellow. I can understand you wanting to argufy about the way in which he came to meet his Maker, because it's a shame and a half. But there's nothing that points to anything other than him being in the wrong place at the wrong time."

"But there are no marks on the walls to indicate where a rock of that size would have come loose," said Susan again, pushing the before-and-after images back toward him. "Look for yourself." She set a magnifying glass by the pictures.

The marshal crossed his arms, as if by refusing to touch them the photographs might magically disappear. "Probably came off the wall from higher up."

"But in that case, he would have heard the rock coming," Inez pointed out. "He would have had time to move out of the way."

"Maybe he decided to try climbin' the cliffs," the marshal countered. "Some of these young fellas, they take on anything close to verticality, just for the sport of it. I've seen 'em do it. And if Calder was up there and grabbed a loose rock, well, that's it. Down they come, and that's the sorry end to it."

Susan opened her mouth again. Inez caught her eye and shook her head. She knew exactly what Susan was going to say, because the same retort was on her lips: *If that were the case, more than his head would have been injured.*

Logic, Inez could see, wasn't going to sway the marshal's take on the incident. His mouth was set in a stubborn straight line. Arms folded across his chest. He was squared up to stand off any opposition, whether a stampede of raging buffalo or a passel of angry petticoats.

"Who found him?" Inez asked.

He uncrossed his arms. "Mrs. Crowson. She'd taken one of the hotel's folks out for a constitutional after breakfast, in the invalid chair, you see. When they happened on the scene, she told me she could see there was no hope for him, so came back and reported to Mr. Lewis, who sent for me."

Mrs. Galbreaith appeared from the kitchen, with a tray of cups. "Coffee, Marshal?" she asked.

"Don't mind if I do. Mrs. Galbreaith, you make the finest Arbuckle's this side of the Mississippi."

She smiled, acknowledging his praise, and set full cups all around, with the cream pitcher near to hand. "I will offer a prayer for Mr. Calder and his family," she said. "How tragic for all of them. First the elder son, and now the younger. I suppose you had a physician determine cause of death? For the family's sake, if nothing else."

He poured a generous amount of cream into his coffee and stirred. The dark liquid faded to caramel brown. "Well, ma'am, as you know, Manitou doesn't have a coroner, but you can't throw a rock without hittin' a sawbones or two. When I arrived at the Mountain Springs House, they'd already rustled up Doc Zuckerman to attend. He came up the canyon with us, gave the situation the eyeball, and determined that it was a sad and sorrowful act of God and Nature that caused Mr. Calder to pass in his chips, and nothing else."

After the unsatisfactory conversation with the marshal, Inez made her way back across Manitou Springs, skirting the Navajo spring, crossing the bridge, and passing the Manitou Soda on her way to the Mountain Springs House. She had hoped that Harmony had somehow succeeded in convincing Aunt Agnes that no bears would come galumphing down into town to snatch them up. But none of the places held her family, so Inez walked on to her hotel.

Her mind picked over the marshal's remarks, turning his comments this way and that, attempting to bring order to disorder.

Why didn't Nurse Crowson say anything to me about having discovered Calder when I saw her this morning? Very convenient that Dr. Zuckerman was there to attend. Why didn't they ask Dr. Prochazka, who is, after all, the hotel's doctor? Was that Lewis' doing, calling Zuckerman to be the attending physician? And just how much "eyeballing" did Dr. Zuckerman do? Not much, I'd wager.

When Inez arrived back at the hotel, she stopped on the veranda, grateful for the shade. She moved along the front porch, choosing a rocker at the far corner, and sat for a moment to rock and cool down from her walk. A waiter carrying a tray stopped to see if she wanted anything. She turned down the offer of iced mint tea—Mrs. Crowson's special blend, the waiter reminded her, and was then offered a lemonade. Again, she demurred. Finally, perhaps more vociferously than required, she turned down a sparkling mineral water concoction that the waiter explained was guaranteed to "animate the vital forces" and was approved by Drs. Prochazka and Zuckerman. She waited until the disappointed waiter left before slipping her handkerchief from her sleeve and tucking it into the seat of the rocker so that a small portion of the linen was visible. When all was set for the next part of her plan, she rose and strolled into the hotel.

She was happy to see that the young desk clerk from the morning was still on duty. A quick glance around the lobby reassured her he was the only other person in the lobby and that the music room across the way was empty.

Her timing was good in other respects: As far as she could tell, the majority of guests seemed to be out, resting in their rooms, or otherwise engaged in after-lunch activities away from the hotel. In any case, the lobby was quite deserted. She halted by the front desk and asked for her room key, making a show of fanning herself and leaning heavily upon the edge of the reception desk. As the clerk handed her the key, she searched her purse before looking at him helplessly. "Oh dear. I must have dropped my handkerchief on the rocker outside when I stopped to rest. I would retrieve it, but am so exhausted from traipsing about this morning."

"I'll be glad to fetch it for you, ma'am." The young man hurried from behind the counter. "Which chair?"

"To the right as you exit the door, at the end of the veranda."

"Would you like to sit in the music room until I return?" His hand hovered near her elbow, as if uncertain whether he should offer aid or not.

"I think it's better if I just remain here and catch my breath. I do appreciate your coming to my aid."

"I'll be back immediately." He hurried out the front door.

Inez glanced around once more. No one was in sight. She reached over the desk and felt for the drawer she knew was there. Grasping the knob, Inez slid the drawer open. A smile bloomed on her face as not one, but three large rings came into view—each holding an identical skeleton key.

Inez hooked one of the rings with a finger, lifted it from the drawer, and slid the drawer shut. She dropped ring and key into her purse, and commenced fanning herself again, feeling quite pleased with herself.

The front door opened, and the clerk returned, triumphant, with Inez's embroidered handkerchief held on high. She thanked him profusely, causing his cheeks to pink in the most endearing manner. She almost felt guilty for the ruse.

Almost.

She made as if to start up the stairs, and then turned around as if she'd just thought of something. "Excuse me, but is Nurse Crowson around this afternoon? Nothing urgent, I had a small question for her."

"She's taken a guest up to the Ute Iron spring," the ever-so-helpful clerk explained.

"Ah, the Ute Iron. That is quite a ways up Ruxton Avenue, is it not?"

"Yes, a bit of a walk, but well worth it," he added. "Some physicians feel it is one of the most medically beneficial springs in the area. Although all have their benefits. It depends on the ailment, of course, as to what treatments the doctors recommend."

"Of course. Any thought on when the nurse might return?"

He twisted around to glance at the wall clock behind the desk. "They left perhaps half an hour ago. The springs can be crowded this time of day, and it is a bit of a stroll…I'd guess they won't return for a good hour or two."

She nodded, more and more pleased. "Thank you."

"Shall I send Mrs. Crowson up to your room when she returns?"

"Oh, no need of that," Inez said hastily. "I will find her at dinner time. That is quite soon enough. Thank you so much. I shall make a point of telling Mr. Lewis what an asset you are to the hotel."

He brightened noticeably and stood a little straighter at his post behind the desk. "If there is anything else I can do for you, Mrs. Stannert, just ask."

She beamed. "Thank you! You have been immensely helpful."

More than you can possibly know.

Chapter Thirty-nine

Upstairs, in front of her suite, Inez pulled out the passkey. Into the lock, a twist of the wrist, and the door clicked open.

Good. So I know it fits the regular rooms. I hope they didn't go so far as to put different locks on the bottom-floor rooms.

Inez entered her stifling bedroom, poured water into the basin, dampened a corner of the hand towel and patted her face to remove the dried sweat. She could imagine the sun, beating down on the rooftop, pushing the heat into the second-story rooms. She wondered how Harmony, Aunt Agnes, Lily, and William were faring.

She cracked the window sash to bring in a bit of outside air. Turning away from the window, she took a deep breath to prepare herself. *I must have a ready story, in case I am caught wandering about.*

The first problem was quickly solved as she recalled the women's staircase that led from her floor to the dining area. No one would be in the dining hall at this between-hour, so she was certain she'd be able to slip down without being seen and avoid the lobby altogether. As for the second problem, Inez took Harmony's empty tonic bottle out of her reticule and smiled. "Thank you, dear sister, for your help," she said aloud to the empty room and pocketed the bottle. Inez placed room and skeleton keys in her purse and exited her suite, taking care to lock the door behind her. From there, it was only a few steps to the end of the hall and a quick descent down the women's stairs to the dining room. At the bottom of the stairs, Inez paused to get her bearings.

It was the dead time between the noon and dinner hour. Tables were prepared for the evening meal, napkins folded into arrow-like peaks and set over crystal goblets. Silverware reflected the mountain motif, with forks and knives balanced into small "teepees" at each place setting, and the menu set square for viewing. All was silent and waiting.

Inez skirted the edge of the room, slipped out the doors and into the corridor between the dining area and the music room. She moved quickly down the corridor, away from the lobby, grateful for the window at the end of the long hall for the afternoon light it shed into the long doorless tunnel. Mrs. Pace's directions had been clear: The stairs were nearly at the end of the corridor. There were no doors along the way, no reason for guests to be in that particular hallway.

Sure enough, a stroll along the empty hall yielded a set of stairs, leading down. Inez paused, gripping her purse in hands which were suddenly sweaty inside her kid gloves. In the hallway, deserted though it was, explanations for her presence came easily. *Just taking a turn around the hotel, looking for a little solitude. Strolling to the window, to look outside.* All believable, understandable, quickly accepted and forgotten.

But the minute she set foot on the stairs and, even more so, once she had entered the dark and shadowed underworld—a world where she did not, by any stretch of imagination, belong—it would be much harder to explain her presence. Her hand snaked into her pocket, touched her sister's empty tonic bottle. *This is my talisman. My passage back to the upper world, should I need it.*

With a deep breath, she headed down the stairs.

At the bottom, feet on unfinished wood planks she paused again, looking to left and right. To the left was the storage area—shadowy shapes of crates, cans, and bags lined up along the floor and in ranks of shelves. She could understand why a small child would instantly take to a game of hide-and-seek in this world beneath. To the right, shelf-lined walls guarded an entry to a passageway that ended in a door. A door, she felt certain, tucked under the veranda.

She held her breath, listening.

Nothing.

Not even the squeak of footsteps on the boards above.

She moved into the hallway until she reached two doors, set with lockplates that looked encouragingly like the plates on the doors to all the hotel rooms upstairs. To left or to right?

According to Mrs. Pace, Lewis' rooms were to the left. *He is safely out all day, no doubt busy pouring tales of Manitou's marvelous future into Mark's ear.* The unknown rooms, perhaps belonging to Nurse Crowson, were to the right. The smell of mint was strong in that direction, almost mesmerizing in its promise. Open me, the door seemed to whisper. Open me.

With that, she turned and inserted the key into the door on the right. She released her breath with a sigh when the key turned, the lock clicked, and the door swung ajar. Without thinking any further, Inez stepped in and pushed the door closed. She stood in a small sitting room. A small window with heavy dark green curtains pulled back an arm's width to reveal sheer voile panels underneath, looked out on a shadowed world under the veranda. A couple of mahogany chairs covered in worn green velvet shared a set of nesting tables. One of the tables was missing, judging by the gap. Inez identified the chairs as cast-offs from the women's parlor upstairs. Two empty teacups sat on the topmost table.

The smell of mint was even stronger inside. Aware that she shouldn't tarry, she scanned the room, which was almost Quaker in its simplicity, then focused on a door opposite from the window, leading further back into the building's lower floor. It turned out to be the entrance to the nurse's sleeping quarters. Inez left the door open to shed some light into the interior. Even so, it was quite dim. Inez wished she could light the candle that sat in its brass holder on the bedstand, but was concerned that, should Nurse Crowson return from her walk and come directly to her apartments, she would detect the smoke, even through the mint.

The bedstand held a tintype, framed in paper. Curious, she carried it to the door for more light. The image showed two men in front of a tent, one sitting on a camp chair, the other on a box. Both stared straight ahead into the camera. A board hanging on the front of the tent said "Surgery." Given that the men were in uniform and kepis, Inez guessed it was the Civil War, most likely the Union side.

Inez readily identified one of the men as a younger Franklin Lewis, right down to the sideburns. The other man, a stranger, sported a chin beard and the smooth unlined face of untested youth. A table between the two men held a dark bag. Inez squinted, sighed, and fished around in her purse, finally pulling out her reading glasses, so she could bring the image into focus. It looked like a physician's instrument bag. She flipped the photograph over. The backing was blank, but the glue that had sealed it to the front had long since lost its adhesiveness. She cautiously lifted the backing to expose the reverse side of the tintype. Scratched into the metal in tiny letters were two sets of initials: *VLF* and *SCF.*

"Huh," Inez said aloud, puzzled. She smoothed down the backing and returned to the image. If the man on the left was Lewis, as she felt certain it was, the initials didn't quite match up. V mostly likely stood for Victor, the name the nurse had let slip and which Lewis had chastised her for uttering. But LF? Victor Lewis Franklin, perhaps? A slightly skewed version of his current name? And who was the second man? *Since the final initial is common to them both, perhaps he is a brother.* Examining the faces of the two, she detected a definite resemblance. Inez shook her head, and focused again on the physician's bag and the sign above the tent.

Lewis swears he knows nothing of the medical profession. This photograph suggests otherwise.

She frowned. Why would Nurse Crowson have this by her bedside? She thought back to what Epperley had said and the interactions she'd observed. *They are related, brother and sister. Perhaps working in the medical field runs in the family: her brothers were doctors and she became a nurse and married at some point along the way.*

Mindful of time passing, Inez retreated to the bedroom and returned the photograph to the stand. She glanced around to see if anything else might catch her eye. Her gaze snagged on a simple pine box sitting by the washbasin and jug. Curiosity overcame her nervousness, and she opened it for a brief peek. The box revealed a soft mass of graying hair, twisted into a neat spiral. Inez immediately thought of *momento mori* or mourning jewelry: locks of hair of those dearly departed, twisted and braided into earrings, bracelets, brooches, and pendants. *Perhaps the second brother or Mr. Crowson is no more? Or perhaps the hair isn't destined for mourning jewelry, but for something else, such as a love token?*

She glanced around the room, anxious to finish her search and move on to Lewis' quarters across the hall. Two doors were left. She twisted the ivory knob on the door next to the nightstand. As expected, it was a closet. Two or three gray, serviceable dresses, a pair of heavy men's boots, coated with red Manitou dust, and a large, almost mannish overcoat. A lumpish shape drew her attention and she bent down for a closer look in the gloom. Inez guessed it was dark woolen clothes, bundled for laundry. She nudged them aside and, to her astonishment, uncovered a doctor's bag. Inez retreated a step and her assumptions about Mrs. Crowson and her life backtracked as well. The lock of hair, the doctor's bag, the photograph by the bed, Inez felt certain now that the second brother must have died, perhaps the husband as well, and that these items were all mementos of a happier time.

A surge of sympathy—and a twinge of shame—made her close the closet door firmly on the nurse's private past. *Perhaps I've been hasty in judging her.*

She vowed the next door would be the last. Even if there was another room beyond, she did not want to tarry any longer nor delve any deeper into Nurse Crowson's private affairs. As she approached the last door, the smell of mint intensified. Inez wondered how the nurse could sleep under such olfactory conditions.

Her hand closed around the round knob and turned. The door creaked open, and Inez was hit with a mentholated wave so intense, she gasped. The sharp odor tore through her sinuses and her lungs like an aromatic knife.

Clapping a hand over nose and mouth, she pulled the door open all the way, trying to see inside the gloomy room. She spotted plants, she assumed they were mint, hanging from ceiling joists and beams. Inez took three steps into the dim room and couldn't talk herself into advancing any farther.

A table extended along the far wall. In addition to three lamps placed at strategic points along its length, the surface was filled with small boxes, bags, dishes of what looked like dried herbs, and several different sets of chemist scales. From table top to ceiling, the back wall supported row upon row of shelves, with glass jars and bottles of varying sizes, shapes, and colors marching along their lengths. It reminded her of a smaller version of what she'd glimpsed in Dr. Prochazka's clinic. Small white labels were affixed to each container. *I should see what's written on those labels. Could Herb Paris be among them?*

The task of searching out one item from what appeared to be hundreds was too overwhelming, and the time available was all too short. She turned to flee the room and blundered into an invalid chair to side of the door. Her hand fell on the seat as she momentarily lost her balance, the rattan almost giving way beneath the pressure. She stepped back hastily as the chair rolled away from her and into the light beyond with an alarmed squeak.

Now, Inez could see that the seat was bowed and broken and strands of rattan frayed, as if it had borne someone or something very heavy. She touched the seat again, tentatively, and brought her gloved fingers closer to her face:

Grit.

Red and dusty.

She recoiled, shoved the chair out of the way and escaped, pulling each door closed behind her until she stood in the parlor room once more.

Inez doubted she would ever be able to rid herself of the smell of mint, and hoped that she wouldn't run into Mrs. Crowson until she'd had a chance to give herself a thorough scrub with soap back in her room and douse herself liberally with rosewater.

She yanked open the door to the hallway, not caring if someone on the other side might see her exiting the quarters. After locking the door behind her, she used the same passkey to enter Lewis' rooms.

The setup here was different from across the hallway. Upon entering, she stood in a study, nearly the size of Nurse Crowson's parlor and bedroom combined. Books lined one wall behind a large desk overflowing with papers. Three leather club chairs, much like the ones she'd glimpsed in her brief foray into the gentlemen's parlor, clustered on the near side of the desk, while a simple ladder-backed wooden chair sat behind. A door at one end of the room, led, she surmised, into his living quarters. The curtains were looped back, allowing the room to be flooded with a diffuse light.

She decided to start at the back this time, and move forward. *I want to be in a position to hear Nurse Crowson open her door, should she return. That will be my signal to abandon this underworld of secrets and head up to the light.* Inez's experience in the nurse's apartment had been unnerving, to say the least. Her heart pounded as if it would shake itself loose from behind her ribs and burst through her stays. She placed one hand over her breast and took a deep breath, trying to calm herself. It was as if the mint had attacked and killed her sense of smell. Lewis could have sprinkled the room with the most powerfully scented bay rum available and she doubted she'd be able to even tell.

The study had one other door toward the back, slightly ajar, providing a slice of blackness beyond. Trying not to shudder at moving into the dark, she pushed through the opening into a bedroom, as simply furnished as Nurse Crowson's. Again, she left the door wide open, to admit the available light and to hear if anyone should come down the hall and turn a key in the lock. She couldn't ignore the feeling of being in a trap with only one way out—back through the study and into the hallway.

She took a turn around the room. Again, a closet. Opening it up, she found a surprisingly large number of somber suits—winter and summer weight trousers, waistcoats, jackets—nothing too flashy, perfect for an obsequious hotelier. Several pairs of well-polished boots lined the floor. Up above, a shelf held a top hat, a straw boater and a variety of other men's hats. Musing that Lewis had far more fashion variety than the nurse, who had nothing aside from her gray uniform-style frocks, Inez abandoned the closet. After looking around, she decided there was nothing more to see in what had to be a quick examination, and returned to Lewis' study, specifically, his desk.

A quick audit revealed that the drift of papers seemed mostly dominated by accounts payable and bills of lading marked "due" or "overdue" mixed in with urgent requests for payment for goods previously sent and received. Only a few papers bore the notation "paid."

Inez, sensitive to the vagaries of a business skating on the edge between profit and loss, having been there herself in the not too distant past, shuffled through the papers with a growing sense of horror. *No wonder Lewis is desperate for investors. If even half of what is here has yet to be paid for, the Mountain Springs House is in very deep trouble.* She paused over a receipt of several hundred dollars of fine wines and liquors from June, which held a scribbled pencil notation that read "Pay in September?" and shook her head.

She set the paper down, covering it with a letter from a local dairy, asking for payment for four months' deliveries of milk and cheeses, and began searching the drawers, wondering if she might find a ledger or bankbook that would give a more coherent picture of the financial state of the hotel.

All she found were older bills of sale and receipts, most dating from winter, a half-empty bottle of port, and a glass. A drawer on the other side of the desk yielded a framed picture, face down. Curious, she picked it up and turned it over.

It was identical to the one in Nurse Crowson's rooms—a young, somber-faced Lewis stared back at her from under his soldier's cap. The unknown man beside him stared back, yielding not a clue to his identity. "Are you Doctor Franklin the younger, then?" she asked softly. The eyes, captured forever in a straight-forward gaze, gave not a hint if she was right or wrong.

Inez slid the drawer open further to replace the photograph. Only then did she realize that a wooden box lay inside, filling the floor of the drawer. She pulled it out and set it atop of the papers. Glancing nervously out the window, the view shadowed by the veranda above, she judged that about an hour had passed since she started her explorations. Returning to the box, she realized it was bottom side up. She flipped it over, and saw two brass plates affixed to the top. One read *U.S.A. Hosp. Dept.* Below it, on the second plate and engraved in a different font, was *V.L.F.* Her mind tumbling with questions, her hands automatically, as if directed by an unseen force, lifted the latch and opened the lid.

Knives, saws, forceps, scissors—instruments meant for snipping, cutting, sawing through flesh and bone and for plucking foreign objects from living tissue gleamed from their beds of maroon velvet. She could almost hear the screams of the injured and sounds of battle in the distance. It was as if the surgical kit were some Pandora's Box from Lewis' past, releasing tortured memories of pain, blood, and death.

She shut the surgical kit, latched it hastily and slipped it back into the drawer. *So, Mr. Lewis, or perhaps it is Dr. Franklin. You lied about the hotel. You lied about your past. And you appear to not be telling the entire truth about your name—as it was in the past or in the present, or perhaps even both. What else are you hiding? And why?*

She set the photograph, face down, on top of the kit, and closed the drawer. Just as the drawer slid shut, she heard a sound out in the hallway. She froze, staring at the door. Sure enough, she heard someone sigh on the other side, a rustling, and a muffled thump as something was set down on the wood floor in the hallway. Inez darted out from behind the desk, and dashed to the bedroom door. She pushed it open and slipped inside, cursing silently as she did.

If the room had felt like a trap before, it felt doubly so now. She pushed the door almost closed, leaving it slightly ajar so she could see out, but hopefully not be seen. Inez stepped to the side, reminding herself that the closet door was within reach. That she could, if necessary, duck inside and bury herself behind the suits or off in a corner. Such a move would, of course, only drag her deeper and deeper into a situation where there would be no room to maneuver. *If I'm discovered, there is no plausible explanation I could give for being here.*

A cold sweat slicked her neck that had nothing to do with the still air of the cellar.

The hall door swung inward. Inez tensed, recalling that she had not locked it behind her when she stole into Lewis' quarters.

Nurse Crowson walked in, a slight frown on her face, key forward. Inez guessed the door had released of its own accord as she put key to lock. The nurse was carrying the inevitable basket; Inez heard the clink of bottles as she set it on the floor.

Crowson straightened up. "Franklin?" she called out. "Are you here?" She paused, head cocked, listening.

Inez held her breath as if the sound of a simple exhale would somehow reach Nurse Crowson's ears.

The nurse looked around the room, hands folded before her. Finally, she moved to the window and tugged the curtains together, leaving only a narrow band for light to leak through. She returned to the center of the room and stood still, except for her head, which swiveled from side to side. Finally, her eyes rested on the door to the bedroom. Although Inez was certain she was invisible in the shadows, it felt as though the nurse could sense her presence, right through the darkness.

Inez stepped to the side, further into the gloom, away from the opening between the two rooms. Her hand searched out and closed around the knob of the closet door. She turned it slowly, silently.

Although she could no longer see the nurse, she heard the no-nonsense tread as the nurse approached the bedroom.

An unfamiliar feminine voice came from without. "Mrs. Crowson? Ma'am?" Inez pulled the closet door open and slipped inside, grateful that the hinges were well-oiled and nothing squeaked. She held the door slightly ajar so she could hear, palm flat against the wood panel.

The footsteps had stopped. Inez could imagine the nurse turning slowly toward the open door to the subterranean hallway. "Yes? What is it?"

"Mr. Weatherby from room two-ought-five is having great difficulty breathing. I think it's serious. He looks blue around the mouth."

The tread reversed, moving away from the bedroom door. Inez sagged against the jamb, limp with relief.

Bottles clinked as the nurse picked up the basket. "Where is he?"

"In the music room."

"Was he outside when the attack happened?"

The door swung shut with a decisive click, cutting off the response.

Inez inhaled, picking up the scent of cedar, and coughed once, covering her mouth too late to hold it in. She stood for a moment in Franklin Lewis' closet, surrounded by his hollow suits. Artifices of fashion and display, they pressed against her, and she had the sudden notion that they were moving slightly, that it was only a matter of seconds, and a sleeve from a jacket would slide around her throat of its own accord.

Inez lunged out of the closet and hastened to the bedroom door. She eased open the apartment door a crack, listened, heard nothing, slid out, and locked it behind her with the skeleton key. She hastened to the staircase, feeling the darkness inside her lighten with each step, as if a long winter were changing into spring. Up the flight of stairs—still no one stopped her. As she rose, her heart rose as well. *Should someone appear at the top of the stairs, I can simply say I was looking for the nurse, to return an empty bottle, that I was told I could find her down here.*

Her presence was reasonable. She could explain without arousing suspicion. At the top of the stairs, she paused, extracted Harmony's empty bottle from her pocket, and holding it before her like an amulet, she emerged into the hall of the main floor. She was almost sorry that no one was there that she could offer her explanation to. She leaned against the florid wallpaper, never so glad to be standing in a carpeted, public corridor. *It's probably best if I don't go back the way I came. Wandering around the dining room doesn't make sense, should someone find me there.* Before heading to the lobby, she walked first to the window at the end of the passageway, to look out at the veranda and steady her nerves.

"Why, Mrs. Stannert. Are you looking for something?"

Nurse Crowson's voice behind her made her skin crawl, but Inez turned smoothly, keeping a neutral smile on her face.

The nurse stood by the staircase, one hand on the corner, apparently preparing to descend.

"Why, Mrs. Crowson," Inez responded, "I was actually looking for you, to return this." She held out the bottle. "My sister, Mrs. DuChamps, gave this to me yesterday, and I just remembered now I needed to get it back to you. One of the staff said she thought I could find you down this way, but I must have not heard her correctly."

"Well, here I am." Nurse Crowson moved forward, black-gloved hand extended.

Inez dropped the bottle into her palm.

The bottle disappeared into the basket. Nurse Crowson continued, "Next time, you should leave the empty bottle with the front desk. Or you can give it to anyone working at the hotel, and they will give it to me. It will save you from wandering all over the hotel."

"I shall remember that," said Inez.

Mrs. Crowson remained where she was, head cocked, gray eyes lingering on Inez. Her expression gave no hint as to what thoughts lay behind. Her stance reminded Inez uncomfortably of what had transpired in Lewis' rooms.

The nurse continued, "There are areas at this end of the hotel that are off-limits to guests. These stairs, for example, lead down to storerooms, laundry, and staff quarters and so on. I shouldn't want you to inadvertently end up someplace that is unsuitable to a guest."

"I understand," said Inez, and smiled.

"Of course you do," said Nurse Crowson, and smiled back—a stretch of the lips with no humor—and stepped aside to let Inez pass.

Inez strolled down the hall, clutching the purse with the skeleton key before her and fighting the urge to walk faster and faster. It was almost as if she moved quickly enough, she could somehow outpace the lingering suspicion she sensed behind her, dogging her like a relentless shadow as she approached the light-filled lobby.

Chapter Forty

Once back in the lobby area, Inez searched out a maid and asked for hot water to be delivered to her room, enough for a thorough sponge bath. The maid looked at her strangely, no doubt wondering who would take a bath in the afternoon. But water was duly delivered, along with an extra basin for rinsing. Between soap and water, flesh-brush, and a vigorous drying with a Turkish towel, the taint of mint began to disappear. Inez examined her shoulder-length hair in the mirror, and decided that a good brushing and perhaps a little cologne water would be enough. She rummaged around and found the eau de cologne Bridgette had prepared for her. She gave it a good shake, unstoppered it, and inhaled. Lavender, rosemary, orange, and bergamot greeted her.

She was working it through her hair when the door to the suite clicked open and Mark walked in.

Inez clutched the collar of her wrapper tight around her neck and said, "What are you doing back so early? I didn't expect you until after dinner."

"Glad to see you too, darlin'." He offered her a crooked grin.

She set down the brush. "What did you find out?"

"I'll tell you everything on our drive to Colorado Springs."

"Our drive to where?" She glanced out the window at the waning summer light. "It's nearly time to meet the family downstairs for dinner."

"We're dining elsewhere tonight. It's an opportunity that, I guarantee, you will thank me for later." Mark walked to the door of her bedroom and leaned against the frame. "And was your day profitable?"

"Very. But I can explain that later, since you're in such a hurry. If you'll pardon me, I'll get dressed. What kind of affair is this?"

Mark strolled into her room and opened the door to the hotel's closet to examine its contents. "Is this all you have?"

She bristled. "I thought it sufficient for a holiday in the country. Please leave my room."

"When you indicated in your telegram to me I was to bring my fancy duds, I figured you'd done the same. But, as luck would have it, I decided to leave nothing to chance. Glad I didn't." He strolled out, adding without looking back, "Don't lock the door on me."

Determined to keep him from entering her room again, Inez put the heavy silver-backed brush down on the washstand, and followed him out, across the sitting room, and paused at the entrance to his sleeping chamber. "Well, something out of the closet will have to do, because it's all I have. Just how formal is this dinner?"

"Very. Epperley arranged it for your benefit, I'll add, but it will be lucrative for us both, I have no doubt."

"Lucrative." She crossed her arms. "When you say that word in that particular tone of voice, I know it means gambling. What is it? Cards, dice, roulette? I hate roulette. No advantage to it, unless you run the wheel."

"Don't talk to me as if I'm some greenhorn off the train, Inez. I know my own business. Cards. Maybe dice, but I'm thinkin' not." He opened one of his two trunks. "Hold out your arms, Inez. I brought these from Leadville, just in case."

Inez held out one hand, keeping the other clutched to the robe's collar. "Who will be there? Any others of interest, besides Epperley? Lewis? Zuckerman? Not Prochazka...he doesn't do anything besides work in that clinic of his." A horrifying thought struck her. "Not Jonathan!"

Mark shook his head. "Not your brother-in-law. Mercy in Heavens, I do believe he feels guilty when taking a glass of port.

Can't imagine him even picking up a game of whist without feeling great personal distress. Epperley asked me strictly on the quiet. Zuckerman is staying in 'Little London' tonight to see some patients and says he's catching the train to Denver tomorrow. Lewis indicated he had business to catch up on here at the hotel. He's been pushin' hard for me to join the table and ante up on this business proposition of his, so I had to finally dig in my heels. Pointed out that glowing personal endorsements are well and good, but I'd not sign anything without seeing hard numbers on the Mountain Springs House and where it stands."

"Given what I learned today, Lewis will probably be burning the midnight oil manufacturing numbers tonight," said Inez, watching as Mark carefully removed several starched shirts, a pair of trousers to a morning suit, two tissue-wrapped waistcoats—one simple black and obviously expensive, the other a particularly handsome silver-teal hue. She could imagine him dealing cards in that one. "So, who will be there, besides Epperley?"

"We'll be dinin' with English nobility," Mark said. "I won't say more. It's supposed to be a surprise for you, and I want you to be properly astonished and gracious when you see what's been arranged." He set his clothing on the bed, and returned to plumbing the trunk.

A disquieting twist plucked deep inside her at the sight of Mark's bed, covered, but with the dent still visible of where he had slept the previous night. She could smell the scent of him in the room—the castile soap he'd always favored, the faint citrus of his hair oil, and a whiff of cigar and brandy about him. The combination of sight and smell brought a visceral reaction as strong as if he had taken her in his arms.

The twist turned into an involuntary shiver, and she snugged the collar of the robe still tighter.

Mark glanced up from his trunk. "A mite chilled? Don't be gettin' the ague, Inez. Tonight, of all nights, you need to be on your game." He laid a neatly folded evening jacket to one side, and then with an exclamation of satisfaction pulled out a slithering evening dress, appropriate for the ballroom, in scarlet and slate.

Inez stared. "That's mine!"

"And has always been a favorite of mine," He held it up, and let the long, perfect length of it spill to the rug. The satin gleamed under lamplight. "Perfect for tonight, under the gaslights. I was mighty glad to see you kept this outfit at the Silver Queen, that it wasn't destroyed in the house fire."

"You went into my rooms at the saloon. After I expressly told you to stay out." Black rage at the invasion curled inside her. "How did you get in? I changed the locks. I took the key. Did you pick the lock?"

"Darlin', you know I don't have that kind of talent." Mark draped the dress on the bed, and added a scarlet silk corset. "Abe loosened the lock and Bridgette gathered your things, after I told her what to look for. So, you see, I did not invade your sanctuary."

From the trunk, he extracted a pair of slate and scarlet patterned silk stockings, matching garters, and her most elegant evening slippers and laid them next to the pile. He stood back, viewing the dress and its appurtenances. "Did I forget anything?"

When she didn't respond, he looked at her. "Shall I bring these to your room?"

"I'll take care of it." She swept everything up in one arm, and hooked the shoes with two fingers. "I don't suppose you brought gloves. Or a hat."

"Of course I did, darlin'. They're in a hat box, in the other trunk. Bridgette said you brought your black cloak, so I'm figuring that'll work for the drive."

"And you *will* explain all this to me. So, we are to play cards with a collection of Epperley's expatriate friends. Does this evening have anything to do with the hotel? Will it help Harmony and her husband? What about Calder? This isn't just some little fun-and-games for your own pleasure, is it? I warn you, I won't play along, if it is."

"All in good time. You need to dress, and I need to prepare as well." With a sweep of his hand, he shepherded her out of his room and shut the door firmly after her.

Not entirely mollified, Inez returned to her room. *Well, what have I got to lose? I can tell him what I uncovered today. He promises this isn't some wild goose chase. He knows I will be furious if it is. I don't believe he would chance that.*

She set the clothes down on her own bed, tossed the wrapper on a chair, and dressed, stopping only to turn up the gas light as the summer dusk faded further into evening. When she was done, she looked through the jewelry she'd brought—most of it somber stuff, not really suited to the impression she was certain that Mark wanted her to make. Finally, she chose the seed-pearl and garnet necklace, a gift from her mother on her eighteenth birthday. It was one of the few items from her life in New York that Inez still possessed. She clasped it around her neck, feeling the cool pearls begin to warm against her flesh.

She stood in front of the mirror over the washstand, stepping back to see as much as she could. Smooth dark hair done up in a French knot. Hazel eyes that glowed pale in the gaslight, and olive skin that smoothed down over her collarbones to swell slightly at the top of her low-cut dress. It was the perfect ensemble for entertaining the gentlemen at the Silver Queen's exclusive gaming room or for one of Leadville's more elegant society balls. Not so appropriate for swanning around a family resort in the wide-open spaces of Manitou. *I'm glad I have the cloak.*

She went into the sitting room and found the hat box that Mark had placed out for her. She had just finished pinning the small slate-colored hat in place and was working on her long gloves when Mark walked out in his evening clothes, swinging the silver-topped cane. He stopped, gave her the once-over, smoothed his mustache with a smile, and said, "Yes, darlin', that will do," in a tone that said much, much more.

She offered up her gloves for him to button. "Are we ready to go?"

Having him help with her gloves was a habit from old. She nearly pulled her arms back when she realized what she'd done, but he stepped up before she could change her mind.

"Nearly." His quick fingers completed the task of in short order and lingered a moment longer than necessary on her wrist. "I'll need to bring the buggy around. I need to talk with Lewis about something quickly. Why don't I take you to the music room. I'll have a porter fetch you, when I'm around front."

He escorted her down to the deserted music room. The murmur of conversation and clink of silverware on china floated to her from the dining room across the hall. Fluttering gaslight played against the frosted glass of the closed dining hall doors.

Inez looked around the quiet room, lights turned low, furniture shadowed. Her gaze settled on the square grand piano at the far end. The promise of music whispered to her, as seductive as a lover's lingering caress.

She surrendered, walked over to the instrument and sat down, flexing her fingers in their tight gloves. She allowed herself to place fingers lightly on the keys, and flow into the opening chord of Shubert's "Serenade," and beyond, into its magical river of sound and feeling. As the echoes of the final notes died, she released a contented sigh.

"And *that* is how it should be played!"

Dr. Prochazka's voice from behind shattered her illusion of solitude.

She twisted around on the stool to find the physician standing a few feet away. He was dressed in dinner clothes, neat, pressed, formal, although she noticed that his cravat was slightly askew, as if done in haste. His wild dark curls were beaten, but not entirely bowed, by some hair grease application or other. The normally aloof expression was missing, replaced by, if not a smile, at least by obvious admiration. A peculiar intensity shone from eyes trapped behind the small spectacles.

He said, "Come." And actually snapped his fingers.

She rose, affronted. "I'm waiting for someone."

"No, no, this will only take a moment. Come." He abruptly grabbed her arm and pulled her out the door, adding, "I apologize. I am not saying this correctly. But there is something you must see. I know you will appreciate it. No one else here cares about the music. They do not hear how a clumsy performance can slaughter the essence of a piece, as surely as a sloppy surgeon can butcher a patient and harm instead of heal."

Carried away on the unexpected torrent of words and the force of his enthusiasm, Inez allowed him to hurry her out the back of the hotel, through the gardens, and to his clinic. During the walk he peppered her with questions. How long had she been playing? Who was her instructor? What did she think of the piano in the music room? "Needs tuning, *neh*?" He didn't wait for answers, but launched into a soliloquy on the differences between uprights and grands and baby grands and square grands. "The horizontal strings have a lesser degree of inharmonicity, purer sound…when played well and properly tuned, of course."

The spigot of commentary, question, and observation ceased abruptly after he unlocked the clinic door, and ushered her in. "Wait," he said.

He strode further into the long building, turning up lights as he went, until he reached the door that lead to the back room. Another key came out of the pocket, he opened the door, disappeared. A light flickered on in the interior, and he reappeared, waving her forward. "This way."

He disappeared inside.

Wary, but curious to get a glimpse of the inner sanctum, Inez moved toward the room.

As she approached, she heard something. Something strange and ghostly, scratchy and not quite clear. Finally, it resolved itself into the sound of musical notes. A piano, ghostly and insubstantial. She slowly pushed open the door to the back room. There was Dr. Prochazka, seated by the oddest contraption she had ever seen. She had a confused impression of brass, polished wood, springs, levers, tubes, a cylinder rotating slowly in the middle, all surmounted by a large horn, facing her way, from which the annoying scratching and an indistinct rendition of Beethoven's "Moonlight Sonata" emerged. It was as if a pianist playing well, but distantly, had to contend with an army of crickets intent on overlaying his music with their own skritching and crikking. Prochazka slowly, methodically cranked a small handwheel mounted on one end. Then he stopped cranking. The flywheel slowed, the cylinder's rotation decreased, the music drifted down in pitch, speed, and volume…and died.

"What is that?" she asked.

Prochazka bounced to his feet, flexing his hands and gazing at the instrument as ardently as a child at a treasured toy. "A phonograph. Invented by your Thomas Edison. And improved by me to be vastly superior."

She tried to ignore his audacious assertion that he had bettered a device created by the greatest inventor of the modern-day world. "It makes music?"

"Not makes. Records. Then plays it back." He looked at her. "Do you see what this means. What is now possible?" The sheer intensity of his gaze, his obvious desire that she understand and anticipate the answer, made her consider carefully before responding.

"So, with this phonograph, one can perform a piece of music and listen to it later?"

"Yes! But not music by just *any*one. Not the horrible display of the previous evening. But the best the world has to offer. Liszt, in his prime. Clara Schumann. Chopin, Tausig—if they were only still alive! Think of it!"

She did. Overwhelmed by the enormity of the idea, Inez glanced at the contraption on the table. "But the sound is not… optimal."

"Work is needed—by Edison, by myself, perhaps by your Alexander Graham Bell; he is also interested in this phonograph invention. Once perfected, what a gift to the world of music!" He seized her hands. "Then talented performers, such as yourself, your performances will reach the far corners of the world with this marvelous machine. And your music, your interpretation of it, will never die."

Inez withdrew her hands from his grasp. His vision dazzled her. It was like looking into the sun—hard to do, possible only for the briefest of moments. Now that he was open to talking to her, she searched for a way to guide the conversation to the subjects closest to her heart. "You are too kind to include me in such a list of luminaries," she said. "I thank you." She looked around the room, long and narrow. "I am impressed that you find time to do this among all your other endeavors."

Counters extended the length of both long walls. At the far end of the room sat a stove. The phonograph occupied a table by itself in the center of the room—a line of demarcation between two countries. One counter was full of strange objects: rows of flat covered glass plates, stacked up in towering pillars. Several microscopes, much like the one in his front office. Only these were clearly working microscopes, and not for show. They had more glass plates stacked around them, some of the plates in groupings covered with bell jars. Clear flasks empty and partially filled, bottles, and, just at the limit of the light, something that looked to be a camera. A magnifying glass at the close end of the table. Scribbled papers were tacked to the wall above the jumble.

On the other side of the room, the counter held a soldier's column of tonic bottles. Above the bottles, orderly shelves were filled with bottles, tins, small containers, all with white paper labels. It reminded Inez of Nurse Crowson's back room, without the overpowering smell of mint.

"Yes, my endeavors." Dr. Prochazka threw himself back down on the chair by the phonograph, gestured for Inez to take the chair opposite. "My work is nearly done. Another reason to celebrate tonight."

"Done?" Inez was perplexed. "Do you mean…" She looked around at the equipment. The bottles. "…you have worked out some elixir to restore health to those with the wasting disease?"

He stared at her as if she was crazy. "A cure? For phthisis? There is no cure." He leaned forward, hands clasped as if in prayer. "But I have found the cause."

"The cause? But, I thought is was a constitutional ailment."

He waved a hand impatiently. "All myths and theories, put forth by desperate people. Yes, even we physicians, we are desperate to offer hope, reasons, explanations, cures. No matter what we say, what we advise, some improve under our direction and indeed seem cured, while others follow the same regimens and are consumed by the disease. And we don't know why." He gazed at the phonograph. "We are blind men, stumbling about in the dark, hearing a phantom music, but unable to detect its source."

He looked at Inez, and said, "I ramble. You do not care to hear the history of discovery. Suffice to say, the evidence has shown that tuberculosis is a specific, inoculable disease. I have worked here and seen it. Dr. Koch, a colleague of mine in Germany, is working on the same questions. We have been corresponding. I shall write to him, tell him what I have learned. I have done all I can here in the States. I shall return to Germany to work with him, and we will transform the future, now that I have discovered the truth."

"Which is what?"

"I have found the bacteria that cause the disease. I have cultivated them in the test tube, photographed them, followed their evolution through their life cycles. I did not invent the procedure," he added matter-of-factly. "Dr. Koch did this for the anthrax disease, ten years ago. I simply followed his procedures."

She tried to come to grips with what he was saying. "But, what does this mean, if it isn't a cure?"

"What it means is that we can see it. We can identify it." He held out his open hand toward her. Inez almost expected to see something tangible resting in his palm. "We have it, at last: the greatest killer of mankind, over the centuries." His hand closed into a fist. "Now, we know what we are fighting."

"So, all of this?" She gestured behind him, to the tonic bottles and medicinals.

"All of that," He turned to look at the shelves and countertop. "The tonics and inhalants. The cod liver oils, mineral waters, vapors of creosote, carbolic acid, mercurial salts...They can provide relief. For some. But they do not cure."

It was the opening she'd been looking for. "What of Herb Paris?"

He raised his eyebrows. "So many want to know, this past day. Yes, I have a store of Herb Paris. It is helpful, for some. Those who suffer from bronchitis, spasmodic coughs. Also for headaches and neuralgia. The seeds and the berries have something of the nature of opium."

"And it is a poison." Inez added. "How could it have ended up in the livery, in a horse's nosebag?"

Prochazka shrugged. She could tell his attention was waning, drifting away from her and her questions. He was disappearing back into indifference. "It is shipped to me from overseas, specifically for my studies and for use in this clinic. I keep it here, in the laboratory."

"Who has access?"

"I keep this room locked at all times."

A delicate cough interrupted them. Inez started and looked toward the entrance to the front of the clinic. Nurse Crowson stepped into the room and into the light. "Excuse me, doctor. I'm here to pick up the medicines." She presented the basket.

He leaped to his feet. "Of course, of course. Time for the evening doses."

Mrs. Crowson slipped in, and headed to the far side, setting her basket on the counter next to the tonic bottles.

"Mrs. Stannert, I apologize for keeping you from your evening." His stiff formality and indifference evaporated. "I hope to hear you play again. Perhaps tomorrow? You might indulge me with a little Beethoven, perhaps?"

She smiled. "'Moonlight Sonata'? I believe it can be arranged."

He took her gloved hand and bowed low over it. "*Dekuji*, madam. Thank you." His voice was fervent.

Inez surveyed the laboratory for the last time. On one side, impenetrable science with its bewildering confusion of glass vessels, curious instruments, and cryptic papers. On the other, orderly palliative treatments with their deceptively clear labels and falsely reassuring tonics. Prochazka stood in the middle, one hand resting on the phonograph. Mrs. Crowson stood a little behind, lifting one bottle at time, setting them in her basket.

Prochazka added, "Forgive me for not escorting you back to the hotel, but I must help Mrs. Crowson. There are a couple new therapeutics we must talk about."

Inez smiled. "I can find my way, doctor. Thank you." She left, pulling the clinic door closed behind her before hurrying across the gardens, into the hotel, and out to the front, where Mark and buggy awaited.

Chapter Forty-one

Inez quickly explained why she had kept Mark waiting and then plunged into her day's happenings. Mark had lit the buggy's lanterns for the night ride, so she was able to see his smile of approval as she detailed how she managed to procure a passkey. When she described her descent to the hotel's underworld, he sobered. "You took a chance there, darlin'. What would you have done if you'd been caught?"

"I don't know," she confessed. "I would have thought of something. If not, well, what would they do, after all? Shoot me?"

"I'd hate to guess. Desperate folks do desperate things when in desperate situations. Although, you do seem to have more lives than a feline and able to talk yourself out of tight corners I'd not thought possible."

She warmed at the compliment. "You always did say that words were my best weapon and defense, with my pocket pistol running in second place. In any case, we now know more about Lewis, and the truth about the financial state of affairs at the hotel. Lewis was a physician during the War. He must have been. The photo. The box of, of…" In her mind, she saw the cutting edges again—the saw, the knives, all blades and teeth, hungry for blood and bone.

"Surgeon's kit."

She looked over at Mark, his profile against the night. "What?"

He said, "The box you described. It's a surgeon's kit."

"How do you know that?"

"Well, darlin', South or North, the army sawbones lugged the same tools."

"Oh, of course." She faced forward again. "In any case, he is a doctor or *was* a doctor, but won't own up to it. Something must have happened that he won't even acknowledge as part of his past. Too, there is the matter of the initials, which seem to indicate his name back then was not the same as the one he currently uses, and the fact that he does not want the name 'Victor' associated with him here in Manitou. Something is awry. Maybe he was a doctor before and something went wrong, or he was incompetent and it all caught up with him. Either way, he's definitely incompetent as a businessman and hotelier. The finances of the Mountain Springs House are a complete disaster, if what is on his desk is any indication." She shot another look at him. "Don't you dare sign any sort of agreement with them. And don't let Jonathan either."

"I'm doing my level best, Inez. It's a dicey situation. I want them to believe I'm serious in my interest, but at the same time not willing to put pen to paper yet. I can't play gull to their game much longer. They know I own the Silver Queen, that I'm not adverse to a gamble, so obviously, I know something about businesses, cheats, and cons. They're probably wondering if I'm on to them, as it is."

"Yes, yes. I understand. You're walking a tightrope in all this." Inez frowned. "It's the photograph, I'll admit, that has me most perplexed. Two men posed in front of a surgeon's tent. One is clearly Lewis, or Franklin, or whatever his name really is. I'm assuming he is the VLF indicated on the back. The second man has the same last initial, looks younger, and there is a definite family resemblance. I suspect they are brothers, and perhaps Mrs. Crowson is their sister. She has the identical photograph in her room by her bed, so obviously, it is important to her."

"Well, I suspect you reckoned right on that. Makes sense they might be brothers who joined up and served in the War together. Two surgeons assigned to the same unit."

"Maybe." She stared straight ahead, deep in thought. The lights of Colorado City straggled by. "Here's another possibility: maybe Mrs. Crowson herself was in the War."

"As a nurse? It's possible."

"I was thinking more that she might be the other person in the photograph. That she might have disguised herself as a man."

"Inez. Not all women have your propensity for wearin' trousers."

"Well, just consider it for a moment. Her brother goes off to war. Maybe he is her only family. She decides to go as well, and the best way to stay by his side is to pretend to be his brother and medical assistant." She glanced at Mark sideways. "It's not so difficult to do, to pretend to be a man."

"For an evening's lark, I can see your point. But you're talkin' about the War, Inez. That's living a ruse under hard conditions, day and night, month after month…or however long afore someone realizes that the doctor with soft hands and gentle voice isn't the comrade-in-arms everyone believes."

"Have you heard Mrs. Crowson speak? Her voice is in the lower register for a woman. I believe you don't give her enough credit. I believe she could have pulled it off." Inez couldn't believe that here she was, defending the nurse's ability to be devious. She shook her head, irritated. "It's just a possibility, that's all."

"Well, sounds like we've got our sights trained on Lewis in any case. It pretty much matches up with what I've been suspecting myself. Maybe Mrs. Crowson is in cahoots with him, supplies the ready poison or some such. I do believe I'll send a telegram to Doc Cramer tomorrow and see if the initials VLF and SCF and the names Victor, Franklin, and Lewis in some combination ring any bells from his old War days. Doc's got a mighty long memory. If Lewis was anywhere near the Union's medical corps, I'm wagering he'll at least know the name. Although Lewis and Franklin are powerful common names."

"Asking Doc is an excellent idea." She brightened. "Add the name Galloway, and ask if he recollects two brothers who served together at doctors, side by side, possibly with the last name Franklin. Now here is something that just occurred to me:

What if the second brother isn't dead? Maybe he's alive, living in Colorado Springs under an alias, and he and Mrs. Crowson are 'taking care' of problem patients for the Mountain Springs House, at Lewis' direction. Maybe this second brother is Dr. Galloway!"

Mark chuckled. "Don't let your horses run too wild, Inez. That's a pretty far reach. Although I do and always did admire how you can take hold on some notion everyone else takes for granted, turn it around and upside down, shake it some, and come up something totally different. You just keep thinking up those wild ideas. One is bound to be the jackpot. Now, before we get to Colorado Springs, let me tell you what I've uncovered for you."

"I'm all ears."

"You'll like this. The private party tonight happens to be at the Colorado Springs Hotel."

"Where Calder's brother was!" she exclaimed.

"Just so. Epperley, Lewis, and a couple of local big bugs took us poor suckers—by that I mean Mr. DuChamps and me—there as part of their tour of the city. Had a cigar there and a sit-down. The El Paso Club they took us to afterwards was much superior, but that's beside the point now. So guess who's stayin' at the Colorado Springs Hotel?"

Her mind was a blank. "Who?"

"Someone you told me about in passing, who recently left the Mountain Springs House. Someone in a poor state of health, who was not responding to Dr. Prochazka's magical prescriptions."

She blinked. "Mr. Travers?"

"The very man."

"How on earth did you winkle that out?"

He flipped the reins. The horse obediently turned onto a wide dirt street. "Pike's Peak Boulevard. We're nearly there, darlin'. As for Travers," he grinned. "Even a blind hog finds an acorn now and then. Call it luck and a hunch. I went to the desk clerk, asked if Mr. Travers was staying there. Fellow's memory improved considerably after I slipped him a buck. Travers is at the hotel, but in a bad way. He has an attendant day and night to help him. The clerk said Travers usually bestirs himself shortly after midnight, rings for the bellboy, and the bellboy and night attendant carry Travers down to the lobby. He sits up most of the night, then is carried back to his room before dawn. I gave the clerk another buck and my card. Wrote on the back I was referred by Dr. Galloway, and hoped to see him later. Clerk promised to deliver my card and keep him in the lobby until the party's over."

"So, we're talking with Travers before dawn. It's going to be *that* sort of a party?"

"I expect so."

Even though Inez judged it to be only around ten at night, the boulevard was silent and empty of traffic. Spindly little trees—no more than saplings—stood tenuous guard before the frame and brick buildings lining the street. To the west and at a distance, Pike's Peak, its highest reaches still snow-powdered in the August moonlight, rose above the darkling lower range.

Mark pulled up in front of a three-story frame building, lights blazing from dormer windows, and announced, "Colorado Springs Hotel."

Once the horse and buggy had been accepted by the hotel's liveryman, Mark walked Inez up the stairs of the broad front porch and escorted her in, one hand resting lightly on her back. He smiled at the clerk, who intoned, "Welcome, Mr. and Mrs. Stannert. Room two-aught-eight. You are expected."

"How am I supposed to play this?" Inez inquired as she lifted the hems of her cloak and skirts a modest inch to climb the stairs.

"This is just a friendly game," he said. "We're not out to skin anyone. I'm more interested in hearing what Epperley and his cronies say about local prospects once they're ginned up and talkative."

She raised her eyebrows. "Ginned up? I thought Colorado Springs was a dry town."

"Don't believe everything you hear. Apparently anything goes as long as it's for medicinal purposes." Mark halted in front of the door displaying the brass numbers two-zero-eight.

Inez heard the rumble of male voices on the other side. Mark gave a little syncopated knock and stepped back, deferring the door to her. "It's your Colorado Springs debut, darlin'. Play it for what it's worth."

The voices inside ceased. Quick steps sounded, and the door swung open. Epperley stood on the sill, face a little flushed, his impressive handlebar mustache not quite on the horizontal. In fact, one of the twisted ends of his facespanner definitely tilted upwards. From this neglect of his most prized physical attribute, Inez surmised that the hotel manager must have partaken heavily of whatever spirits were available in the ostensibly dry town.

Epperley placed a hand over his heart, and bowed deeply. "Mrs. Stannert. You and your gallant escort do us great honor with your presence. Welcome to this, our bastion of British civility and fine spirits in Colorado Springs, otherwise known as Little London."

With a sudden scraping of chairs, the men in the room, all attired in proper evening clothes, bounded to their feet. The fumes inside poured out to greet her—a heady mix of brandy, port, sherry, and other high-quality liquors blended with a fog of cigar, cigarette and pipe smoke. She counted six men standing, all of whom she recognized. The lot of them—she thought of them collectively as the "Lost Lads of London"—appeared at the Silver Queen once a month, like clockwork, when their remittance checks came in. They would spend a night and a day and often another night carousing through Leadville with special attention paid to State Street's red-light district. Most of their time was spent drinking, gambling, quarreling amongst themselves and occasionally with others before they slunk out of town again, wallets and spirits exhausted.

"I was not aware that you were part of this merry band, Mr. Epperley," Inez said. "You are not part of their monthly forays to Leadville."

"That is because, unlike all of these chaps," he glanced toward the men standing at attention, "*I* work for a living."

One of the lads, whom Inez recognized as "the Squire," lifted his glass on high. The liquid, either red wine or an equally deep-colored port, sloshed dangerously as he waved it about. "God bless the Queen!" he bellowed.

"Lord Percy over there has come into an inheritance from his Uncle Charles in Suffolk," said Epperley, nodding toward a chap, who was horizontal on an overstuffed divan. "Every time we toasted 'To his lordship!' this evening, Percy would hop to his feet and down a shot of imperial scotch. Now, look at him."

They all looked.

Muffled snores escaped from the opera hat covering Percy's face from the light.

Another of the lads, whom Inez knew by the sobriquet of Sir Daniel, said, "Never mind. A thousand pounds from home arrived today. That'll keep us celebrating Percy's deliverance from poverty 'til the Second Coming and beyond."

Epperley squinted at him in amazement. The Squire exclaimed, "You don't say! In fact, you didn't say, until now. How'd you manage that?"

"Told the lord of the manor back home that I'd just purchased a gopher ranch, having had no luck with cattle, and that I needed the extra funds to fatten the gophers for market," said Sir Daniel. "Old man doesn't know a Hereford cow from a rodent gopher, and sent it on. As to why I didn't mention it until now—" he glanced at Epperley. "Epperley here wouldn't've let up until I'd promised to toss it into that blasted sinkhole of a hotel of his in Manitou."

Epperley wasn't so drunk as to not look guilty and alarmed. "Dash it all, Daniel! It's no sinkhole. I put my own inheritance into it, as you bloody well know." He turned back to the door, his gaze traveling over Inez's shoulder to Mark, standing behind her. "Daniel's deep in his cups. Don't listen to him."

Sir Daniel weaved his way to the entry. "Oh, button it, Epperley. Felicitations, Mrs. Stannert. Is that Mr. Stannert back there? Don't believe we've met. Pleasure. Is this reprobate Epperley stuffing your head with twaddle about his precious resort along with the odious Lewis and Zuckerman? If so, don't believe him."

"Daniel," said Epperley, dangerously calm. "You talk too much."

Sir Daniel clapped Epperley on the shoulder. "If you were in charge of the place, we'd all jump in with both feet and back you to the hilt. You know that. But not with that insufferable not to mention incompetent Lewis in charge." He addressed Mark. "If you're going to take the plunge and fund the hotel's future, I'd say your best move would be to stage a revolution—you Yanks are good at that—depose the reigning monarch at the Mountain Springs House, and crown Epperley here as king. With Epperley at the helm, she would sail true."

The Squire, who had lowered himself into a chair at the table, chimed in. "But Daniel, Epperley's not in charge, and not likely to ever be, short of an epidemic that affects only the upper management. Say, a form of specialized plague that only attacks unfashionable sideburns. And Epperley, to be frank, we get bloody well tired of hearing you bang on about the wonders of the place and trying to get your sticky fingers into our pockets so we must join you on that particular sinking ship. I'd rather invest in Daniel's gopher farm."

"The gopher farm is a fantasy," snapped Epperley.

"Just so." The Squire tapped his now-empty glass on the table surface, impatient. "Now, for God's sake, are we gentlemen to keep our guests standing at the door? Let the Stannerts in and give the lady a chair. She came all this way, to *us*, so we wouldn't have to go to *her* to do our monthly tithing at the bar."

Epperley stepped to the side and invited the Stannerts in with a grand sweep of his arm. Mark, standing behind her, rested his hands on her shoulders and leaned in, saying in a low voice, "I got what I came for, darlin'. Now, it's your turn."

Inez turned her head and smiled at him. From inches away, he returned her smile with one of his own, raised her hand to his lips, and kissed the inside of her wrist. Even through the glove, she felt a sudden, unexpected thrill of response curl through her body. His blue eyes—warm, eager, filled with anticipation of the coming game—generated a corresponding heat within her.

Wordlessly, she undid the clasp of her cloak. Mark lifted it from her shoulders, and she stepped into the room.

All the lads—the conscious ones, in any case—were riveted, eyes upon her.

She lifted a hand and began to unbutton one glove. "I am so honored to be here, that you would think to invite me to your gathering," she said in a low, musical voice. "It's been a long ride from Manitou, and I find I am much in need of a glass of the best brandy you might have—for medicinal purposes, of course, for I'm feeling a little faint. And, I am positively *dying* for a leisurely evening of cards and clever conversation. What do you say to a game of poker?"

Drawing off the glove, finger by finger, she moved toward the table, Mark following at her back.

Chapter Forty-two

"Just like old times, darlin'. You were magnificent." Mark settled Inez's cloak back about her shoulders.

The Stannerts were outside the infamous room of two-aught-eight, preparing to leave. They had said their goodbyes to the Brits who were still standing. Of the original six, three had dropped away as the darkest hours of the night ticked by, victims of waning funds and indiscriminate drinking. The various bottles had emptied, only to be replaced by full ones, which emptied again, and were again replaced. It was like the cycle of an hour-glass, in which the level of sand drops, the glass is turned, and the level drops again.

The card playing was, as Mark had presupposed, more a friendly pastime than a money-making proposition. Even so, they were walking away with far more than they had brought to the table, despite their concerted efforts to go easy on the lads. The players had imbibed enough to be sloppy in their calculations. Sir Daniel, who appeared to have the most to spend, seemed intent on hanging onto his "gopher endowment" and was the only one of the group, besides the Stannerts, to finish with a full purse.

The night had been profitable in other ways. Through various remarks and asides, Inez was now certain that Epperley was itching to take over the Mountain Springs House and that he had no respect for how Lewis was handling business but was doing his level best to keep things afloat, even so.

As for delicate inquiries regarding Lewis and Crowson's relationship, he added bits to the backstory. "Siblings, or maybe cousins. Whenever someone even dares to say something against the nurse, he springs to her defense in a way that is positively brotherly."

As to a possible spouse for Mrs. Crowson? "Haven't heard a peep," Epperley said shortly. "If there was a marriage, it must have been long ago. I say, she doesn't strike me as the type, though. She's devoted to Lewis now and to Dr. P, of course. She's his right-hand woman, I suppose you'd say."

What about a second brother?

Epperley screwed up his face, setting his mustache even more askew. "Never heard of one. I'd say it's just the two of them. Who knows about the past, though. They never talk about where they were or what they did before they came to Manitou." He slanted a suspicious look at her. "Why?"

She hastily changed the subject. After some time passed in desultory small talk, she dared to bring up the incident with the Herb Paris.

"Oh yes. Heard that claptrap about the horse. Must have been a mistake. Did you see this berry Calder was prattling on about? No evidence of it now, so who's to say what it was. Probably from one of the local plants. Locoweed, maybe. Calder always thought he knew everything about everything. Not to speak ill of the dead. Why do you ask?" His eyes narrowed dangerously, and for a moment, he looked almost sober. Inez veered away from the topic, and inquired instead about Mr. Travers.

"Right, right. He's taken up residence in this hotel," said Epperley. "Never a good sign, when they leave Dr. P's care in that sort of state. Poor chap. Last gasp, is my take on it. I've seen enough lungers to know when their number's up."

Had he ever heard of a Dr. Galloway?

"Can't say that I have. But, the Springs area draws doctors the way your city in the clouds draws lawyers. I understand you can't throw a stone across Leadville's main avenue without hitting half a dozen solicitors."

Even as they added more dollars to their winnings, Inez added more pieces to the puzzle. Only a few pieces were still missing, she mused. Unfortunately, they were the most important ones.

"Shall we pay a visit to Mr. Travers?" Mark asked as they started down the stairs.

"I suppose so." She stifled a yawn. "It may be our only opportunity to find out about Dr. Galloway."

Travers was not hard to spot. The lobby was empty, the night clerk dozing behind the desk, settled in one chair with his feet up on another. Off to one side, a hunched figure sat in an invalid chair. A single oil lamp, turned low, shed a weak light. A Negro boy, of about fourteen years and all long legs and arms, was curled up on a nearby sofa, asleep. As Inez and Mark approached, Inez wondered if perhaps they weren't too late, and Mr. Travers had already passed from this life to the next.

As they drew near, however, Mr. Travers' chest visibly heaved, and he began a tortured cough. The boy stirred and sprang up, pulling a cloth from his pocket. He hurried to hold it up to Mr. Travers' mouth. Once Travers stopped coughing, the boy carefully wiped the man's face. "Is it time, Mr. Travers?" he asked in a timid voice.

Travers nodded and motioned with one skeletal hand.

The attendant fished around in his pocket again, pulled out a bottle, and shook a pill into the outstretched claw.

"Mr. Travers?" Inez inquired.

He looked up with sunken rheumy eyes. Sparse hair lay slicked across his sweating skull. He was so emaciated that Inez thought that, when Charon did invite him into his boat to cross the river Styx, the boatman could take Travers' body as well as his soul, for they would be equally insubstantial.

Travers' gaze swept past Inez to Mark. Mark stepped forward. "Mr. Travers, I'm Mr. Stannert. I left a card for you with the clerk today. About Dr. Galloway?"

"You don't look like you suffer from the white plague." His voice was the merest of whispers, a breeze intimating death in the wings.

Mark spoke. "I was inquiring for my wife's uncle." He put a hand on Inez's arm, a signal that he would steer the conversation. "He is doing very poorly from the wasting disease. We came to the Mountain Springs House to see if the physician there might cure him. He says not. But then, we heard that Galloway might be the one who can help."

"A cure. A cure," Travers wheezed, triumphant. "Yes! Galloway is a genius. All the rest—charlatans. He has eased my breathing, brought me back from the brink. Hemlock extract for inhalation. Injections of mercury salts. And calomel," he held out a shaky hand, disclosing the chalk white pill, "chloride of mercury, just as in the War. It worked then, and it will now. Mercury! Ah now, that's the ticket. Galloway understands."

Inez scrutinized Travers, who beamed up at them with fevered, shiny eyes. The dried blood at the corners of his mouth. The emaciation, flushed skin stretched over cheekbones. The laboring chest, rising, falling, with each hard-won breath.

Anger coiled within her. *Wasting away from the wasting disease. Consumed by consumption. Who is this Galloway, who is so cold-hearted as to raise false hopes in a dying man?*

Travers grasped Mark's wrist. Thin fingers with swollen joints tightened. Fingernails thickened and curved dug into Mark's snow-white cuff. "You talked to Mrs. Crowson? She gave you the card?"

Mark nodded.

"Then, you know what I know, for I'm certain she told you. The doctor comes twice a week to start with. More often, if you send word to the nurse. He comes at night. She assists in his stead, brings the medications, performs the injections, when he is busy. The man with a cure is a busy man. A very busy man."

"What does he look like?" Inez asked.

Mark shot her a warning glance, but Travers answered readily.

"Wears his jacket from the army. Showed me his green sash, his surgical bag, with eagle on the lock. Yes, from the War."

"But his appearance," she persisted. "Tall? Short? Gray hair? Mustache?"

He frowned, perplexed.

"So we may recognize him," she added hastily.

He nodded, closed his eyes. Inez wasn't certain if he was exhausted and trying to recapture lost energy, or calling up an image behind his fluttering paper-thin lids. He finally responded, "Much like the nurse. Same eyes. Same broad forehead. A relative? I do not inquire. That he provides the cure is enough. Beard." He drew a vague arc at his throat. "Chin beard."

His eyes opened and refocused on Mark. "You could have seen for yourself, if you'd been here an hour earlier. Dr. Galloway came, gave me an injection. I told him of your interest. I gave him your card. He thanked me. Said he would find you."

A cold breath of fear, like a winter wind, sighed up Inez's spine. "Do you ever see them, together? The nurse and the physician?"

He shook his head. "No. Different nights." He smiled, lost in vague memory. "Another thing. Like the nurse, this Dr. Galloway, he smells of…mint."

Chapter Forty-three

"I guess I was wrong and you were right about women in trousers," Mark said, as he urged the horse the last mile to Manitou.

Inez clutched his arm, leaning forward as if leaning would encourage the horse to pick up the pace. "Can't you make him go a little faster?"

"Darlin', fast horses on a road we don't know, that's how horses break legs and riders break necks. I'm going as fast as is safe."

"The road is straight here," Inez said.

Mark sighed, and urged the horse into a slow and cautious trot. "What's got you so wound up, Inez? Mrs. Crowson and Lewis aren't likely to do anything tonight. They may know we're on to something—I guess leavin' my card for Travers wasn't the best move I've ever made—but how much we know, that's got to be a mystery to them."

"Don't bet on it. Mrs. Crowson may have overheard me ask Dr. Prochazka about herb Paris tonight. She knows that Calder spoke to me before he died. She was there when we were walking in the garden. She knew I was up to something when she cornered me in the hallway after I'd been downstairs looking around. At least, thank goodness, she didn't catch me in Lewis' rooms—or hers, for that matter."

"Remember, darlin', they see me as a likely investor. It's not reasonable that they'd turn around and bite my hand at this point."

"I don't know, Mark. I just don't know. As you said, she's not likely to run. Everything she values is here, as far as I can see. Her garden, her brother, her herbs, teas, and potions. The invalids need her and count on her. If she is, indeed, living a double life as a male physician, she must be doing it for a reason. Why not just hire herself out as a nurse and tend to others in that way? Why don trousers and a fake beard," the carefully boxed coil of gray hair in the nurse's rooms now made sense, "unless she's doing something she wants to be kept secret?"

"Don't forget she probably gave you that not-so-gentle shove down the stairs."

She frowned. "Could be. But, it doesn't fit. As you said, you and Jonathan DuChamps are their most promising prospects to pull them out of this financial disaster they're in. Just look at their situation: up to their necks in debt, yet still building, planning on a bowling alley, billiard room, adding cottages and another floor, hiring a telegraphist so they can have their own telegraph station here. How do they expect to pay? Who will take them on credit, if they don't pay up on what they owe now? They must desperately want your money, and of course, Jonathan DuChamps'. So the question is, what will she or they do next? Who is the next likely target? The person who knows too much and is expendable, if it isn't you, me, or Jonathan and his family?"

In an agony of impatience and worry, Inez twisted her hands into the fabric of her cloak, gazing ahead into the waning night. *When is dawn going to come? When will the skies lighten up so we can see?*

She recognized buildings that heralded the outskirts of the Manitou hamlet. "The telegraph office is on the way, at the Manitou House," she said abruptly. "We'll stop there, and you can send a message to Doc. Tell him it is urgent and ask him to respond quickly, that the situation is dire. Ask him if he knew any physicians with initials VLF and SCF from the days of the War. Mention the names Crowson and Galloway and as well as Victor, Lewis, and Franklin."

"You'll wait while I parse this out?"

"I cannot. I cannot sit and dither, not the way I feel. I'll take the buggy back to the Mountain Springs House. I feel something is going to happen, and if so, I want to be there. It won't take you more than a handful of minutes to walk to the hotel."

"So, tell me what you are going to do and where you'll be. You plan on taking the buggy to the livery and then what? You going up to our rooms, or plan on pitchin' a tent outside your sister's or William's room?"

"I could actually watch them both at the same time from the hallway. No, I'll head up to our rooms. You will find me there."

"I surely hope so, darlin'. If you're not there, I'm going to tear the place apart looking for you, starting with the lower floor and workin' my way up."

After dropping Mark off at the Manitou House and promising several times over that, yes, she would be waiting in their rooms, Inez returned to the Mountain Springs House. Dawn was finally approaching. Not yet arrived, but the sky was lightening from impenetrable black to a darkling gray, with the shapes of the foothills just taking on substance against the sky.

She drove the buggy to the livery and delivered care of the horse up to a very sleepy Billy. She was disappointed that Morrow wasn't on duty that night. Somehow, she would have felt better, knowing that he was there with his keen eye and calm ways.

She walked out of the livery, to the edge of the garden, and paused. Ahead of her, the hotel kept its silence, its occupants still deep in sleep. At least, that's what she assumed. But behind some of the plants screening the lower story from idle eyes, she thought she detected a glimmer of light corresponding to the location of Lewis' study.

So, he is still awake. Probably still trying to 'fix' the numbers for this morning's meeting with Mark and Jonathan.

One foot on the path to the hotel, she hesitated, and glanced toward the clinic. Lights still burned through drawn window blinds. *Dr. Prochazka should be told. The sooner the better. Who knows what the nurse might do, if she thinks he's worked out her part in all this? He seems almost oblivious to her. An invisible person can be more dangerous than someone who is an outright enemy.*

Decision made, she hurried to the clinic. She pushed on the door, which swung open. Moving silently inside, she entered the dark waiting room and moved into the office. The door to the backroom was partially ajar, with lamplight blazing. She saw a shadow moving within. Heartened, she walked forward as quickly as she could in her slim evening skirts.

"Dr. Prochazka?" she called, setting one hand on the door and pushing. "I must speak with you."

She stopped. The room revealed a long, lank figure on the floor, pool of red spreading around his head. Nurse Crowson, enveloped in a long cloak, crouched by him, hand on wrist as if searching a pulse, but eyes lifted, gazing straight at Inez.

Chapter Forty-four

Inez took a quick step back. "What happened?" was all she could think of saying.

Nurse Crowson rose. The long cloak fell back to reveal the nurse was dressed in men's jacket and trousers. The heavy statuette of Asclepius was clutched in one hand.

One end of the white marble statue was stained with blood.

"Excellent. You're here." Mrs. Crowson sounded as if she had been expecting her, as if she'd rung a bell and the bellboy had arrived.

Inez snuck her hand through the side slit of her cloak and into her secret dress pocket. She almost swore out loud.

No pocket pistol.

Then, she recalled Mark earlier that evening, his fingers warm on her wrist, saying, "You won't need that tonight."

"Please, pull your hand out of your pocket slowly," said Crowson. "I want to see it empty."

Inez eyed her, wondering if she could, perhaps, physically subdue the nurse. Obviously, Mrs. Crowson was strong. And she was in trousers, whereas Inez was hampered by her evening dress. Tight skirts didn't make for swift movements, so Inez didn't think she could outrun the nurse. Of course, there was always screaming for help.

Crowson sighed, shifted the bloody statue to her other hand, reached into the basket next to the phonograph and pulled out a revolver. "I really don't want to use this, Mrs. Stannert.

Makes far too much noise. But I will if I must. Now, I'll keep Dr. Prochazka company, and you do the housekeeping. Then, we will decide what to do with you."

Inez slowly pulled her empty hand out of her pocket.

"Better," said the nurse with a nod, as if commending a patient for swallowing a particularly evil-tasting dose. "Now, please remove your cloak. I want to be able to see your hands and what they are doing at every moment. You are too fast and clever by half. It's not good for a woman to be so clever. I know."

"What do you mean?" Inez slowly, so as to not antagonize her, unfastened the clasp and let the cloak slither to the floor.

"Lovely," said Crowson. Inez wasn't certain if she meant her dress or the fact that she'd obeyed with a minimum of fuss. "I know because I, too, am a clever woman, and the only way I've been able to utilize that talent is by disguise and subterfuge. It was not the life I wanted."

"The War? Dr. Galloway?"

"Ah yes. You've learned a great deal in a few days. Yes, the War. Everyone believed Victor was a brilliant surgeon."

Inez swallowed hard. *She called him Victor to my face. This cannot be good.* She glanced around furtively, for something close at hand that could be used as a weapon.

Crowson continued, "I made myself be content to be his shadow, his younger brother, the assistant surgeon, but he and I, we both knew the truth. I was the hands behind the healing, the one who guided the blade he held at each and every surgery and amputation. I whispered the words he was to use, told him what treatments to apply. In this way, I was able to stay in the unit with him and assist in the operations, be an equal of the other men, looked up to for my abilities. Until Galloway." Her hand shook, then steadied. "But that won't happen again. Now, we have a second chance. I know he will listen to me when I explain the situation, show him the opportunity. He owes me that much. I gave up my life for him, and now it is his turn."

"You have committed murder and mayhem in the name of medicine," said Inez. "A true healer would shrink away in horror and disgust. I cannot imagine he will listen to you, once he finds out what you have done."

"He'll never know. He believes whatever I say. You've given me a splendid idea, which I will explain so you are not tempted to do something stupid. If I must shoot you, I shall simply put the revolver in the doctor's hand. The story can be that you killed each other. A little messy to explain, but one can always conjecture. The motivation will be clear, however. I know, as did the doctor, that the DuChamps boy is really your son. I know the doctor told the DuChamps that he strongly advises that your son not go back to Leadville. Too high, you know. You learn of this. You are a passionate woman. You become incensed, distraught. And you are prone to drink. Yes, I know that. So did Dr. Prochazka, and he warned your husband of the dangers you were in, soon after his arrival. If I'm not wrong, I believe you have been drinking earlier this night. Again, excellent. We all know that alcohol quickens, excites, and animates the vital forces. So, in your passion and determination, you come to the doctor's clinic to seduce him and convince him to change his mind."

The gun rose and fell, indicating Inez's evening dress. "Perhaps it can even be suggested that your husband put you up to this act of immorality. He will deny it, of course. But his background is such that who will believe him?"

She nodded, pleased. "I hate to lose Mr. Stannert as a possible investor, but there is no hope for it, so I might as well destroy any credibility he has here and drive a wedge between him and Mr. DuChamps. Yes, it is brilliant. It will work."

Her eyes snapped back into focus, glinting in the light from the table lamp. "So, Mrs. Stannert. You had best obey my every word, if you hope to convince me that it isn't more advantageous to kill you. Now, to work."

"What am I to do?" *Whatever it is, I'll do it slowly as possible, and hope that I get an opportunity to act.*

Crowson pointed with the gun to a large crate below the counter where Prochazka conducted his research. "Just take everything on the surface, pull the photographs and notes from the wall, and toss them in. Be careful. The doctor was culturing various strains of tuberculosis on the Petri dishes. I don't know what might happen if you cut yourself on the glass and some gets under your skin."

Glad that she was wearing evening gloves, Inez moved slowly over to the counter. "Since I'm to be your housemaid, perhaps you can explain to me why you killed Dr. Prochazka. He said he'd found the mechanism for consumption. He was thinking of leaving Manitou. If you wanted him out of the way, why not simply let him go?"

Inez picked up one glass dish between two fingers and dropped it into the crate with a crash.

"No, no, silently please. Why Dr. Prochazka? He told me of his research success this evening. He was exuberant, of course. But he didn't see what that would mean to us. All the tonics and medicines would be useless. What good is a mineral springs against a bacterium? All the people who flock here would stop coming. Dr. Prochazka was correct about one thing: once the enemy is identified, it is just a matter of time before someone comes up with the proper weapon. We would be truly ruined, and Victor would not recover from such a devastation."

"But Dr. Prochazka's colleague, Dr. Koch, is on the same trail." Inez picked up a half-full flask and lowered it into the crate. "It's just a matter of time."

"I'll take some time over none. All I want to do is convince Victor he must return to the medical field and we will do as we did before. We have Prochazka's tonics. I kept his receipt book. Victor can turn the running of the hotel over to someone else, and he can become the hotel's physician and I will once again be his hands and guide him. We don't need Prochazka anymore, and we certainly don't need his 'research' on phthisis." She gestured with the pistol. "A little faster, Mrs. Stannert. Dawn will be here soon."

"How did you kill him?"

"Easy enough. Unlike Robert Calder, who refused my tea— and I knew he would, so I had prepared—Dr. Prochazka has some every night at about three in the morning, to help him sleep. He is an insomniac and finds the mint relaxes him. This time, there was more than mint."

"Why the statue?"

"When I came in, expecting he would be in a swoon, he wasn't. Alas, I had no choice." She sounded sad. "Violence is not my way."

"Is not your way? What about Calder?"

"Well, you know about the herb Paris. I had access. I had keys. By the way, right after you and your husband left this evening, I went into your rooms." She reached into the basket and pulled out a passkey to the hotel. "So, I knew it was you. You were in Victor's rooms yesterday and mine as well. I sensed someone had been there. The chair had been moved. There was a disturbance of things. Then, Mr. Travers showed me your husband's card." She shook her head. "How much wiser you would both have been to simply take your walks and enjoy the scenery."

"So, Calder." Inez removed a tower of Petri dishes, bent to bring them close to the floor of the crate. They slithered in, clattering.

"I thought if his horse became ill, he would stop his silly questions. Perhaps he would be injured as well, or at least inconvenienced. I didn't know events would unfold as they did. Then, he became wild. You saw him in the garden. I knew I had to take direct action, because eventually he would destroy Victor and perhaps uncover my part as well. So, I made certain I was out walking that evening. He stopped, as any proper gentleman would, and offered me a ride to the hotel. I told him my conscience would not rest, I'd been out walking, trying to decide what to do, and that I had to confide in him about his brother. He came to my rooms with great eagerness to hear what I had to say. He refused my tea, and instead took the offer of a glass of port from a sealed bottle." A pale smile ghosted across her round face. "Sealed. Do you not see the folly of his choice, Mrs. Stannert?"

"You poisoned the bottle of port."

"There was no other way to quiet him. It was quick, painless. He became unconscious. I injected his heart with air, just to be sure. I put him in the invalid chair and rolled him up the canyon. I didn't want him to be found near the hotel. I didn't want any connection with the hotel. We have had enough troubles as it is, and I do not want to drive paying visitors away. No one saw me. If they did, well, so what? The pre-dawn air can be beneficial for some, easing the breathing. That would have been my story."

"So you dumped his body in Williams' Canyon, maneuvered the boulder on that bench of rock into the invalid chair." Inez's hand shook. She picked up a heavy microscope.

"No, no, leave those there. I've decided it will be better for the story I'm to tell. So, yes, I used the chair. However, I miscalculated. The boulder was so heavy, it nearly broke the chair's mechanisms. Still, it all worked. You needn't mourn Calder too much. As I said, he was well dead by that time."

Inez shuddered. "Did you want Mrs. Pace to die also?"

"Absolutely not. As with the horses, events that were supposed to unfold in a certain way, did not. After the mishap in the Garden of the Gods, I determined I would be in control of all the factors."

"What was supposed to happen with Mrs. Pace?"

"I extracted the digitalis from the foxglove. Measured the amount carefully. Pulled out only as much tonic as needed, and injected the digitalis in its place. If Kirsten Pace had taken the proper dosage, her heart would have weakened at altitude, but that is all. She would have become short of breath, and they would have returned quickly, contritely. The Paces would have seen that we were right and they were wrong: it was dangerous for them to go to Leadville. Why would Mr. Pace want to look for investment opportunities there, when the Mountain Springs House is here? Leadville doesn't need his money, *we* do!"

The naked ferocity in her voice caused Inez to clutch the doctor's notebook to her breast, as if paper and leather could be armor against a moving bullet. Her mind raced, trying to see things the way the nurse might.

"So, it was just supposed to be a lesson," offered Inez. "Not lethal at all. Because, after all, you want the Paces to be on your side."

"Yes, yes. That's it. A lesson." Mrs. Crowson's head bobbed. "But things went awry. Mr. Pace took ill. I assume the altitude, although why he and not his wife felt the effects, I don't understand. And then, he drank the entire bottle! The entire bottle! I made it very clear: only a teaspoon, and only three times a day."

"So, he essentially killed himself."

"Exactly, Mrs. Stannert." She sounded pleased that Inez understood.

"The notebooks too?" Inez held it out to her, as if she might want to keep them. "Seems such a waste. All his work."

"Toss them. Especially them."

She did. "How are we to explain the doctor's death?" *Assuming I can stay alive and not become a part of this ghastly tableau.*

"My plan is this. He needs to be taken out of here." She looked down at the crumpled body and mess of blood on the floor. "His papers and experiments must be destroyed too. I was thinking that a fire in the clinic would do. Perhaps they will think he simply died in the fire."

"But people will rally and attempt to put out the flames," pointed out Inez, a half-empty flask dangling innocently in one hand. "If you are going to hide the body, perhaps just put out that he left in the night? Just disappeared? People do that all the time." *Mark did.* "We can suggest that he was planning on returning to Germany. Perhaps, being the eccentric sort he is, he just gathered up his papers and left. He might have mentioned his success at his experiments and plans to return to others, so, while it might seem odd for him to vanish, it might not be entirely out of character."

Crowson thought, then smiled broadly, approvingly. "I knew I did the right thing in not shooting you when you walked in the door. We will be most excellent confederates, and you will convince your husband to invest well and heavily in the hotel." Her eyes narrowed. "But I will tell you this, lest you might be tempted to cross me and talk to your husband, your sister, the marshal, my brother, anyone at all. Mr. DuChamps has agreed to allow his wife, that is, your sister, and your son to winter over in Manitou, at our hotel. What a tragedy it would be if either your sister or your son should, well, suddenly fail dangerously in health. You may think that by telling them to not take the tonic, you could save them. But they must eat. They must drink. They must breathe. And I have all the keys."

Inez stared, horrified. "You would kill an innocent child?"

"Not I. You would by your own indiscretion. You would kill your own son. I know you don't want to do that, do you? Now, quickly, time is passing." She hitched the gun meaningfully.

Just then, a groan at her feet.

Inez stared, incredulous, as Prochazka's outstretched fingers twitched. She wanted to scream: Be silent! Don't move!

But it was too late. The nurse looked down and said, "Dear me." She brought the statue up high and whipped it down.

Inez threw the half-full flask at the nurse.

The statue contacted the doctor's skull with a sickening thud, just as the flask's contents splashed over the nurse.

Mrs. Crowson screamed. She staggered and dropped the statue, then grabbed the edge of her cloak to wipe her face.

Inez grabbed another flask, hiked her skirts up to her knees, and headed for the door, flinging the second glass as she dashed past Mrs. Crowson, who dodged and lifted her gun.

The shot cracked throughout the clinic. Inez swore she could feel the bullet buzz past her head. She broke into a hobbled run, only to find a bulky male figure looming at the clinic's door, silhouetted by the dawning light.

Lewis grabbed Inez and spun her out of the way, shouting, "Shelby! Stop!"

The second bullet, meant for Inez, hit him square in the neck.

The scream came not from Lewis but from Crowson.

Inez flattened herself to the floor next to the hotelier, who was bubbling up blood. She scrabbled in his pockets for a pistol, a knife, anything.

He was unarmed.

Crowson bore down upon them, eyes wild. She grabbed Inez by her silk-clad shoulder and shoved her away from the dying man.

Sister knelt by brother. She set the gun down and tried to staunch the wound with her hands. Blood oozed between her fingers to the floor, soaking into the thirsty dry wood.

Inez backed away, on gloved hands and stockinged knees, and gripped a chair leg, dragging the chair around so she could swing it. She was determined to take down the nurse with hardwood, if nothing else. Assuming she got the chance before the next shot.

Crowson ignored Inez. Whispering low to her brother, she put an arm behind his back and pulled him up to a half-seated position. Lewis choked and a surge of blood spilled from his lips, splashing over his jacket. He went still.

Through the open door, Inez could see the back porch of the hotel. Several men were gathered in a knot. The knot loosened, and one figure limped down the steps and came through the garden, moving quickly: Mark.

Mrs. Crowson lowered Lewis to the floor, gripped his wrist as if seeking a pulse, and closed her eyes. Inez dragged the chair toward herself and rose on her knees, tensing to swing.

The nurse opened her eyes and gazed at Inez. Her expression was as one who lived through battles and wars, only to be brought down by an invisible burden, too heavy to bear.

"I did everything I could, everything in my power to bring him back to who he needed to be, so we could return to who we were," she whispered, still clutching his wrist. "Now that he's gone, that can never happen." She raised her revolver.

The final shot shattered the air before Inez could bring the chair around.

But it didn't matter.

After all, the bullet was not meant for her.

Chapter Forty-five

There was no way to hush up the scatter of bodies in the clinic and the lingering sense of catastrophe that greeted the hotel's patrons and patients at the dawning of the day.

Epperley did the next best thing and closed the clinic building, putting a hefty lock on the door. The hotel manager then put out an urgent request to Dr. Zuckerman, who agreed to put off his trip to Denver and take over the Mountain Springs House's patients immediately.

Epperley stepped into the breach, deciding that it was best to put it out and about that the whole sorry business was a family affair, brought on by Crowson's sudden mental collapse. As he explained privately to Inez and Mark that evening, from behind a screen of cigarette smoke and during a shared bottle of brandy in the manager's small but comfortable office on the main floor, "All the people who matter, including the marshal, know about Mrs. Crowson's unceasing work here at the hotel and in the community. They won't blink an eye at the suggestion that all the strain brought her to the edge of hysteria and that something simple pushed her over. The overwhelming responsibilities of being on the front line of the healing profession and what not. Besides, Dr. Prochazka was not the easiest chap to answer to. He'd drive anyone to madness, honestly. I'm certain the hotel's reputation can survive this unfortunate incident, provided I can count on your discretion." He raised an eyebrow and added another generous tot to their glasses.

When Inez inquired as to what would happen to Prochazka's research, Epperley waved a desultory hand, sending a coil of cigarette smoke into a swirling chaos. "You started the job quite neatly with your enforced housekeeping in the back room. I had a maid I trust finish the task. Burned the papers to keep them away from prying eyes."

Inez couldn't help it. She gasped.

Epperley continued. "Threw the rest of the glassware away. Oh, gave the microscopes and Dr. P's tonic recipes to Zuckerman, at his request. It was all he wanted, and he's welcome to them. By-the-by, as you probably know, Zuckerman is as heavily invested in the hotel as I am. He's backing up this sorry tale of woe with his considerable reputation, so we'll have no problem from the medical side of things."

"But Dr. Prochazka told me he'd discovered the cause of tuberculosis," Inez said. "Think of the lives that could be saved, if his work could be salvaged."

Smoke puffed from Epperley's nostrils in a derisive snort. "Assuming he really did, who would present those results to the medical establishment and the world?" He tapped the growing ash into a crystal ashtray. "Are you volunteering for the assignment, Mrs. Stannert? Or perhaps you're thinking of Dr. Zuckerman? He's no researcher, just the local pill pusher. A well-regarded one, but still, no academic. He'd be laughed out of any serious gathering of medical men. He'll make a mint from all of Dr. P's tonics, and that's all he cares about. As for the building…"

Inez leaned forward. "Will it remain a clinic?"

"No. I have my plans." He leaned back, gazed up at the ceiling, and drew reflectively on his cigarette, sending the resultant plume skyward. "A billiard room for men and women *and* a bowling alley. The building will hold them both nicely, with room to spare. That'll show the Cliff House and Manitou House that we're still a serious competitor and not to be trifled with."

Over the following few days, the real story played out in communications between Doc Cramer in Leadville and the Stannerts in Manitou.

Doc's initial response to Mark's urgent telegram arrived while Inez was being fussed over by Harmony and Aunt Agnes, who offered up endless glasses of mineral water and cups of mint tea in the women's parlor room. Aunt Agnes kept saying, "I knew it! This barbaric place is full of barbarians. Shooting guns, as if this is some dreadful dime novel come to life. That poor nurse, Mrs. Crowson, was no doubt driven mad living in this wilderness, as any woman with normal sensibilities would be."

Harmony's urgent hush to Agnes went unnoticed. Agnes continued, "Why you won't come with us, Inez, I cannot understand. You are stubborn beyond belief. You could have been killed in the crossfire! If that so-called husband of yours cared about you at all he would have taken the money I offered."

Inez, who was refusing the mineral water, refusing the tea, refusing Harmony's insistence that she "lie down" on the divan in the parlor, bolted upright away from Harmony's gentle hands. "*What?* Aunt Agnes, what did you do?"

Even Harmony looked aghast.

The tumbler of mineral water in Aunt Agnes' hand wavered. Then, she shot a hard defiant stare at Inez. "I offered Mr. Stannert money to let you go, to release you. A considerable sum, I'll add. I told him I would take you back east, effect the divorce, and it needn't concern him at all. He need not do anything, not show up, not place a motion, it would all be taken care of, none would be the wiser, and he'd be free. I even offered that we would arrange for him to see William, when the child was older. Although honestly, it isn't as if he has provided for you and William in a manner befitting descendants of the Underwoods."

"Aunt Agnes, this is the last straw," snapped Inez. "You have meddled in our affairs—mine, my husband's, our son's—and overstepped your bounds completely. I have met card sharps, buffalo hunters, confidence men, *cyprians*—"

Harmony gasped and lay a hand across her bosom. Inez was surprised that Harmony even knew what the term meant.

"—with more honor than you," she finished.

Mark picked that moment to knock on the women's parlor door and venture into the female bastion, bearing Doc's response to the urgent early morning telegram.

From the way her husband and aunt eyed each other—with the thinnest of civilized veneers glossing mutual dislike—Inez surmised that Agnes had been telling the truth about her attempt to bribe Mark and his refusal to rise to the bait.

With the briefest of bows to Agnes and a deeper, more respectful one to Harmony, Mark showed Inez the yellow sheet on which the telegraph operator had printed Doc's reply: "The War and the 'Franke' brothers. Telegraphist incorrectly wrote 'Franklin.' VLF is Surgeon Victor Lewis Franke. SCF is Asst Surgeon Shelby Crowson Franke. Dr. Galloway killed in botched surgery. Why?"

Inez promptly rose to her feet and clutched Mark's arm as if he were her lifeline to sanity. She escaped the parlor and her aunt, only after repeated assurances to her frantic sister that she was, indeed, unharmed and merely needed to rest upstairs. Epperley stopped them both in the hallway, Zuckerman hot on his heels, and said in a low voice, "Please, do not say anything to anyone yet. I shall arrange for us to meet this evening and discuss this unfortunate turn of events. If you could stay mum until then, it would be much appreciated."

In the sitting room of their suite, Inez made a proper recovery with a cup of strong coffee laced with even stronger brandy. She and Mark then drafted another telegram to Doc with a short, circumspect explanation and more questions. Doc promptly sent back an equally short and opaque response.

Later that day, a knock on the Stannerts' hotel door provided a break in the flurry of telegrams back and forth to Leadville. Inez opened the door to find Susan Carothers and Mrs. Pace, accompanied by a distinguished man with intense blue eyes, along with the Pace children and their nanny. "We have come to say good-bye," said Mrs. Pace, lifting her mourning veil. "It will be a relief to head back to our home, now that my husband's brother has arrived." She introduced Eric Pace to Inez and

Mark. He shook hands solemnly all around. Mathilda piped up, "Uncle Eric is going to be like our father now." Inez noted the blush that climbed his face and the glance he sent toward Mrs. Pace as she scolded Mathilda. Maybe, Inez thought, the future would prove the child right, after the proper amount of time had passed.

They offered to wait outside the door so Susan could have a few private words with Inez. Mark excused himself to his bedroom, leaving the two friends alone.

Susan clutched Inez's hand. "This is short notice, but when Kirsten offered that I could share their carriage to the train station in Colorado Springs, I decided to accept. I need to return to Leadville and my studio. It's just too hard to stay here, I keep thinking of Robert." She opened her tote, pulled out a cabinet card, and handed it to Inez. It was one of Mrs. Galbreaith's images of Robert Calder, standing in the narrows of Williams Canyon, cocky smile on his face, arms folded. Even on paper, he radiated life and vitality.

"I understand," said Inez. "He was a good man. He worked hard to find the truth, and I believe he cared quite a bit for you." She handed the card back to her friend.

Susan took the card, tucked it carefully away, and rose. "Didn't someone once say work is the best medicine for troubled souls? I have plenty to do, and am anxious to get started." She leaned forward and brushed Inez's cheek with her lips. "Thank you so much for asking me to come to Manitou with you. Despite all the heartaches, I'm glad I came. I would have never met Robert, if not for you."

Inez held her hand a moment longer. "I'll see you back in Leadville, Susan. We shall have tea and talk. But not mint tea," she added quickly.

A few days later, after a third unsatisfactory round of telegrams, Inez and Mark finally received a letter from Doc. He laid out his story with a preponderance of ink blots and enthusiasm that Inez suspected was due to an overabundant late-night consumption of liquor for nonmedicinal purposes.

Doc began with "I did not know the Franke brothers personally. But the unfolding of events and theories that I provide to you in this letter came from men who knew the surgeons in question. Medical men who labored in the hospital tents alongside me, men I will forever vouchsafe as honest and reliable as any I've known throughout my life."

He then launched into an explanation that had Inez exclaiming with force and Mark shaking his head. The Franke brothers had enlisted together and, at their request, were assigned to the same unit. "As it was explained to me later, they always operated together," Doc said. "It was assumed by those in the medical fraternity that they were brothers trained at the same school, practiced together. They were extremely private and not given to talking about themselves or their past. For a long time, it was believed that Victor Franke was the brilliant physician. He handled the worst of cases with apparent ease and skill. Little did we know that it wasn't the brilliance of the surgeon, but the *assistant* surgeon, that was responsible for the heroic medical deeds. Since the two of them always worked together, they managed to keep the fiction going for quite a while."

The subterfuge unraveled when Victor Franke was called in to perform a standard amputation on colleague Dr. Galloway. Shelby Franke was not there to attend, so an impartial assistant surgeon stepped in and witnessed the carnage unfold on the operating table. According to everything the assistant said later, the operation should have been a simple matter, but Victor Franke botched it horribly.

The assistant surgeon realized too late that the so-called brilliant Dr. Franke was standing motionless, bone saw in hand, blood draining from his face, as his patient expired. The assistant physician jumped in and tried and save Galloway, but Galloway died on the operating table.

"It was a horrible outcome. Still, there was nothing to be done. We were in the middle of a war, after all. Men died and were dying all around us, every minute of the day and night. But the assistant surgeon spoke to his colleagues, and Victor

Franke's light was dimmed. Instead of admitting his mistake and his ineptitude, squaring up, picking up the pieces and marching on, Franke said nothing. He and his brother disappeared soon after—deserters, which branded them yet again, most finally. I have not heard of the pair of them until now, hence my astonishment upon receiving your initial telegram. I look forward with great interest to hearing what brought their names to your attention in Manitou, when you return."

Chapter Forty-six

Inez finished reading Doc's opus in the sitting room of their suite and lowered the last sheet of onionskin paper carefully atop the others. Mark sat opposite her, reading the Colorado Springs' *Gazette*, cigar balanced between two fingers. "All this time," she said, "Mrs. Crowson was angling to return to her glory days, with her brother as her puppet. But why would she think he would agree to return to being a physician? He demurred to me time and time again that he had absolutely no interest in medicine."

"Doesn't mean he couldn't have been persuaded by her, when all is said and done," Mark observed. "Maybe he was even willing to go along with it, up to a point. Until the end. Who knows? All we know is what we heard, not what passed between them. Like a con game, if you're bein' taken by experts, you'll never know." He returned to his paper.

"Maybe." Inez tapped a finger on Doc's letter. "It obviously all went wrong when she left him to cope on his own, so she was no doubt setting it up so that wouldn't happen again."

With a sigh, Mark set his paper aside. "Darlin', she didn't need him. If she was even half as good as Doc and the folks around here say, she could have been brilliant on her own. Even Leadville has its lady doctor, Dr. Mary Barker Bates."

"Maybe it was her brother's idea that she not step forward as a physician, thus drawing attention to herself and to him. Too, it is not an easy life for a woman to openly take on a man's role."

Inez thought briefly about her own experience and struggles of running the saloon during Mark's long absence.

A knock on the door interrupted her musings. Mark opened the door to reveal Lily on the other side, eyes downcast.

Inez sat up straighter. "Is William awake and ready for the afternoon?"

It had become a routine for the Stannerts to take William out after his afternoon rest. Inez was simultaneously heartened by his increasing acceptance of them—at least, he no longer cried at great length when separated from Lily and the DuChamps—but also discouraged by what she viewed as her own incompetence as a mother. When witnessing Harmony's gentle and loving interactions with William, Inez had to fight to keep the green stab of jealousy from developing into a mortal wound.

"No'm." Lily kept her eyes downcast. Inez realized she was dressed in a long cloak, ready to go outside. "Missus and I are going out for a walk. The mister wants to talk to you, ma'am. He said he'd wake Wilkie for you, if he is still asleep when you're done."

Inez looked at Mark. "Are you coming?"

Mark picked up his paper and rustled the papers. "Sounds like the invitation is just for you, Mrs. Stannert."

She and Lily left Mark with his paper and cigar, and started down the hall. Inez followed a few steps behind Lily, wondering what Jonathon DuChamps could possibly want to talk to her in private about. Her gaze sharpened as something about Lily—her slight stature, the billowing of her lightweight summer cloak, the way she glided with small determined steps—put Inez in mind of a ghost floating down the hall. That observation brought back a most unwelcome memory.

Inez stopped by the tall niche holding the statue of Hermes at the top of the stairs, and spoke sharply. "Lily!"

William's young nanny started and turned. Her gaze involuntarily shifted to the statue, then back to Inez. For a moment, Lily looked wild-eyed, like some small animal, trapped in a corner and blinded by a sudden light. Her hands, which had been folded before her, separated, and twisted into the dark fabric of her summer cloak. It was as if she held to the cloth to keep those hands from flying out and forward in an involuntary push. A savage, desperate push that would send an unaware adversary plunging down the stairs. A push to save the family she loved more than anything else on earth.

Inez had seen all she needed to see.

Arms folded, she walked slowly forward. "So, it was you that night."

Lily retreated a single step. "I'm sorry, ma'am." The words were barely a whisper. "I just wanted Wilkie to stay with us. I just wanted him to be happy."

Inez stopped her words with a hand on her shoulder. "We'll say no more, not to anyone. I understand you did this through love, no matter how misguided it was. My only request in exchange for my silence is that you continue to love and take care of William for as long as he stays with you and my sister, whether that be a week, a month, or a year. That when the time comes to say good-bye, you find a way to hold it in your heart that it is for the best. I and Mr. Stannert will not do anything that isn't in the best interests of our son. Do you understand?"

Lily nodded. She wouldn't look at Inez, but Inez saw a tear slide down her cheek, past the shadow of the hood.

Lily and Inez continued toward the DuChamps' rooms. Just short of Harmony and Jonathan's suite, a door flew open. "Inez Marie, I must talk with you." It was, of course, Aunt Agnes.

Inez pursed her lips in annoyance. "Aunt Agnes, I'm on my way to see Jonathan."

"This will take but a moment." Agnes clutched her arm and drew her inside, telling Lily, "Go tell Mr. DuChamps that she will be there directly." Agnes closed the door in Lily's dumb-founded face.

Inez sighed, leaned her back against the door and crossed her arms. "What is this all about?"

Agnes, garbed in her pre-Raphaelite costume, bustled to the windows facing the second-story veranda and drew the shades down, casting the room into secluded gloom. "I wanted to talk with you alone, away from prying ears and eyes." She turned and faced Inez, her loose gown swirling about her like an eddy in a stream. For a moment, looking into her aunt's calculating eyes, Inez was put in mind of the Greek goddess Athena, weaving her plots and stratagems.

"We have unfinished business," her aunt continued. "Goodness, stand up straight, Inez, and uncross your arms. You are slouching like a hooligan."

Inez didn't alter her stance. "Say what you want to say. I need to talk to Jonathan, and then Mr. Stannert and I are taking William out for his afternoon constitutional."

"As to William," Agnes paused by the corner table and picked something up. "This involves him."

Inez straightened up. "What does?"

Agnes floated toward her, holding out the paper for Inez to read. It was a railway ticket from Colorado Springs, heading east. Inez stared at it, then at Aunt Agnes, not quite believing what she was seeing.

"This is your chance to come home with us," Agnes said, "with William, your sister, your family." She held the ticket up, face-level. "This is my gift to you: your freedom. Come home, and we'll straighten out the business of your marriage, so you need never worry about him bothering you again. You will never want, you will never need, you can spend all your time with your son and your true family. We only want what's best for you, Inez."

Agnes scrutinized her as if she were dissecting every flicker of emotion that crossed Inez's face. "All is forgiven. Your parents are expecting you. All you need to do is come to the station the morning we leave. You needn't tell your husband anything. You needn't even bring any clothes. Everything will be provided. You can walk away from this," she waved the ticket summarily at the curtained window, which shut out the foothills of Pike's Peak and the dusty trails, rivers, and rocks of the Manitou area and Colorado's high country beyond, "as if it were a bad dream."

Inez closed her eyes against Agnes' determined gaze and imagined, in a tumbling rush, what it would be like, should she say yes. It would be simple, as Aunt Agnes said. Show up at the station, board the east-bound train. This time, she would be holding her son; she would not have to give him up to anyone. There would be no need to look back, only look into his eyes and see her future there. She would return to New York, to her mother and her father. Agnes said they had forgiven her, and Inez knew that what Aunt Agnes wanted, she got. Her aunt had somehow finagled forgiveness from her iron-willed father, and her mother would be waiting with open arms, Inez knew this to be true. She would simply place her marital trials and tribulations into the competent hands of the Underwoods' family lawyers, and she would never need to think on it again. Never think on Mark, on Leadville, on Reverend Sands, the saloon, any of it. It would all be as a dream.

Life would settle back into the comfort and cocoon of family wealth and privilege, accompanied, of course, by the expectations that such a life extracts. And everything, everything, would be taken care of.

She opened her eyes onto Aunt Agnes' expectant face. "Are you finished?" Inez asked.

"Yes. Except to say, this is your one chance. Should you decline, you will never hear from me again. I shall not be able to broker another agreement between you and your father, so you will remain an outcast, left to your own devices to handle your own problems and messes."

Inez plucked the ticket from Agnes' hand, examined it, then set it down on the table by the door. "I have been handling my own messes, as you call them, for over a decade now. I can take care of myself, Aunt Agnes. This is my home, here in the West. As for William, he is my son, and he will return to me some day. Blood calls blood and, I will never, ever turn my back on him." Inez's hand settled on the doorknob. "No more than I would turn my back on you or any other of my family, should you be in need or should you come here to visit me. I have, you see, forgiven you all. Now, I must go meet with Jonathan." Inez bent over and kissed Agnes' smooth cheek. "I know you do this through love, however misguided, and I thank you for it."

Before her aunt could say another word, Inez pulled the door open and slipped outside into the hall. Taking a deep, shaking breath, Inez moved down to the next door and knocked. She heard Jonathan call, "Enter!"

Inez opened the door to find Jonathan standing and facing her, hands clasped behind him as if preparing to address a boardroom of hostile investors. "Thank you, Mrs. Stannert, for coming. Please, make yourself comfortable." He gestured to one of a pair of the chairs.

She entered, closed the door, and moved to the chair, saying, "What did you want to discuss?"

"I must speak with you, frankly, and in confidence, about my wife—that is, about your sister—and your son."

Inez sat and tried to quiet her anxiously beating heart. "Whatever you say I will hold close and not speak of to anyone, if that is what you wish."

He nodded once, his magnified eyes behind the spectacles pinned to the far wall, as if he'd taken her acquiescence as a given, and was preparing his words. He finally returned to the empty chair and sat, pushing his glasses up his nose as he did so. He looked straight at her. "Your sister thinks the world of you. More than you probably realize. Back home, she awaits each of your letters, and if there is too long a silence, begins to fret and worry. Although she never says so to me, I can see how she brightens at receiving words from you and pines when she does not."

"I love her as well," said Inez. "I cannot imagine a world without her."

"Yes. Well. That leads to…" He almost seemed to choke, and stopped, clearing his throat. He withdrew his handkerchief and held it to his lips for a moment.

He finally said, "You know we came here not just for your son's health, but for hers as well. She told you that, did she not?"

Inez nodded, feeling a sudden shroud of fear descending over her heart and stopping her breath. "Of course. She said it was a simple cough. That the mountain air was doing her well along with the exercise."

"It is not a simple cough." He said it with such vehemence, such hopelessness, that Inez knew. What she had, at some level, feared all through the visit now loomed before her.

She could hardly say the words. "Wasting disease?"

"Consumption. Phthisis. The white plague. Tuberculosis. Whatever name you call it, it is the same damnable disease."

Inez was so caught up in his agony and her own, she didn't even blink at his expletive. "Does she know?"

"Of course not!" Vehemence again. "She is not to know. It would cause her to lose hope. She needs all her strength, her will, to fight. She *must* fight. Her physicians and I assure her it is a stubborn cough, a non-fatal weakness of the lungs, that with careful attention, prescription, and time will improve."

Inez stood up, walked to the window to gather her composure, then returned and sat down again. "You haven't told her. So this is why there is talk of her coming back and staying in Colorado for a longer time?"

"Yes." His lips tightened below his pencil mustache. "I could not bear to be apart from her for so long, except that it will bring a possible cure. A possible retreat of the disease. That is one reason I agreed we could come here, to Manitou, to Dr. Prochazka. I'd heard from very reliable sources of his work and that there might be a cure, a true cure, as a result. Now, all for naught."

Inez covered her mouth with her hand, holding back the exclamation of pain and anger. *Damn you, Epperley and Crowson! You destroyed his work and have killed my sister as surely as if you put a bullet in her breast.*

"I may still set her up here for an extended stay, once I have consulted with the doctors back home," Jonathan said. "She has improved considerably, perhaps due to the weather, the air, your presence. And, of course," he pinned her once again with his spectacle-enhanced stare, "due to your son."

Inez's heart, which had been beating rapidly, lurched as he continued, "Wilkie, that is your William, has brought her joy. Reason to live."

"I know she loves him dearly," said Inez, her mind racing frantically in various directions, looking for alternate resolutions to the one she sensed bearing down upon her like a train.

Jonathan continued, "If you say it is time, and you want to take him back, she would wave good-bye with a smile on her face and her heart breaking. I do not think she would recover from the loss."

Inez said desperately, "She has such a wonderful way with him. She would be a wonderful mother to her own children. Why don't you—"

She stopped herself from saying, "have children of your own?"

He answered as if she'd asked. "There can be no children between us."

"None?" It was a stupid response, but the only word that came to mind.

"None." His tone said that was all he would say on the subject. "So, I have a request, a plea, an entreaty, to make of you."

Inez gripped the arms of the chair, but her frantic hold could not stop the words from being said.

"Please, Mrs. Stannert. Inez, if I may. I am begging you." He removed his spectacles, rubbed his eyes with one hand, and looked at her with unguarded eyes. "Tell her that you want William to stay with us."

She closed her eyes. "Mr. DuChamps. Jonathan. You ask a great deal of me."

"I do not mean forever," he added hastily. "But let her know, you will not call for him in a month, a year. That a way will be found such that they can stay together."

Inez observed him, silent. Then, "I am not the only one involved in this decision. There is William's father, Mr. Stannert, who also has a say in the matter."

Jonathan sat back in the chair, and hooked the glasses back over his ears. "I have spoken to Mr. Stannert. He said the verdict is entirely yours, and that he will abide by whatever you say." He clasped his hands, then unclasped them, and pulled out his pocket watch. "Harmony and Lily will return soon from their walk, and I should wake up William as promised." He glanced at her and away. "If you cannot offer me your decision now, I can understand you need time. I'm sorry to have sprung such a weighty topic on you at what is essentially the last moment."

She reached over and placed a hand upon Jonathan's tailored sleeve. "No. Do not apologize. So much has happened, so quickly, how could you know how this trip would unfold? Besides, I know my decision. It is the only one that a loving mother and sister could possibly make."

His expression, filled with fear, filled with hope, filled her vision, waiting for the words that would bring him peace or set his world crashing down into darkness.

Chapter Forty-seven

"So, you decided that William could stay with the DuChamps," said Mark.

The Stannerts, appearing as any normal family of three out for a short afternoon walk, strolled over the small wood bridge leading to the Manitou Soda spring.

"How could I not?" Inez gazed down at the top of her son's head. Light brown curls escaped his straw hat, curling about his round face. He grabbed one of the bridge rails and squatted, peering down at the rushing Fountain Creek waters. Inez leaned down and grabbed the back of his kilt skirt. "No, William!" she said sharply. "You could fall in and drown!"

Mark chuckled. "You sounded like my own momma when you said that, Inez."

She hauled William upright, then took his hand. He said, "No!" and tried to pull his hand away.

"Is this how you responded to her as well?" Inez tightened her grip on his hand as he wiggled his fingers furiously, trying to escape her grip. "William, be good. When we get to the other side, I'll let you climb some rocks."

"Rocks!" William said happily, his voice almost covered by the sound of rushing water.

"My momma would've strapped me good for saying 'no.' Probably why I was such a rascal back when. I learned early how to preserve my own skin and still get my way." He leaned over, bracing himself with the cane, and picked up William with one arm. "On up, Wilkie. Let's find the rocks."

"Besides," Inez continued, tipping her parasol to block the sun, "Jonathan promised to consult with the doctors back home. If they agree, he said he'd give serious consideration to allowing Harmony and William to settle in the area. Not that they'd be alone. If they come, I'm certain Jonathan would see to it that they have a sizeable retinue, which will no doubt include Lily, a cook, a maid, and a man of some kind to drive and help as needed. Maybe even a nurse or personal physician."

"We could come out of the mountains to visit as often as you please," said Mark. "The Springs are only a short train ride from Leadville."

Over the bridge at last, he set William back on his feet. William wavered a moment, then started toward the rustic pavilion by the spring, followed closely by his parents.

"About 'we.'" Inez slowed her step and stopped by William. "We need to discuss that."

Mark started talking fast, as if hoping to get it all said before she cut him off. "All I ask is that you hold off on pressing for a divorce. Give me a chance to show we can still make a go of it. You know, I told Jonathan DuChamps that the decision about William was up to you. I didn't insist on paternal prerogative, which he clearly expected me to do. In Manitou, I've been here for you, helped you at every turn. I know you, Inez. I'd never make you someone you didn't want to be—like some men do to their women. We have years, a life, a child together. So all I'm saying is that you give me—us—time. Enough time to see if we can't find our way back."

Inez took a deep breath. The fresh smell and sounds of fast-rushing water filled her senses. Even her skin seemed to soften, welcoming the moisture from the air. Her thoughts seemed to be as on the surface of the turbulent water—rushing downstream, whether she willed it or not.

She looked at Mark.

He waited. His blue eyes stayed steady on her face. Stillness waited in his expression, as if he was purposely holding back the charm, the twinkle in the eye, the sly half-smile that toppled hearts so fast they scarcely missed a beat between being free and being captured.

She looked down at his hands, covering the head of his cane. Even through his gloves, she could tell he gripped the silver knob tight. It was the only indication of tension in his immobile demeanor.

She finally spoke. "How long do you have in mind?"

He answered promptly. "Two years."

She shook her head. "Too long."

"Well, we've been apart a long time, Inez. Keep in mind, we had ten years together, through good times and bad. We had some very good times, along with the bad, and we stuck together through it all. That's got to count for something." He leaned over his cane. "I'll rebuild our house and give it to you. You'll have a proper place to live. I won't have a key, it'll be yours, no matter what you finally decide to do. I'll sign papers to that effect, if you want."

She squinted. "Where will you stay?"

"I'll stay in a hotel or maybe move into the saloon…but not your rooms," he added hastily. "I'll work out something. I don't need much space, after all."

She looked away. The peaked roof of the rustic pavilion reminded her of the high mountains of Colorado, and she felt a sudden pang of homesickness for Leadville.

"You won't have a key," she said slowly.

"That's right, darlin'. We'll lead our separate lives."

She shook her head. "I don't think you understand."

She glanced at her husband, and saw Reverend Sands' face imposed over Mark's. They did, she realized ruefully, look a lot alike. Thoughts of the reverend sent a wave of longing crashing over her, so intense, that she had to struggle to keep her voice even as she said, "You know about Reverend Sands. This isn't a fly-by-night, Mark." She hesitated, then continued, "We have made plans. For the future."

He tipped his head to one side, considering. His gaze swept over her, evaluated her anew, weighing her words, her posture, her tone of voice. She sensed he weighed other things as well. He didn't brush her off. He was taking what she said, straight on and at face value, realizing she was serious, and not to be cajoled with a few 'darlin's' and a smile or two.

She said, "Six months. Because six months after you were bushwhacked, you were completely recovered and able to get about on your own. You could have come up to Leadville in person. Sent a telegram. Posted your own letter. But you did none of that, and instead settled into your new life with this Josephine."

He nodded and smoothed his mustache. "That's true. But more than eight months ago, you first heard tell I might still be alive. Abe told me about that. And you didn't ask, you didn't search. Seems we both have reasons to atone, darlin', to make amends, and compromise. A year. That's the least we owe each other, and our son."

Inez closed her eyes. Exhaled slowly. With her eyes shut, she said, "A year. More time than it takes to birth a child."

She opened her eyes. "After a year, if I decide I want a divorce, you won't fight. You will agree to plead guilty of adultery, desertion, whatever charges my lawyer decides will be best."

His brow furrowed. "What about William?"

"I won't take him from you, Mark. But neither will I give him up. We will have to work out a compromise of some kind."

He nodded. "A year, then."

Her heart lifted.

"But," he continued, "during that year, you give me an honest chance. I won't play a rube against the house. You and I, we have one evening a week together, just the two of us. No ghosts of dancehall girls or men of God hoverin' over our shoulders or whisperin' in our ears. Once a week, we go over the accounts together, talk about the business, and then…we go out to dinner, or the theater. Sit and talk. Play cards, just the two of us, like old times. It doesn't matter to me what we do. You decide." He threw down his last card. "It's only fair, darlin'."

Fair. She couldn't walk away, thinking she'd been unfair.

"How can I trust you?" she finally asked. "A year is a long time. What's to keep you from 'forgetting' about all this and fighting me in the courts?"

"When we get back, we can draw up an agreement. Just between us, dictating the terms. We can have someone we both trust do the witnessing, maybe Abe. We'll give it to him for safekeeping."

She nodded slowly. "A year. Very well, Mr. Stannert. We have a deal. You will have your chance, such as it is."

She held out a gloved hand. He took her hand, but instead of shaking, simply held it. His eyes crinkled up in a smile, the old charm she remembered so well, showing through. "That's all I asked for, Mrs. Stannert, was a chance."

"Your odds are not good," she warned, hand still resting in his. "Whether two months, four months, or twelve, I'm not about to change my mind. Truly, Mark. I no longer hate you, but I don't love you anymore, and I don't trust you, really. I wish I could make you see that. It's just business between us, now."

He nodded. "Darlin', I understand. But don't forget. I'm a gambling man. I'm used to playin' the odds, and this is too important a game for me to walk away from." The old grin appeared, with a hint of boyish mischief. "Fair warning, Mrs. Stannert. As you recall, I only play to win."

Inez couldn't help but smile back as she slid her hand from his grasp. "Of course, Mr. Stannert. And as you recall, so do I."

She twirled her parasol, one complete revolution of white lace and fringe. With that, Inez faced forward and, with Mark at her side, strolled down toward the spring and their son.

Author's Note

To all who turn to the Author's Note first: Spoilers ahead! If you like to experience a mystery in your mysteries, wait to read this until you're done with *Mercury's Rise*.

You have been warned.

Several forces were at work in the formation of this story. There was the history of Manitou Springs and Colorado Springs. There was my interest in tuberculosis and the state of medicine during Inez's time. And, there was the ending to the preceding book, *Leaden Skies*, and Inez's admittedly precarious situation. All pitched me forward into new territory.

First, a quick overview of what's real and what isn't in terms of places, people, and events in this book. Colorado Springs and Manitou Springs exist. They are five miles apart, and about an hour and a half drive south from Denver, and two and a half hours from Leadville (*much* quicker by car than stagecoach!). Leadville is a real place (if you don't know about Leadville, author's notes in the earlier Silver Rush historical mysteries provide some background). Many of the hotels mentioned in *Mercury's Rise*—the Cliff House, Manitou House, and the Colorado Springs Hotel, for instance—existed in 1880. The Mountain Springs House is entirely fictional, although I was so taken with the Cliff House after a couple of stays there that I promptly borrowed many of its features and architecture. My fictional hotel/health resort is situated where the U.S. Post

Office now stands in Manitou, which itself is on land once part of the estate of Jerome Wheeler, a former president of Macy's Department Store and an Aspen mining magnate. Mrs. Anna Galbreaith is real, but a bit of an enigma, despite determined, nearly obsessive Internet research on my part. Since she uses the initial of her given name (A for Anna) on her photographs, I assume she was a widow or divorcee, but have had little luck plumbing her story, except that she was a photographer and also ran the Ohio House, a boarding house in Manitou, in the 1880s. I was so enchanted by Anna and her photos that I decided to nudge her and her boarding house into my story. As for geological features, the mineral springs at Manitou exist today, mostly buried under concrete as the city "grew up and over" them. There is a Williams Cañon or Canyon (although The Narrows aren't quite as narrow as portrayed here), and the Garden of the Gods is known the world over. Today, you can stroll about Manitou and taste the various mineral waters, walk up Williams Canyon, and visit the Garden of the Gods and gaze upon the majestic sandstone features, just as Inez, Susan, and Harmony do in these pages. If you are lucky, you might even hear a bagpiper playing atop one of the sandstone formations, as I did one day.

Location and historical events led the way in creating the story of *Mercury's Rise*. My interest in Colorado Springs and Manitou Springs was initially piqued by my research into William Jackson Palmer, a general on the Union side in the Civil War and founder of the Denver & Rio Grande Railroad, for my second Silver Rush book, *Iron Ties*. From Palmer, it was a natural progression to his friend and business partner, Dr. William Bell. Palmer is usually credited with founding the town of Colorado Springs, and Bell with founding Manitou Springs. As I nosed about, getting my bearings, I became intrigued with the "selling" of the area—particularly of Manitou Springs—as a health resort and tourist destination in the mid-to-late 1800s. Promotion and puffery was hot and heavy in nearly every period piece of documentation I read, from the backs of cabinet cards (such as the one I possess of Williams Canyon taken by Mrs. Galbreaith) to books such as *Tourist Guide to Colorado in 1879* by Frank Fossett and *New Colorado and the Santa Fe Trail* by A.A. Hayes, Jr., published 1880. Here's a sample from the latter book (for which I owe many thanks to George McCluny for sending to me):

"Of course we went to Manitou, for every one goes thither. It is called the 'Saratoga of the West'—an appellation which pleases Manitou and does not hurt Saratoga. There are some baths and some mineral springs there…Manitou is a 'health resort,' 'Why, they keep me here for an example of the effects of the climate,' said a worthy and busy man at Colorado Springs. 'I came here from Chicago on a mattress.'"

Many more did come to this growing health and spa resort area, hoping that the mineral waters, the climate, and the location would cure what ailed them. For those interested in learning more about Manitou Springs, the Cliff House, and Colorado Springs, *Images of America: Manitou Springs* by Deborah Harrison, *Images of America: Colorado Springs* by Elizabeth Wallace, *Selected Colorado Writings* by Helen Hunt Jackson, and *The Cliff House: Pikes Peak Hospitality* by Betty Jo Cardona and Deborah Harrison are very accessible. In addition, through the magic of Google books, you can read effervescent promotional patter about Manitou Springs, its resorts, scenery, and healthful attributes, as well as enthusiastic descriptions of the area's natural wonders as it was written in the 1870s and 1880s. I recommend *Marvels of the New West* by William M. Thayer (1887), which also includes some mighty fine engravings; *The National Magazine: A Monthly Journal of American History, Vol. 11* (1889–1890); and *My first holiday: or, Letters home from Colorado, Utah, and California* by Caroline H. Dall (1881), for starters. As an author of promotional patter myself in the not-so-distant past, I recognized and appreciated (in a professional way) the verbal sleight of hand employed by these writers to lure those east of the Hudson to visit and mayhap to stay in the West.

The tourist and health resort boom in Manitou Springs had not quite arrived in 1880, but it was coming. As I explored the area, I heard over and over, "Oh, if only you could set your story a little later!" In 1880, there was no cog railroad up Pike's Peak, no Broadmoor Hotel, not even the Antlers Hotel in Colorado Springs (1880 was one year too early). But that's okay: in fiction, one can always have characters who see the opportunities coming. Other real historical tidbits: from the 1870s on, the big resorts in Manitou engaged in an escalating competition for visitors through frequent redecorating, adding rooms and entire floors, increasing amenities, adding ever more lavish entertainments, and increasing the luxury of their accommodations, with ruinous results when expenses outpaced income. Burros were used to go up Pike's Peak and to explore the area. Runaway buggies were a common cause of death (if you discount dying of consumption and related diseases), and rockfall was common.

Many of those coming to Colorado were "chasing the cure," looking for relief, hoping for a cure from tuberculosis, also known as consumption, the white plague, the wasting disease, and so on. You need only read about the scourge of the disease, before the discovery of antibiotics effected a true cure, to shudder and pray that "superbug" tuberculosis does not breach the current spectrum of antibiotics. For histories on the disease, I turned to Katherine Ott's *Fevered Lives*, Sheila M. Rothman's *Living in the Shadow of Death*, and René and Jean Dubos' *The White Plague*. If you want to gain a sense of the desperation of doctors during this time, go online for the *Transactions of the American Medical Association*, 1880, and even later documents such as the *JAMA Society Proceedings*, 1888. As a science writer, I appreciate the power of metaphor and analogy to make a point, and found this passage in the *Transactions* from Ephraim Cutter, M.D., to his colleagues a real eye-opener:

"It is estimated that one-quarter of the human deaths is caused directly or indirectly by what is commonly called consumption... I find I can write my name readily ten times in one minute...it would take 1 year, 213 days, and 16 hours of unintermitted writing to inscribe the names of this host, if on the average they consisted of thirteen letters. Suppose the vast company could be marshaled in rows four deep and two feet apart, this host would reach 770 miles in length, and occupy 10 days and 17 hours in passing a given point at a continuous rate of three miles an hour." These particular transactions are full of papers on tuberculosis, treatment and research, such as "The Salisbury Plans in Consumption—Production in Animals—Rationale and Treatment," "Artificial Inflation as a Remedial Agent in Diseases of the Lungs," A Further Contribution to the Local Treatment of Pulmonary Cavities," "Some Remarks on the Lesions of the Larynx in Phthisis," etc.

The so-called causes and cures ranged far and wide. For instance, in 1881 in the textbook *The Principles and Practice of Medicine*, some of the causes put forth were hereditary disposition, unfavorable climate, sedentary indoor life, defective ventilation, deficiency of light and "depressing emotions." Cure routines ranged from reliance on nourishing food, fresh air, and exercise, to the "slaughterhouse cure," i.e., drinking the blood of freshly slaughtered oxen and cows (reported in Denver in 1879), to patent medicines and nostrums containing such ingredients as cod-liver oil, lime, arsenic, chloroform, the ever-present alcohol, and yes, mercury, even into the 1920s. *Nostrums and Quackery* by Arthur J. Cramp, M.D. is very disturbing, particularly since it was published in 1921, long after Robert Koch's discovery that tuberculosis is caused by a bacterium. Another "cure" proposed by a well-respected physician in 1875 was—I kid you not—growing a beard. (See Addison Porter Dutcher's *Pulmonary Tuberculosis: Its Pathology, Nature, Symptoms, Diagnosis, Prognosis, Causes, Hygiene, and Medical Treatment*, "Chapter 30: A Plea for the Beards; Its Influence in Protecting the Throat and Lungs from Disease," pg. 304.)

So, for those of you who are shocked that, at the end of *Mercury's Rise*, Inez allows her son to stay with her consumptive sister, keep in mind the state of medical knowledge of the day. Scientists as early as the late 1700s were theorizing about what became the basis for germ theory. By the time of the Civil War, the best minds were conscious of the dangers of sepsis, and Robert Lister had begun using carbolic acid as an antibacterial agent (hence Listerine). However, that did not prevent the re-use of bandages, and horribly septic conditions in medicine in general. Physicians after the War and into the 1880s were generally aware of the idea of contagion, but the idea of bacteria spreading disease really did not become commonly accepted among doctors until much later. Even with Koch's 1882 discovery of the *Mycobacterium tuberculosis* (if you knew this, you probably guessed correctly that Dr. Prochazka wasn't going to make it out alive in *Mercury's Rise*), it took until 1920 for the first human trials of the BCG vaccine to occur and until 1944 for streptomycin—the first antibiotic to successfully treat tuberculosis—to be discovered. There are photos taken in the 1890s, showing people at the various springs in Manitou all sharing the same public tin cup to drink the waters. Makes you shudder to think of it. So please, do not judge Inez's decision harshly; she's doing the best that she can, given the era in which she lives.

For information on poisons and nasty plants, I turned to *Book of Poisons*, by Serita Stevens and Anne Bannon, *This Will Kill You*, by H. P. Newquist and Rich Maloof, *Wicked Plants*, by Amy Stewart, *Deadly Doses*, by Serita Deborah Stevens with Anne Klarner, *Murder and Mayhem* by D.P. Lyle, M.D. For what grows where, I used *Manitou Springs Wildflowers* by Nicholas D. Weiner and Brent I. Weiner, *Rocky Mountain Wildflowers* by Ronald J. Taylor, *Colorado Trees and Wildflowers* by Waterford Press, and a whole lot of online references to see if particular plants existed in Colorado in 1880 and what they were called at the time. (I did the best I could, folks, but sometimes, you just have to know when to call it quits.)

For insight into the life of British remittance men in the West, I recommend *Marmalade and Whiskey* by Lee Olson.

Now, about women and women's roles. Be glad, fellow females, that you are not a woman in the mid-to-late 1800s trying to obtain a divorce. I pity Inez, and you will too, after reading *Governing the Hearth* by Michael Grossberg, *Man and Wife in America* by Hendrik Hartog, *A Judgment for Solomon* by Michael Grossberg, and Ruth Rymer Miller's dissertation *Alimony and Divorce: An Historical-Comparative Study of Gender Conflict.* In crafting Inez's discussion with her lawyer, I relied heavily on Chapter 8 of Hartog's *Man and Wife in America*, titled "The Right to Kill." Hartog uses a telling quote by lawyer Edwin Stanton from the 1859 trial of Daniel E. Sickles to introduce this chapter: "By the contemplation of the law, the wife is always in the husband's presence, always under his wing; and any movement against her person is a movement against his right and may be resisted as such." For more about the Sickels trial, the McFarland-Richardson trial and others—in which men killed their wives' lovers and, for the most part, got away with it—I urge you to look up this book and this particular chapter. I have more references, but will stop there. Suffice it to say, Inez has an uphill battle should she continue to pursue a divorce.

As for women in the Civil War, a fascinating look at the roles they played in the medical services (and in some cases, the disguises they employed) can be found in *They Fought Like Demons* by DeAnne Blanton and Lauren M. Cook. *Doctors in Blue* by George Worthington Adams has a sobering section on nurses in the Civil War. As Adams notes, "The war opened the gates of a great profession to women at a time when their economic opportunities were scarce." Hand in hand with the opportunities came difficulties. Many surgeons did not take to the idea or reality of women in the nursing roll. Adams explains, "The usual attitude of medical officers was that they [female nurses] were 'permitted nuisances,' especially at hospitals near the front." In my searches, I found some mention of women physicians in the Civil War, but they appeared "scarcer than hen's teeth." Mary Edwards Walker was one such unusual woman; you can read an online profile of her written by the St. Lawrence County, NY Branch of the American Association of University Women. Clearly, if a woman openly took that road, she had to be strong in any number of ways and ready to deal with a storm of controversy and disapproval. Fifteen years later, the situation for women in the medical field was changing, albeit very slowly.

For example in the Leadville 1880 census, there were four women who were physicians/surgeons, four counted as nurses/hospital workers, and thirteen Sisters of Charity (at least some of whom were acting in the capacity of nurses in Leadville's St. Vincent's Hospital). That same census counted sixty-nine male physicians/surgeons, and, interestingly, only one nurse.

For mixed drinks circa 1880s, the *New and Improved Bartender's Manual: Or How to Mix Drinks of the Present Style* by Harry Johnson (1888) was very handy.

In case you are curious, Ayer's Cherry Pectoral ("Cures Colds, Coughs and all Diseases of the Throat and Lungs") for infants, children and adults was real. Users were instructed to take liberal doses, night and morning, for a cold, and to commence with a medium dose for a cough, increasing the quantity until it produces nausea or depression. According to the *Journal of the American Medical Association*, Volume 58 (1912), Ayer's Cherry Pectoral in its pre-1905 formulary contained morphine and alcohol.

It is tempting to keep pulling out references from my bookshelves and referring to my virtual bookmarks—I have more, many more!—but I'm thinking, no, I need to call a halt to this or I'll end up writing a thirty-page Author's Note. So, I'll finish up by saying thank you to all the *Leaden Skies* readers who contacted me with earnest pleas for the next in the series and admonitions to be quick about it. I hope you enjoyed *Mercury's Rise*. Inez and I now need to return our attentions to Leadville and contemplate her rather convoluted future. At the same time, keep in mind that, as far as William and Harmony are concerned, we are saying goodbye to them for just a while. They will be back, and that's a promise.

To receive a free catalog of Poisoned Pen Press titles, please contact us in one of the following ways:

Phone: 1-800-421-3976
Facsimile: 1-480-949-1707
Email: info@poisonedpenpress.com
Website: www.poisonedpenpress.com

Poisoned Pen Press
6962 E. First Ave. Ste 103
Scottsdale, AZ 85251